C000149712

Jack London

John Griffith London (born John Griffith Chaney; January 12, 1876 – November 22, 1916) was an American novelist, journalist, and social activist. A pioneer in the world of commercial magazine fiction, he was one of the first writers to become a worldwide celebrity and earn a large fortune from writing. He was also an innovator in the genre that would later become known as science fiction. His most famous works include The Call of the Wild and White Fang, both set in the Klondike Gold Rush, as well as the short stories "To Build a Fire", "An Odyssey of the North", and "Love of Life". He also wrote about the South Pacific in stories such as "The Pearls of Parlay" and "The Heathen". London was part of the radical literary group "The Crowd" in San Francisco and a passionate advocate of unionization, socialism, and the rights of workers. He wrote several powerful works dealing with these topics, such as his dystopian novel The Iron Heel, his non-fiction exposé The People of the Abyss, and The War of the Classes. (Source: Wikipedia)

Literary works:

The Cruise of the Dazzler (1902)
A Daughter of the Snows (1902)
The Call of the Wild (1903)
The Kempton-Wace Letters (1903)
The Sea-Wolf (1904)
The Game (1905)
White Fang (1906)
Before Adam (1907)
The Iron Heel (1908)
Martin Eden (1909)
Burning Daylight (1910)
Adventure (1911)
The Scarlet Plague (1912)
A Son of the Sun (1912)
The Abysmal Brute (1913)
The Valley of the Moon (1913)

BOOKLAND
CLASSICS

THE COLLECTED WORKS
OF
JACK LONDON
VOL. 06 (OF 25)

THE IRON HEEL
SOUTH SEA TALES

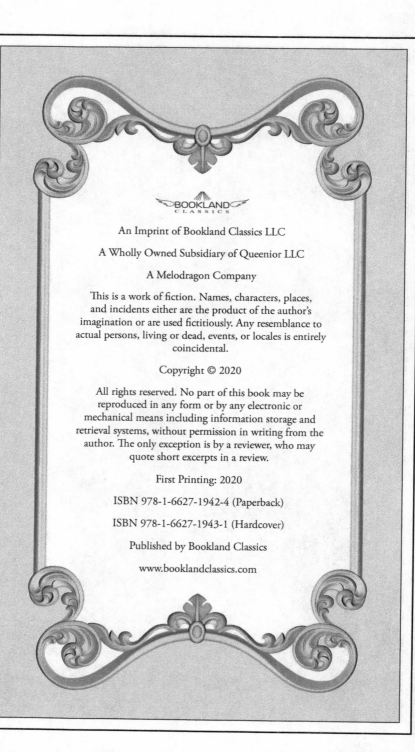

BOOKLAND
CLASSICS

An Imprint of Bookland Classics LLC

A Wholly Owned Subsidiary of Queenior LLC

A Melodragon Company

This is a work of fiction. Names, characters, places, and incidents either are the product of the author's imagination or are used fictitiously. Any resemblance to actual persons, living or dead, events, or locales is entirely coincidental.

Copyright © 2020

All rights reserved. No part of this book may be reproduced in any form or by any electronic or mechanical means including information storage and retrieval systems, without permission in writing from the author. The only exception is by a reviewer, who may quote short excerpts in a review.

First Printing: 2020

ISBN 978-1-6627-1942-4 (Paperback)

ISBN 978-1-6627-1943-1 (Hardcover)

Published by Bookland Classics

www.booklandclassics.com

Contents

THE COLLECTED WORKS

OF

JACK LONDON

VOL. 06 (OF 25)

THE IRON HEEL

"At first, this Earth, a stage so gloomed with woe

You almost sicken at the shifting of the scenes.

And yet be patient. Our Playwright may show

In some fifth act what this Wild Drama means."

FOREWORD

It cannot be said that the Everhard Manuscript is an important historical document. To the historian it bristles with errors—not errors of fact, but errors of interpretation. Looking back across the seven centuries that have lapsed since Avis Everhard completed her manuscript, events, and the bearings of events, that were confused and veiled to her, are clear to us. She lacked perspective. She was too close to the events she writes about. Nay, she was merged in the events she has described.

Nevertheless, as a personal document, the Everhard Manuscript is of inestimable value. But here again enter error of perspective, and vitiation due to the bias of love. Yet we smile, indeed, and forgive Avis Everhard for the heroic lines upon which she modelled her husband. We know to-day that he was not so colossal, and that he loomed among the events of his times less largely than the Manuscript would lead us to believe.

We know that Ernest Everhard was an exceptionally strong man, but not so exceptional as his wife thought him to be. He was, after all, but one of a large number of heroes who, throughout the world, devoted their lives to the Revolution; though it must be conceded that he did unusual work, especially in his elaboration and interpretation of working-class philosophy. "Proletarian science" and "proletarian philosophy" were his phrases for it, and therein he shows the provincialism of his mind—a defect, however, that was due to the times and that none in that day could escape.

But to return to the Manuscript. Especially valuable is it in communicating to us the FEEL of those terrible times. Nowhere do we find more vividly portrayed the psychology of the persons that lived in that turbulent period embraced between the years 1912 and 1932—their mistakes and ignorance, their doubts and fears and misapprehensions, their ethical delusions, their violent passions, their inconceivable sordidness and selfishness. These are the things that are so hard for us of this enlightened age to understand. History tells us that these things were, and biology and psychology tell us why they

were; but history and biology and psychology do not make these things alive. We accept them as facts, but we are left without sympathetic comprehension of them.

This sympathy comes to us, however, as we peruse the Everhard Manuscript. We enter into the minds of the actors in that long-ago world-drama, and for the time being their mental processes are our mental processes. Not alone do we understand Avis Everhard's love for her hero-husband, but we feel, as he felt, in those first days, the vague and terrible loom of the Oligarchy. The Iron Heel (well named) we feel descending upon and crushing mankind.

And in passing we note that that historic phrase, the Iron Heel, originated in Ernest Everhard's mind. This, we may say, is the one moot question that this new-found document clears up. Previous to this, the earliest-known use of the phrase occurred in the pamphlet, "Ye Slaves," written by George Milford and published in December, 1912. This George Milford was an obscure agitator about whom nothing is known, save the one additional bit of information gained from the Manuscript, which mentions that he was shot in the Chicago Commune. Evidently he had heard Ernest Everhard make use of the phrase in some public speech, most probably when he was running for Congress in the fall of 1912. From the Manuscript we learn that Everhard used the phrase at a private dinner in the spring of 1912. This is, without discussion, the earliest-known occasion on which the Oligarchy was so designated.

The rise of the Oligarchy will always remain a cause of secret wonder to the historian and the philosopher. Other great historical events have their place in social evolution. They were inevitable. Their coming could have been predicted with the same certitude that astronomers to-day predict the outcome of the movements of stars. Without these other great historical events, social evolution could not have proceeded. Primitive communism, chattel slavery, serf slavery, and wage slavery were necessary stepping-stones in the evolution of society. But it were ridiculous to assert that the Iron Heel was a necessary stepping-stone. Rather, to-day, is it adjudged a step aside, or a step backward, to the social tyrannies that made the early world a hell, but that were as necessary as the Iron Heel was unnecessary.

Black as Feudalism was, yet the coming of it was inevitable. What else than Feudalism could have followed upon the breakdown of that great centralized governmental machine known as the Roman Empire? Not so, however, with the Iron Heel. In the orderly procedure of social evolution there was no place for it. It was not necessary, and it was not inevitable. It must always remain the great curiosity of history—a whim, a fantasy, an apparition, a thing unexpected and undreamed; and it should serve as a warning to those rash political theorists of to-day who speak with certitude of social processes.

Capitalism was adjudged by the sociologists of the time to be the culmination of bourgeois rule, the ripened fruit of the bourgeois revolution. And we of to-day can but applaud that judgment. Following upon Capitalism, it was held, even by such intellectual and antagonistic giants as Herbert Spencer, that Socialism would come. Out of the decay of self-seeking capitalism, it was held, would arise that flower of the ages, the Brotherhood of Man. Instead of which, appalling alike to us who look back and to those that lived at the time, capitalism, rotten-ripe, sent forth that monstrous offshoot, the Oligarchy.

Too late did the socialist movement of the early twentieth century divine the coming of the Oligarchy. Even as it was divined, the Oligarchy was there—a fact established in blood, a stupendous and awful reality. Nor even then, as the Everhard Manuscript well shows, was any permanence attributed to the Iron Heel. Its overthrow was a matter of a few short years, was the judgment of the revolutionists. It is true, they realized that the Peasant Revolt was unplanned, and that the First Revolt was premature; but they little realized that the Second Revolt, planned and mature, was doomed to equal futility and more terrible punishment.

It is apparent that Avis Everhard completed the Manuscript during the last days of preparation for the Second Revolt; hence the fact that there is no mention of the disastrous outcome of the Second Revolt. It is quite clear that she intended the Manuscript for immediate publication, as soon as the Iron Heel was overthrown, so that her husband, so recently dead, should receive full credit for all that he had ventured and accomplished. Then came the frightful crushing of the Second Revolt, and it is probable that in the moment of danger, ere she fled or was captured by the Mercenaries, she hid the Manuscript in the hollow oak at Wake Robin Lodge.

Of Avis Everhard there is no further record. Undoubtedly she was executed by the Mercenaries; and, as is well known, no record of such executions was kept by the Iron Heel. But little did she realize, even then, as she hid the Manuscript and prepared to flee, how terrible had been the breakdown of the Second Revolt. Little did she realize that the tortuous and distorted evolution of the next three centuries would compel a Third Revolt and a Fourth Revolt, and many Revolts, all drowned in seas of blood, ere the world-movement of labor should come into its own. And little did she dream that for seven long centuries the tribute of her love to Ernest Everhard would repose undisturbed in the heart of the ancient oak of Wake Robin Lodge.

ANTHONY MEREDITH

Ardis,

November 27, 419 B.O.M.

CHAPTER I. MY EAGLE

The soft summer wind stirs the redwoods, and Wild-Water ripples sweet cadences over its mossy stones. There are butterflies in the sunshine, and from everywhere arises the drowsy hum of bees. It is so quiet and peaceful, and I sit here, and ponder, and am restless. It is the quiet that makes me restless. It seems unreal. All the world is quiet, but it is the quiet before the storm. I strain my ears, and all my senses, for some betrayal of that impending storm. Oh, that it may not be premature! That it may not be premature!*

> * *The Second Revolt was largely the work of Ernest Everhard,*
>
> *though he cooperated, of course, with the European leaders.*
>
> *The capture and secret execution of Everhard was the great*
>
> *event of the spring of 1932 A.D. Yet so thoroughly had he*
>
> *prepared for the revolt, that his fellow-conspirators were*
>
> *able, with little confusion or delay, to carry out his*
>
> *plans. It was after Everhard's execution that his wife went*
>
> *to Wake Robin Lodge, a small bungalow in the Sonoma Hills of*
>
> *California.*

Small wonder that I am restless. I think, and think, and I cannot cease from thinking. I have been in the thick of life so long that I am oppressed by the peace and quiet, and I cannot forbear from dwelling upon that mad maelstrom of death and destruction so soon to burst forth. In my ears are the cries of the stricken; and I can see, as I have seen in the past,* all the marring and mangling of the sweet, beautiful flesh, and the souls torn with violence from proud bodies and hurled to God. Thus do we poor humans attain our ends, striving through carnage and destruction to bring lasting peace and happiness upon the earth.

Without doubt she here refers to the Chicago Commune.

And then I am lonely. When I do not think of what is to come, I think of what has been and is no more—my Eagle, beating with tireless wings the void, soaring toward what was ever his sun, the flaming ideal of human freedom. I cannot sit idly by and wait the great event that is his making, though he is not here to see. He devoted all the years of his manhood to it, and for it he gave his life. It is his handiwork. He made it.*

With all respect to Avis Everhard, it must be pointed out that Everhard was but one of many able leaders who planned the Second Revolt. And we to-day, looking back across the centuries, can safely say that even had he lived, the Second Revolt would not have been less calamitous in its outcome than it was.

And so it is, in this anxious time of waiting, that I shall write of my husband. There is much light that I alone of all persons living can throw upon his character, and so noble a character cannot be blazoned forth too brightly. His was a great soul, and, when my love grows unselfish, my chiefest regret is that he is not here to witness to-morrow's dawn. We cannot fail. He has built too stoutly and too surely for that. Woe to the Iron Heel! Soon shall it be thrust back from off prostrate humanity. When the word goes forth, the labor hosts of all the world shall rise. There has been nothing like it in the history of the world. The solidarity of labor is assured, and for the first time will there be an international revolution wide as the world is wide.*

* The Second Revolt was truly international. It was a colossal plan—too colossal to be wrought by the genius of one man alone. Labor, in all the oligarchies of the world, was prepared to rise at the signal. Germany, Italy, France, and all Australasia were labor countries—socialist states. They were ready to lend aid to the revolution. Gallantly they did; and it was for this reason, when the Second Revolt was crushed, that they, too, were crushed by the united oligarchies of the world, their socialist governments being replaced by oligarchical governments.

You see, I am full of what is impending. I have lived it day and night utterly and for so long that it is ever present in my mind. For that matter, I cannot think of my husband without thinking of it. He was the soul of it, and how can I possibly separate the two in thought?

As I have said, there is much light that I alone can throw upon his character. It is well known that he toiled hard for liberty and suffered sore. How hard he toiled and how greatly he suffered, I well know; for I have been with him during these twenty anxious years and I know his patience, his untiring effort, his infinite devotion to the Cause for which, only two months gone, he laid down his life.

I shall try to write simply and to tell here how Ernest Everhard entered my life—how I first met him, how he grew until I became a part of him, and the tremendous changes he wrought in my life. In this way may you look at him through my eyes and learn him as I learned him—in all save the things too secret and sweet for me to tell.

It was in February, 1912, that I first met him, when, as a guest of my father's* at dinner, he came to our house in Berkeley. I cannot say that my very first impression of him was favorable. He was one of many at dinner, and in the drawing-room where we gathered and waited for all to arrive, he made a rather incongruous appearance. It was "preacher's night," as my father privately called it, and Ernest was certainly out of place in the midst of the churchmen.

*John Cunningham, Avis Everhard's father, was a professor at the State University at Berkeley, California. His chosen field was physics, and in addition he did much original research and was greatly distinguished as a scientist. His chief contribution to science was his studies of the electron and his monumental work on the "Identification of Matter and Energy," wherein he established, beyond cavil and for all time, that the ultimate unit of matter and the ultimate unit of force were identical. This idea had been earlier advanced, but not demonstrated, by Sir Oliver Lodge and other students in the new field of radio-activity.

In the first place, his clothes did not fit him. He wore a ready-made suit of dark cloth that was ill adjusted to his body. In fact, no ready-made suit of clothes ever could fit his body. And on this night, as always, the cloth bulged with his muscles, while the coat between the shoulders, what of the heavy shoulder-development, was a maze of wrinkles. His neck was the neck of a prize-fighter,* thick and strong. So this was the social philosopher and ex-horseshoer my father had discovered, was my thought. And he certainly looked it with those bulging muscles and that bull-throat. Immediately I classified him—a sort of prodigy, I thought, a Blind Tom** of the working class.

In that day it was the custom of men to compete for purses of money. They fought with their hands. When one was beaten into insensibility or killed, the survivor took the money.

** *This obscure reference applies to a blind negro musician who took the world by storm in the latter half of the nineteenth century of the Christian Era.*

And then, when he shook hands with me! His handshake was firm and strong, but he looked at me boldly with his black eyes—too boldly, I thought. You see, I was a creature of environment, and at that time had strong class instincts. Such boldness on the part of a man of my own class would have been almost unforgivable. I know that I could not avoid dropping my eyes, and I was quite relieved when I passed him on and turned to greet Bishop Morehouse—a favorite of mine, a sweet and serious man of middle age, Christ-like in appearance and goodness, and a scholar as well.

But this boldness that I took to be presumption was a vital clew to the nature of Ernest Everhard. He was simple, direct, afraid of nothing, and he refused to waste time on conventional mannerisms. "You pleased me," he explained long afterward; "and why should I not fill my eyes with that which pleases me?" I have said that he was afraid of nothing. He was a natural aristocrat—and this in spite of the fact that he was in the camp of the non-aristocrats. He was a superman, a blond beast such as Nietzsche* has described, and in addition he was aflame with democracy.

23

* Friederich Nietzsche, the mad philosopher of the

nineteenth century of the Christian Era, who caught wild

glimpses of truth, but who, before he was done, reasoned

himself around the great circle of human thought and off

into madness.

In the interest of meeting the other guests, and what of my unfavorable impression, I forgot all about the working-class philosopher, though once or twice at table I noticed him—especially the twinkle in his eye as he listened to the talk first of one minister and then of another. He has humor, I thought, and I almost forgave him his clothes. But the time went by, and the dinner went by, and he never opened his mouth to speak, while the ministers talked interminably about the working class and its relation to the church, and what the church had done and was doing for it. I noticed that my father was annoyed because Ernest did not talk. Once father took advantage of a lull and asked him to say something; but Ernest shrugged his shoulders and with an "I have nothing to say" went on eating salted almonds.

But father was not to be denied. After a while he said:

"We have with us a member of the working class. I am sure that he can present things from a new point of view that will be interesting and refreshing. I refer to Mr. Everhard."

The others betrayed a well-mannered interest, and urged Ernest for a statement of his views. Their attitude toward him was so broadly tolerant and kindly that it was really patronizing. And I saw that Ernest noted it and was amused. He looked slowly about him, and I saw the glint of laughter in his eyes.

"I am not versed in the courtesies of ecclesiastical controversy," he began, and then hesitated with modesty and indecision.

"Go on," they urged, and Dr. Hammerfield said: "We do not mind the truth that is in any man. If it is sincere," he amended.

"Then you separate sincerity from truth?" Ernest laughed quickly.

Dr. Hammerfield gasped, and managed to answer, "The best of us may be mistaken, young man, the best of us."

Ernest's manner changed on the instant. He became another man.

"All right, then," he answered; "and let me begin by saying that you are all mistaken. You know nothing, and worse than nothing, about the working class. Your sociology is as vicious and worthless as is your method of thinking."

It was not so much what he said as how he said it. I roused at the first sound of his voice. It was as bold as his eyes. It was a clarion-call that thrilled me. And the whole table was aroused, shaken alive from monotony and drowsiness.

"What is so dreadfully vicious and worthless in our method of thinking, young man?" Dr. Hammerfield demanded, and already there was something unpleasant in his voice and manner of utterance.

"You are metaphysicians. You can prove anything by metaphysics; and having done so, every metaphysician can prove every other metaphysician wrong—to his own satisfaction. You are anarchists in the realm of thought. And you are mad cosmos-makers. Each of you dwells in a cosmos of his own making, created out of his own fancies and desires. You do not know the real world in which you live, and your thinking has no place in the real world except in so far as it is phenomena of mental aberration.

"Do you know what I was reminded of as I sat at table and listened to you talk and talk? You reminded me for all the world of the scholastics of the Middle Ages who gravely and learnedly debated the absorbing question of how many angels could dance on the point of a needle. Why, my dear sirs, you are as remote from the intellectual life of the twentieth century as an Indian medicine-man making incantation in the primeval forest ten thousand years ago."

As Ernest talked he seemed in a fine passion; his face glowed, his eyes snapped and flashed, and his chin and jaw were eloquent with aggressiveness. But it was only a way he had. It always aroused people. His smashing, sledge-hammer manner of attack invariably made them forget themselves. And they were forgetting themselves now. Bishop Morehouse was leaning forward and listening intently. Exasperation and anger were flushing the face of Dr. Hammerfield. And others were exasperated, too, and some were smiling in an amused and superior way. As for myself, I found it most enjoyable. I glanced at father, and I was afraid he was going to giggle at the effect of this human bombshell he had been guilty of launching amongst us.

"Your terms are rather vague," Dr. Hammerfield interrupted. "Just precisely what do you mean when you call us metaphysicians?"

"I call you metaphysicians because you reason metaphysically," Ernest went on. "Your method of reasoning is the opposite to that of science. There is no validity to your conclusions. You can prove everything and nothing, and no two of you can agree upon anything. Each of you goes into his own consciousness to explain himself and the universe. As well may you lift yourselves by your own bootstraps as to explain consciousness by consciousness."

"I do not understand," Bishop Morehouse said. "It seems to me that all things of the mind are metaphysical. That most exact and convincing of all sciences, mathematics, is sheerly metaphysical. Each and every thought-process of the scientific reasoner is metaphysical. Surely you will agree with me?"

"As you say, you do not understand," Ernest replied. "The metaphysician reasons deductively out of his own subjectivity. The scientist reasons inductively from the facts of experience. The metaphysician reasons from theory to facts, the scientist reasons from facts to theory. The metaphysician explains the universe by himself, the scientist explains himself by the universe."

"Thank God we are not scientists," Dr. Hammerfield murmured complacently.

"What are you then?" Ernest demanded.

"Philosophers."

"There you go," Ernest laughed. "You have left the real and solid earth and are up in the air with a word for a flying machine. Pray come down to earth and tell me precisely what you do mean by philosophy."

"Philosophy is—" (Dr. Hammerfield paused and cleared his throat)— "something that cannot be defined comprehensively except to such minds and temperaments as are philosophical. The narrow scientist with his nose in a test-tube cannot understand philosophy."

Ernest ignored the thrust. It was always his way to turn the point back upon an opponent, and he did it now, with a beaming brotherliness of face and utterance.

"Then you will undoubtedly understand the definition I shall now make of philosophy. But before I make it, I shall challenge you to point out error in it or to remain a silent metaphysician. Philosophy is merely the widest science of all. Its reasoning method is the same as that of any particular science and of all particular sciences. And by that same method of reasoning, the inductive method, philosophy fuses all particular sciences into one great science. As Spencer says, the data of any particular science are partially unified knowledge. Philosophy unifies the knowledge that is contributed by all the sciences. Philosophy is the science of science, the master science, if you please. How do you like my definition?"

"Very creditable, very creditable," Dr. Hammerfield muttered lamely.

But Ernest was merciless.

"Remember," he warned, "my definition is fatal to metaphysics. If you do not now point out a flaw in my definition, you are disqualified later on from advancing metaphysical arguments. You must go through life seeking that flaw and remaining metaphysically silent until you have found it."

Ernest waited. The silence was painful. Dr. Hammerfield was pained. He was also puzzled. Ernest's sledge-hammer attack disconcerted him. He was not used to the simple and direct method of controversy. He looked appealingly around the table, but no one answered for him. I caught father grinning into his napkin.

"There is another way of disqualifying the metaphysicians," Ernest said, when he had rendered Dr. Hammerfield's discomfiture complete. "Judge them by their works. What have they done for mankind beyond the spinning of airy fancies and the mistaking of their own shadows for gods? They have added to the gayety of mankind, I grant; but what tangible good have they wrought for mankind? They philosophized, if you will pardon my misuse of the word, about the heart as the seat of the emotions, while the scientists were formulating the circulation of the blood. They declaimed about famine and pestilence as being scourges of God, while the scientists were building granaries and draining cities. They builded gods in their own shapes and out of their own desires, while the scientists were building roads and bridges. They were describing the earth as the centre of the universe, while the scientists were discovering America and probing space for the stars and the laws of the stars. In short, the metaphysicians have done nothing, absolutely nothing, for mankind. Step by step, before the advance of science, they have been driven back. As fast as the ascertained facts of science have overthrown their subjective explanations of things, they have made new subjective explanations of things, including explanations of the latest ascertained facts. And this, I doubt not, they will go on doing to the end of time. Gentlemen, a metaphysician is a medicine man. The difference between you and the Eskimo who makes a fur-clad blubber-eating god is merely a difference of several thousand years of ascertained facts. That is all."

"Yet the thought of Aristotle ruled Europe for twelve centuries," Dr. Ballingford announced pompously. "And Aristotle was a metaphysician."

Dr. Ballingford glanced around the table and was rewarded by nods and smiles of approval.

"Your illustration is most unfortunate," Ernest replied. "You refer to a very dark period in human history. In fact, we call that period the Dark Ages. A period wherein science was raped by the metaphysicians, wherein physics became a search for the Philosopher's Stone, wherein chemistry became alchemy, and astronomy became astrology. Sorry the domination of Aristotle's thought!"

Dr. Ballingford looked pained, then he brightened up and said:

"Granted this horrible picture you have drawn, yet you must confess that metaphysics was inherently potent in so far as it drew humanity out of this dark period and on into the illumination of the succeeding centuries."

"Metaphysics had nothing to do with it," Ernest retorted.

"What?" Dr. Hammerfield cried. "It was not the thinking and the speculation that led to the voyages of discovery?"

"Ah, my dear sir," Ernest smiled, "I thought you were disqualified. You have not yet picked out the flaw in my definition of philosophy. You are now on an unsubstantial basis. But it is the way of the metaphysicians, and I forgive you. No, I repeat, metaphysics had nothing to do with it. Bread and butter, silks and jewels, dollars and cents, and, incidentally, the closing up of the overland trade-routes to India, were the things that caused the voyages of discovery. With the fall of Constantinople, in 1453, the Turks blocked the way of the caravans to India. The traders of Europe had to find another route. Here was the original cause for the voyages of discovery. Columbus sailed to find a new route to the Indies. It is so stated in all the history books. Incidentally, new facts were learned about the nature, size, and form of the earth, and the Ptolemaic system went glimmering."

Dr. Hammerfield snorted.

"You do not agree with me?" Ernest queried. "Then wherein am I wrong?"

"I can only reaffirm my position," Dr. Hammerfield retorted tartly. "It is too long a story to enter into now."

"No story is too long for the scientist," Ernest said sweetly. "That is why the scientist gets to places. That is why he got to America."

29

I shall not describe the whole evening, though it is a joy to me to recall every moment, every detail, of those first hours of my coming to know Ernest Everhard.

Battle royal raged, and the ministers grew red-faced and excited, especially at the moments when Ernest called them romantic philosophers, shadow-projectors, and similar things. And always he checked them back to facts. "The fact, man, the irrefragable fact!" he would proclaim triumphantly, when he had brought one of them a cropper. He bristled with facts. He tripped them up with facts, ambuscaded them with facts, bombarded them with broadsides of facts.

"You seem to worship at the shrine of fact," Dr. Hammerfield taunted him.

"There is no God but Fact, and Mr. Everhard is its prophet," Dr. Ballingford paraphrased.

Ernest smilingly acquiesced.

"I'm like the man from Texas," he said. And, on being solicited, he explained. "You see, the man from Missouri always says, 'You've got to show me.' But the man from Texas says, 'You've got to put it in my hand.' From which it is apparent that he is no metaphysician."

Another time, when Ernest had just said that the metaphysical philosophers could never stand the test of truth, Dr. Hammerfield suddenly demanded:

"What is the test of truth, young man? Will you kindly explain what has so long puzzled wiser heads than yours?"

"Certainly," Ernest answered. His cocksureness irritated them. "The wise heads have puzzled so sorely over truth because they went up into the air after it. Had they remained on the solid earth, they would have found it easily enough—ay, they would have found that they themselves were precisely testing truth with every practical act and thought of their lives."

"The test, the test," Dr. Hammerfield repeated impatiently. "Never mind the preamble. Give us that which we have sought so long—the test of truth. Give it us, and we will be as gods."

There was an impolite and sneering scepticism in his words and manner that secretly pleased most of them at the table, though it seemed to bother Bishop Morehouse.

"Dr. Jordan* has stated it very clearly," Ernest said. "His test of truth is: 'Will it work? Will you trust your life to it?'"

> *A noted educator of the late nineteenth and early
>
> twentieth centuries of the Christian Era. He was president
>
> of the Stanford University, a private benefaction of the
>
> times.

"Pish!" Dr. Hammerfield sneered. "You have not taken Bishop Berkeley* into account. He has never been answered."

> *An idealistic monist who long puzzled the philosophers of
>
> that time with his denial of the existence of matter, but
>
> whose clever argument was finally demolished when the new
>
> empiric facts of science were philosophically generalized.

"The noblest metaphysician of them all," Ernest laughed. "But your example is unfortunate. As Berkeley himself attested, his metaphysics didn't work."

Dr. Hammerfield was angry, righteously angry. It was as though he had caught Ernest in a theft or a lie.

"Young man," he trumpeted, "that statement is on a par with all you have uttered to-night. It is a base and unwarranted assumption."

"I am quite crushed," Ernest murmured meekly. "Only I don't know what hit me. You'll have to put it in my hand, Doctor."

"I will, I will," Dr. Hammerfield spluttered. "How do you know? You do not know that Bishop Berkeley attested that his metaphysics did not work. You have no proof. Young man, they have always worked."

"I take it as proof that Berkeley's metaphysics did not work, because—" Ernest paused calmly for a moment. "Because Berkeley made an invariable practice of going through doors instead of walls. Because he trusted his life to solid bread and butter and roast beef. Because he shaved himself with a razor that worked when it removed the hair from his face."

"But those are actual things!" Dr. Hammerfield cried. "Metaphysics is of the mind."

"And they work—in the mind?" Ernest queried softly.

The other nodded.

"And even a multitude of angels can dance on the point of a needle—in the mind," Ernest went on reflectively. "And a blubber-eating, fur-clad god can exist and work—in the mind; and there are no proofs to the contrary—in the mind. I suppose, Doctor, you live in the mind?"

"My mind to me a kingdom is," was the answer.

"That's another way of saying that you live up in the air. But you come back to earth at meal-time, I am sure, or when an earthquake happens along. Or, tell me, Doctor, do you have no apprehension in an earthquake that that incorporeal body of yours will be hit by an immaterial brick?"

Instantly, and quite unconsciously, Dr. Hammerfield's hand shot up to his head, where a scar disappeared under the hair. It happened that Ernest had blundered on an apposite illustration. Dr. Hammerfield had been nearly killed in the Great Earthquake* by a falling chimney. Everybody broke out into roars of laughter.

* *The Great Earthquake of 1906 A.D. that destroyed San*

Francisco.

"Well?" Ernest asked, when the merriment had subsided. "Proofs to the contrary?"

And in the silence he asked again, "Well?" Then he added, "Still well, but not so well, that argument of yours."

But Dr. Hammerfield was temporarily crushed, and the battle raged on in new directions. On point after point, Ernest challenged the ministers. When they affirmed that they knew the working class, he told them fundamental truths about the working class that they did not know, and challenged them for disproofs. He gave them facts, always facts, checked their excursions into the air, and brought them back to the solid earth and its facts.

How the scene comes back to me! I can hear him now, with that war-note in his voice, flaying them with his facts, each fact a lash that stung and stung again. And he was merciless. He took no quarter,* and gave none. I can never forget the flaying he gave them at the end:

* *This figure arises from the customs of the times. When,*

among men fighting to the death in their wild-animal way, a

beaten man threw down his weapons, it was at the option of

the victor to slay him or spare him.

"You have repeatedly confessed to-night, by direct avowal or ignorant statement, that you do not know the working class. But you are not to be blamed for this. How can you know anything about the working class? You

33

do not live in the same locality with the working class. You herd with the capitalist class in another locality. And why not? It is the capitalist class that pays you, that feeds you, that puts the very clothes on your backs that you are wearing to-night. And in return you preach to your employers the brands of metaphysics that are especially acceptable to them; and the especially acceptable brands are acceptable because they do not menace the established order of society."

Here there was a stir of dissent around the table.

"Oh, I am not challenging your sincerity," Ernest continued. "You are sincere. You preach what you believe. There lies your strength and your value—to the capitalist class. But should you change your belief to something that menaces the established order, your preaching would be unacceptable to your employers, and you would be discharged. Every little while some one or another of you is so discharged.* Am I not right?"

During this period there were many ministers cast out of the church for preaching unacceptable doctrine. Especially were they cast out when their preaching became tainted with socialism.

This time there was no dissent. They sat dumbly acquiescent, with the exception of Dr. Hammerfield, who said:

"It is when their thinking is wrong that they are asked to resign."

"Which is another way of saying when their thinking is unacceptable," Ernest answered, and then went on. "So I say to you, go ahead and preach and earn your pay, but for goodness' sake leave the working class alone. You belong in the enemy's camp. You have nothing in common with the working class. Your hands are soft with the work others have performed for you. Your stomachs are round with the plenitude of eating." (Here Dr. Ballingford winced, and every eye glanced at his prodigious girth. It was said he had not seen his own feet in years.) "And your minds are filled with doctrines that are buttresses of the established order. You are as much mercenaries (sincere mercenaries, I grant) as were the men of the Swiss Guard.* Be true to your salt and your hire; guard, with your preaching, the interests of your employers; but do not come down to the working class and serve as false leaders. You cannot honestly be in the two camps at once. The working class has done without you. Believe me, the working class will continue to do without you. And, furthermore, the working class can do better without you than with you."

The hired foreign palace guards of Louis XVI, a king of France that was beheaded by his people.

CHAPTER II. CHALLENGES.

After the guests had gone, father threw himself into a chair and gave vent to roars of Gargantuan laughter. Not since the death of my mother had I known him to laugh so heartily.

"I'll wager Dr. Hammerfield was never up against anything like it in his life," he laughed. "'The courtesies of ecclesiastical controversy!' Did you notice how he began like a lamb—Everhard, I mean, and how quickly he became a roaring lion? He has a splendidly disciplined mind. He would have made a good scientist if his energies had been directed that way."

I need scarcely say that I was deeply interested in Ernest Everhard. It was not alone what he had said and how he had said it, but it was the man himself. I had never met a man like him. I suppose that was why, in spite of my twenty-four years, I had not married. I liked him; I had to confess it to myself. And my like for him was founded on things beyond intellect and argument. Regardless of his bulging muscles and prize-fighter's throat, he impressed me as an ingenuous boy. I felt that under the guise of an intellectual swashbuckler was a delicate and sensitive spirit. I sensed this, in ways I knew not, save that they were my woman's intuitions.

There was something in that clarion-call of his that went to my heart. It still rang in my ears, and I felt that I should like to hear it again—and to see again that glint of laughter in his eyes that belied the impassioned seriousness of his face. And there were further reaches of vague and indeterminate feelings that stirred in me. I almost loved him then, though I am confident, had I never seen him again, that the vague feelings would have passed away and that I should easily have forgotten him.

But I was not destined never to see him again. My father's new-born interest in sociology and the dinner parties he gave would not permit. Father was not a sociologist. His marriage with my mother had been very happy, and in the researches of his own science, physics, he had been very happy. But when mother died, his own work could not fill the emptiness. At first, in a mild way, he had dabbled in philosophy; then, becoming interested, he had drifted on into economics and sociology. He had a strong sense of justice, and he soon became fired with a passion to redress wrong. It was with gratitude that I hailed these signs of a new interest in life, though I little dreamed what the outcome would be. With the enthusiasm of a boy he plunged excitedly into these new pursuits, regardless of whither they led him.

He had been used always to the laboratory, and so it was that he turned the dining room into a sociological laboratory. Here came to dinner all sorts and conditions of men,—scientists, politicians, bankers, merchants, professors, labor leaders, socialists, and anarchists. He stirred them to discussion, and analyzed their thoughts of life and society.

He had met Ernest shortly prior to the "preacher's night." And after the guests were gone, I learned how he had met him, passing down a street at night and stopping to listen to a man on a soap-box who was addressing a crowd of workingmen. The man on the box was Ernest. Not that he was a mere soap-box orator. He stood high in the councils of the socialist party, was one of the leaders, and was the acknowledged leader in the philosophy of socialism. But he had a certain clear way of stating the abstruse in simple language, was a born expositor and teacher, and was not above the soap-box as a means of interpreting economics to the workingmen.

My father stopped to listen, became interested, effected a meeting, and, after quite an acquaintance, invited him to the ministers' dinner. It was after the dinner that father told me what little he knew about him. He had been born in the working class, though he was a descendant of the old line of Everhards that for over two hundred years had lived in America.* At ten years of age he had gone to work in the mills, and later he served his apprenticeship and became a horseshoer. He was self-educated, had taught himself German and French, and at that time was earning a meagre living by translating scientific and philosophical works for a struggling socialist publishing house in Chicago. Also, his earnings were added to by the royalties from the small sales of his own economic and philosophic works.

** The distinction between being native born and foreign born
was sharp and invidious in those days.*

This much I learned of him before I went to bed, and I lay long awake, listening in memory to the sound of his voice. I grew frightened at my thoughts. He was so unlike the men of my own class, so alien and so strong. His masterfulness delighted me and terrified me, for my fancies wantonly roved until I found myself considering him as a lover, as a husband. I had always heard that the strength of men was an irresistible attraction to women; but he was too strong. "No! no!" I cried out. "It is impossible, absurd!" And on the morrow I awoke to find in myself a longing to see him again. I wanted to see him mastering men in discussion, the war-note in his voice; to see him, in all his certitude and strength, shattering their complacency, shaking them out of their ruts of thinking. What if he did swashbuckle? To use his own phrase, "it worked," it produced effects. And, besides, his swashbuckling was a fine thing to see. It stirred one like the onset of battle.

Several days passed during which I read Ernest's books, borrowed from my father. His written word was as his spoken word, clear and convincing. It was its absolute simplicity that convinced even while one continued to doubt. He had the gift of lucidity. He was the perfect expositor. Yet, in spite of his style, there was much that I did not like. He laid too great stress on what he called the class struggle, the antagonism between labor and capital, the conflict of interest.

Father reported with glee Dr. Hammerfield's judgment of Ernest, which was to the effect that he was "an insolent young puppy, made bumptious by a little and very inadequate learning." Also, Dr. Hammerfield declined to meet Ernest again.

But Bishop Morehouse turned out to have become interested in Ernest, and was anxious for another meeting. "A strong young man," he said; "and very much alive, very much alive. But he is too sure, too sure."

Ernest came one afternoon with father. The Bishop had already arrived, and we were having tea on the veranda. Ernest's continued presence in Berkeley, by the way, was accounted for by the fact that he was taking special courses in biology at the university, and also that he was hard at work on a new book entitled "Philosophy and Revolution." *

This book continued to be secretly printed throughout the three centuries of the Iron Heel. There are several copies of various editions in the National Library of Ardis.

The veranda seemed suddenly to have become small when Ernest arrived. Not that he was so very large—he stood only five feet nine inches; but that he seemed to radiate an atmosphere of largeness. As he stopped to meet me, he betrayed a certain slight awkwardness that was strangely at variance with his bold-looking eyes and his firm, sure hand that clasped for a moment in greeting. And in that moment his eyes were just as steady and sure. There seemed a question in them this time, and as before he looked at me over long.

"I have been reading your 'Working-class Philosophy,'" I said, and his eyes lighted in a pleased way.

"Of course," he answered, "you took into consideration the audience to which it was addressed."

"I did, and it is because I did that I have a quarrel with you," I challenged.

"I, too, have a quarrel with you, Mr. Everhard," Bishop Morehouse said.

Ernest shrugged his shoulders whimsically and accepted a cup of tea.

The Bishop bowed and gave me precedence.

"You foment class hatred," I said. "I consider it wrong and criminal to appeal to all that is narrow and brutal in the working class. Class hatred is anti-social, and, it seems to me, anti-socialistic."

"Not guilty," he answered. "Class hatred is neither in the text nor in the spirit of anything I have ever written."

"Oh!" I cried reproachfully, and reached for his book and opened it.

He sipped his tea and smiled at me while I ran over the pages.

"Page one hundred and thirty-two," I read aloud: "'The class struggle, therefore, presents itself in the present stage of social development between the wage-paying and the wage-paid classes.'"

I looked at him triumphantly.

"No mention there of class hatred," he smiled back.

"But," I answered, "you say 'class struggle.'"

"A different thing from class hatred," he replied. "And, believe me, we foment no hatred. We say that the class struggle is a law of social development. We are not responsible for it. We do not make the class struggle. We merely explain it, as Newton explained gravitation. We explain the nature of the conflict of interest that produces the class struggle."

"But there should be no conflict of interest!" I cried.

"I agree with you heartily," he answered. "That is what we socialists are trying to bring about,—the abolition of the conflict of interest. Pardon me. Let me read an extract." He took his book and turned back several pages. "Page one hundred and twenty-six: 'The cycle of class struggles which began with the dissolution of rude, tribal communism and the rise of private property will end with the passing of private property in the means of social existence.'"

"But I disagree with you," the Bishop interposed, his pale, ascetic face betraying by a faint glow the intensity of his feelings. "Your premise is wrong. There is no such thing as a conflict of interest between labor and capital—or, rather, there ought not to be."

"Thank you," Ernest said gravely. "By that last statement you have given me back my premise."

"But why should there be a conflict?" the Bishop demanded warmly.

Ernest shrugged his shoulders. "Because we are so made, I guess."

"But we are not so made!" cried the other.

"Are you discussing the ideal man?" Ernest asked, "—unselfish and godlike, and so few in numbers as to be practically non-existent, or are you discussing the common and ordinary average man?"

"The common and ordinary man," was the answer.

"Who is weak and fallible, prone to error?"

Bishop Morehouse nodded.

"And petty and selfish?"

Again he nodded.

"Watch out!" Ernest warned. "I said 'selfish.'"

"The average man IS selfish," the Bishop affirmed valiantly.

"Wants all he can get?"

"Wants all he can get—true but deplorable."

"Then I've got you." Ernest's jaw snapped like a trap. "Let me show you. Here is a man who works on the street railways."

"He couldn't work if it weren't for capital," the Bishop interrupted.

"True, and you will grant that capital would perish if there were no labor to earn the dividends."

The Bishop was silent.

"Won't you?" Ernest insisted.

The Bishop nodded.

"Then our statements cancel each other," Ernest said in a matter-of-fact tone, "and we are where we were. Now to begin again. The workingmen on the street railway furnish the labor. The stockholders furnish the capital. By the joint effort of the workingmen and the capital, money is earned.* They divide between them this money that is earned. Capital's share is called 'dividends.' Labor's share is called 'wages.'"

In those days, groups of predatory individuals controlled all the means of transportation, and for the use of same levied toll upon the public.

"Very good," the Bishop interposed. "And there is no reason that the division should not be amicable."

"You have already forgotten what we had agreed upon," Ernest replied. "We agreed that the average man is selfish. He is the man that is. You have gone up in the air and are arranging a division between the kind of men that ought to be but are not. But to return to the earth, the workingman, being selfish, wants all he can get in the division. The capitalist, being selfish, wants all he can get in the division. When there is only so much of the same thing, and when two men want all they can get of the same thing, there is a conflict of interest between labor and capital. And it is an irreconcilable conflict. As long as workingmen and capitalists exist, they will continue to quarrel over the division. If you were in San Francisco this afternoon, you'd have to walk. There isn't a street car running."

"Another strike?" * the Bishop queried with alarm.

These quarrels were very common in those irrational and anarchic times. Sometimes the laborers refused to work. Sometimes the capitalists refused to let the laborers work. In the violence and turbulence of such disagreements much property was destroyed and many lives lost. All this is inconceivable to us—as inconceivable as another custom of that time, namely, the habit the men of the lower classes had of breaking the furniture when they quarrelled with their wives.

"Yes, they're quarrelling over the division of the earnings of the street railways."

Bishop Morehouse became excited.

"It is wrong!" he cried. "It is so short-sighted on the part of the workingmen. How can they hope to keep our sympathy—"

"When we are compelled to walk," Ernest said slyly.

But Bishop Morehouse ignored him and went on:

"Their outlook is too narrow. Men should be men, not brutes. There will be violence and murder now, and sorrowing widows and orphans. Capital and labor should be friends. They should work hand in hand and to their mutual benefit."

"Ah, now you are up in the air again," Ernest remarked dryly. "Come back to earth. Remember, we agreed that the average man is selfish."

"But he ought not to be!" the Bishop cried.

"And there I agree with you," was Ernest's rejoinder. "He ought not to be selfish, but he will continue to be selfish as long as he lives in a social system that is based on pig-ethics."

The Bishop was aghast, and my father chuckled.

"Yes, pig-ethics," Ernest went on remorselessly. "That is the meaning of the capitalist system. And that is what your church is standing for, what you are preaching for every time you get up in the pulpit. Pig-ethics! There is no other name for it."

Bishop Morehouse turned appealingly to my father, but he laughed and nodded his head.

"I'm afraid Mr. Everhard is right," he said. "LAISSEZ-FAIRE, the let-alone policy of each for himself and devil take the hindmost. As Mr. Everhard said the other night, the function you churchmen perform is to maintain the established order of society, and society is established on that foundation."

"But that is not the teaching of Christ!" cried the Bishop.

"The Church is not teaching Christ these days," Ernest put in quickly. "That is why the workingmen will have nothing to do with the Church. The Church condones the frightful brutality and savagery with which the capitalist class treats the working class."

"The Church does not condone it," the Bishop objected.

"The Church does not protest against it," Ernest replied. "And in so far as the Church does not protest, it condones, for remember the Church is supported by the capitalist class."

"I had not looked at it in that light," the Bishop said naively. "You must be wrong. I know that there is much that is sad and wicked in this world. I know that the Church has lost the—what you call the proletariat." *

* *Proletariat: Derived originally from the Latin PROLETARII, the name given in the census of Servius Tullius to those who were of value to the state only as the rearers of offspring (PROLES); in other words, they were of no importance either for wealth, or position, or exceptional ability.*

"You never had the proletariat," Ernest cried. "The proletariat has grown up outside the Church and without the Church."

"I do not follow you," the Bishop said faintly.

"Then let me explain. With the introduction of machinery and the factory system in the latter part of the eighteenth century, the great mass of the working people was separated from the land. The old system of labor was broken down. The working people were driven from their villages and herded in factory towns. The mothers and children were put to work at the new machines. Family life ceased. The conditions were frightful. It is a tale of blood."

"I know, I know," Bishop Morehouse interrupted with an agonized expression on his face. "It was terrible. But it occurred a century and a half ago."

"And there, a century and a half ago, originated the modern proletariat," Ernest continued. "And the Church ignored it. While a slaughter-house was made of the nation by the capitalist, the Church was dumb. It did not protest, as to-day it does not protest. As Austin Lewis* says, speaking of that time, those to whom the command 'Feed my lambs' had been given, saw those lambs sold into slavery and worked to death without a protest.** The Church was dumb, then, and before I go on I want you either flatly to agree with me or flatly to disagree with me. Was the Church dumb then?"

*Candidate for Governor of California on the Socialist ticket in the fall election of 1906 Christian Era. An Englishman by birth, a writer of many books on political economy and philosophy, and one of the Socialist leaders of the times.

** There is no more horrible page in history than the treatment of the child and women slaves in the English factories in the latter half of the eighteenth century of the Christian Era. In such industrial hells arose some of the proudest fortunes of that day.

Bishop Morehouse hesitated. Like Dr. Hammerfield, he was unused to this fierce "infighting," as Ernest called it.

"The history of the eighteenth century is written," Ernest prompted. "If the Church was not dumb, it will be found not dumb in the books."

"I am afraid the Church was dumb," the Bishop confessed.

"And the Church is dumb to-day."

"There I disagree," said the Bishop.

Ernest paused, looked at him searchingly, and accepted the challenge.

"All right," he said. "Let us see. In Chicago there are women who toil all the week for ninety cents. Has the Church protested?"

"This is news to me," was the answer. "Ninety cents per week! It is horrible!"

"Has the Church protested?" Ernest insisted.

"The Church does not know." The Bishop was struggling hard.

"Yet the command to the Church was, 'Feed my lambs,'" Ernest sneered. And then, the next moment, "Pardon my sneer, Bishop. But can you wonder that we lose patience with you? When have you protested to your capitalistic congregations at the working of children in the Southern cotton mills?*

Children, six and seven years of age, working every night at twelve-hour shifts? They never see the blessed sunshine. They die like flies. The dividends are paid out of their blood. And out of the dividends magnificent churches are built in New England, wherein your kind preaches pleasant platitudes to the sleek, full-bellied recipients of those dividends."

Everhard might have drawn a better illustration from the Southern Church's outspoken defence of chattel slavery prior to what is known as the "War of the Rebellion." Several such illustrations, culled from the documents of the times, are here appended. In 1835 A.D., the General Assembly of the Presbyterian Church resolved that: "slavery is recognized in both the Old and the New Testaments, and is not condemned by the authority of God." The Charleston Baptist Association issued the following, in an address, in 1835 A.D.: "The right of masters to dispose of the time of their slaves has been distinctly recognized by the Creator of all things, who is surely at liberty to vest the right of property over any object whomsoever He pleases." The Rev. E. D. Simon, Doctor of Divinity and professor in the Randolph-Macon Methodist College of Virginia, wrote: "Extracts from Holy Writ unequivocally assert the right of property in slaves, together with the usual incidents to that right. The right to buy and sell is clearly stated.

47

Upon the whole, then, whether we consult the Jewish policy instituted by God himself, or the uniform opinion and practice of mankind in all ages, or the injunctions of the New Testament and the moral law, we are brought to the conclusion that slavery is not immoral. Having established the point that the first African slaves were legally brought into bondage, the right to detain their children in bondage follows as an indispensable consequence. Thus we see that the slavery that exists in America was founded in right."

It is not at all remarkable that this same note should have been struck by the Church a generation or so later in relation to the defence of capitalistic property. In the great museum at Asgard there is a book entitled "Essays in Application," written by Henry van Dyke. The book was published in 1905 of the Christian Era. From what we can make out, Van Dyke must have been a churchman. The book is a good example of what Everhard would have called bourgeois thinking. Note the similarity between the utterance of the Charleston Baptist Association quoted above, and the following utterance of Van Dyke seventy years later: "The Bible teaches that God owns the world. He distributes to every man according to His own good pleasure, conformably to general laws."

"I did not know," the Bishop murmured faintly. His face was pale, and he seemed suffering from nausea.

"Then you have not protested?"

The Bishop shook his head.

"Then the Church is dumb to-day, as it was in the eighteenth century?"

The Bishop was silent, and for once Ernest forbore to press the point.

"And do not forget, whenever a churchman does protest, that he is discharged."

"I hardly think that is fair," was the objection.

"Will you protest?" Ernest demanded.

"Show me evils, such as you mention, in our own community, and I will protest."

"I'll show you," Ernest said quietly. "I am at your disposal. I will take you on a journey through hell."

"And I shall protest." The Bishop straightened himself in his chair, and over his gentle face spread the harshness of the warrior. "The Church shall not be dumb!"

"You will be discharged," was the warning.

"I shall prove the contrary," was the retort. "I shall prove, if what you say is so, that the Church has erred through ignorance. And, furthermore, I hold that whatever is horrible in industrial society is due to the ignorance of the capitalist class. It will mend all that is wrong as soon as it receives the message. And this message it shall be the duty of the Church to deliver."

Ernest laughed. He laughed brutally, and I was driven to the Bishop's defence.

"Remember," I said, "you see but one side of the shield. There is much good in us, though you give us credit for no good at all. Bishop Morehouse is right. The industrial wrong, terrible as you say it is, is due to ignorance. The divisions of society have become too widely separated."

"The wild Indian is not so brutal and savage as the capitalist class," he answered; and in that moment I hated him.

"You do not know us," I answered. "We are not brutal and savage."

"Prove it," he challenged.

"How can I prove it . . . to you?" I was growing angry.

He shook his head. "I do not ask you to prove it to me. I ask you to prove it to yourself."

"I know," I said.

"You know nothing," was his rude reply.

"There, there, children," father said soothingly.

"I don't care—" I began indignantly, but Ernest interrupted.

"I understand you have money, or your father has, which is the same thing—money invested in the Sierra Mills."

"What has that to do with it?" I cried.

"Nothing much," he began slowly, "except that the gown you wear is stained with blood. The food you eat is a bloody stew. The blood of little children and of strong men is dripping from your very roof-beams. I can close my eyes, now, and hear it drip, drop, drip, drop, all about me."

And suiting the action to the words, he closed his eyes and leaned back in his chair. I burst into tears of mortification and hurt vanity. I had never been so brutally treated in my life. Both the Bishop and my father were embarrassed and perturbed. They tried to lead the conversation away into easier channels; but Ernest opened his eyes, looked at me, and waved them aside. His mouth was stern, and his eyes too; and in the latter there was no glint of laughter. What he was about to say, what terrible castigation he was going to give me, I never knew; for at that moment a man, passing along the sidewalk, stopped and glanced in at us. He was a large man, poorly dressed, and on his back was a great load of rattan and bamboo stands, chairs, and screens. He looked at the house as if debating whether or not he should come in and try to sell some of his wares.

"That man's name is Jackson," Ernest said.

"With that strong body of his he should be at work, and not peddling," * I answered curtly.

> * In that day there were many thousands of these poor
>
> merchants called PEDLERS. They carried their whole stock in
>
> trade from door to door. It was a most wasteful expenditure
>
> of energy. Distribution was as confused and irrational as
>
> the whole general system of society.

"Notice the sleeve of his left arm," Ernest said gently.

I looked, and saw that the sleeve was empty.

"It was some of the blood from that arm that I heard dripping from your roof-beams," Ernest said with continued gentleness. "He lost his arm in the Sierra Mills, and like a broken-down horse you turned him out on the highway to die. When I say 'you,' I mean the superintendent and the officials that you and the other stockholders pay to manage the mills for you. It was an accident. It was caused by his trying to save the company a few dollars. The toothed drum of the picker caught his arm. He might have let the small flint that he saw in the teeth go through. It would have smashed out a double row of spikes. But he reached for the flint, and his arm was picked and clawed to shreds from the finger tips to the shoulder. It was at night. The mills were working overtime. They paid a fat dividend that quarter. Jackson had been working many hours, and his muscles had lost their resiliency and snap. They made his movements a bit slow. That was why the machine caught him. He had a wife and three children."

"And what did the company do for him?" I asked.

"Nothing. Oh, yes, they did do something. They successfully fought the damage suit he brought when he came out of hospital. The company employs very efficient lawyers, you know."

"You have not told the whole story," I said with conviction. "Or else you do not know the whole story. Maybe the man was insolent."

"Insolent! Ha! ha!" His laughter was Mephistophelian. "Great God! Insolent! And with his arm chewed off! Nevertheless he was a meek and lowly servant, and there is no record of his having been insolent."

"But the courts," I urged. "The case would not have been decided against him had there been no more to the affair than you have mentioned."

"Colonel Ingram is leading counsel for the company. He is a shrewd lawyer." Ernest looked at me intently for a moment, then went on. "I'll tell you what you do, Miss Cunningham. You investigate Jackson's case."

"I had already determined to," I said coldly.

"All right," he beamed good-naturedly, "and I'll tell you where to find him. But I tremble for you when I think of all you are to prove by Jackson's arm."

And so it came about that both the Bishop and I accepted Ernest's challenges. They went away together, leaving me smarting with a sense of injustice that had been done me and my class. The man was a beast. I hated him, then, and consoled myself with the thought that his behavior was what was to be expected from a man of the working class.

CHAPTER III. JACKSON'S ARM.

Little did I dream the fateful part Jackson's arm was to play in my life. Jackson himself did not impress me when I hunted him out. I found him in a crazy, ramshackle* house down near the bay on the edge of the marsh. Pools of stagnant water stood around the house, their surfaces covered with a green and putrid-looking scum, while the stench that arose from them was intolerable.

> *An adjective descriptive of ruined and dilapidated houses
>
>   in which great numbers of the working people found shelter
>
>   in those days. They invariably paid rent, and, considering
>
>   the value of such houses, enormous rent, to the landlords.

I found Jackson the meek and lowly man he had been described. He was making some sort of rattan-work, and he toiled on stolidly while I talked with him. But in spite of his meekness and lowliness, I fancied I caught the first note of a nascent bitterness in him when he said:

"They might a-given me a job as watchman,* anyway."

> *In those days thievery was incredibly prevalent.
>
>   Everybody stole property from everybody else. The lords of
>
>   society stole legally or else legalized their stealing,
>
>   while the poorer classes stole illegally. Nothing was safe
>
>   unless guarded. Enormous numbers of men were employed as

watchmen to protect property. The houses of the well-to-do were a combination of safe deposit vault and fortress. The appropriation of the personal belongings of others by our own children of to-day is looked upon as a rudimentary survival of the theft-characteristic that in those early times was universal.

I got little out of him. He struck me as stupid, and yet the deftness with which he worked with his one hand seemed to belie his stupidity. This suggested an idea to me.

"How did you happen to get your arm caught in the machine?" I asked.

He looked at me in a slow and pondering way, and shook his head. "I don't know. It just happened."

"Carelessness?" I prompted.

"No," he answered, "I ain't for callin' it that. I was workin' overtime, an' I guess I was tired out some. I worked seventeen years in them mills, an' I've took notice that most of the accidents happens just before whistle-blow.* I'm willin' to bet that more accidents happens in the hour before whistle-blow than in all the rest of the day. A man ain't so quick after workin' steady for hours. I've seen too many of 'em cut up an' gouged an' chawed not to know."

* The laborers were called to work and dismissed by savage, screaming, nerve-racking steam-whistles.

"Many of them?" I queried.

"Hundreds an' hundreds, an' children, too."

With the exception of the terrible details, Jackson's story of his accident was the same as that I had already heard. When I asked him if he had broken some rule of working the machinery, he shook his head.

"I chucked off the belt with my right hand," he said, "an' made a reach for the flint with my left. I didn't stop to see if the belt was off. I thought my right hand had done it—only it didn't. I reached quick, and the belt wasn't all the way off. And then my arm was chewed off."

"It must have been painful," I said sympathetically.

"The crunchin' of the bones wasn't nice," was his answer.

His mind was rather hazy concerning the damage suit. Only one thing was clear to him, and that was that he had not got any damages. He had a feeling that the testimony of the foremen and the superintendent had brought about the adverse decision of the court. Their testimony, as he put it, "wasn't what it ought to have ben." And to them I resolved to go.

One thing was plain, Jackson's situation was wretched. His wife was in ill health, and he was unable to earn, by his rattan-work and peddling, sufficient food for the family. He was back in his rent, and the oldest boy, a lad of eleven, had started to work in the mills.

"They might a-given me that watchman's job," were his last words as I went away.

By the time I had seen the lawyer who had handled Jackson's case, and the two foremen and the superintendent at the mills who had testified, I began to feel that there was something after all in Ernest's contention.

He was a weak and inefficient-looking man, the lawyer, and at sight of him I did not wonder that Jackson's case had been lost. My first thought was that it had served Jackson right for getting such a lawyer. But the next moment two of Ernest's statements came flashing into my consciousness: "The company employs very efficient lawyers" and "Colonel Ingram is a shrewd lawyer." I did some rapid thinking. It dawned upon me that of course the company could afford finer legal talent than could a workingman like Jackson. But this was merely a minor detail. There was some very good reason, I was sure, why Jackson's case had gone against him.

"Why did you lose the case?" I asked.

The lawyer was perplexed and worried for a moment, and I found it in my heart to pity the wretched little creature. Then he began to whine. I do believe his whine was congenital. He was a man beaten at birth. He whined about the testimony. The witnesses had given only the evidence that helped the other side. Not one word could he get out of them that would have helped Jackson. They knew which side their bread was buttered on. Jackson was a fool. He had been brow-beaten and confused by Colonel Ingram. Colonel Ingram was brilliant at cross-examination. He had made Jackson answer damaging questions.

"How could his answers be damaging if he had the right on his side?" I demanded.

"What's right got to do with it?" he demanded back. "You see all those books." He moved his hand over the array of volumes on the walls of his tiny office. "All my reading and studying of them has taught me that law is one thing and right is another thing. Ask any lawyer. You go to Sunday-school to learn what is right. But you go to those books to learn . . . law."

"Do you mean to tell me that Jackson had the right on his side and yet was beaten?" I queried tentatively. "Do you mean to tell me that there is no justice in Judge Caldwell's court?"

The little lawyer glared at me a moment, and then the belligerence faded out of his face.

"I hadn't a fair chance," he began whining again. "They made a fool out of Jackson and out of me, too. What chance had I? Colonel Ingram is a great lawyer. If he wasn't great, would he have charge of the law business of the Sierra Mills, of the Erston Land Syndicate, of the Berkeley Consolidated, of the Oakland, San Leandro, and Pleasanton Electric? He's a corporation lawyer, and corporation lawyers are not paid for being fools.* What do you think the Sierra Mills alone give him twenty thousand dollars a year for?

Because he's worth twenty thousand dollars a year to them, that's what for. I'm not worth that much. If I was, I wouldn't be on the outside, starving and taking cases like Jackson's. What do you think I'd have got if I'd won Jackson's case?"

* *The function of the corporation lawyer was to serve, by corrupt methods, the money-grabbing propensities of the corporations. It is on record that Theodore Roosevelt, at that time President of the United States, said in 1905 A.D., in his address at Harvard Commencement: "We all know that, as things actually are, many of the most influential and most highly remunerated members of the Bar in every centre of wealth, make it their special task to work out bold and ingenious schemes by which their wealthy clients, individual or corporate, can evade the laws which were made to regulate, in the interests of the public, the uses of great wealth."*

"You'd have robbed him, most probably," I answered.

"Of course I would," he cried angrily. "I've got to live, haven't I?" *

* *A typical illustration of the internecine strife that permeated all society. Men preyed upon one another like ravening wolves. The big wolves ate the little wolves, and*

in the social pack Jackson was one of the least of the

little wolves.

"He has a wife and children," I chided.

"So have I a wife and children," he retorted. "And there's not a soul in this world except myself that cares whether they starve or not."

His face suddenly softened, and he opened his watch and showed me a small photograph of a woman and two little girls pasted inside the case.

"There they are. Look at them. We've had a hard time, a hard time. I had hoped to send them away to the country if I'd won Jackson's case. They're not healthy here, but I can't afford to send them away."

When I started to leave, he dropped back into his whine.

"I hadn't the ghost of a chance. Colonel Ingram and Judge Caldwell are pretty friendly. I'm not saying that if I'd got the right kind of testimony out of their witnesses on cross-examination, that friendship would have decided the case. And yet I must say that Judge Caldwell did a whole lot to prevent my getting that very testimony. Why, Judge Caldwell and Colonel Ingram belong to the same lodge and the same club. They live in the same neighborhood— one I can't afford. And their wives are always in and out of each other's houses. They're always having whist parties and such things back and forth."

"And yet you think Jackson had the right of it?" I asked, pausing for the moment on the threshold.

"I don't think; I know it," was his answer. "And at first I thought he had some show, too. But I didn't tell my wife. I didn't want to disappoint her. She had her heart set on a trip to the country hard enough as it was."

"Why did you not call attention to the fact that Jackson was trying to save the machinery from being injured?" I asked Peter Donnelly, one of the foremen who had testified at the trial.

He pondered a long time before replying. Then he cast an anxious look about him and said:

"Because I've a good wife an' three of the sweetest children ye ever laid eyes on, that's why."

"I do not understand," I said.

"In other words, because it wouldn't a-ben healthy," he answered.

"You mean—" I began.

But he interrupted passionately.

"I mean what I said. It's long years I've worked in the mills. I began as a little lad on the spindles. I worked up ever since. It's by hard work I got to my present exalted position. I'm a foreman, if you please. An' I doubt me if there's a man in the mills that'd put out a hand to drag me from drownin'. I used to belong to the union. But I've stayed by the company through two strikes. They called me 'scab.' There's not a man among 'em to-day to take a drink with me if I asked him. D'ye see the scars on me head where I was struck with flying bricks? There ain't a child at the spindles but what would curse me name. Me only friend is the company. It's not me duty, but me bread an' butter an' the life of me children to stand by the mills. That's why."

"Was Jackson to blame?" I asked.

"He should a-got the damages. He was a good worker an' never made trouble."

"Then you were not at liberty to tell the whole truth, as you had sworn to do?"

He shook his head.

"The truth, the whole truth, and nothing but the truth?" I said solemnly.

Again his face became impassioned, and he lifted it, not to me, but to heaven.

"I'd let me soul an' body burn in everlastin' hell for them children of mine," was his answer.

Henry Dallas, the superintendent, was a vulpine-faced creature who regarded me insolently and refused to talk. Not a word could I get from him concerning the trial and his testimony. But with the other foreman I had better luck. James Smith was a hard-faced man, and my heart sank as I encountered him. He, too, gave me the impression that he was not a free agent, as we talked I began to see that he was mentally superior to the average of his kind. He agreed with Peter Donnelly that Jackson should have got damages, and he went farther and called the action heartless and cold-blooded that had turned the worker adrift after he had been made helpless by the accident. Also, he explained that there were many accidents in the mills, and that the company's policy was to fight to the bitter end all consequent damage suits.

"It means hundreds of thousands a year to the stockholders," he said; and as he spoke I remembered the last dividend that had been paid my father, and the pretty gown for me and the books for him that had been bought out of that dividend. I remembered Ernest's charge that my gown was stained with blood, and my flesh began to crawl underneath my garments.

"When you testified at the trial, you didn't point out that Jackson received his accident through trying to save the machinery from damage?" I said.

"No, I did not," was the answer, and his mouth set bitterly. "I testified to the effect that Jackson injured himself by neglect and carelessness, and that the company was not in any way to blame or liable."

"Was it carelessness?" I asked.

"Call it that, or anything you want to call it. The fact is, a man gets tired after he's been working for hours."

I was becoming interested in the man. He certainly was of a superior kind.

"You are better educated than most workingmen," I said.

"I went through high school," he replied. "I worked my way through doing janitor-work. I wanted to go through the university. But my father died, and I came to work in the mills.

60

"I wanted to become a naturalist," he explained shyly, as though confessing a weakness. "I love animals. But I came to work in the mills. When I was promoted to foreman I got married, then the family came, and . . . well, I wasn't my own boss any more."

"What do you mean by that?" I asked.

"I was explaining why I testified at the trial the way I did—why I followed instructions."

"Whose instructions?"

"Colonel Ingram. He outlined the evidence I was to give."

"And it lost Jackson's case for him."

He nodded, and the blood began to rise darkly in his face.

"And Jackson had a wife and two children dependent on him."

"I know," he said quietly, though his face was growing darker.

"Tell me," I went on, "was it easy to make yourself over from what you were, say in high school, to the man you must have become to do such a thing at the trial?"

The suddenness of his outburst startled and frightened me. He ripped* out a savage oath, and clenched his fist as though about to strike me.

* It is interesting to note the virilities of language that
were common speech in that day, as indicative of the life,
'red of claw and fang,' that was then lived. Reference is
here made, of course, not to the oath of Smith, but to the
verb ripped used by Avis Everhard.

"I beg your pardon," he said the next moment. "No, it was not easy. And now I guess you can go away. You've got all you wanted out of me. But let me tell you this before you go. It won't do you any good to repeat anything I've said. I'll deny it, and there are no witnesses. I'll deny every word of it; and if I have to, I'll do it under oath on the witness stand."

After my interview with Smith I went to my father's office in the Chemistry Building and there encountered Ernest. It was quite unexpected, but he met me with his bold eyes and firm hand-clasp, and with that curious blend of his awkwardness and ease. It was as though our last stormy meeting was forgotten; but I was not in the mood to have it forgotten.

"I have been looking up Jackson's case," I said abruptly.

He was all interested attention, and waited for me to go on, though I could see in his eyes the certitude that my convictions had been shaken.

"He seems to have been badly treated," I confessed. "I—I—think some of his blood is dripping from our roof-beams."

"Of course," he answered. "If Jackson and all his fellows were treated mercifully, the dividends would not be so large."

"I shall never be able to take pleasure in pretty gowns again," I added.

I felt humble and contrite, and was aware of a sweet feeling that Ernest was a sort of father confessor. Then, as ever after, his strength appealed to me. It seemed to radiate a promise of peace and protection.

"Nor will you be able to take pleasure in sackcloth," he said gravely. "There are the jute mills, you know, and the same thing goes on there. It goes on everywhere. Our boasted civilization is based upon blood, soaked in blood, and neither you nor I nor any of us can escape the scarlet stain. The men you talked with—who were they?"

I told him all that had taken place.

"And not one of them was a free agent," he said. "They were all tied to the merciless industrial machine. And the pathos of it and the tragedy is that they are tied by their heartstrings. Their children—always the young life that it is their instinct to protect. This instinct is stronger than any ethic they possess. My father! He lied, he stole, he did all sorts of dishonorable things to put bread into my mouth and into the mouths of my brothers and sisters. He was a slave to the industrial machine, and it stamped his life out, worked him to death."

"But you," I interjected. "You are surely a free agent."

"Not wholly," he replied. "I am not tied by my heartstrings. I am often thankful that I have no children, and I dearly love children. Yet if I married I should not dare to have any."

"That surely is bad doctrine," I cried.

"I know it is," he said sadly. "But it is expedient doctrine. I am a revolutionist, and it is a perilous vocation."

I laughed incredulously.

"If I tried to enter your father's house at night to steal his dividends from the Sierra Mills, what would he do?"

"He sleeps with a revolver on the stand by the bed," I answered. "He would most probably shoot you."

"And if I and a few others should lead a million and a half of men* into the houses of all the well-to-do, there would be a great deal of shooting, wouldn't there?"

* *This reference is to the socialist vote cast in the United States in 1910. The rise of this vote clearly indicates the swift growth of the party of revolution. Its voting strength in the United States in 1888 was 2068; in 1902, 127,713; in 1904, 435,040; in 1908, 1,108,427; and in 1910, 1,688,211.*

"Yes, but you are not doing that," I objected.

"It is precisely what I am doing. And we intend to take, not the mere wealth in the houses, but all the sources of that wealth, all the mines, and railroads, and factories, and banks, and stores. That is the revolution. It is truly perilous. There will be more shooting, I am afraid, than even I dream of. But as I was saying, no one to-day is a free agent. We are all caught up in the wheels and cogs of the industrial machine. You found that you were, and that the men you talked with were. Talk with more of them. Go and see Colonel Ingram. Look up the reporters that kept Jackson's case out of the papers, and the editors that run the papers. You will find them all slaves of the machine."

A little later in our conversation I asked him a simple little question about the liability of workingmen to accidents, and received a statistical lecture in return.

"It is all in the books," he said. "The figures have been gathered, and it has been proved conclusively that accidents rarely occur in the first hours of the morning work, but that they increase rapidly in the succeeding hours as the workers grow tired and slower in both their muscular and mental processes.

"Why, do you know that your father has three times as many chances for safety of life and limb than has a working-man? He has. The insurance* companies know. They will charge him four dollars and twenty cents a year on a thousand-dollar accident policy, and for the same policy they will charge a laborer fifteen dollars."

> *In the terrible wolf-struggle of those centuries, no man
> was permanently safe, no matter how much wealth he amassed.
> Out of fear for the welfare of their families, men devised
> the scheme of insurance. To us, in this intelligent age,

*such a device is laughably absurd and primitive. But in
that age insurance was a very serious matter. The amusing
part of it is that the funds of the insurance companies were
frequently plundered and wasted by the very officials who
were intrusted with the management of them.*

"And you?" I asked; and in the moment of asking I was aware of a solicitude that was something more than slight.

"Oh, as a revolutionist, I have about eight chances to the workingman's one of being injured or killed," he answered carelessly. "The insurance companies charge the highly trained chemists that handle explosives eight times what they charge the workingmen. I don't think they'd insure me at all. Why did you ask?"

My eyes fluttered, and I could feel the blood warm in my face. It was not that he had caught me in my solicitude, but that I had caught myself, and in his presence.

Just then my father came in and began making preparations to depart with me. Ernest returned some books he had borrowed, and went away first. But just as he was going, he turned and said:

"Oh, by the way, while you are ruining your own peace of mind and I am ruining the Bishop's, you'd better look up Mrs. Wickson and Mrs. Pertonwaithe. Their husbands, you know, are the two principal stockholders in the Mills. Like all the rest of humanity, those two women are tied to the machine, but they are so tied that they sit on top of it."

CHAPTER IV. SLAVES OF THE MACHINE

The more I thought of Jackson's arm, the more shaken I was. I was confronted by the concrete. For the first time I was seeing life. My university life, and study and culture, had not been real. I had learned nothing but theories of life and society that looked all very well on the printed page, but now I had seen life itself. Jackson's arm was a fact of life. "The fact, man, the irrefragable fact!" of Ernest's was ringing in my consciousness.

It seemed monstrous, impossible, that our whole society was based upon blood. And yet there was Jackson. I could not get away from him. Constantly my thought swung back to him as the compass to the Pole. He had been monstrously treated. His blood had not been paid for in order that a larger dividend might be paid. And I knew a score of happy complacent families that had received those dividends and by that much had profited by Jackson's blood. If one man could be so monstrously treated and society move on its way unheeding, might not many men be so monstrously treated? I remembered Ernest's women of Chicago who toiled for ninety cents a week, and the child slaves of the Southern cotton mills he had described. And I could see their wan white hands, from which the blood had been pressed, at work upon the cloth out of which had been made my gown. And then I thought of the Sierra Mills and the dividends that had been paid, and I saw the blood of Jackson upon my gown as well. Jackson I could not escape. Always my meditations led me back to him.

Down in the depths of me I had a feeling that I stood on the edge of a precipice. It was as though I were about to see a new and awful revelation of life. And not I alone. My whole world was turning over. There was my father. I could see the effect Ernest was beginning to have on him. And then there was the Bishop. When I had last seen him he had looked a sick man. He was at high nervous tension, and in his eyes there was unspeakable horror. From the little I learned I knew that Ernest had been keeping his promise of taking him through hell. But what scenes of hell the Bishop's eyes had seen, I knew not, for he seemed too stunned to speak about them.

Once, the feeling strong upon me that my little world and all the world was turning over, I thought of Ernest as the cause of it; and also I thought, "We were so happy and peaceful before he came!" And the next moment I was aware that the thought was a treason against truth, and Ernest rose before me transfigured, the apostle of truth, with shining brows and the fearlessness of one of Gods own angels, battling for the truth and the right, and battling for the succor of the poor and lonely and oppressed. And then there arose before me another figure, the Christ! He, too, had taken the part of the lowly and oppressed, and against all the established power of priest and pharisee. And I remembered his end upon the cross, and my heart contracted with a pang as I thought of Ernest. Was he, too, destined for a cross?—he, with his clarion call and war-noted voice, and all the fine man's vigor of him!

And in that moment I knew that I loved him, and that I was melting with desire to comfort him. I thought of his life. A sordid, harsh, and meagre life it must have been. And I thought of his father, who had lied and stolen for him and been worked to death. And he himself had gone into the mills when he was ten! All my heart seemed bursting with desire to fold my arms around him, and to rest his head on my breast—his head that must be weary with so many thoughts; and to give him rest—just rest—and easement and forgetfulness for a tender space.

I met Colonel Ingram at a church reception. Him I knew well and had known well for many years. I trapped him behind large palms and rubber plants, though he did not know he was trapped. He met me with the conventional gayety and gallantry. He was ever a graceful man, diplomatic, tactful, and considerate. And as for appearance, he was the most distinguished-looking man in our society. Beside him even the venerable head of the university looked tawdry and small.

And yet I found Colonel Ingram situated the same as the unlettered mechanics. He was not a free agent. He, too, was bound upon the wheel. I shall never forget the change in him when I mentioned Jackson's case. His smiling good nature vanished like a ghost. A sudden, frightful expression distorted his well-bred face. I felt the same alarm that I had felt when James Smith broke out. But Colonel Ingram did not curse. That was the slight difference that was left between the workingman and him. He was famed as a wit, but he had no wit now. And, unconsciously, this way and that he glanced for avenues of escape. But he was trapped amid the palms and rubber trees.

Oh, he was sick of the sound of Jackson's name. Why had I brought the matter up? He did not relish my joke. It was poor taste on my part, and very inconsiderate. Did I not know that in his profession personal feelings did not count? He left his personal feelings at home when he went down to the office. At the office he had only professional feelings.

"Should Jackson have received damages?" I asked.

"Certainly," he answered. "That is, personally, I have a feeling that he should. But that has nothing to do with the legal aspects of the case."

He was getting his scattered wits slightly in hand.

"Tell me, has right anything to do with the law?" I asked.

"You have used the wrong initial consonant," he smiled in answer.

"Might?" I queried; and he nodded his head. "And yet we are supposed to get justice by means of the law?"

"That is the paradox of it," he countered. "We do get justice."

"You are speaking professionally now, are you not?" I asked.

Colonel Ingram blushed, actually blushed, and again he looked anxiously about him for a way of escape. But I blocked his path and did not offer to move.

"Tell me," I said, "when one surrenders his personal feelings to his professional feelings, may not the action be defined as a sort of spiritual mayhem?"

I did not get an answer. Colonel Ingram had ingloriously bolted, overturning a palm in his flight.

Next I tried the newspapers. I wrote a quiet, restrained, dispassionate account of Jackson's case. I made no charges against the men with whom I had talked, nor, for that matter, did I even mention them. I gave the actual facts of the case, the long years Jackson had worked in the mills, his effort to save the machinery from damage and the consequent accident, and his own present wretched and starving condition. The three local newspapers rejected my communication, likewise did the two weeklies.

I got hold of Percy Layton. He was a graduate of the university, had gone in for journalism, and was then serving his apprenticeship as reporter on the most influential of the three newspapers. He smiled when I asked him the reason the newspapers suppressed all mention of Jackson or his case.

"Editorial policy," he said. "We have nothing to do with that. It's up to the editors."

"But why is it policy?" I asked.

"We're all solid with the corporations," he answered. "If you paid advertising rates, you couldn't get any such matter into the papers. A man who tried to smuggle it in would lose his job. You couldn't get it in if you paid ten times the regular advertising rates."

"How about your own policy?" I questioned. "It would seem your function is to twist truth at the command of your employers, who, in turn, obey the behests of the corporations."

"I haven't anything to do with that." He looked uncomfortable for the moment, then brightened as he saw his way out. "I, myself, do not write untruthful things. I keep square all right with my own conscience. Of course, there's lots that's repugnant in the course of the day's work. But then, you see, that's all part of the day's work," he wound up boyishly.

"Yet you expect to sit at an editor's desk some day and conduct a policy."

"I'll be case-hardened by that time," was his reply.

"Since you are not yet case-hardened, tell me what you think right now about the general editorial policy."

"I don't think," he answered quickly. "One can't kick over the ropes if he's going to succeed in journalism. I've learned that much, at any rate."

And he nodded his young head sagely.

"But the right?" I persisted.

"You don't understand the game. Of course it's all right, because it comes out all right, don't you see?"

"Delightfully vague," I murmured; but my heart was aching for the youth of him, and I felt that I must either scream or burst into tears.

I was beginning to see through the appearances of the society in which I had always lived, and to find the frightful realities that were beneath. There seemed a tacit conspiracy against Jackson, and I was aware of a thrill of sympathy for the whining lawyer who had ingloriously fought his case. But this tacit conspiracy grew large. Not alone was it aimed against Jackson. It was aimed against every workingman who was maimed in the mills. And if against every man in the mills, why not against every man in all the other mills and factories? In fact, was it not true of all the industries?

And if this was so, then society was a lie. I shrank back from my own conclusions. It was too terrible and awful to be true. But there was Jackson, and Jackson's arm, and the blood that stained my gown and dripped from my own roof-beams. And there were many Jacksons—hundreds of them in the mills alone, as Jackson himself had said. Jackson I could not escape.

I saw Mr. Wickson and Mr. Pertonwaithe, the two men who held most of the stock in the Sierra Mills. But I could not shake them as I had shaken the mechanics in their employ. I discovered that they had an ethic superior to that of the rest of society. It was what I may call the aristocratic ethic or the master ethic.* They talked in large ways of policy, and they identified policy and right. And to me they talked in fatherly ways, patronizing my youth and inexperience. They were the most hopeless of all I had encountered in my quest. They believed absolutely that their conduct was right. There was no question about it, no discussion. They were convinced that they were the saviours of society, and that it was they who made happiness for the many. And they drew pathetic pictures of what would be the sufferings of the working class were it not for the employment that they, and they alone, by their wisdom, provided for it.

Before Avis Everhard was born, John Stuart Mill, in his essay, ON LIBERTY, wrote: "Wherever there is an ascendant class, a large portion of the morality emanates from its class interests and its class feelings of superiority."

Fresh from these two masters, I met Ernest and related my experience. He looked at me with a pleased expression, and said:

"Really, this is fine. You are beginning to dig truth for yourself. It is your own empirical generalization, and it is correct. No man in the industrial machine is a free-will agent, except the large capitalist, and he isn't, if you'll pardon the Irishism.* You see, the masters are quite sure that they are right in what they are doing. That is the crowning absurdity of the whole situation. They are so tied by their human nature that they can't do a thing unless they think it is right. They must have a sanction for their acts.

Verbal contradictions, called BULLS, were long an amiable weakness of the ancient Irish.

"When they want to do a thing, in business of course, they must wait till there arises in their brains, somehow, a religious, or ethical, or scientific, or philosophic, concept that the thing is right. And then they go ahead and do it, unwitting that one of the weaknesses of the human mind is that the wish is parent to the thought. No matter what they want to do, the sanction always comes. They are superficial casuists. They are Jesuitical. They even see their way to doing wrong that right may come of it. One of the pleasant and axiomatic fictions they have created is that they are superior to the rest of mankind in wisdom and efficiency. Therefrom comes their sanction to manage the bread and butter of the rest of mankind. They have even resurrected the theory of the divine right of kings—commercial kings in their case.*

> *The newspapers, in 1902 of that era, credited the president of the Anthracite Coal Trust, George F. Baer, with the enunciation of the following principle: "The rights and interests of the laboring man will be protected by the Christian men to whom God in His infinite wisdom has given the property interests of the country."*

"The weakness in their position lies in that they are merely business men. They are not philosophers. They are not biologists nor sociologists. If they were, of course all would be well. A business man who was also a biologist and a sociologist would know, approximately, the right thing to do for humanity. But, outside the realm of business, these men are stupid. They know only business. They do not know mankind nor society, and yet they set themselves up as arbiters of the fates of the hungry millions and all the other millions thrown in. History, some day, will have an excruciating laugh at their expense."

I was not surprised when I had my talk out with Mrs. Wickson and Mrs. Pertonwaithe. They were society women.* Their homes were palaces. They had many homes scattered over the country, in the mountains, on lakes, and by the sea. They were tended by armies of servants, and their social activities were bewildering. They patronized the university and the churches, and the pastors especially bowed at their knees in meek subservience.** They were powers, these two women, what of the money that was theirs. The power of subsidization of thought was theirs to a remarkable degree, as I was soon to learn under Ernest's tuition.

*SOCIETY is here used in a restricted sense, a common usage

of the times to denote the gilded drones that did no labor,

but only glutted themselves at the honey-vats of the

workers. Neither the business men nor the laborers had time

or opportunity for SOCIETY. SOCIETY was the creation of the

idle rich who toiled not and who in this way played.

** "Bring on your tainted money," was the expressed

sentiment of the Church during this period.

They aped their husbands, and talked in the same large ways about policy, and the duties and responsibilities of the rich. They were swayed by the same ethic that dominated their husbands—the ethic of their class; and they uttered glib phrases that their own ears did not understand.

Also, they grew irritated when I told them of the deplorable condition of Jackson's family, and when I wondered that they had made no voluntary provision for the man. I was told that they thanked no one for instructing them in their social duties. When I asked them flatly to assist Jackson, they as flatly refused. The astounding thing about it was that they refused in almost identically the same language, and this in face of the fact that I interviewed them separately and that one did not know that I had seen or was going to see the other. Their common reply was that they were glad of the opportunity to make it perfectly plain that no premium would ever be put on carelessness by them; nor would they, by paying for accident, tempt the poor to hurt themselves in the machinery.*

** In the files of the OUTLOOK, a critical weekly of the
period, in the number dated August 18, 1906, is related the
circumstance of a workingman losing his arm, the details of
which are quite similar to those of Jackson's case as
related by Avis Everhard.*

And they were sincere, these two women. They were drunk with conviction of the superiority of their class and of themselves. They had a sanction, in their own class-ethic, for every act they performed. As I drove away from Mrs. Pertonwaithe's great house, I looked back at it, and I remembered Ernest's expression that they were bound to the machine, but that they were so bound that they sat on top of it.

CHAPTER V. THE PHILOMATHS

Ernest was often at the house. Nor was it my father, merely, nor the controversial dinners, that drew him there. Even at that time I flattered myself that I played some part in causing his visits, and it was not long before I learned the correctness of my surmise. For never was there such a lover as Ernest Everhard. His gaze and his hand-clasp grew firmer and steadier, if that were possible; and the question that had grown from the first in his eyes, grew only the more imperative.

My impression of him, the first time I saw him, had been unfavorable. Then I had found myself attracted toward him. Next came my repulsion, when he so savagely attacked my class and me. After that, as I saw that he had not maligned my class, and that the harsh and bitter things he said about it were justified, I had drawn closer to him again. He became my oracle. For me he tore the sham from the face of society and gave me glimpses of reality that were as unpleasant as they were undeniably true.

As I have said, there was never such a lover as he. No girl could live in a university town till she was twenty-four and not have love experiences. I had been made love to by beardless sophomores and gray professors, and by the athletes and the football giants. But not one of them made love to me as Ernest did. His arms were around me before I knew. His lips were on mine before I could protest or resist. Before his earnestness conventional maiden dignity was ridiculous. He swept me off my feet by the splendid invincible rush of him. He did not propose. He put his arms around me and kissed me and took it for granted that we should be married. There was no discussion about it. The only discussion—and that arose afterward—was when we should be married.

It was unprecedented. It was unreal. Yet, in accordance with Ernest's test of truth, it worked. I trusted my life to it. And fortunate was the trust. Yet during those first days of our love, fear of the future came often to me when I thought of the violence and impetuosity of his love-making. Yet such fears were groundless. No woman was ever blessed with a gentler, tenderer husband. This gentleness and violence on his part was a curious blend similar to the one in his carriage of awkwardness and ease. That slight awkwardness! He never got over it, and it was delicious. His behavior in our drawing-room reminded me of a careful bull in a china shop.*

In those days it was still the custom to fill the living rooms with bric-a-brac. They had not discovered simplicity of living. Such rooms were museums, entailing endless labor to keep clean. The dust-demon was the lord of the household. There were a myriad devices for catching dust, and only a few devices for getting rid of it.

It was at this time that vanished my last doubt of the completeness of my love for him (a subconscious doubt, at most). It was at the Philomath Club—a wonderful night of battle, wherein Ernest bearded the masters in their lair. Now the Philomath Club was the most select on the Pacific Coast. It was the creation of Miss Brentwood, an enormously wealthy old maid; and it was her husband, and family, and toy. Its members were the wealthiest in the community, and the strongest-minded of the wealthy, with, of course, a sprinkling of scholars to give it intellectual tone.

The Philomath had no club house. It was not that kind of a club. Once a month its members gathered at some one of their private houses to listen to a lecture. The lecturers were usually, though not always, hired. If a chemist in New York made a new discovery in say radium, all his expenses across the continent were paid, and as well he received a princely fee for his time. The same with a returning explorer from the polar regions, or the latest literary or artistic success. No visitors were allowed, while it was the Philomath's policy to permit none of its discussions to get into the papers. Thus great statesmen—and there had been such occasions—were able fully to speak their minds.

I spread before me a wrinkled letter, written to me by Ernest twenty years ago, and from it I copy the following:

"Your father is a member of the Philomath, so you are able to come. Therefore come next Tuesday night. I promise you that you will have the time of your life. In your recent encounters, you failed to shake the masters. If you come, I'll shake them for you. I'll make them snarl like wolves. You merely questioned their morality. When their morality is questioned, they grow only the more complacent and superior. But I shall menace their money-bags. That will shake them to the roots of their primitive natures. If you can come, you will see the cave-man, in evening dress, snarling and snapping over a bone. I promise you a great caterwauling and an illuminating insight into the nature of the beast.

"They've invited me in order to tear me to pieces. This is the idea of Miss Brentwood. She clumsily hinted as much when she invited me. She's given them that kind of fun before. They delight in getting trustful-souled gentle reformers before them. Miss Brentwood thinks I am as mild as a kitten and as good-natured and stolid as the family cow. I'll not deny that I helped to give her that impression. She was very tentative at first, until she divined my harmlessness. I am to receive a handsome fee—two hundred and fifty dollars—as befits the man who, though a radical, once ran for governor. Also, I am to wear evening dress. This is compulsory. I never was so apparelled in my life. I suppose I'll have to hire one somewhere. But I'd do more than that to get a chance at the Philomaths."

Of all places, the Club gathered that night at the Pertonwaithe house. Extra chairs had been brought into the great drawing-room, and in all there must have been two hundred Philomaths that sat down to hear Ernest. They were truly lords of society. I amused myself with running over in my mind the sum of the fortunes represented, and it ran well into the hundreds of millions. And the possessors were not of the idle rich. They were men of affairs who took most active parts in industrial and political life.

We were all seated when Miss Brentwood brought Ernest in. They moved at once to the head of the room, from where he was to speak. He was in evening dress, and, what of his broad shoulders and kingly head, he looked magnificent. And then there was that faint and unmistakable touch of awkwardness in his movements. I almost think I could have loved him for that alone. And as I looked at him I was aware of a great joy. I felt again the pulse of his palm on mine, the touch of his lips; and such pride was mine that I felt I must rise up and cry out to the assembled company: "He is mine! He has held me in his arms, and I, mere I, have filled that mind of his to the exclusion of all his multitudinous and kingly thoughts!"

At the head of the room, Miss Brentwood introduced him to Colonel Van Gilbert, and I knew that the latter was to preside. Colonel Van Gilbert was a great corporation lawyer. In addition, he was immensely wealthy. The smallest fee he would deign to notice was a hundred thousand dollars. He was a master of law. The law was a puppet with which he played. He moulded it like clay, twisted and distorted it like a Chinese puzzle into any design he chose. In appearance and rhetoric he was old-fashioned, but in imagination and knowledge and resource he was as young as the latest statute. His first prominence had come when he broke the Shardwell will.* His fee for this one act was five hundred thousand dollars. From then on he had risen like a rocket. He was often called the greatest lawyer in the country—corporation lawyer, of course; and no classification of the three greatest lawyers in the United States could have excluded him.

*This breaking of wills was a peculiar feature of the period. With the accumulation of vast fortunes, the problem of disposing of these fortunes after death was a vexing one to the accumulators. Will-making and will-breaking became complementary trades, like armor-making and gun-making. The shrewdest will-making lawyers were called in to make wills that could not be broken. But these wills were always *broken, and very often by the very lawyers that had drawn*

them up. Nevertheless the delusion persisted in the wealthy

class that an absolutely unbreakable will could be cast; and

so, through the generations, clients and lawyers pursued the

illusion. It was a pursuit like unto that of the Universal

Solvent of the mediaeval alchemists.

He arose and began, in a few well-chosen phrases that carried an undertone of faint irony, to introduce Ernest. Colonel Van Gilbert was subtly facetious in his introduction of the social reformer and member of the working class, and the audience smiled. It made me angry, and I glanced at Ernest. The sight of him made me doubly angry. He did not seem to resent the delicate slurs. Worse than that, he did not seem to be aware of them. There he sat, gentle, and stolid, and somnolent. He really looked stupid. And for a moment the thought rose in my mind, What if he were overawed by this imposing array of power and brains? Then I smiled. He couldn't fool me. But he fooled the others, just as he had fooled Miss Brentwood. She occupied a chair right up to the front, and several times she turned her head toward one or another of her CONFRERES and smiled her appreciation of the remarks.

Colonel Van Gilbert done, Ernest arose and began to speak. He began in a low voice, haltingly and modestly, and with an air of evident embarrassment. He spoke of his birth in the working class, and of the sordidness and wretchedness of his environment, where flesh and spirit were alike starved and tormented. He described his ambitions and ideals, and his conception of the paradise wherein lived the people of the upper classes. As he said:

"Up above me, I knew, were unselfishnesses of the spirit, clean and noble thinking, keen intellectual living. I knew all this because I read 'Seaside Library' * novels, in which, with the exception of the villains and adventuresses, all men and women thought beautiful thoughts, spoke a beautiful tongue, and performed glorious deeds. In short, as I accepted the rising of the sun, I accepted that up above me was all that was fine and noble and gracious, all that gave decency and dignity to life, all that made life worth living and that remunerated one for his travail and misery."

A curious and amazing literature that served to make the working class utterly misapprehend the nature of the leisure class.

He went on and traced his life in the mills, the learning of the horseshoeing trade, and his meeting with the socialists. Among them, he said, he had found keen intellects and brilliant wits, ministers of the Gospel who had been broken because their Christianity was too wide for any congregation of mammon-worshippers, and professors who had been broken on the wheel of university subservience to the ruling class. The socialists were revolutionists, he said, struggling to overthrow the irrational society of the present and out of the material to build the rational society of the future. Much more he said that would take too long to write, but I shall never forget how he described the life among the revolutionists. All halting utterance vanished. His voice grew strong and confident, and it glowed as he glowed, and as the thoughts glowed that poured out from him. He said:

"Amongst the revolutionists I found, also, warm faith in the human, ardent idealism, sweetnesses of unselfishness, renunciation, and martyrdom— all the splendid, stinging things of the spirit. Here life was clean, noble, and alive. I was in touch with great souls who exalted flesh and spirit over dollars and cents, and to whom the thin wail of the starved slum child meant more than all the pomp and circumstance of commercial expansion and world empire. All about me were nobleness of purpose and heroism of effort, and my days and nights were sunshine and starshine, all fire and dew, with before my eyes, ever burning and blazing, the Holy Grail, Christ's own Grail, the warm human, long-suffering and maltreated but to be rescued and saved at the last."

As before I had seen him transfigured, so now he stood transfigured before me. His brows were bright with the divine that was in him, and brighter yet shone his eyes from the midst of the radiance that seemed to envelop him as a mantle. But the others did not see this radiance, and I assumed that it was due to the tears of joy and love that dimmed my vision. At any rate, Mr. Wickson, who sat behind me, was unaffected, for I heard him sneer aloud, "Utopian." *

* The people of that age were phrase slaves. The abjectness of their servitude is incomprehensible to us. There was a magic in words greater than the conjurer's art. So befuddled and chaotic were their minds that the utterance of a single word could negative the generalizations of a lifetime of serious research and thought. Such a word was the adjective UTOPIAN. The mere utterance of it could damn any scheme, no matter how sanely conceived, of economic amelioration or regeneration. Vast populations grew frenzied over such phrases as "an honest dollar" and "a full dinner pail." The coinage of such phrases was considered strokes of genius.

Ernest went on to his rise in society, till at last he came in touch with members of the upper classes, and rubbed shoulders with the men who sat in the high places. Then came his disillusionment, and this disillusionment he described in terms that did not flatter his audience. He was surprised at the commonness of the clay. Life proved not to be fine and gracious. He was appalled by the selfishness he encountered, and what had surprised

81

him even more than that was the absence of intellectual life. Fresh from his revolutionists, he was shocked by the intellectual stupidity of the master class. And then, in spite of their magnificent churches and well-paid preachers, he had found the masters, men and women, grossly material. It was true that they prattled sweet little ideals and dear little moralities, but in spite of their prattle the dominant key of the life they lived was materialistic. And they were without real morality—for instance, that which Christ had preached but which was no longer preached.

"I met men," he said, "who invoked the name of the Prince of Peace in their diatribes against war, and who put rifles in the hands of Pinkertons* with which to shoot down strikers in their own factories. I met men incoherent with indignation at the brutality of prize-fighting, and who, at the same time, were parties to the adulteration of food that killed each year more babes than even red-handed Herod had killed.

> *Originally, they were private detectives; but they quickly
> became hired fighting men of the capitalists, and ultimately
> developed into the Mercenaries of the Oligarchy.*

"This delicate, aristocratic-featured gentleman was a dummy director and a tool of corporations that secretly robbed widows and orphans. This gentleman, who collected fine editions and was a patron of literature, paid blackmail to a heavy-jowled, black-browed boss of a municipal machine. This editor, who published patent medicine advertisements, called me a scoundrelly demagogue because I dared him to print in his paper the truth about patent medicines.* This man, talking soberly and earnestly about the beauties of idealism and the goodness of God, had just betrayed his comrades in a business deal. This man, a pillar of the church and heavy contributor to foreign missions, worked his shop girls ten hours a day on a starvation wage and thereby directly encouraged prostitution. This man, who endowed chairs in universities and erected magnificent chapels, perjured himself in courts of law over dollars and cents. This railroad magnate broke his word as a citizen, as a gentleman, and as a Christian, when he granted a secret rebate, and he granted many secret rebates. This senator was the tool and the slave, the little puppet, of a brutal uneducated machine boss;** so was this governor and this supreme court judge; and all three rode on railroad passes; and, also, this sleek capitalist owned the machine, the machine boss, and the railroads that issued the passes.

* PATENT MEDICINES were patent lies, but, like the charms and indulgences of the Middle Ages, they deceived the people. The only difference lay in that the patent medicines were more harmful and more costly.

** Even as late as 1912, A.D., the great mass of the people still persisted in the belief that they ruled the country by virtue of their ballots. In reality, the country was ruled by what were called POLITICAL MACHINES. At first the machine bosses charged the master capitalists extortionate tolls for legislation; but in a short time the master capitalists found it cheaper to own the political machines themselves and to hire the machine bosses.

"And so it was, instead of in paradise, that I found myself in the arid desert of commercialism. I found nothing but stupidity, except for business. I found none clean, noble, and alive, though I found many who were alive—with rottenness. What I did find was monstrous selfishness and heartlessness, and a gross, gluttonous, practised, and practical materialism."

Much more Ernest told them of themselves and of his disillusionment. Intellectually they had bored him; morally and spiritually they had sickened him; so that he was glad to go back to his revolutionists, who were clean, noble, and alive, and all that the capitalists were not.

"And now," he said, "let me tell you about that revolution."

But first I must say that his terrible diatribe had not touched them. I looked about me at their faces and saw that they remained complacently superior to what he had charged. And I remembered what he had told me: that no indictment of their morality could shake them. However, I could see that the boldness of his language had affected Miss Brentwood. She was looking worried and apprehensive.

Ernest began by describing the army of revolution, and as he gave the figures of its strength (the votes cast in the various countries), the assemblage began to grow restless. Concern showed in their faces, and I noticed a tightening of lips. At last the gage of battle had been thrown down. He described the international organization of the socialists that united the million and a half in the United States with the twenty-three millions and a half in the rest of the world.

"Such an army of revolution," he said, "twenty-five millions strong, is a thing to make rulers and ruling classes pause and consider. The cry of this army is: 'No quarter! We want all that you possess. We will be content with nothing less than all that you possess. We want in our hands the reins of power and the destiny of mankind. Here are our hands. They are strong hands. We are going to take your governments, your palaces, and all your purpled ease away from you, and in that day you shall work for your bread even as the peasant in the field or the starved and runty clerk in your metropolises. Here are our hands. They are strong hands!'"

And as he spoke he extended from his splendid shoulders his two great arms, and the horseshoer's hands were clutching the air like eagle's talons. He was the spirit of regnant labor as he stood there, his hands outreaching to rend and crush his audience. I was aware of a faintly perceptible shrinking on the part of the listeners before this figure of revolution, concrete, potential, and menacing. That is, the women shrank, and fear was in their faces. Not so with the men. They were of the active rich, and not the idle, and they were fighters. A low, throaty rumble arose, lingered on the air a moment, and ceased. It was the forerunner of the snarl, and I was to hear it many times that night—the token of the brute in man, the earnest of his primitive passions. And they were unconscious that they had made this sound. It was the growl of the pack, mouthed by the pack, and mouthed in all unconsciousness. And in that moment, as I saw the harshness form in their faces and saw the fight-light flashing in their eyes, I realized that not easily would they let their lordship of the world be wrested from them.

Ernest proceeded with his attack. He accounted for the existence of the million and a half of revolutionists in the United States by charging the capitalist class with having mismanaged society. He sketched the economic condition of the cave-man and of the savage peoples of to-day, pointing out that they possessed neither tools nor machines, and possessed only a natural efficiency of one in producing power. Then he traced the development of machinery and social organization so that to-day the producing power of civilized man was a thousand times greater than that of the savage.

"Five men," he said, "can produce bread for a thousand. One man can produce cotton cloth for two hundred and fifty people, woollens for three hundred, and boots and shoes for a thousand. One would conclude from this that under a capable management of society modern civilized man would be a great deal better off than the cave-man. But is he? Let us see. In the United States to-day there are fifteen million* people living in poverty; and by poverty is meant that condition in life in which, through lack of food and adequate shelter, the mere standard of working efficiency cannot be maintained. In the United States to-day, in spite of all your so-called labor legislation, there are three millions of child laborers.** In twelve years their numbers have been doubled. And in passing I will ask you managers of society why you did not make public the census figures of 1910? And I will answer for you, that you were afraid. The figures of misery would have precipitated the revolution that even now is gathering.

* Robert Hunter, in 1906, in a book entitled "Poverty," pointed out that at that time there were ten millions in the United States living in poverty.

** In the United States Census of 1900 (the last census the figures of which were made public), the number of child laborers was placed at 1,752,187.

"But to return to my indictment. If modern man's producing power is a thousand times greater than that of the cave-man, why then, in the United States to-day, are there fifteen million people who are not properly sheltered and properly fed? Why then, in the United States to-day, are there three million child laborers? It is a true indictment. The capitalist class has mismanaged. In face of the facts that modern man lives more wretchedly than the cave-man, and that his producing power is a thousand times greater than that of the cave-man, no other conclusion is possible than that the capitalist class has mismanaged, that you have mismanaged, my masters, that you have criminally and selfishly mismanaged. And on this count you cannot answer me here to-night, face to face, any more than can your whole class answer the million and a half of revolutionists in the United States. You cannot answer. I challenge you to answer. And furthermore, I dare to say to you now that when I have finished you will not answer. On that point you will be tongue-tied, though you will talk wordily enough about other things.

"You have failed in your management. You have made a shambles of civilization. You have been blind and greedy. You have risen up (as you to-day rise up), shamelessly, in our legislative halls, and declared that profits were impossible without the toil of children and babes. Don't take my word for it. It is all in the records against you. You have lulled your conscience to sleep with prattle of sweet ideals and dear moralities. You are fat with power and possession, drunken with success; and you have no more hope against us than have the drones, clustered about the honey-vats, when the worker-bees spring upon them to end their rotund existence. You have failed in your management of society, and your management is to be taken away from you. A million and a half of the men of the working class say that they are going to get the rest of the working class to join with them and take the management away from you. This is the revolution, my masters. Stop it if you can."

For an appreciable lapse of time Ernest's voice continued to ring through the great room. Then arose the throaty rumble I had heard before, and a dozen men were on their feet clamoring for recognition from Colonel Van Gilbert. I noticed Miss Brentwood's shoulders moving convulsively, and for the moment I was angry, for I thought that she was laughing at Ernest. And then I discovered that it was not laughter, but hysteria. She was appalled by what she had done in bringing this firebrand before her blessed Philomath Club.

Colonel Van Gilbert did not notice the dozen men, with passion-wrought faces, who strove to get permission from him to speak. His own face was passion-wrought. He sprang to his feet, waving his arms, and for a moment could utter only incoherent sounds. Then speech poured from him. But it was not the speech of a one-hundred-thousand-dollar lawyer, nor was the rhetoric old-fashioned.

"Fallacy upon fallacy!" he cried. "Never in all my life have I heard so many fallacies uttered in one short hour. And besides, young man, I must tell you that you have said nothing new. I learned all that at college before you were born. Jean Jacques Rousseau enunciated your socialistic theory nearly two centuries ago. A return to the soil, forsooth! Reversion! Our biology teaches the absurdity of it. It has been truly said that a little learning is a dangerous thing, and you have exemplified it to-night with your madcap theories. Fallacy upon fallacy! I was never so nauseated in my life with overplus of fallacy. That for your immature generalizations and childish reasonings!"

He snapped his fingers contemptuously and proceeded to sit down. There were lip-exclamations of approval on the part of the women, and hoarser notes of confirmation came from the men. As for the dozen men who were clamoring for the floor, half of them began speaking at once. The confusion and babel was indescribable. Never had Mrs. Pertonwaithe's spacious walls beheld such a spectacle. These, then, were the cool captains of industry and lords of society, these snarling, growling savages in evening clothes. Truly Ernest had shaken them when he stretched out his hands for their moneybags, his hands that had appeared in their eyes as the hands of the fifteen hundred thousand revolutionists.

But Ernest never lost his head in a situation. Before Colonel Van Gilbert had succeeded in sitting down, Ernest was on his feet and had sprung forward.

"One at a time!" he roared at them.

The sound arose from his great lungs and dominated the human tempest. By sheer compulsion of personality he commanded silence.

"One at a time," he repeated softly. "Let me answer Colonel Van Gilbert. After that the rest of you can come at me—but one at a time, remember. No mass-plays here. This is not a football field.

"As for you," he went on, turning toward Colonel Van Gilbert, "you have replied to nothing I have said. You have merely made a few excited and dogmatic assertions about my mental caliber. That may serve you in your business, but you can't talk to me like that. I am not a workingman, cap in hand, asking you to increase my wages or to protect me from the machine at which I work. You cannot be dogmatic with truth when you deal with me. Save that for dealing with your wage-slaves. They will not dare reply to you because you hold their bread and butter, their lives, in your hands.

"As for this return to nature that you say you learned at college before I was born, permit me to point out that on the face of it you cannot have learned anything since. Socialism has no more to do with the state of nature than has differential calculus with a Bible class. I have called your class stupid when outside the realm of business. You, sir, have brilliantly exemplified my statement."

This terrible castigation of her hundred-thousand-dollar lawyer was too much for Miss Brentwood's nerves. Her hysteria became violent, and she was helped, weeping and laughing, out of the room. It was just as well, for there was worse to follow.

"Don't take my word for it," Ernest continued, when the interruption had been led away. "Your own authorities with one unanimous voice will prove you stupid. Your own hired purveyors of knowledge will tell you that you are wrong. Go to your meekest little assistant instructor of sociology and ask him what is the difference between Rousseau's theory of the return to nature and the theory of socialism; ask your greatest orthodox bourgeois political economists and sociologists; question through the pages of every text-book written on the subject and stored on the shelves of your subsidized libraries; and from one and all the answer will be that there is nothing congruous between the return to nature and socialism. On the other hand, the unanimous affirmative answer will be that the return to nature and socialism are diametrically opposed to each other. As I say, don't take my word for it. The record of your stupidity is there in the books, your own books that you never read. And so far as your stupidity is concerned, you are but the exemplar of your class.

"You know law and business, Colonel Van Gilbert. You know how to serve corporations and increase dividends by twisting the law. Very good. Stick to it. You are quite a figure. You are a very good lawyer, but you are a poor historian, you know nothing of sociology, and your biology is contemporaneous with Pliny."

Here Colonel Van Gilbert writhed in his chair. There was perfect quiet in the room. Everybody sat fascinated—paralyzed, I may say. Such fearful treatment of the great Colonel Van Gilbert was unheard of, undreamed of, impossible to believe—the great Colonel Van Gilbert before whom judges trembled when he arose in court. But Ernest never gave quarter to an enemy.

"This is, of course, no reflection on you," Ernest said. "Every man to his trade. Only you stick to your trade, and I'll stick to mine. You have specialized. When it comes to a knowledge of the law, of how best to evade the law or make new law for the benefit of thieving corporations, I am down in the dirt at your feet. But when it comes to sociology—my trade—you are down in the dirt at my feet. Remember that. Remember, also, that your law is the stuff of a day, and that you are not versatile in the stuff of more than a day. Therefore your dogmatic assertions and rash generalizations on things historical and sociological are not worth the breath you waste on them."

Ernest paused for a moment and regarded him thoughtfully, noting his face dark and twisted with anger, his panting chest, his writhing body, and his slim white hands nervously clenching and unclenching.

"But it seems you have breath to use, and I'll give you a chance to use it. I indicted your class. Show me that my indictment is wrong. I pointed out to you the wretchedness of modern man—three million child slaves in the United States, without whose labor profits would not be possible, and fifteen million under-fed, ill-clothed, and worse-housed people. I pointed out that modern man's producing power through social organization and the use of machinery was a thousand times greater than that of the cave-man. And I stated that from these two facts no other conclusion was possible than that the capitalist class had mismanaged. This was my indictment, and I specifically and at length challenged you to answer it. Nay, I did more. I prophesied that you would not answer. It remains for your breath to smash my prophecy. You called my speech fallacy. Show the fallacy, Colonel Van Gilbert. Answer the indictment that I and my fifteen hundred thousand comrades have brought against your class and you."

Colonel Van Gilbert quite forgot that he was presiding, and that in courtesy he should permit the other clamorers to speak. He was on his feet, flinging his arms, his rhetoric, and his control to the winds, alternately abusing Ernest for his youth and demagoguery, and savagely attacking the working class, elaborating its inefficiency and worthlessness.

"For a lawyer, you are the hardest man to keep to a point I ever saw," Ernest began his answer to the tirade. "My youth has nothing to do with what I have enunciated. Nor has the worthlessness of the working class. I charged the capitalist class with having mismanaged society. You have not answered.

You have made no attempt to answer. Why? Is it because you have no answer? You are the champion of this whole audience. Every one here, except me, is hanging on your lips for that answer. They are hanging on your lips for that answer because they have no answer themselves. As for me, as I said before, I know that you not only cannot answer, but that you will not attempt an answer."

"This is intolerable!" Colonel Van Gilbert cried out. "This is insult!"

"That you should not answer is intolerable," Ernest replied gravely. "No man can be intellectually insulted. Insult, in its very nature, is emotional. Recover yourself. Give me an intellectual answer to my intellectual charge that the capitalist class has mismanaged society."

Colonel Van Gilbert remained silent, a sullen, superior expression on his face, such as will appear on the face of a man who will not bandy words with a ruffian.

"Do not be downcast," Ernest said. "Take consolation in the fact that no member of your class has ever yet answered that charge." He turned to the other men who were anxious to speak. "And now it's your chance. Fire away, and do not forget that I here challenge you to give the answer that Colonel Van Gilbert has failed to give."

It would be impossible for me to write all that was said in the discussion. I never realized before how many words could be spoken in three short hours. At any rate, it was glorious. The more his opponents grew excited, the more Ernest deliberately excited them. He had an encyclopaedic command of the field of knowledge, and by a word or a phrase, by delicate rapier thrusts, he punctured them. He named the points of their illogic. This was a false syllogism, that conclusion had no connection with the premise, while that next premise was an impostor because it had cunningly hidden in it the conclusion that was being attempted to be proved. This was an error, that was an assumption, and the next was an assertion contrary to ascertained truth as printed in all the text-books.

And so it went. Sometimes he exchanged the rapier for the club and went smashing amongst their thoughts right and left. And always he demanded facts and refused to discuss theories. And his facts made for them a Waterloo. When they attacked the working class, he always retorted, "The pot calling the kettle black; that is no answer to the charge that your own face is dirty." And to one and all he said: "Why have you not answered the charge that your class has mismanaged? You have talked about other things and things concerning other things, but you have not answered. Is it because you have no answer?"

It was at the end of the discussion that Mr. Wickson spoke. He was the only one that was cool, and Ernest treated him with a respect he had not accorded the others.

"No answer is necessary," Mr. Wickson said with slow deliberation. "I have followed the whole discussion with amazement and disgust. I am disgusted with you gentlemen, members of my class. You have behaved like foolish little schoolboys, what with intruding ethics and the thunder of the common politician into such a discussion. You have been outgeneralled and outclassed. You have been very wordy, and all you have done is buzz. You have buzzed like gnats about a bear. Gentlemen, there stands the bear" (he pointed at Ernest), "and your buzzing has only tickled his ears.

"Believe me, the situation is serious. That bear reached out his paws tonight to crush us. He has said there are a million and a half of revolutionists in the United States. That is a fact. He has said that it is their intention to take away from us our governments, our palaces, and all our purpled ease. That, also, is a fact. A change, a great change, is coming in society; but, haply, it may not be the change the bear anticipates. The bear has said that he will crush us. What if we crush the bear?"

The throat-rumble arose in the great room, and man nodded to man with indorsement and certitude. Their faces were set hard. They were fighters, that was certain.

"But not by buzzing will we crush the bear," Mr. Wickson went on coldly and dispassionately. "We will hunt the bear. We will not reply to the bear in words. Our reply shall be couched in terms of lead. We are in power. Nobody will deny it. By virtue of that power we shall remain in power."

He turned suddenly upon Ernest. The moment was dramatic.

"This, then, is our answer. We have no words to waste on you. When you reach out your vaunted strong hands for our palaces and purpled ease, we will show you what strength is. In roar of shell and shrapnel and in whine of machine-guns will our answer be couched.* We will grind you revolutionists down under our heel, and we shall walk upon your faces. The world is ours, we are its lords, and ours it shall remain. As for the host of labor, it has been in the dirt since history began, and I read history aright. And in the dirt it shall remain so long as I and mine and those that come after us have the power. There is the word. It is the king of words—Power. Not God, not Mammon, but Power. Pour it over your tongue till it tingles with it. Power."

*To show the tenor of thought, the following definition is quoted from "The Cynic's Word Book" (1906 A.D.), written by one Ambrose Bierce, an avowed and confirmed misanthrope of the period: "Grapeshot, n. An argument which the future is preparing in answer to the demands of American Socialism."

"I am answered," Ernest said quietly. "It is the only answer that could be given. Power. It is what we of the working class preach. We know, and well we know by bitter experience, that no appeal for the right, for justice, for humanity, can ever touch you. Your hearts are hard as your heels with which you tread upon the faces of the poor. So we have preached power. By the power of our ballots on election day will we take your government away from you—"

"What if you do get a majority, a sweeping majority, on election day?" Mr. Wickson broke in to demand. "Suppose we refuse to turn the government over to you after you have captured it at the ballot-box?"

"That, also, have we considered," Ernest replied. "And we shall give you an answer in terms of lead. Power you have proclaimed the king of words. Very good. Power it shall be. And in the day that we sweep to victory at the ballot-box, and you refuse to turn over to us the government we have constitutionally and peacefully captured, and you demand what we are going to do about it—in that day, I say, we shall answer you; and in roar of shell and shrapnel and in whine of machine-guns shall our answer be couched.

"You cannot escape us. It is true that you have read history aright. It is true that labor has from the beginning of history been in the dirt. And it is equally true that so long as you and yours and those that come after you have power, that labor shall remain in the dirt. I agree with you. I agree with all that you have said. Power will be the arbiter, as it always has been the arbiter. It is a struggle of classes. Just as your class dragged down the old feudal nobility, so shall it be dragged down by my class, the working class. If you will read your biology and your sociology as clearly as you do your history, you will see that this end I have described is inevitable. It does not matter whether it is in one year, ten, or a thousand—your class shall be dragged down. And it shall be done by power. We of the labor hosts have conned that word over till our minds are all a-tingle with it. Power. It is a kingly word."

And so ended the night with the Philomaths.

CHAPTER VI. ADUMBRATIONS

It was about this time that the warnings of coming events began to fall about us thick and fast. Ernest had already questioned father's policy of having socialists and labor leaders at his house, and of openly attending socialist meetings; and father had only laughed at him for his pains. As for myself, I was learning much from this contact with the working-class leaders and thinkers. I was seeing the other side of the shield. I was delighted with the unselfishness and high idealism I encountered, though I was appalled by the vast philosophic and scientific literature of socialism that was opened up to me. I was learning fast, but I learned not fast enough to realize then the peril of our position.

There were warnings, but I did not heed them. For instance, Mrs. Pertonwaithe and Mrs. Wickson exercised tremendous social power in the university town, and from them emanated the sentiment that I was a too-forward and self-assertive young woman with a mischievous penchant for officiousness and interference in other persons' affairs. This I thought no more than natural, considering the part I had played in investigating the case of Jackson's arm. But the effect of such a sentiment, enunciated by two such powerful social arbiters, I underestimated.

True, I noticed a certain aloofness on the part of my general friends, but this I ascribed to the disapproval that was prevalent in my circles of my intended marriage with Ernest. It was not till some time afterward that Ernest pointed out to me clearly that this general attitude of my class was something more than spontaneous, that behind it were the hidden springs of an organized conduct. "You have given shelter to an enemy of your class," he said. "And not alone shelter, for you have given your love, yourself. This is treason to your class. Think not that you will escape being penalized."

But it was before this that father returned one afternoon. Ernest was with me, and we could see that father was angry—philosophically angry. He was rarely really angry; but a certain measure of controlled anger he allowed himself. He called it a tonic. And we could see that he was tonic-angry when he entered the room.

"What do you think?" he demanded. "I had luncheon with Wilcox."

Wilcox was the superannuated president of the university, whose withered mind was stored with generalizations that were young in 1870, and which he had since failed to revise.

"I was invited," father announced. "I was sent for."

He paused, and we waited.

"Oh, it was done very nicely, I'll allow; but I was reprimanded. I! And by that old fossil!"

"I'll wager I know what you were reprimanded for," Ernest said.

"Not in three guesses," father laughed.

"One guess will do," Ernest retorted. "And it won't be a guess. It will be a deduction. You were reprimanded for your private life."

"The very thing!" father cried. "How did you guess?"

"I knew it was coming. I warned you before about it."

"Yes, you did," father meditated. "But I couldn't believe it. At any rate, it is only so much more clinching evidence for my book."

"It is nothing to what will come," Ernest went on, "if you persist in your policy of having these socialists and radicals of all sorts at your house, myself included."

"Just what old Wilcox said. And of all unwarranted things! He said it was in poor taste, utterly profitless, anyway, and not in harmony with university traditions and policy. He said much more of the same vague sort, and I couldn't pin him down to anything specific. I made it pretty awkward for him, and he could only go on repeating himself and telling me how much he honored me, and all the world honored me, as a scientist. It wasn't an agreeable task for him. I could see he didn't like it."

"He was not a free agent," Ernest said. "The leg-bar* is not always worn graciously."

> *LEG-BAR—the African slaves were so manacled; also
> criminals. It was not until the coming of the Brotherhood
> of Man that the leg-bar passed out of use.

"Yes. I got that much out of him. He said the university needed ever so much more money this year than the state was willing to furnish; and that it must come from wealthy personages who could not but be offended by the swerving of the university from its high ideal of the passionless pursuit of passionless intelligence. When I tried to pin him down to what my home life had to do with swerving the university from its high ideal, he offered me a two years' vacation, on full pay, in Europe, for recreation and research. Of course I couldn't accept it under the circumstances."

"It would have been far better if you had," Ernest said gravely.

"It was a bribe," father protested; and Ernest nodded.

"Also, the beggar said that there was talk, tea-table gossip and so forth, about my daughter being seen in public with so notorious a character as you, and that it was not in keeping with university tone and dignity. Not that he personally objected—oh, no; but that there was talk and that I would understand."

Ernest considered this announcement for a moment, and then said, and his face was very grave, withal there was a sombre wrath in it:

"There is more behind this than a mere university ideal. Somebody has put pressure on President Wilcox."

"Do you think so?" father asked, and his face showed that he was interested rather than frightened.

"I wish I could convey to you the conception that is dimly forming in my own mind," Ernest said. "Never in the history of the world was society in so terrific flux as it is right now. The swift changes in our industrial system are causing equally swift changes in our religious, political, and social structures. An unseen and fearful revolution is taking place in the fibre and structure of society. One can only dimly feel these things. But they are in the air, now, to-day. One can feel the loom of them—things vast, vague, and terrible. My mind recoils from contemplation of what they may crystallize into. You heard Wickson talk the other night. Behind what he said were the same nameless, formless things that I feel. He spoke out of a superconscious apprehension of them."

"You mean . . . ?" father began, then paused.

"I mean that there is a shadow of something colossal and menacing that even now is beginning to fall across the land. Call it the shadow of an oligarchy, if you will; it is the nearest I dare approximate it. What its nature may be I refuse to imagine.* But what I wanted to say was this: You are in a perilous position—a peril that my own fear enhances because I am not able even to measure it. Take my advice and accept the vacation."

* *Though, like Everhard, they did not dream of the nature of it, there were men, even before his time, who caught glimpses of the shadow. John C. Calhoun said: "A power has risen up in the government greater than the people themselves, consisting of many and various and powerful interests, combined into one mass, and held together by the cohesive power of the vast surplus in the banks." And that great humanist, Abraham Lincoln, said, just before his assassination: "I see in the near future a crisis*

approaching that unnerves me and causes me to tremble for the safety of my country. . . . Corporations have been enthroned, an era of corruption in high places will follow, and the money-power of the country will endeavor to prolong its reign by working upon the prejudices of the people until the wealth is aggregated in a few hands and the Republic is destroyed."

"But it would be cowardly," was the protest.

"Not at all. You are an old man. You have done your work in the world, and a great work. Leave the present battle to youth and strength. We young fellows have our work yet to do. Avis will stand by my side in what is to come. She will be your representative in the battle-front."

"But they can't hurt me," father objected. "Thank God I am independent. Oh, I assure you, I know the frightful persecution they can wage on a professor who is economically dependent on his university. But I am independent. I have not been a professor for the sake of my salary. I can get along very comfortably on my own income, and the salary is all they can take away from me."

"But you do not realize," Ernest answered. "If all that I fear be so, your private income, your principal itself, can be taken from you just as easily as your salary."

Father was silent for a few minutes. He was thinking deeply, and I could see the lines of decision forming in his face. At last he spoke.

"I shall not take the vacation." He paused again. "I shall go on with my book.* You may be wrong, but whether you are wrong or right, I shall stand by my guns."

This book, "Economics and Education," was published in that year. Three copies of it are extant; two at Ardis, and one at Asgard. It dealt, in elaborate detail, with one factor in the persistence of the established, namely, the capitalistic bias of the universities and common schools. It was a logical and crushing indictment of the whole system of education that developed in the minds of the students only such ideas as were favorable to the capitalistic regime, to the exclusion of all ideas that were inimical and subversive. The book created a furor, and was promptly suppressed by the Oligarchy.

"All right," Ernest said. "You are travelling the same path that Bishop Morehouse is, and toward a similar smash-up. You'll both be proletarians before you're done with it."

The conversation turned upon the Bishop, and we got Ernest to explain what he had been doing with him.

"He is soul-sick from the journey through hell I have given him. I took him through the homes of a few of our factory workers. I showed him the human wrecks cast aside by the industrial machine, and he listened to their life stories. I took him through the slums of San Francisco, and in drunkenness, prostitution, and criminality he learned a deeper cause than innate depravity. He is very sick, and, worse than that, he has got out of hand. He is too ethical. He has been too severely touched. And, as usual, he is unpractical. He is up in the air with all kinds of ethical delusions and plans for mission work among the cultured. He feels it is his bounden duty to resurrect the ancient spirit of the Church and to deliver its message to the masters. He is overwrought. Sooner or later he is going to break out, and then there's going to be a smash-up. What form it will take I can't even guess. He is a pure, exalted soul, but he is so unpractical. He's beyond me. I can't keep his feet on the earth. And through the air he is rushing on to his Gethsemane. And after this his crucifixion. Such high souls are made for crucifixion."

"And you?" I asked; and beneath my smile was the seriousness of the anxiety of love.

"Not I," he laughed back. "I may be executed, or assassinated, but I shall never be crucified. I am planted too solidly and stolidly upon the earth."

"But why should you bring about the crucifixion of the Bishop?" I asked. "You will not deny that you are the cause of it."

"Why should I leave one comfortable soul in comfort when there are millions in travail and misery?" he demanded back.

"Then why did you advise father to accept the vacation?"

"Because I am not a pure, exalted soul," was the answer. "Because I am solid and stolid and selfish. Because I love you and, like Ruth of old, thy people are my people. As for the Bishop, he has no daughter. Besides, no matter how small the good, nevertheless his little inadequate wail will be productive of some good in the revolution, and every little bit counts."

I could not agree with Ernest. I knew well the noble nature of Bishop Morehouse, and I could not conceive that his voice raised for righteousness would be no more than a little inadequate wail. But I did not yet have the harsh facts of life at my fingers' ends as Ernest had. He saw clearly the futility of the Bishop's great soul, as coming events were soon to show as clearly to me.

It was shortly after this day that Ernest told me, as a good story, the offer he had received from the government, namely, an appointment as United States Commissioner of Labor. I was overjoyed. The salary was comparatively large, and would make safe our marriage. And then it surely was congenial work for Ernest, and, furthermore, my jealous pride in him made me hail the proffered appointment as a recognition of his abilities.

Then I noticed the twinkle in his eyes. He was laughing at me.

"You are not going to . . . to decline?" I quavered.

"It is a bribe," he said. "Behind it is the fine hand of Wickson, and behind him the hands of greater men than he. It is an old trick, old as the class struggle is old—stealing the captains from the army of labor. Poor betrayed labor! If you but knew how many of its leaders have been bought out in similar ways in the past. It is cheaper, so much cheaper, to buy a general than to fight him and his whole army. There was—but I'll not call any names. I'm bitter enough over it as it is. Dear heart, I am a captain of labor. I could not sell out. If for no other reason, the memory of my poor old father and the way he was worked to death would prevent."

The tears were in his eyes, this great, strong hero of mine. He never could forgive the way his father had been malformed—the sordid lies and the petty thefts he had been compelled to, in order to put food in his children's mouths.

"My father was a good man," Ernest once said to me. "The soul of him was good, and yet it was twisted, and maimed, and blunted by the savagery of his life. He was made into a broken-down beast by his masters, the arch-beasts. He should be alive to-day, like your father. He had a strong constitution. But he was caught in the machine and worked to death—for profit. Think of it. For profit—his life blood transmuted into a wine-supper, or a jewelled gewgaw, or some similar sense-orgy of the parasitic and idle rich, his masters, the arch-beasts."

CHAPTER VII. THE BISHOP'S VISION

"The Bishop is out of hand," Ernest wrote me. "He is clear up in the air. Tonight he is going to begin putting to rights this very miserable world of ours. He is going to deliver his message. He has told me so, and I cannot dissuade him. To-night he is chairman of the I.P.H.,* and he will embody his message in his introductory remarks.

There is no clew to the name of the organization for which these initials stand.

"May I bring you to hear him? Of course, he is foredoomed to futility. It will break your heart—it will break his; but for you it will be an excellent object lesson. You know, dear heart, how proud I am because you love me. And because of that I want you to know my fullest value, I want to redeem, in your eyes, some small measure of my unworthiness. And so it is that my pride desires that you shall know my thinking is correct and right. My views are harsh; the futility of so noble a soul as the Bishop will show you the compulsion for such harshness. So come to-night. Sad though this night's happening will be, I feel that it will but draw you more closely to me."

The I.P.H. held its convention that night in San Francisco.* This convention had been called to consider public immorality and the remedy for it. Bishop Morehouse presided. He was very nervous as he sat on the platform, and I could see the high tension he was under. By his side were Bishop Dickinson; H. H. Jones, the head of the ethical department in the University of California; Mrs. W. W. Hurd, the great charity organizer; Philip Ward, the equally great philanthropist; and several lesser luminaries in the field of morality and charity. Bishop Morehouse arose and abruptly began:

** It took but a few minutes to cross by ferry from Berkeley
to San Francisco. These, and the other bay cities,
practically composed one community.*

"I was in my brougham, driving through the streets. It was night-time. Now and then I looked through the carriage windows, and suddenly my eyes seemed to be opened, and I saw things as they really are. At first I covered my eyes with my hands to shut out the awful sight, and then, in the darkness, the question came to me: What is to be done? What is to be done? A little later the question came to me in another way: What would the Master do? And with the question a great light seemed to fill the place, and I saw my duty sun-clear, as Saul saw his on the way to Damascus.

"I stopped the carriage, got out, and, after a few minutes' conversation, persuaded two of the public women to get into the brougham with me. If Jesus was right, then these two unfortunates were my sisters, and the only hope of their purification was in my affection and tenderness.

"I live in one of the loveliest localities of San Francisco. The house in which I live cost a hundred thousand dollars, and its furnishings, books, and works of art cost as much more. The house is a mansion. No, it is a palace, wherein there are many servants. I never knew what palaces were good for. I had thought they were to live in. But now I know. I took the two women of the street to my palace, and they are going to stay with me. I hope to fill every room in my palace with such sisters as they."

The audience had been growing more and more restless and unsettled, and the faces of those that sat on the platform had been betraying greater and greater dismay and consternation. And at this point Bishop Dickinson arose, and with an expression of disgust on his face, fled from the platform and the hall. But Bishop Morehouse, oblivious to all, his eyes filled with his vision, continued:

"Oh, sisters and brothers, in this act of mine I find the solution of all my difficulties. I didn't know what broughams were made for, but now I know. They are made to carry the weak, the sick, and the aged; they are made to show honor to those who have lost the sense even of shame.

"I did not know what palaces were made for, but now I have found a use for them. The palaces of the Church should be hospitals and nurseries for those who have fallen by the wayside and are perishing."

He made a long pause, plainly overcome by the thought that was in him, and nervous how best to express it.

"I am not fit, dear brethren, to tell you anything about morality. I have lived in shame and hypocrisies too long to be able to help others; but my action with those women, sisters of mine, shows me that the better way is easy to find. To those who believe in Jesus and his gospel there can be no other relation between man and man than the relation of affection. Love alone is stronger than sin—stronger than death. I therefore say to the rich among you that it is their duty to do what I have done and am doing. Let each one of you who is prosperous take into his house some thief and treat him as his brother, some unfortunate and treat her as his sister, and San Francisco will need no police force and no magistrates; the prisons will be turned into hospitals, and the criminal will disappear with his crime.

"We must give ourselves and not our money alone. We must do as Christ did; that is the message of the Church today. We have wandered far from the Master's teaching. We are consumed in our own flesh-pots. We have put mammon in the place of Christ. I have here a poem that tells the whole story. I should like to read it to you. It was written by an erring soul who yet saw clearly.* It must not be mistaken for an attack upon the Catholic Church. It is an attack upon all churches, upon the pomp and splendor of all churches that have wandered from the Master's path and hedged themselves in from his lambs. Here it is:

"*The silver trumpets rang across the Dome;*

The people knelt upon the ground with awe;

And borne upon the necks of men I saw,

Like some great God, the Holy Lord of Rome.

"Priest-like, he wore a robe more white than foam,

And, king-like, swathed himself in royal red,

Three crowns of gold rose high upon his head;

In splendor and in light the Pope passed home.

"My heart stole back across wide wastes of years

To One who wandered by a lonely sea;

And sought in vain for any place of rest:

'Foxes have holes, and every bird its nest,

I, only I, must wander wearily,

And bruise my feet, and drink wine salt with tears.'"

* Oscar Wilde, one of the lords of language of the

nineteenth century of the Christian Era.

The audience was agitated, but unresponsive. Yet Bishop Morehouse was not aware of it. He held steadily on his way.

"And so I say to the rich among you, and to all the rich, that bitterly you oppress the Master's lambs. You have hardened your hearts. You have closed your ears to the voices that are crying in the land—the voices of pain and sorrow that you will not hear but that some day will be heard. And so I say—"

But at this point H. H. Jones and Philip Ward, who had already risen from their chairs, led the Bishop off the platform, while the audience sat breathless and shocked.

Ernest laughed harshly and savagely when he had gained the street. His laughter jarred upon me. My heart seemed ready to burst with suppressed tears.

"He has delivered his message," Ernest cried. "The manhood and the deep-hidden, tender nature of their Bishop burst out, and his Christian audience, that loved him, concluded that he was crazy! Did you see them leading him so solicitously from the platform? There must have been laughter in hell at the spectacle."

"Nevertheless, it will make a great impression, what the Bishop did and said to-night," I said.

"Think so?" Ernest queried mockingly.

"It will make a sensation," I asserted. "Didn't you see the reporters scribbling like mad while he was speaking?"

"Not a line of which will appear in to-morrow's papers."

"I can't believe it," I cried.

"Just wait and see," was the answer. "Not a line, not a thought that he uttered. The daily press? The daily suppressage!"

"But the reporters," I objected. "I saw them."

"Not a word that he uttered will see print. You have forgotten the editors. They draw their salaries for the policy they maintain. Their policy is to print nothing that is a vital menace to the established. The Bishop's utterance was a violent assault upon the established morality. It was heresy. They led him from the platform to prevent him from uttering more heresy. The newspapers will purge his heresy in the oblivion of silence. The press of the United States? It is a parasitic growth that battens on the capitalist class. Its function is to serve the established by moulding public opinion, and right well it serves it.

"Let me prophesy. To-morrow's papers will merely mention that the Bishop is in poor health, that he has been working too hard, and that he broke down last night. The next mention, some days hence, will be to the effect that he is suffering from nervous prostration and has been given a vacation by his grateful flock. After that, one of two things will happen: either the Bishop will see the error of his way and return from his vacation a well man in whose eyes there are no more visions, or else he will persist in his madness, and then you may expect to see in the papers, couched pathetically and tenderly, the announcement of his insanity. After that he will be left to gibber his visions to padded walls."

"Now there you go too far!" I cried out.

"In the eyes of society it will truly be insanity," he replied. "What honest man, who is not insane, would take lost women and thieves into his house to dwell with him sisterly and brotherly? True, Christ died between two thieves, but that is another story. Insanity? The mental processes of the man with whom one disagrees, are always wrong. Therefore the mind of the man is wrong. Where is the line between wrong mind and insane mind? It is inconceivable that any sane man can radically disagree with one's most sane conclusions.

"There is a good example of it in this evening's paper. Mary McKenna lives south of Market Street. She is a poor but honest woman. She is also patriotic. But she has erroneous ideas concerning the American flag and the protection it is supposed to symbolize. And here's what happened to her. Her husband had an accident and was laid up in hospital three months. In spite of taking in washing, she got behind in her rent. Yesterday they evicted her. But first, she hoisted an American flag, and from under its folds she announced that by virtue of its protection they could not turn her out on to the cold street. What was done? She was arrested and arraigned for insanity. To-day she was examined by the regular insanity experts. She was found insane. She was consigned to the Napa Asylum."

"But that is far-fetched," I objected. "Suppose I should disagree with everybody about the literary style of a book. They wouldn't send me to an asylum for that."

"Very true," he replied. "But such divergence of opinion would constitute no menace to society. Therein lies the difference. The divergence of opinion on the parts of Mary McKenna and the Bishop do menace society. What if all the poor people should refuse to pay rent and shelter themselves under the American flag? Landlordism would go crumbling. The Bishop's views are just as perilous to society. Ergo, to the asylum with him."

But still I refused to believe.

"Wait and see," Ernest said, and I waited.

Next morning I sent out for all the papers. So far Ernest was right. Not a word that Bishop Morehouse had uttered was in print. Mention was made in one or two of the papers that he had been overcome by his feelings. Yet the platitudes of the speakers that followed him were reported at length.

Several days later the brief announcement was made that he had gone away on a vacation to recover from the effects of overwork. So far so good, but there had been no hint of insanity, nor even of nervous collapse. Little did I dream the terrible road the Bishop was destined to travel—the Gethsemane and crucifixion that Ernest had pondered about.

CHAPTER VIII. THE MACHINE BREAKERS

It was just before Ernest ran for Congress, on the socialist ticket, that father gave what he privately called his "Profit and Loss" dinner. Ernest called it the dinner of the Machine Breakers. In point of fact, it was merely a dinner for business men—small business men, of course. I doubt if one of them was interested in any business the total capitalization of which exceeded a couple of hundred thousand dollars. They were truly representative middle-class business men.

There was Owen, of Silverberg, Owen & Company—a large grocery firm with several branch stores. We bought our groceries from them. There were both partners of the big drug firm of Kowalt & Washburn, and Mr. Asmunsen, the owner of a large granite quarry in Contra Costa County. And there were many similar men, owners or part-owners in small factories, small businesses and small industries—small capitalists, in short.

They were shrewd-faced, interesting men, and they talked with simplicity and clearness. Their unanimous complaint was against the corporations and trusts. Their creed was, "Bust the Trusts." All oppression originated in the trusts, and one and all told the same tale of woe. They advocated government ownership of such trusts as the railroads and telegraphs, and excessive income taxes, graduated with ferocity, to destroy large accumulations. Likewise they advocated, as a cure for local ills, municipal ownership of such public utilities as water, gas, telephones, and street railways.

Especially interesting was Mr. Asmunsen's narrative of his tribulations as a quarry owner. He confessed that he never made any profits out of his quarry, and this, in spite of the enormous volume of business that had been caused by the destruction of San Francisco by the big earthquake. For six years the rebuilding of San Francisco had been going on, and his business had quadrupled and octupled, and yet he was no better off.

"The railroad knows my business just a little bit better than I do," he said. "It knows my operating expenses to a cent, and it knows the terms of my contracts. How it knows these things I can only guess. It must have spies in my employ, and it must have access to the parties to all my contracts. For look you, when I place a big contract, the terms of which favor me a goodly profit, the freight rate from my quarry to market is promptly raised. No explanation is made. The railroad gets my profit. Under such circumstances I have never succeeded in getting the railroad to reconsider its raise. On the other hand, when there have been accidents, increased expenses of operating, or contracts with less profitable terms, I have always succeeded in getting the railroad to lower its rate. What is the result? Large or small, the railroad always gets my profits."

"What remains to you over and above," Ernest interrupted to ask, "would roughly be the equivalent of your salary as a manager did the railroad own the quarry."

"The very thing," Mr. Asmunsen replied. "Only a short time ago I had my books gone through for the past ten years. I discovered that for those ten years my gain was just equivalent to a manager's salary. The railroad might just as well have owned my quarry and hired me to run it."

"But with this difference," Ernest laughed; "the railroad would have had to assume all the risk which you so obligingly assumed for it."

"Very true," Mr. Asmunsen answered sadly.

Having let them have their say, Ernest began asking questions right and left. He began with Mr. Owen.

"You started a branch store here in Berkeley about six months ago?"

"Yes," Mr. Owen answered.

"And since then I've noticed that three little corner groceries have gone out of business. Was your branch store the cause of it?"

Mr. Owen affirmed with a complacent smile. "They had no chance against us."

"Why not?"

"We had greater capital. With a large business there is always less waste and greater efficiency."

"And your branch store absorbed the profits of the three small ones. I see. But tell me, what became of the owners of the three stores?"

"One is driving a delivery wagon for us. I don't know what happened to the other two."

Ernest turned abruptly on Mr. Kowalt.

"You sell a great deal at cut-rates.* What have become of the owners of the small drug stores that you forced to the wall?"

> *A lowering of selling price to cost, and even to less than
>
> cost. Thus, a large company could sell at a loss for a
>
> longer period than a small company, and so drive the small
>
> company out of business. A common device of competition.

"One of them, Mr. Haasfurther, has charge now of our prescription department," was the answer.

"And you absorbed the profits they had been making?"

"Surely. That is what we are in business for."

"And you?" Ernest said suddenly to Mr. Asmunsen. "You are disgusted because the railroad has absorbed your profits?"

Mr. Asmunsen nodded.

"What you want is to make profits yourself?"

Again Mr. Asmunsen nodded.

"Out of others?"

There was no answer.

"Out of others?" Ernest insisted.

"That is the way profits are made," Mr. Asmunsen replied curtly.

"Then the business game is to make profits out of others, and to prevent others from making profits out of you. That's it, isn't it?"

Ernest had to repeat his question before Mr. Asmunsen gave an answer, and then he said:

"Yes, that's it, except that we do not object to the others making profits so long as they are not extortionate."

"By extortionate you mean large; yet you do not object to making large profits yourself? . . . Surely not?"

And Mr. Asmunsen amiably confessed to the weakness. There was one other man who was quizzed by Ernest at this juncture, a Mr. Calvin, who had once been a great dairy-owner.

"Some time ago you were fighting the Milk Trust," Ernest said to him; "and now you are in Grange politics.* How did it happen?"

Many efforts were made during this period to organize the perishing farmer class into a political party, the aim of which was destroy the trusts and corporations by drastic legislation. All such attempts ended in failure.

"Oh, I haven't quit the fight," Mr. Calvin answered, and he looked belligerent enough. "I'm fighting the Trust on the only field where it is possible to fight—the political field. Let me show you. A few years ago we dairymen had everything our own way."

"But you competed among yourselves?" Ernest interrupted.

"Yes, that was what kept the profits down. We did try to organize, but independent dairymen always broke through us. Then came the Milk Trust."

"Financed by surplus capital from Standard Oil," * Ernest said.

> *The first successful great trust—almost a generation in
> advance of the rest.*

"Yes," Mr. Calvin acknowledged. "But we did not know it at the time. Its agents approached us with a club. "Come in and be fat," was their proposition, "or stay out and starve." Most of us came in. Those that didn't, starved. Oh, it paid us . . . at first. Milk was raised a cent a quart. One-quarter of this cent came to us. Three-quarters of it went to the Trust. Then milk was raised another cent, only we didn't get any of that cent. Our complaints were useless. The Trust was in control. We discovered that we were pawns. Finally, the additional quarter of a cent was denied us. Then the Trust began to squeeze us out. What could we do? We were squeezed out. There were no dairymen, only a Milk Trust."

"But with milk two cents higher, I should think you could have competed," Ernest suggested slyly.

"So we thought. We tried it." Mr. Calvin paused a moment. "It broke us. The Trust could put milk upon the market more cheaply than we. It could sell still at a slight profit when we were selling at actual loss. I dropped fifty thousand dollars in that venture. Most of us went bankrupt.* The dairymen were wiped out of existence."

> *Bankruptcy—a peculiar institution that enabled an
> individual, who had failed in competitive industry, to

> *forego paying his debts. The effect was to ameliorate the*
>
> *too savage conditions of the fang-and-claw social struggle.*

"So the Trust took your profits away from you," Ernest said, "and you've gone into politics in order to legislate the Trust out of existence and get the profits back?"

Mr. Calvin's face lighted up. "That is precisely what I say in my speeches to the farmers. That's our whole idea in a nutshell."

"And yet the Trust produces milk more cheaply than could the independent dairymen?" Ernest queried.

"Why shouldn't it, with the splendid organization and new machinery its large capital makes possible?"

"There is no discussion," Ernest answered. "It certainly should, and, furthermore, it does."

Mr. Calvin here launched out into a political speech in exposition of his views. He was warmly followed by a number of the others, and the cry of all was to destroy the trusts.

"Poor simple folk," Ernest said to me in an undertone. "They see clearly as far as they see, but they see only to the ends of their noses."

A little later he got the floor again, and in his characteristic way controlled it for the rest of the evening.

"I have listened carefully to all of you," he began, "and I see plainly that you play the business game in the orthodox fashion. Life sums itself up to you in profits. You have a firm and abiding belief that you were created for the sole purpose of making profits. Only there is a hitch. In the midst of your own profit-making along comes the trust and takes your profits away from you. This is a dilemma that interferes somehow with the aim of creation, and the only way out, as it seems to you, is to destroy that which takes from you your profits.

"I have listened carefully, and there is only one name that will epitomize you. I shall call you that name. You are machine-breakers. Do you know what a machine-breaker is? Let me tell you. In the eighteenth century, in England, men and women wove cloth on hand-looms in their own cottages. It was a slow, clumsy, and costly way of weaving cloth, this cottage system of manufacture. Along came the steam-engine and labor-saving machinery. A thousand looms assembled in a large factory, and driven by a central engine wove cloth vastly more cheaply than could the cottage weavers on their hand-looms. Here in the factory was combination, and before it competition faded away. The men and women who had worked the hand-looms for themselves now went into the factories and worked the machine-looms, not for themselves, but for the capitalist owners. Furthermore, little children went to work on the machine-looms, at lower wages, and displaced the men. This made hard times for the men. Their standard of living fell. They starved. And they said it was all the fault of the machines. Therefore, they proceeded to break the machines. They did not succeed, and they were very stupid.

"Yet you have not learned their lesson. Here are you, a century and a half later, trying to break machines. By your own confession the trust machines do the work more efficiently and more cheaply than you can. That is why you cannot compete with them. And yet you would break those machines. You are even more stupid than the stupid workmen of England. And while you maunder about restoring competition, the trusts go on destroying you.

"One and all you tell the same story,—the passing away of competition and the coming on of combination. You, Mr. Owen, destroyed competition here in Berkeley when your branch store drove the three small groceries out of business. Your combination was more effective. Yet you feel the pressure of other combinations on you, the trust combinations, and you cry out. It is because you are not a trust. If you were a grocery trust for the whole United States, you would be singing another song. And the song would be, 'Blessed are the trusts.' And yet again, not only is your small combination not a trust, but you are aware yourself of its lack of strength. You are beginning to divine your own end. You feel yourself and your branch stores a pawn in the game. You see the powerful interests rising and growing more powerful day by day;

you feel their mailed hands descending upon your profits and taking a pinch here and a pinch there—the railroad trust, the oil trust, the steel trust, the coal trust; and you know that in the end they will destroy you, take away from you the last per cent of your little profits.

"You, sir, are a poor gamester. When you squeezed out the three small groceries here in Berkeley by virtue of your superior combination, you swelled out your chest, talked about efficiency and enterprise, and sent your wife to Europe on the profits you had gained by eating up the three small groceries. It is dog eat dog, and you ate them up. But, on the other hand, you are being eaten up in turn by the bigger dogs, wherefore you squeal. And what I say to you is true of all of you at this table. You are all squealing. You are all playing the losing game, and you are all squealing about it.

"But when you squeal you don't state the situation flatly, as I have stated it. You don't say that you like to squeeze profits out of others, and that you are making all the row because others are squeezing your profits out of you. No, you are too cunning for that. You say something else. You make small-capitalist political speeches such as Mr. Calvin made. What did he say? Here are a few of his phrases I caught: 'Our original principles are all right,' 'What this country requires is a return to fundamental American methods—free opportunity for all,' 'The spirit of liberty in which this nation was born,' 'Let us return to the principles of our forefathers.'

"When he says 'free opportunity for all,' he means free opportunity to squeeze profits, which freedom of opportunity is now denied him by the great trusts. And the absurd thing about it is that you have repeated these phrases so often that you believe them. You want opportunity to plunder your fellow-men in your own small way, but you hypnotize yourselves into thinking you want freedom. You are piggish and acquisitive, but the magic of your phrases leads you to believe that you are patriotic. Your desire for profits, which is sheer selfishness, you metamorphose into altruistic solicitude for suffering humanity. Come on now, right here amongst ourselves, and be honest for once. Look the matter in the face and state it in direct terms."

There were flushed and angry faces at the table, and withal a measure of awe. They were a little frightened at this smooth-faced young fellow, and the swing and smash of his words, and his dreadful trait of calling a spade a spade. Mr. Calvin promptly replied.

"And why not?" he demanded. "Why can we not return to ways of our fathers when this republic was founded? You have spoken much truth, Mr. Everhard, unpalatable though it has been. But here amongst ourselves let us speak out. Let us throw off all disguise and accept the truth as Mr. Everhard has flatly stated it. It is true that we smaller capitalists are after profits, and that the trusts are taking our profits away from us. It is true that we want to destroy the trusts in order that our profits may remain to us. And why can we not do it? Why not? I say, why not?"

"Ah, now we come to the gist of the matter," Ernest said with a pleased expression. "I'll try to tell you why not, though the telling will be rather hard. You see, you fellows have studied business, in a small way, but you have not studied social evolution at all. You are in the midst of a transition stage now in economic evolution, but you do not understand it, and that's what causes all the confusion. Why cannot you return? Because you can't. You can no more make water run up hill than can you cause the tide of economic evolution to flow back in its channel along the way it came. Joshua made the sun stand still upon Gibeon, but you would outdo Joshua. You would make the sun go backward in the sky. You would have time retrace its steps from noon to morning.

"In the face of labor-saving machinery, of organized production, of the increased efficiency of combination, you would set the economic sun back a whole generation or so to the time when there were no great capitalists, no great machinery, no railroads—a time when a host of little capitalists warred with each other in economic anarchy, and when production was primitive, wasteful, unorganized, and costly. Believe me, Joshua's task was easier, and he had Jehovah to help him. But God has forsaken you small capitalists. The sun of the small capitalists is setting. It will never rise again. Nor is it in your power even to make it stand still. You are perishing, and you are doomed to perish utterly from the face of society.

"This is the fiat of evolution. It is the word of God. Combination is stronger than competition. Primitive man was a puny creature hiding in the crevices of the rocks. He combined and made war upon his carnivorous enemies. They were competitive beasts. Primitive man was a combinative beast, and because of it he rose to primacy over all the animals. And man has been achieving greater and greater combinations ever since. It is combination versus competition, a thousand centuries long struggle, in which competition has always been worsted. Whoso enlists on the side of competition perishes."

"But the trusts themselves arose out of competition," Mr. Calvin interrupted.

"Very true," Ernest answered. "And the trusts themselves destroyed competition. That, by your own word, is why you are no longer in the dairy business."

The first laughter of the evening went around the table, and even Mr. Calvin joined in the laugh against himself.

"And now, while we are on the trusts," Ernest went on, "let us settle a few things. I shall make certain statements, and if you disagree with them, speak up. Silence will mean agreement. Is it not true that a machine-loom will weave more cloth and weave more cheaply than a hand-loom?" He paused, but nobody spoke up. "Is it not then highly irrational to break the machine-loom and go back to the clumsy and more costly hand-loom method of weaving?" Heads nodded in acquiescence. "Is it not true that that known as a trust produces more efficiently and cheaply than can a thousand competing small concerns?" Still no one objected. "Then is it not irrational to destroy that cheap and efficient combination?"

No one answered for a long time. Then Mr. Kowalt spoke.

"What are we to do, then?" he demanded. "To destroy the trusts is the only way we can see to escape their domination."

Ernest was all fire and aliveness on the instant.

"I'll show you another way!" he cried. "Let us not destroy those wonderful machines that produce efficiently and cheaply. Let us control them. Let us profit by their efficiency and cheapness. Let us run them for ourselves. Let us oust the present owners of the wonderful machines, and let us own the wonderful machines ourselves. That, gentlemen, is socialism, a greater combination than the trusts, a greater economic and social combination than any that has as yet appeared on the planet. It is in line with evolution. We meet combination with greater combination. It is the winning side. Come on over with us socialists and play on the winning side."

Here arose dissent. There was a shaking of heads, and mutterings arose.

"All right, then, you prefer to be anachronisms," Ernest laughed. "You prefer to play atavistic roles. You are doomed to perish as all atavisms perish. Have you ever asked what will happen to you when greater combinations than even the present trusts arise? Have you ever considered where you will stand when the great trusts themselves combine into the combination of combinations—into the social, economic, and political trust?"

He turned abruptly and irrelevantly upon Mr. Calvin.

"Tell me," Ernest said, "if this is not true. You are compelled to form a new political party because the old parties are in the hands of the trusts. The chief obstacle to your Grange propaganda is the trusts. Behind every obstacle you encounter, every blow that smites you, every defeat that you receive, is the hand of the trusts. Is this not so? Tell me."

Mr. Calvin sat in uncomfortable silence.

"Go ahead," Ernest encouraged.

"It is true," Mr. Calvin confessed. "We captured the state legislature of Oregon and put through splendid protective legislation, and it was vetoed by the governor, who was a creature of the trusts. We elected a governor of Colorado, and the legislature refused to permit him to take office. Twice we have passed a national income tax, and each time the supreme court smashed it as unconstitutional. The courts are in the hands of the trusts. We, the people, do not pay our judges sufficiently. But there will come a time—"

"When the combination of the trusts will control all legislation, when the combination of the trusts will itself be the government," Ernest interrupted.

"Never! never!" were the cries that arose. Everybody was excited and belligerent.

"Tell me," Ernest demanded, "what will you do when such a time comes?"

"We will rise in our strength!" Mr. Asmunsen cried, and many voices backed his decision.

"That will be civil war," Ernest warned them.

"So be it, civil war," was Mr. Asmunsen's answer, with the cries of all the men at the table behind him. "We have not forgotten the deeds of our forefathers. For our liberties we are ready to fight and die."

Ernest smiled.

"Do not forget," he said, "that we had tacitly agreed that liberty in your case, gentlemen, means liberty to squeeze profits out of others."

The table was angry, now, fighting angry; but Ernest controlled the tumult and made himself heard.

"One more question. When you rise in your strength, remember, the reason for your rising will be that the government is in the hands of the trusts. Therefore, against your strength the government will turn the regular army, the navy, the militia, the police—in short, the whole organized war machinery of the United States. Where will your strength be then?"

Dismay sat on their faces, and before they could recover, Ernest struck again.

"Do you remember, not so long ago, when our regular army was only fifty thousand? Year by year it has been increased until to-day it is three hundred thousand."

Again he struck.

"Nor is that all. While you diligently pursued that favorite phantom of yours, called profits, and moralized about that favorite fetich of yours, called competition, even greater and more direful things have been accomplished by combination. There is the militia."

"It is our strength!" cried Mr. Kowalt. "With it we would repel the invasion of the regular army."

"You would go into the militia yourself," was Ernest's retort, "and be sent to Maine, or Florida, or the Philippines, or anywhere else, to drown in blood your own comrades civil-warring for their liberties. While from Kansas, or Wisconsin, or any other state, your own comrades would go into the militia and come here to California to drown in blood your own civil-warring."

Now they were really shocked, and they sat wordless, until Mr. Owen murmured:

"We would not go into the militia. That would settle it. We would not be so foolish."

Ernest laughed outright.

"You do not understand the combination that has been effected. You could not help yourself. You would be drafted into the militia."

"There is such a thing as civil law," Mr. Owen insisted.

"Not when the government suspends civil law. In that day when you speak of rising in your strength, your strength would be turned against yourself. Into the militia you would go, willy-nilly. Habeas corpus, I heard some one mutter just now. Instead of habeas corpus you would get post mortems. If you refused to go into the militia, or to obey after you were in, you would be tried by drumhead court martial and shot down like dogs. It is the law."

"It is not the law!" Mr. Calvin asserted positively. "There is no such law. Young man, you have dreamed all this. Why, you spoke of sending the militia to the Philippines. That is unconstitutional. The Constitution especially states that the militia cannot be sent out of the country."

"What's the Constitution got to do with it?" Ernest demanded. "The courts interpret the Constitution, and the courts, as Mr. Asmunsen agreed, are the creatures of the trusts. Besides, it is as I have said, the law. It has been the law for years, for nine years, gentlemen."

"That we can be drafted into the militia?" Mr. Calvin asked incredulously. "That they can shoot us by drumhead court martial if we refuse?"

"Yes," Ernest answered, "precisely that."

"How is it that we have never heard of this law?" my father asked, and I could see that it was likewise new to him.

"For two reasons," Ernest said. "First, there has been no need to enforce it. If there had, you'd have heard of it soon enough. And secondly, the law was rushed through Congress and the Senate secretly, with practically no discussion. Of course, the newspapers made no mention of it. But we socialists knew about it. We published it in our papers. But you never read our papers."

"I still insist you are dreaming," Mr. Calvin said stubbornly. "The country would never have permitted it."

"But the country did permit it," Ernest replied. "And as for my dreaming—" he put his hand in his pocket and drew out a small pamphlet— "tell me if this looks like dream-stuff."

He opened it and began to read:

"'Section One, be it enacted, and so forth and so forth, that the militia shall consist of every able-bodied male citizen of the respective states, territories, and District of Columbia, who is more than eighteen and less than forty-five years of age.'

"'Section Seven, that any officer or enlisted man'—remember Section One, gentlemen, you are all enlisted men—'that any enlisted man of the militia who shall refuse or neglect to present himself to such mustering officer upon being called forth as herein prescribed, shall be subject to trial by court martial, and shall be punished as such court martial shall direct.'

"'Section Eight, that courts martial, for the trial of officers or men of the militia, shall be composed of militia officers only.'

"'Section Nine, that the militia, when called into the actual service of the United States, shall be subject to the same rules and articles of war as the regular troops of the United States.'

"There you are gentlemen, American citizens, and fellow-militiamen. Nine years ago we socialists thought that law was aimed against labor. But it would seem that it was aimed against you, too. Congressman Wiley, in the brief discussion that was permitted, said that the bill 'provided for a reserve force to take the mob by the throat'—you're the mob, gentlemen—'and protect at all hazards life, liberty, and property.' And in the time to come, when you rise in your strength, remember that you will be rising against the property of the trusts, and the liberty of the trusts, according to the law, to squeeze you. Your teeth are pulled, gentlemen. Your claws are trimmed. In the day you rise in your strength, toothless and clawless, you will be as harmless as any army of clams."

"I don't believe it!" Kowalt cried. "There is no such law. It is a canard got up by you socialists."

"This bill was introduced in the House of Representatives on July 30, 1902," was the reply. "It was introduced by Representative Dick of Ohio. It was rushed through. It was passed unanimously by the Senate on January 14, 1903. And just seven days afterward was approved by the President of the United States." *

*Everhard was right in the essential particulars, though his date of the introduction of the bill is in error. The bill was introduced on June 30, and not on July 30. The Congressional Record is here in Ardis, and a reference to it shows mention of the bill on the following dates: June 30, December 9, 15, 16, and 17, 1902, and January 7 and 14, 1903. The ignorance evidenced by the business men at the *dinner was nothing unusual. Very few people knew of the existence of this law. E. Untermann, a revolutionist, in July, 1903, published a pamphlet at Girard, Kansas, on the "Militia Bill." This pamphlet had a small circulation among workingmen; but already had the segregation of classes proceeded so far, that the members of the middle class never heard of the pamphlet at all, and so remained in ignorance of the law.*

CHAPTER IX. THE MATHEMATICS OF A DREAM

In the midst of the consternation his revelation had produced, Ernest began again to speak.

"You have said, a dozen of you to-night, that socialism is impossible. You have asserted the impossible, now let me demonstrate the inevitable. Not only is it inevitable that you small capitalists shall pass away, but it is inevitable that the large capitalists, and the trusts also, shall pass away. Remember, the tide of evolution never flows backward. It flows on and on, and it flows from competition to combination, and from little combination to large combination, and from large combination to colossal combination, and it flows on to socialism, which is the most colossal combination of all.

"You tell me that I dream. Very good. I'll give you the mathematics of my dream; and here, in advance, I challenge you to show that my mathematics are wrong. I shall develop the inevitability of the breakdown of the capitalist system, and I shall demonstrate mathematically why it must break down. Here goes, and bear with me if at first I seem irrelevant.

"Let us, first of all, investigate a particular industrial process, and whenever I state something with which you disagree, please interrupt me. Here is a shoe factory. This factory takes leather and makes it into shoes. Here is one hundred dollars' worth of leather. It goes through the factory and comes out in the form of shoes, worth, let us say, two hundred dollars. What has happened? One hundred dollars has been added to the value of the leather. How was it added? Let us see.

"Capital and labor added this value of one hundred dollars. Capital furnished the factory, the machines, and paid all the expenses. Labor furnished labor. By the joint effort of capital and labor one hundred dollars of value was added. Are you all agreed so far?"

Heads nodded around the table in affirmation.

"Labor and capital having produced this one hundred dollars, now proceed to divide it. The statistics of this division are fractional; so let us, for the sake of convenience, make them roughly approximate. Capital takes fifty dollars as its share, and labor gets in wages fifty dollars as its share. We will not enter into the squabbling over the division.* No matter how much squabbling takes place, in one percentage or another the division is arranged. And take notice here, that what is true of this particular industrial process is true of all industrial processes. Am I right?"

> *Everhard here clearly develops the cause of all the labor troubles of that time. In the division of the joint-product, capital wanted all it could get, and labor wanted all it could get. This quarrel over the division was irreconcilable. So long as the system of capitalistic production existed, labor and capital continued to quarrel over the division of the joint-product. It is a ludicrous spectacle to us, but we must not forget that we have seven centuries' advantage over those that lived in that time.

Again the whole table agreed with Ernest.

"Now, suppose labor, having received its fifty dollars, wanted to buy back shoes. It could only buy back fifty dollars' worth. That's clear, isn't it?

"And now we shift from this particular process to the sum total of all industrial processes in the United States, which includes the leather itself, raw material, transportation, selling, everything. We will say, for the sake of round figures, that the total production of wealth in the United States is one year is four billion dollars. Then labor has received in wages, during the same period, two billion dollars. Four billion dollars has been produced. How much of this can labor buy back? Two billions. There is no discussion of this, I am sure. For that matter, my percentages are mild. Because of a thousand capitalistic devices, labor cannot buy back even half of the total product.

"But to return. We will say labor buys back two billions. Then it stands to reason that labor can consume only two billions. There are still two billions to be accounted for, which labor cannot buy back and consume."

"Labor does not consume its two billions, even," Mr. Kowalt spoke up. "If it did, it would not have any deposits in the savings banks."

"Labor's deposits in the savings banks are only a sort of reserve fund that is consumed as fast as it accumulates. These deposits are saved for old age, for sickness and accident, and for funeral expenses. The savings bank deposit is simply a piece of the loaf put back on the shelf to be eaten next day. No, labor consumes all of the total product that its wages will buy back.

"Two billions are left to capital. After it has paid its expenses, does it consume the remainder? Does capital consume all of its two billions?"

Ernest stopped and put the question point blank to a number of the men. They shook their heads.

"I don't know," one of them frankly said.

"Of course you do," Ernest went on. "Stop and think a moment. If capital consumed its share, the sum total of capital could not increase. It would remain constant. If you will look at the economic history of the United States, you will see that the sum total of capital has continually increased. Therefore capital does not consume its share. Do you remember when England owned so much of our railroad bonds? As the years went by, we bought back those bonds. What does that mean? That part of capital's unconsumed share bought back the bonds. What is the meaning of the fact that to-day the capitalists of the United States own hundreds and hundreds of millions of dollars of Mexican bonds, Russian bonds, Italian bonds, Grecian bonds? The meaning is that those hundreds and hundreds of millions were part of capital's share which capital did not consume. Furthermore, from the very beginning of the capitalist system, capital has never consumed all of its share.

"And now we come to the point. Four billion dollars of wealth is produced in one year in the United States. Labor buys back and consumes two billions. Capital does not consume the remaining two billions. There is a large balance left over unconsumed. What is done with this balance? What can be done with it? Labor cannot consume any of it, for labor has already spent all its wages. Capital will not consume this balance, because, already, according to its nature, it has consumed all it can. And still remains the balance. What can be done with it? What is done with it?"

"It is sold abroad," Mr. Kowalt volunteered.

"The very thing," Ernest agreed. "Because of this balance arises our need for a foreign market. This is sold abroad. It has to be sold abroad. There is no other way of getting rid of it. And that unconsumed surplus, sold abroad, becomes what we call our favorable balance of trade. Are we all agreed so far?"

"Surely it is a waste of time to elaborate these A B C's of commerce," Mr. Calvin said tartly. "We all understand them."

"And it is by these A B C's I have so carefully elaborated that I shall confound you," Ernest retorted. "There's the beauty of it. And I'm going to confound you with them right now. Here goes.

"The United States is a capitalist country that has developed its resources. According to its capitalist system of industry, it has an unconsumed surplus that must be got rid of, and that must be got rid of abroad.* What is true of the United States is true of every other capitalist country with developed resources. Every one of such countries has an unconsumed surplus. Don't forget that they have already traded with one another, and that these surpluses yet remain. Labor in all these countries has spent its wages, and cannot buy any of the surpluses. Capital in all these countries has already consumed all it is able according to its nature. And still remain the surpluses. They cannot dispose of these surpluses to one another. How are they going to get rid of them?"

> ** Theodore Roosevelt, President of the United States a few*
>
> *years prior to this time, made the following public*
>
> *declaration: "A more liberal and extensive reciprocity in*
>
> *the purchase and sale of commodities is necessary, so that*
>
> *the overproduction of the United States can be*
>
> *satisfactorily disposed of to foreign countries." Of*
>
> *course, this overproduction he mentions was the profits of*
>
> *the capitalist system over and beyond the consuming power of*
>
> *the capitalists. It was at this time that Senator Mark*
>
> *Hanna said: "The production of wealth in the United States*
>
> *is one-third larger annually than its consumption." Also a*
>
> *fellow-Senator, Chauncey Depew, said: "The American people*
>
> *produce annually two billions more wealth than they*
>
> *consume."*

"Sell them to countries with undeveloped resources," Mr. Kowalt suggested.

"The very thing. You see, my argument is so clear and simple that in your own minds you carry it on for me. And now for the next step. Suppose the United States disposes of its surplus to a country with undeveloped resources like, say, Brazil. Remember this surplus is over and above trade, which articles of trade have been consumed. What, then, does the United States get in return from Brazil?"

"Gold," said Mr. Kowalt.

"But there is only so much gold, and not much of it, in the world," Ernest objected.

"Gold in the form of securities and bonds and so forth," Mr. Kowalt amended.

"Now you've struck it," Ernest said. "From Brazil the United States, in return for her surplus, gets bonds and securities. And what does that mean? It means that the United States is coming to own railroads in Brazil, factories, mines, and lands in Brazil. And what is the meaning of that in turn?"

Mr. Kowalt pondered and shook his head.

"I'll tell you," Ernest continued. "It means that the resources of Brazil are being developed. And now, the next point. When Brazil, under the capitalist system, has developed her resources, she will herself have an unconsumed surplus. Can she get rid of this surplus to the United States? No, because the United States has herself a surplus. Can the United States do what she previously did—get rid of her surplus to Brazil? No, for Brazil now has a surplus, too.

"What happens? The United States and Brazil must both seek out other countries with undeveloped resources, in order to unload the surpluses on them. But by the very process of unloading the surpluses, the resources of those countries are in turn developed. Soon they have surpluses, and are seeking other countries on which to unload. Now, gentlemen, follow me. The planet is only so large. There are only so many countries in the world. What will happen when every country in the world, down to the smallest and last, with a surplus in its hands, stands confronting every other country with surpluses in their hands?"

He paused and regarded his listeners. The bepuzzlement in their faces was delicious. Also, there was awe in their faces. Out of abstractions Ernest had conjured a vision and made them see it. They were seeing it then, as they sat there, and they were frightened by it.

"We started with A B C, Mr. Calvin," Ernest said slyly. "I have now given you the rest of the alphabet. It is very simple. That is the beauty of it. You surely have the answer forthcoming. What, then, when every country in the world has an unconsumed surplus? Where will your capitalist system be then?"

But Mr. Calvin shook a troubled head. He was obviously questing back through Ernest's reasoning in search of an error.

"Let me briefly go over the ground with you again," Ernest said. "We began with a particular industrial process, the shoe factory. We found that the division of the joint product that took place there was similar to the division that took place in the sum total of all industrial processes. We found that labor could buy back with its wages only so much of the product, and that capital did not consume all of the remainder of the product. We found that when labor had consumed to the full extent of its wages, and when capital had consumed all it wanted, there was still left an unconsumed surplus. We agreed that this surplus could only be disposed of abroad. We agreed, also, that the effect of unloading this surplus on another country would be to develop the resources of that country, and that in a short time that country would have an unconsumed surplus. We extended this process to all the countries on the planet, till every country was producing every year, and every day, an unconsumed surplus, which it could dispose of to no other country. And now I ask you again, what are we going to do with those surpluses?"

Still no one answered.

"Mr. Calvin?" Ernest queried.

"It beats me," Mr. Calvin confessed.

"I never dreamed of such a thing," Mr. Asmunsen said. "And yet it does seem clear as print."

It was the first time I had ever heard Karl Marx's* doctrine of surplus value elaborated, and Ernest had done it so simply that I, too, sat puzzled and dumbfounded.

* Karl Marx—the great intellectual hero of Socialism. A German Jew of the nineteenth century. A contemporary of John Stuart Mill. It seems incredible to us that whole generations should have elapsed after the enunciation of Marx's economic discoveries, in which time he was sneered at by the world's accepted thinkers and scholars. Because of his discoveries he was banished from his native country, and he died an exile in England.

"I'll tell you a way to get rid of the surplus," Ernest said. "Throw it into the sea. Throw every year hundreds of millions of dollars' worth of shoes and wheat and clothing and all the commodities of commerce into the sea. Won't that fix it?"

"It will certainly fix it," Mr. Calvin answered. "But it is absurd for you to talk that way."

Ernest was upon him like a flash.

"Is it a bit more absurd than what you advocate, you machine-breaker, returning to the antediluvian ways of your forefathers? What do you propose in order to get rid of the surplus? You would escape the problem of the surplus by not producing any surplus. And how do you propose to avoid producing a surplus? By returning to a primitive method of production, so confused and disorderly and irrational, so wasteful and costly, that it will be impossible to produce a surplus."

Mr. Calvin swallowed. The point had been driven home. He swallowed again and cleared his throat.

"You are right," he said. "I stand convicted. It is absurd. But we've got to do something. It is a case of life and death for us of the middle class. We refuse to perish. We elect to be absurd and to return to the truly crude and wasteful methods of our forefathers. We will put back industry to its pre-trust stage. We will break the machines. And what are you going to do about it?"

"But you can't break the machines," Ernest replied. "You cannot make the tide of evolution flow backward. Opposed to you are two great forces, each of which is more powerful than you of the middle class. The large capitalists, the trusts, in short, will not let you turn back. They don't want the machines destroyed. And greater than the trusts, and more powerful, is labor. It will not let you destroy the machines. The ownership of the world, along with the machines, lies between the trusts and labor. That is the battle alignment. Neither side wants the destruction of the machines. But each side wants to possess the machines. In this battle the middle class has no place. The middle class is a pygmy between two giants. Don't you see, you poor perishing middle class, you are caught between the upper and nether millstones, and even now has the grinding begun.

"I have demonstrated to you mathematically the inevitable breakdown of the capitalist system. When every country stands with an unconsumed and unsalable surplus on its hands, the capitalist system will break down under the terrific structure of profits that it itself has reared. And in that day there won't be any destruction of the machines. The struggle then will be for the ownership of the machines. If labor wins, your way will be easy. The United States, and the whole world for that matter, will enter upon a new and tremendous era. Instead of being crushed by the machines, life will be made fairer, and happier, and nobler by them. You of the destroyed middle class, along with labor—there will be nothing but labor then; so you, and all the rest of labor, will participate in the equitable distribution of the products of the wonderful machines. And we, all of us, will make new and more wonderful machines. And there won't be any unconsumed surplus, because there won't be any profits."

"But suppose the trusts win in this battle over the ownership of the machines and the world?" Mr. Kowalt asked.

"Then," Ernest answered, "you, and labor, and all of us, will be crushed under the iron heel of a despotism as relentless and terrible as any despotism that has blackened the pages of the history of man. That will be a good name for that despotism, the Iron Heel." *

The earliest known use of that name to designate the

Oligarchy.

There was a long pause, and every man at the table meditated in ways unwonted and profound.

"But this socialism of yours is a dream," Mr. Calvin said; and repeated, "a dream."

"I'll show you something that isn't a dream, then," Ernest answered. "And that something I shall call the Oligarchy. You call it the Plutocracy. We both mean the same thing, the large capitalists or the trusts. Let us see where the power lies today. And in order to do so, let us apportion society into its class divisions.

"There are three big classes in society. First comes the Plutocracy, which is composed of wealthy bankers, railway magnates, corporation directors, and trust magnates. Second, is the middle class, your class, gentlemen, which is composed of farmers, merchants, small manufacturers, and professional men. And third and last comes my class, the proletariat, which is composed of the wage-workers.*

This division of society made by Everhard is in accordance

with that made by Lucien Sanial, one of the statistical

authorities of that time. His calculation of the membership

of these divisions by occupation, from the United States

135

Census of 1900, is as follows: Plutocratic class, 250,251;

Middle class, 8,429,845; and Proletariat class, 20,393,137.

"You cannot but grant that the ownership of wealth constitutes essential power in the United States to-day. How is this wealth owned by these three classes? Here are the figures. The Plutocracy owns sixty-seven billions of wealth. Of the total number of persons engaged in occupations in the United States, only nine-tenths of one per cent are from the Plutocracy, yet the Plutocracy owns seventy per cent of the total wealth. The middle class owns twenty-four billions. Twenty-nine per cent of those in occupations are from the middle class, and they own twenty-five per cent of the total wealth. Remains the proletariat. It owns four billions. Of all persons in occupations, seventy per cent come from the proletariat; and the proletariat owns four per cent of the total wealth. Where does the power lie, gentlemen?"

"From your own figures, we of the middle class are more powerful than labor," Mr. Asmunsen remarked.

"Calling us weak does not make you stronger in the face of the strength of the Plutocracy," Ernest retorted. "And furthermore, I'm not done with you. There is a greater strength than wealth, and it is greater because it cannot be taken away. Our strength, the strength of the proletariat, is in our muscles, in our hands to cast ballots, in our fingers to pull triggers. This strength we cannot be stripped of. It is the primitive strength, it is the strength that is to life germane, it is the strength that is stronger than wealth, and that wealth cannot take away.

"But your strength is detachable. It can be taken away from you. Even now the Plutocracy is taking it away from you. In the end it will take it all away from you. And then you will cease to be the middle class. You will descend to us. You will become proletarians. And the beauty of it is that you will then add to our strength. We will hail you brothers, and we will fight shoulder to shoulder in the cause of humanity.

"You see, labor has nothing concrete of which to be despoiled. Its share of the wealth of the country consists of clothes and household furniture, with here and there, in very rare cases, an unencumbered home. But you have the concrete wealth, twenty-four billions of it, and the Plutocracy will take it away from you. Of course, there is the large likelihood that the proletariat will take it away first. Don't you see your position, gentlemen? The middle class is a wobbly little lamb between a lion and a tiger. If one doesn't get you, the other will. And if the Plutocracy gets you first, why it's only a matter of time when the Proletariat gets the Plutocracy.

"Even your present wealth is not a true measure of your power. The strength of your wealth at this moment is only an empty shell. That is why you are crying out your feeble little battle-cry, 'Return to the ways of our fathers.' You are aware of your impotency. You know that your strength is an empty shell. And I'll show you the emptiness of it.

"What power have the farmers? Over fifty per cent are thralls by virtue of the fact that they are merely tenants or are mortgaged. And all of them are thralls by virtue of the fact that the trusts already own or control (which is the same thing only better)—own and control all the means of marketing the crops, such as cold storage, railroads, elevators, and steamship lines. And, furthermore, the trusts control the markets. In all this the farmers are without power. As regards their political and governmental power, I'll take that up later, along with the political and governmental power of the whole middle class.

"Day by day the trusts squeeze out the farmers as they squeezed out Mr. Calvin and the rest of the dairymen. And day by day are the merchants squeezed out in the same way. Do you remember how, in six months, the Tobacco Trust squeezed out over four hundred cigar stores in New York City alone? Where are the old-time owners of the coal fields? You know today, without my telling you, that the Railroad Trust owns or controls the entire anthracite and bituminous coal fields. Doesn't the Standard Oil Trust* own a score of the ocean lines? And does it not also control copper, to say nothing of running a smelter trust as a little side enterprise? There are ten thousand cities in the United States to-night lighted by the companies owned or controlled by Standard Oil, and in as many cities all the electric transportation,—urban, suburban, and interurban,—is in the hands of Standard Oil. The small capitalists who were in these thousands of enterprises are gone. You know that. It's the same way that you are going.

* *Standard Oil and Rockefeller—see upcoming footnote:*

"Rockefeller began as a member . . ."

"The small manufacturer is like the farmer; and small manufacturers and farmers to-day are reduced, to all intents and purposes, to feudal tenure. For that matter, the professional men and the artists are at this present moment villeins in everything but name, while the politicians are henchmen. Why do you, Mr. Calvin, work all your nights and days to organize the farmers, along with the rest of the middle class, into a new political party? Because the politicians of the old parties will have nothing to do with your atavistic ideas; and with your atavistic ideas, they will have nothing to do because they are what I said they are, henchmen, retainers of the Plutocracy.

"I spoke of the professional men and the artists as villeins. What else are they? One and all, the professors, the preachers, and the editors, hold their jobs by serving the Plutocracy, and their service consists of propagating only such ideas as are either harmless to or commendatory of the Plutocracy. Whenever they propagate ideas that menace the Plutocracy, they lose their jobs, in which case, if they have not provided for the rainy day, they descend into the proletariat and either perish or become working-class agitators. And don't forget that it is the press, the pulpit, and the university that mould public opinion, set the thought-pace of the nation. As for the artists, they merely pander to the little less than ignoble tastes of the Plutocracy.

"But after all, wealth in itself is not the real power; it is the means to power, and power is governmental. Who controls the government to-day? The proletariat with its twenty millions engaged in occupations? Even you laugh at the idea. Does the middle class, with its eight million occupied members? No more than the proletariat. Who, then, controls the government? The Plutocracy, with its paltry quarter of a million of occupied members. But this quarter of a million does not control the government, though it renders yeoman service. It is the brain of the Plutocracy that controls the government, and this brain consists of seven* small and powerful groups of men. And do not forget that these groups are working to-day practically in unison.

*Even as late as 1907, it was considered that eleven groups dominated the country, but this number was reduced by the amalgamation of the five railroad groups into a supreme combination of all the railroads. These five groups so amalgamated, along with their financial and political allies, were (1) James J. Hill with his control of the Northwest; (2) the Pennsylvania railway group, Schiff financial manager, with big banking firms of Philadelphia and New York; (3) Harriman, with Frick for counsel and Odell as political lieutenant, controlling the central continental, Southwestern and Southern Pacific Coast lines of transportation; (4) the Gould family railway interests; and (5) Moore, Reid, and Leeds, known as the "Rock Island crowd." These strong oligarchs arose out of the conflict of competition and travelled the inevitable road toward combination.

"Let me point out the power of but one of them, the railroad group. It employs forty thousand lawyers to defeat the people in the courts. It issues countless thousands of free passes to judges, bankers, editors, ministers, university men, members of state legislatures, and of Congress. It maintains luxurious lobbies* at every state capital, and at the national capital; and in all the cities and towns of the land it employs an immense army of pettifoggers and small politicians whose business is to attend primaries, pack conventions, get on juries, bribe judges, and in every way to work for its interests.**

> * Lobby—a peculiar institution for bribing, bulldozing, and corrupting the legislators who were supposed to represent the people's interests.

> ** A decade before this speech of Everhard's, the New York Board of Trade issued a report from which the following is quoted: "The railroads control absolutely the legislatures of a majority of the states of the Union; they make and unmake United States Senators, congressmen, and governors, and are practically dictators of the governmental policy of the United States."

"Gentlemen, I have merely sketched the power of one of the seven groups that constitute the brain of the Plutocracy.* Your twenty-four billions of wealth does not give you twenty-five cents' worth of governmental power. It is an empty shell, and soon even the empty shell will be taken away from you. The Plutocracy has all power in its hands to-day. It to-day makes the laws, for it owns the Senate, Congress, the courts, and the state legislatures. And not only that. Behind law must be force to execute the law. To-day the Plutocracy makes the law, and to enforce the law it has at its beck and call the, police, the army, the navy, and, lastly, the militia, which is you, and me, and all of us."

Rockefeller began as a member of the proletariat, and through thrift and cunning succeeded in developing the first perfect trust, namely that known as Standard Oil. We cannot forbear giving the following remarkable page from the history of the times, to show how the need for reinvestment of the Standard Oil surplus crushed out small capitalists and hastened the breakdown of the capitalist system. David Graham Phillips was a radical writer of the period, and the quotation, by him, is taken from a copy of the Saturday Evening Post, dated October 4, 1902 A.D. This is the only copy of this publication that has come down to us, and yet, from its appearance and content, we cannot but conclude that it was one of the popular periodicals with a large circulation. The quotation here follows:

"About ten years ago Rockefeller's income was given as thirty millions by an excellent authority. He had reached the limit of profitable investment of profits in the oil industry. Here, then, were these enormous sums in cash pouring in—more than $2,000,000 a month for John Davison Rockefeller alone. The problem of reinvestment became more serious. It became a nightmare. The oil income was swelling, swelling, and the number of sound investments limited, even more limited than it is now. It was through no special eagerness for more gains that the Rockefellers began to branch out from oil into other things. They were forced, swept on by this inrolling tide of wealth which their monopoly magnet irresistibly attracted. They developed a staff of investment seekers and investigators. It is said that the chief of this staff has a salary of $125,000 a year.

"The first conspicuous excursion and incursion of the Rockefellers was into the railway field. By 1895 they controlled one-fifth of the railway mileage of the country. What do they own or, through dominant ownership, control to-day? They are powerful in all the great railways of New York, north, east, and west, except one, where their share is only a few millions. They are in most of the great railways radiating from Chicago. They dominate in several of the systems that extend to the Pacific. It is their *votes that make Mr. Morgan so potent, though, it may be added, they need his brains more than he needs their votes— at present, and the combination of the two constitutes in large measure the 'community of interest.'*

"But railways could not alone absorb rapidly enough those mighty floods of gold. Presently John D. Rockefeller's $2,500,000 a month had increased to four, to five, to six millions a month, to $75,000,000 a year. Illuminating oil was becoming all profit. The reinvestments of income were adding their mite of many annual millions.

"The Rockefellers went into gas and electricity when those industries had developed to the safe investment stage. And now a large part of the American people must begin to enrich the Rockefellers as soon as the sun goes down, no matter what form of illuminant they use. They went into farm mortgages. It is said that when prosperity a few years ago enabled the farmers to rid themselves of their mortgages, John D. Rockefeller was moved almost to tears; eight millions which he had thought taken care of for years to come at a good interest were suddenly dumped upon his doorstep and there set up a-squawking for a new home. This

143

unexpected addition to his worriments in finding places for the progeny of his petroleum and their progeny and their progeny's progeny was too much for the equanimity of a man without a digestion. . . .

"The Rockefellers went into mines—iron and coal and copper and lead; into other industrial companies; into street railways, into national, state, and municipal bonds; into steamships and steamboats and telegraphy; into real estate, into skyscrapers and residences and hotels and business blocks; into life insurance, into banking. There was soon literally no field of industry where their millions were not at work. . . .

"The Rockefeller bank—the National City Bank—is by itself far and away the biggest bank in the United States. It is exceeded in the world only by the Bank of England and the Bank of France. The deposits average more than one hundred millions a day; and it dominates the call loan market on Wall Street and the stock market. But it is not alone; it is the head of the Rockefeller chain of banks, which includes fourteen banks and trust companies in New York City, and banks of great strength and influence in every large money center in the country.

"John D. Rockefeller owns Standard Oil stock worth between four and five hundred millions at the market quotations. He has a hundred millions in the steel trust, almost as much in a single western railway system, half as much in a second, and so on and on and on until the mind wearies of the cataloguing. His income last year was about $100,000,000— it is doubtful if the incomes of all the Rothschilds together make a greater sum. And it is going up by leaps and bounds."

Little discussion took place after this, and the dinner soon broke up. All were quiet and subdued, and leave-taking was done with low *voices. It seemed almost that they were scared by the vision of the times they had seen.*

"The situation is, indeed, serious," Mr. Calvin said to Ernest. "I have little quarrel with the way you have depicted it. Only I disagree with you about the doom of the middle class. We shall survive, and we shall overthrow the trusts."

"And return to the ways of your fathers," Ernest finished for him.

145

"Even so," Mr. Calvin answered gravely. "I know it's a sort of machine-breaking, and that it is absurd. But then life seems absurd to-day, what of the machinations of the Plutocracy. And at any rate, our sort of machine-breaking is at least practical and possible, which your dream is not. Your socialistic dream is . . . well, a dream. We cannot follow you."

"I only wish you fellows knew a little something about evolution and sociology," Ernest said wistfully, as they shook hands. "We would be saved so much trouble if you did."

CHAPTER X. THE VORTEX

Following like thunder claps upon the Business Men's dinner, occurred event after event of terrifying moment; and I, little I, who had lived so placidly all my days in the quiet university town, found myself and my personal affairs drawn into the vortex of the great world-affairs. Whether it was my love for Ernest, or the clear sight he had given me of the society in which I lived, that made me a revolutionist, I know not; but a revolutionist I became, and I was plunged into a whirl of happenings that would have been inconceivable three short months before.

The crisis in my own fortunes came simultaneously with great crises in society. First of all, father was discharged from the university. Oh, he was not technically discharged. His resignation was demanded, that was all. This, in itself, did not amount to much. Father, in fact, was delighted. He was especially delighted because his discharge had been precipitated by the publication of his book, "Economics and Education." It clinched his argument, he contended. What better evidence could be advanced to prove that education was dominated by the capitalist class?

But this proof never got anywhere. Nobody knew he had been forced to resign from the university. He was so eminent a scientist that such an announcement, coupled with the reason for his enforced resignation, would have created somewhat of a furor all over the world. The newspapers showered him with praise and honor, and commended him for having given up the drudgery of the lecture room in order to devote his whole time to scientific research.

At first father laughed. Then he became angry—tonic angry. Then came the suppression of his book. This suppression was performed secretly, so secretly that at first we could not comprehend. The publication of the book had immediately caused a bit of excitement in the country. Father had been politely abused in the capitalist press, the tone of the abuse being to the effect that it was a pity so great a scientist should leave his field and invade the realm of sociology, about which he knew nothing and wherein he had promptly become lost. This lasted for a week, while father chuckled and said the book had touched a sore spot on capitalism. And then, abruptly, the newspapers and the critical magazines ceased saying anything about the book at all. Also, and with equal suddenness, the book disappeared from the market. Not a copy was obtainable from any bookseller. Father wrote to the publishers and was informed that the plates had been accidentally injured. An unsatisfactory correspondence followed. Driven finally to an unequivocal stand, the publishers stated that they could not see their way to putting the book into type again, but that they were willing to relinquish their rights in it.

"And you won't find another publishing house in the country to touch it," Ernest said. "And if I were you, I'd hunt cover right now. You've merely got a foretaste of the Iron Heel."

But father was nothing if not a scientist. He never believed in jumping to conclusions. A laboratory experiment was no experiment if it were not carried through in all its details. So he patiently went the round of the publishing houses. They gave a multitude of excuses, but not one house would consider the book.

When father became convinced that the book had actually been suppressed, he tried to get the fact into the newspapers; but his communications were ignored. At a political meeting of the socialists, where many reporters were present, father saw his chance. He arose and related the history of the suppression of the book. He laughed next day when he read the newspapers, and then he grew angry to a degree that eliminated all tonic qualities. The papers made no mention of the book, but they misreported him beautifully. They twisted his words and phrases away from the context, and turned his subdued and controlled remarks into a howling anarchistic speech. It was done artfully. One instance, in particular, I remember. He had used the phrase "social revolution." The reporter merely dropped out "social." This was sent out all over the country in an Associated Press despatch, and from all over the country arose a cry of alarm. Father was branded as a nihilist and an anarchist, and in one cartoon that was copied widely he was portrayed waving a red flag at the head of a mob of long-haired, wild-eyed men who bore in their hands torches, knives, and dynamite bombs.

He was assailed terribly in the press, in long and abusive editorials, for his anarchy, and hints were made of mental breakdown on his part. This behavior, on the part of the capitalist press, was nothing new, Ernest told us. It was the custom, he said, to send reporters to all the socialist meetings for the express purpose of misreporting and distorting what was said, in order to frighten the middle class away from any possible affiliation with the proletariat. And repeatedly Ernest warned father to cease fighting and to take to cover.

The socialist press of the country took up the fight, however, and throughout the reading portion of the working class it was known that the book had been suppressed. But this knowledge stopped with the working class. Next, the "Appeal to Reason," a big socialist publishing house, arranged with father to bring out the book. Father was jubilant, but Ernest was alarmed.

"I tell you we are on the verge of the unknown," he insisted. "Big things are happening secretly all around us. We can feel them. We do not know what they are, but they are there. The whole fabric of society is a-tremble with them. Don't ask me. I don't know myself. But out of this flux of society something is about to crystallize. It is crystallizing now. The suppression of the book is a precipitation. How many books have been suppressed? We haven't the least idea. We are in the dark. We have no way of learning. Watch out next for the suppression of the socialist press and socialist publishing houses. I'm afraid it's coming. We are going to be throttled."

Ernest had his hand on the pulse of events even more closely than the rest of the socialists, and within two days the first blow was struck. The Appeal to Reason was a weekly, and its regular circulation amongst the proletariat was seven hundred and fifty thousand. Also, it very frequently got out special editions of from two to five millions. These great editions were paid for and distributed by the small army of voluntary workers who had marshalled around the Appeal. The first blow was aimed at these special editions, and it was a crushing one. By an arbitrary ruling of the Post Office, these editions were decided to be not the regular circulation of the paper, and for that reason were denied admission to the mails.

A week later the Post Office Department ruled that the paper was seditious, and barred it entirely from the mails. This was a fearful blow to the socialist propaganda. The Appeal was desperate. It devised a plan of reaching its subscribers through the express companies, but they declined to handle it. This was the end of the Appeal. But not quite. It prepared to go on with its book publishing. Twenty thousand copies of father's book were in the bindery, and the presses were turning off more. And then, without warning, a mob arose one night, and, under a waving American flag, singing patriotic songs, set fire to the great plant of the Appeal and totally destroyed it.

Now Girard, Kansas, was a quiet, peaceable town. There had never been any labor troubles there. The Appeal paid union wages; and, in fact, was the backbone of the town, giving employment to hundreds of men and women. It was not the citizens of Girard that composed the mob. This mob had risen up out of the earth apparently, and to all intents and purposes, its work done, it had gone back into the earth. Ernest saw in the affair the most sinister import.

"The Black Hundreds* are being organized in the United States," he said. "This is the beginning. There will be more of it. The Iron Heel is getting bold."

* *The Black Hundreds were reactionary mobs organized by the perishing Autocracy in the Russian Revolution. These reactionary groups attacked the revolutionary groups, and also, at needed moments, rioted and destroyed property so as to afford the Autocracy the pretext of calling out the Cossacks.*

And so perished father's book. We were to see much of the Black Hundreds as the days went by. Week by week more of the socialist papers were barred from the mails, and in a number of instances the Black Hundreds destroyed the socialist presses. Of course, the newspapers of the land lived up to the reactionary policy of the ruling class, and the destroyed socialist press was misrepresented and vilified, while the Black Hundreds were represented as true patriots and saviours of society. So convincing was all this misrepresentation that even sincere ministers in the pulpit praised the Black Hundreds while regretting the necessity of violence.

History was making fast. The fall elections were soon to occur, and Ernest was nominated by the socialist party to run for Congress. His chance for election was most favorable. The street-car strike in San Francisco had been broken. And following upon it the teamsters' strike had been broken. These two defeats had been very disastrous to organized labor. The whole Water Front Federation, along with its allies in the structural trades, had backed up the teamsters, and all had been smashed down ingloriously. It had been a bloody strike. The police had broken countless heads with their riot clubs; and the death list had been augmented by the turning loose of a machine-gun on the strikers from the barns of the Marsden Special Delivery Company.

In consequence, the men were sullen and vindictive. They wanted blood, and revenge. Beaten on their chosen field, they were ripe to seek revenge by means of political action. They still maintained their labor organization, and this gave them strength in the political struggle that was on. Ernest's chance for election grew stronger and stronger. Day by day unions and more unions voted their support to the socialists, until even Ernest laughed when the Undertakers' Assistants and the Chicken Pickers fell into line. Labor became mulish. While it packed the socialist meetings with mad enthusiasm, it was impervious to the wiles of the old-party politicians. The old-party orators were usually greeted with empty halls, though occasionally they encountered full halls where they were so roughly handled that more than once it was necessary to call out the police reserves.

History was making fast. The air was vibrant with things happening and impending. The country was on the verge of hard times,* caused by a series of prosperous years wherein the difficulty of disposing abroad of the unconsumed surplus had become increasingly difficult. Industries were working short time; many great factories were standing idle against the time when the surplus should be gone; and wages were being cut right and left.

* Under the capitalist regime these periods of hard times were as inevitable as they were absurd. Prosperity always brought calamity. This, of course, was due to the excess of unconsumed profits that was piled up.

Also, the great machinist strike had been broken. Two hundred thousand machinists, along with their five hundred thousand allies in the metalworking trades, had been defeated in as bloody a strike as had ever marred the United States. Pitched battles had been fought with the small armies of armed strike-breakers* put in the field by the employers' associations; the Black Hundreds, appearing in scores of wide-scattered places, had destroyed property; and, in consequence, a hundred thousand regular soldiers of the United States has been called out to put a frightful end to the whole affair. A number of the labor leaders had been executed; many others had been sentenced to prison, while thousands of the rank and file of the strikers had been herded into bull-pens** and abominably treated by the soldiers.

* Strike-breakers—these were, in purpose and practice and everything except name, the private soldiers of the capitalists. They were thoroughly organized and well armed, and they were held in readiness to be hurled in special trains to any part of the country where labor went on strike or was locked out by the employers. Only those curious

times could have given rise to the amazing spectacle of one,

Farley, a notorious commander of strike-breakers, who, in

1906, swept across the United States in special trains from

New York to San Francisco with an army of twenty-five

hundred men, fully armed and equipped, to break a strike of

the San Francisco street-car men. Such an act was in direct

violation of the laws of the land. The fact that this act,

and thousands of similar acts, went unpunished, goes to show

how completely the judiciary was the creature of the

Plutocracy.

** Bull-pen—in a miners' strike in Idaho, in the latter

part of the nineteenth century, it happened that many of the

strikers were confined in a bull-pen by the troops. The

practice and the name continued in the twentieth century.

The years of prosperity were now to be paid for. All markets were glutted; all markets were falling; and amidst the general crumble of prices the price of labor crumbled fastest of all. The land was convulsed with industrial dissensions. Labor was striking here, there, and everywhere; and where it was not striking, it was being turned out by the capitalists. The papers were filled with tales of violence and blood. And through it all the Black Hundreds played their part. Riot, arson, and wanton destruction of property was their function, and well they performed it. The whole regular army was in the field, called there by the actions of the Black Hundreds.* All cities and towns were like armed camps, and laborers were shot down like dogs. Out of the vast army of the unemployed the strike-breakers were recruited; and when the strike-breakers were worsted by the labor unions, the troops always appeared and crushed the unions. Then there was the militia. As yet, it was not necessary to have recourse to the secret militia law. Only the regularly organized militia was out, and it was out everywhere. And in this time of terror, the regular army was increased an additional hundred thousand by the government.

The name only, and not the idea, was imported from Russia. The Black Hundreds were a development out of the secret agents of the capitalists, and their use arose in the labor struggles of the nineteenth century. There is no discussion of this. No less an authority of the times than Carroll D. Wright, United States Commissioner of Labor, is responsible for the statement. From his book, entitled "The Battles of Labor," is quoted the declaration that "in some of the great historic strikes the employers themselves have instigated acts of violence;" that manufacturers have deliberately provoked strikes in order to get rid of surplus stock; and that freight cars have been burned by employers' agents during railroad strikes in order to increase disorder. It was out of these secret agents of the employers that the Black Hundreds arose; and it was they, in turn, that later became that terrible weapon of the Oligarchy, the agents-provocateurs.

Never had labor received such an all-around beating. The great captains of industry, the oligarchs, had for the first time thrown their full weight into the breach the struggling employers' associations had made. These associations were practically middle-class affairs, and now, compelled by hard times and crashing markets, and aided by the great captains of industry, they gave organized labor an awful and decisive defeat. It was an all-powerful alliance, but it was an alliance of the lion and the lamb, as the middle class was soon to learn.

Labor was bloody and sullen, but crushed. Yet its defeat did not put an end to the hard times. The banks, themselves constituting one of the most important forces of the Oligarchy, continued to call in credits. The Wall Street* group turned the stock market into a maelstrom where the values of all the land crumbled away almost to nothingness. And out of all the rack and ruin rose the form of the nascent Oligarchy, imperturbable, indifferent, and sure. Its serenity and certitude was terrifying. Not only did it use its own vast power, but it used all the power of the United States Treasury to carry out its plans.

* Wall Street—so named from a street in ancient New York, where was situated the stock exchange, and where the irrational organization of society permitted underhanded manipulation of all the industries of the country.

The captains of industry had turned upon the middle class. The employers' associations, that had helped the captains of industry to tear and rend labor, were now torn and rent by their quondam allies. Amidst the crashing of the middle men, the small business men and manufacturers, the trusts stood firm. Nay, the trusts did more than stand firm. They were active.

They sowed wind, and wind, and ever more wind; for they alone knew how to reap the whirlwind and make a profit out of it. And such profits! Colossal profits! Strong enough themselves to weather the storm that was largely their own brewing, they turned loose and plundered the wrecks that floated about them. Values were pitifully and inconceivably shrunken, and the trusts added hugely to their holdings, even extending their enterprises into many new fields—and always at the expense of the middle class.

Thus the summer of 1912 witnessed the virtual death-thrust to the middle class. Even Ernest was astounded at the quickness with which it had been done. He shook his head ominously and looked forward without hope to the fall elections.

"It's no use," he said. "We are beaten. The Iron Heel is here. I had hoped for a peaceable victory at the ballot-box. I was wrong. Wickson was right. We shall be robbed of our few remaining liberties; the Iron Heel will walk upon our faces; nothing remains but a bloody revolution of the working class. Of course we will win, but I shudder to think of it."

And from then on Ernest pinned his faith in revolution. In this he was in advance of his party. His fellow-socialists could not agree with him. They still insisted that victory could be gained through the elections. It was not that they were stunned. They were too cool-headed and courageous for that. They were merely incredulous, that was all. Ernest could not get them seriously to fear the coming of the Oligarchy. They were stirred by him, but they were too sure of their own strength. There was no room in their theoretical social evolution for an oligarchy, therefore the Oligarchy could not be.

"We'll send you to Congress and it will be all right," they told him at one of our secret meetings.

"And when they take me out of Congress," Ernest replied coldly, "and put me against a wall, and blow my brains out—what then?"

"Then we'll rise in our might," a dozen voices answered at once.

"Then you'll welter in your gore," was his retort. "I've heard that song sung by the middle class, and where is it now in its might?"

CHAPTER XI. THE GREAT ADVENTURE

Mr. Wickson did not send for father. They met by chance on the ferry-boat to San Francisco, so that the warning he gave father was not premeditated. Had they not met accidentally, there would not have been any warning. Not that the outcome would have been different, however. Father came of stout old Mayflower* stock, and the blood was imperative in him.

One of the first ships that carried colonies to America, after the discovery of the New World. Descendants of these original colonists were for a while inordinately proud of their genealogy; but in time the blood became so widely diffused that it ran in the veins practically of all Americans.

"Ernest was right," he told me, as soon as he had returned home. "Ernest is a very remarkable young man, and I'd rather see you his wife than the wife of Rockefeller himself or the King of England."

"What's the matter?" I asked in alarm.

"The Oligarchy is about to tread upon our faces—yours and mine. Wickson as much as told me so. He was very kind—for an oligarch. He offered to reinstate me in the university. What do you think of that? He, Wickson, a sordid money-grabber, has the power to determine whether I shall or shall not teach in the university of the state. But he offered me even better than that—offered to make me president of some great college of physical sciences that is being planned—the Oligarchy must get rid of its surplus somehow, you see.

"'Do you remember what I told that socialist lover of your daughter's?' he said. 'I told him that we would walk upon the faces of the working class. And so we shall. As for you, I have for you a deep respect as a scientist; but if you throw your fortunes in with the working class—well, watch out for your face, that is all.' And then he turned and left me."

"It means we'll have to marry earlier than you planned," was Ernest's comment when we told him.

I could not follow his reasoning, but I was soon to learn it. It was at this time that the quarterly dividend of the Sierra Mills was paid—or, rather, should have been paid, for father did not receive his. After waiting several days, father wrote to the secretary. Promptly came the reply that there was no record on the books of father's owning any stock, and a polite request for more explicit information.

"I'll make it explicit enough, confound him," father declared, and departed for the bank to get the stock in question from his safe-deposit box.

"Ernest is a very remarkable man," he said when he got back and while I was helping him off with his overcoat. "I repeat, my daughter, that young man of yours is a very remarkable young man."

I had learned, whenever he praised Ernest in such fashion, to expect disaster.

"They have already walked upon my face," father explained. "There was no stock. The box was empty. You and Ernest will have to get married pretty quickly."

Father insisted on laboratory methods. He brought the Sierra Mills into court, but he could not bring the books of the Sierra Mills into court. He did not control the courts, and the Sierra Mills did. That explained it all. He was thoroughly beaten by the law, and the bare-faced robbery held good.

It is almost laughable now, when I look back on it, the way father was beaten. He met Wickson accidentally on the street in San Francisco, and he told Wickson that he was a damned scoundrel. And then father was arrested for attempted assault, fined in the police court, and bound over to keep the peace. It was all so ridiculous that when he got home he had to laugh himself. But what a furor was raised in the local papers! There was grave talk about the bacillus of violence that infected all men who embraced socialism; and father, with his long and peaceful life, was instanced as a shining example of how the bacillus of violence worked. Also, it was asserted by more than one paper that father's mind had weakened under the strain of scientific study, and confinement in a state asylum for the insane was suggested. Nor was this merely talk. It was an imminent peril. But father was wise enough to see it. He had the Bishop's experience to lesson from, and he lessoned well. He kept quiet no matter what injustice was perpetrated on him, and really, I think, surprised his enemies.

There was the matter of the house—our home. A mortgage was foreclosed on it, and we had to give up possession. Of course there wasn't any mortgage, and never had been any mortgage. The ground had been bought outright, and the house had been paid for when it was built. And house and lot had always been free and unencumbered. Nevertheless there was the mortgage, properly and legally drawn up and signed, with a record of the payments of interest through a number of years. Father made no outcry. As he had been robbed of his money, so was he now robbed of his home. And he had no recourse. The machinery of society was in the hands of those who were bent on breaking him. He was a philosopher at heart, and he was no longer even angry.

"I am doomed to be broken," he said to me; "but that is no reason that I should not try to be shattered as little as possible. These old bones of mine are fragile, and I've learned my lesson. God knows I don't want to spend my last days in an insane asylum."

Which reminds me of Bishop Morehouse, whom I have neglected for many pages. But first let me tell of my marriage. In the play of events, my marriage sinks into insignificance, I know, so I shall barely mention it.

"Now we shall become real proletarians," father said, when we were driven from our home. "I have often envied that young man of yours for his actual knowledge of the proletariat. Now I shall see and learn for myself."

159

Father must have had strong in him the blood of adventure. He looked upon our catastrophe in the light of an adventure. No anger nor bitterness possessed him. He was too philosophic and simple to be vindictive, and he lived too much in the world of mind to miss the creature comforts we were giving up. So it was, when we moved to San Francisco into four wretched rooms in the slum south of Market Street, that he embarked upon the adventure with the joy and enthusiasm of a child—combined with the clear sight and mental grasp of an extraordinary intellect. He really never crystallized mentally. He had no false sense of values. Conventional or habitual values meant nothing to him. The only values he recognized were mathematical and scientific facts. My father was a great man. He had the mind and the soul that only great men have. In ways he was even greater than Ernest, than whom I have known none greater.

Even I found some relief in our change of living. If nothing else, I was escaping from the organized ostracism that had been our increasing portion in the university town ever since the enmity of the nascent Oligarchy had been incurred. And the change was to me likewise adventure, and the greatest of all, for it was love-adventure. The change in our fortunes had hastened my marriage, and it was as a wife that I came to live in the four rooms on Pell Street, in the San Francisco slum.

And this out of all remains: I made Ernest happy. I came into his stormy life, not as a new perturbing force, but as one that made toward peace and repose. I gave him rest. It was the guerdon of my love for him. It was the one infallible token that I had not failed. To bring forgetfulness, or the light of gladness, into those poor tired eyes of his—what greater joy could have blessed me than that?

Those dear tired eyes. He toiled as few men ever toiled, and all his lifetime he toiled for others. That was the measure of his manhood. He was a humanist and a lover. And he, with his incarnate spirit of battle, his gladiator body and his eagle spirit—he was as gentle and tender to me as a poet. He was a poet. A singer in deeds. And all his life he sang the song of man. And he did it out of sheer love of man, and for man he gave his life and was crucified.

And all this he did with no hope of future reward. In his conception of things there was no future life. He, who fairly burnt with immortality, denied himself immortality—such was the paradox of him. He, so warm in spirit, was dominated by that cold and forbidding philosophy, materialistic monism. I used to refute him by telling him that I measured his immortality by the wings of his soul, and that I should have to live endless aeons in order to achieve the full measurement. Whereat he would laugh, and his arms would leap out to me, and he would call me his sweet metaphysician; and the tiredness would pass out of his eyes, and into them would flood the happy love-light that was in itself a new and sufficient advertisement of his immortality.

Also, he used to call me his dualist, and he would explain how Kant, by means of pure reason, had abolished reason, in order to worship God. And he drew the parallel and included me guilty of a similar act. And when I pleaded guilty, but defended the act as highly rational, he but pressed me closer and laughed as only one of God's own lovers could laugh. I was wont to deny that heredity and environment could explain his own originality and genius, any more than could the cold groping finger of science catch and analyze and classify that elusive essence that lurked in the constitution of life itself.

I held that space was an apparition of God, and that soul was a projection of the character of God; and when he called me his sweet metaphysician, I called him my immortal materialist. And so we loved and were happy; and I forgave him his materialism because of his tremendous work in the world, performed without thought of soul-gain thereby, and because of his so exceeding modesty of spirit that prevented him from having pride and regal consciousness of himself and his soul.

But he had pride. How could he have been an eagle and not have pride? His contention was that it was finer for a finite mortal speck of life to feel Godlike, than for a god to feel godlike; and so it was that he exalted what he deemed his mortality. He was fond of quoting a fragment from a certain poem. He had never seen the whole poem, and he had tried vainly to learn its authorship. I here give the fragment, not alone because he loved it, but because it epitomized the paradox that he was in the spirit of him, and his conception of his spirit. For how can a man, with thrilling, and burning, and exaltation, recite the following and still be mere mortal earth, a bit of fugitive force, an evanescent form? Here it is:

> *"Joy upon joy and gain upon gain*
>
> *Are the destined rights of my birth,*
>
> *And I shout the praise of my endless days*
>
> *To the echoing edge of the earth.*
>
> *Though I suffer all deaths that a man can die*
>
> *To the uttermost end of time,*
>
> *I have deep-drained this, my cup of bliss,*
>
> *In every age and clime—*

> *"The froth of Pride, the tang of Power,*
>
> *The sweet of Womanhood!*
>
> *I drain the lees upon my knees,*
>
> *For oh, the draught is good;*
>
> *I drink to Life, I drink to Death,*
>
> *And smack my lips with song,*
>
> *For when I die, another 'I' shall pass the cup along.*

> *"The man you drove from Eden's grove*
>
> *Was I, my Lord, was I,*

And I shall be there when the earth and the air

Are rent from sea to sky;

For it is my world, my gorgeous world,

The world of my dearest woes,

From the first faint cry of the newborn

To the rack of the woman's throes.

"Packed with the pulse of an unborn race,

Torn with a world's desire,

The surging flood of my wild young blood

Would quench the judgment fire.

I am Man, Man, Man, from the tingling flesh

To the dust of my earthly goal,

From the nestling gloom of the pregnant womb

To the sheen of my naked soul.

Bone of my bone and flesh of my flesh

The whole world leaps to my will,

And the unslaked thirst of an Eden cursed

Shall harrow the earth for its fill.

Almighty God, when I drain life's glass

Of all its rainbow gleams,

The hapless plight of eternal night

Shall be none too long for my dreams.

"The man you drove from Eden's grove

Was I, my Lord, was I,

And I shall be there when the earth and the air

Are rent from sea to sky;

For it is my world, my gorgeous world,

The world of my dear delight,

From the brightest gleam of the Arctic stream

To the dusk of my own love-night."

Ernest always overworked. His wonderful constitution kept him up; but even that constitution could not keep the tired look out of his eyes. His dear, tired eyes! He never slept more than four and one-half hours a night; yet he never found time to do all the work he wanted to do. He never ceased from his activities as a propagandist, and was always scheduled long in advance for lectures to workingmen's organizations. Then there was the campaign. He did a man's full work in that alone. With the suppression of the socialist publishing houses, his meagre royalties ceased, and he was hard-put to make a living; for he had to make a living in addition to all his other labor. He did a great deal of translating for the magazines on scientific and philosophic subjects; and, coming home late at night, worn out from the strain of the campaign, he would plunge into his translating and toil on well into the morning hours. And in addition to everything, there was his studying. To the day of his death he kept up his studies, and he studied prodigiously.

And yet he found time in which to love me and make me happy. But this was accomplished only through my merging my life completely into his. I learned shorthand and typewriting, and became his secretary. He insisted that I succeeded in cutting his work in half; and so it was that I schooled myself to understand his work. Our interests became mutual, and we worked together and played together.

And then there were our sweet stolen moments in the midst of our work—just a word, or caress, or flash of love-light; and our moments were sweeter for being stolen. For we lived on the heights, where the air was keen and sparkling, where the toil was for humanity, and where sordidness and selfishness never entered. We loved love, and our love was never smirched by anything less than the best. And this out of all remains: I did not fail. I gave him rest—he who worked so hard for others, my dear, tired-eyed mortalist.

CHAPTER XII. THE BISHOP

It was after my marriage that I chanced upon Bishop Morehouse. But I must give the events in their proper sequence. After his outbreak at the I. P. H. Convention, the Bishop, being a gentle soul, had yielded to the friendly pressure brought to bear upon him, and had gone away on a vacation. But he returned more fixed than ever in his determination to preach the message of the Church. To the consternation of his congregation, his first sermon was quite similar to the address he had given before the Convention. Again he said, and at length and with distressing detail, that the Church had wandered away from the Master's teaching, and that Mammon had been instated in the place of Christ.

And the result was, willy-nilly, that he was led away to a private sanitarium for mental disease, while in the newspapers appeared pathetic accounts of his mental breakdown and of the saintliness of his character. He was held a prisoner in the sanitarium. I called repeatedly, but was denied access to him; and I was terribly impressed by the tragedy of a sane, normal, saintly man being crushed by the brutal will of society. For the Bishop was sane, and pure, and noble. As Ernest said, all that was the matter with him was that he had incorrect notions of biology and sociology, and because of his incorrect notions he had not gone about it in the right way to rectify matters.

What terrified me was the Bishop's helplessness. If he persisted in the truth as he saw it, he was doomed to an insane ward. And he could do nothing. His money, his position, his culture, could not save him. His views were perilous to society, and society could not conceive that such perilous views could be the product of a sane mind. Or, at least, it seems to me that such was society's attitude.

But the Bishop, in spite of the gentleness and purity of his spirit, was possessed of guile. He apprehended clearly his danger. He saw himself caught in the web, and he tried to escape from it. Denied help from his friends, such as father and Ernest and I could have given, he was left to battle for himself alone. And in the enforced solitude of the sanitarium he recovered. He became again sane. His eyes ceased to see visions; his brain was purged of the fancy that it was the duty of society to feed the Master's lambs.

As I say, he became well, quite well, and the newspapers and the church people hailed his return with joy. I went once to his church. The sermon was of the same order as the ones he had preached long before his eyes had seen visions. I was disappointed, shocked. Had society then beaten him into submission? Was he a coward? Had he been bulldozed into recanting? Or had the strain been too great for him, and had he meekly surrendered to the juggernaut of the established?

I called upon him in his beautiful home. He was woefully changed. He was thinner, and there were lines on his face which I had never seen before. He was manifestly distressed by my coming. He plucked nervously at his sleeve as we talked; and his eyes were restless, fluttering here, there, and everywhere, and refusing to meet mine. His mind seemed preoccupied, and there were strange pauses in his conversation, abrupt changes of topic, and an inconsecutiveness that was bewildering. Could this, then, be the firm-poised, Christ-like man I had known, with pure, limpid eyes and a gaze steady and unfaltering as his soul? He had been man-handled; he had been cowed into subjection. His spirit was too gentle. It had not been mighty enough to face the organized wolf-pack of society.

I felt sad, unutterably sad. He talked ambiguously, and was so apprehensive of what I might say that I had not the heart to catechise him. He spoke in a far-away manner of his illness, and we talked disjointedly about the church, the alterations in the organ, and about petty charities; and he saw me depart with such evident relief that I should have laughed had not my heart been so full of tears.

The poor little hero! If I had only known! He was battling like a giant, and I did not guess it. Alone, all alone, in the midst of millions of his fellow-men, he was fighting his fight. Torn by his horror of the asylum and his fidelity to truth and the right, he clung steadfastly to truth and the right; but so alone was he that he did not dare to trust even me. He had learned his lesson well—too well.

But I was soon to know. One day the Bishop disappeared. He had told nobody that he was going away; and as the days went by and he did not reappear, there was much gossip to the effect that he had committed suicide while temporarily deranged. But this idea was dispelled when it was learned that he had sold all his possessions,—his city mansion, his country house at Menlo Park, his paintings, and collections, and even his cherished library. It was patent that he had made a clean and secret sweep of everything before he disappeared.

This happened during the time when calamity had overtaken us in our own affairs; and it was not till we were well settled in our new home that we had opportunity really to wonder and speculate about the Bishop's doings. And then, everything was suddenly made clear. Early one evening, while it was yet twilight, I had run across the street and into the butcher-shop to get some chops for Ernest's supper. We called the last meal of the day "supper" in our new environment.

Just at the moment I came out of the butcher-shop, a man emerged from the corner grocery that stood alongside. A queer sense familiarity made me look again. But the man had turned and was walking rapidly away. There was something about the slope of the shoulders and the fringe of silver hair between coat collar and slouch hat that aroused vague memories. Instead of crossing the street, I hurried after the man. I quickened my pace, trying not to think the thoughts that formed unbidden in my brain. No, it was impossible. It could not be—not in those faded overalls, too long in the legs and frayed at the bottoms.

I paused, laughed at myself, and almost abandoned the chase. But the haunting familiarity of those shoulders and that silver hair! Again I hurried on. As I passed him, I shot a keen look at his face; then I whirled around abruptly and confronted—the Bishop.

He halted with equal abruptness, and gasped. A large paper bag in his right hand fell to the sidewalk. It burst, and about his feet and mine bounced and rolled a flood of potatoes. He looked at me with surprise and alarm, then he seemed to wilt away; the shoulders drooped with dejection, and he uttered a deep sigh.

I held out my hand. He shook it, but his hand felt clammy. He cleared his throat in embarrassment, and I could see the sweat starting out on his forehead. It was evident that he was badly frightened.

"The potatoes," he murmured faintly. "They are precious."

Between us we picked them up and replaced them in the broken bag, which he now held carefully in the hollow of his arm. I tried to tell him my gladness at meeting him and that he must come right home with me.

"Father will be rejoiced to see you," I said. "We live only a stone's throw away."

"I can't," he said, "I must be going. Good-by."

He looked apprehensively about him, as though dreading discovery, and made an attempt to walk on.

"Tell me where you live, and I shall call later," he said, when he saw that I walked beside him and that it was my intention to stick to him now that he was found.

"No," I answered firmly. "You must come now."

He looked at the potatoes spilling on his arm, and at the small parcels on his other arm.

"Really, it is impossible," he said. "Forgive me for my rudeness. If you only knew."

He looked as if he were going to break down, but the next moment he had himself in control.

"Besides, this food," he went on. "It is a sad case. It is terrible. She is an old woman. I must take it to her at once. She is suffering from want of it. I must go at once. You understand. Then I will return. I promise you."

"Let me go with you," I volunteered. "Is it far?"

He sighed again, and surrendered.

"Only two blocks," he said. "Let us hasten."

Under the Bishop's guidance I learned something of my own neighborhood. I had not dreamed such wretchedness and misery existed in it. Of course, this was because I did not concern myself with charity. I had become convinced that Ernest was right when he sneered at charity as a poulticing of an ulcer. Remove the ulcer, was his remedy; give to the worker his product; pension as soldiers those who grow honorably old in their toil, and there will be no need for charity. Convinced of this, I toiled with him at the revolution, and did not exhaust my energy in alleviating the social ills that continuously arose from the injustice of the system.

I followed the Bishop into a small room, ten by twelve, in a rear tenement. And there we found a little old German woman—sixty-four years old, the Bishop said. She was surprised at seeing me, but she nodded a pleasant greeting and went on sewing on the pair of men's trousers in her lap. Beside her, on the floor, was a pile of trousers. The Bishop discovered there was neither coal nor kindling, and went out to buy some.

I took up a pair of trousers and examined her work.

"Six cents, lady," she said, nodding her head gently while she went on stitching. She stitched slowly, but never did she cease from stitching. She seemed mastered by the verb "to stitch."

"For all that work?" I asked. "Is that what they pay? How long does it take you?"

"Yes," she answered, "that is what they pay. Six cents for finishing. Two hours' sewing on each pair."

"But the boss doesn't know that," she added quickly, betraying a fear of getting him into trouble. "I'm slow. I've got the rheumatism in my hands. Girls work much faster. They finish in half that time. The boss is kind. He lets me take the work home, now that I am old and the noise of the machine bothers my head. If it wasn't for his kindness, I'd starve.

"Yes, those who work in the shop get eight cents. But what can you do? There is not enough work for the young. The old have no chance. Often one pair is all I can get. Sometimes, like to-day, I am given eight pair to finish before night."

I asked her the hours she worked, and she said it depended on the season.

"In the summer, when there is a rush order, I work from five in the morning to nine at night. But in the winter it is too cold. The hands do not early get over the stiffness. Then you must work later—till after midnight sometimes.

"Yes, it has been a bad summer. The hard times. God must be angry. This is the first work the boss has given me in a week. It is true, one cannot eat much when there is no work. I am used to it. I have sewed all my life, in the old country and here in San Francisco—thirty-three years.

"If you are sure of the rent, it is all right. The houseman is very kind, but he must have his rent. It is fair. He only charges three dollars for this room. That is cheap. But it is not easy for you to find all of three dollars every month."

She ceased talking, and, nodding her head, went on stitching.

"You have to be very careful as to how you spend your earnings," I suggested.

She nodded emphatically.

"After the rent it's not so bad. Of course you can't buy meat. And there is no milk for the coffee. But always there is one meal a day, and often two."

She said this last proudly. There was a smack of success in her words. But as she stitched on in silence, I noticed the sadness in her pleasant eyes and the droop of her mouth. The look in her eyes became far away. She rubbed the dimness hastily out of them; it interfered with her stitching.

"No, it is not the hunger that makes the heart ache," she explained. "You get used to being hungry. It is for my child that I cry. It was the machine that killed her. It is true she worked hard, but I cannot understand. She was strong. And she was young—only forty; and she worked only thirty years. She began young, it is true; but my man died. The boiler exploded down at the works. And what were we to do? She was ten, but she was very strong. But the machine killed her. Yes, it did. It killed her, and she was the fastest worker in the shop. I have thought about it often, and I know. That is why I cannot work in the shop. The machine bothers my head. Always I hear it saying, 'I did it, I did it.' And it says that all day long. And then I think of my daughter, and I cannot work."

The moistness was in her old eyes again, and she had to wipe it away before she could go on stitching.

I heard the Bishop stumbling up the stairs, and I opened the door. What a spectacle he was. On his back he carried half a sack of coal, with kindling on top. Some of the coal dust had coated his face, and the sweat from his exertions was running in streaks. He dropped his burden in the corner by the stove and wiped his face on a coarse bandana handkerchief. I could scarcely accept the verdict of my senses. The Bishop, black as a coal-heaver, in a workingman's cheap cotton shirt (one button was missing from the throat), and in overalls! That was the most incongruous of all—the overalls, frayed at the bottoms, dragged down at the heels, and held up by a narrow leather belt around the hips such as laborers wear.

Though the Bishop was warm, the poor swollen hands of the old woman were already cramping with the cold; and before we left her, the Bishop had built the fire, while I had peeled the potatoes and put them on to boil. I was to learn, as time went by, that there were many cases similar to hers, and many worse, hidden away in the monstrous depths of the tenements in my neighborhood.

We got back to find Ernest alarmed by my absence. After the first surprise of greeting was over, the Bishop leaned back in his chair, stretched out his overall-covered legs, and actually sighed a comfortable sigh. We were the first of his old friends he had met since his disappearance, he told us; and during the intervening weeks he must have suffered greatly from loneliness. He told us much, though he told us more of the joy he had experienced in doing the Master's bidding.

"For truly now," he said, "I am feeding his lambs. And I have learned a great lesson. The soul cannot be ministered to till the stomach is appeased. His lambs must be fed bread and butter and potatoes and meat; after that, and only after that, are their spirits ready for more refined nourishment."

He ate heartily of the supper I cooked. Never had he had such an appetite at our table in the old days. We spoke of it, and he said that he had never been so healthy in his life.

"I walk always now," he said, and a blush was on his cheek at the thought of the time when he rode in his carriage, as though it were a sin not lightly to be laid.

"My health is better for it," he added hastily. "And I am very happy—indeed, most happy. At last I am a consecrated spirit."

And yet there was in his face a permanent pain, the pain of the world that he was now taking to himself. He was seeing life in the raw, and it was a different life from what he had known within the printed books of his library.

"And you are responsible for all this, young man," he said directly to Ernest.

Ernest was embarrassed and awkward.

"I—I warned you," he faltered.

"No, you misunderstand," the Bishop answered. "I speak not in reproach, but in gratitude. I have you to thank for showing me my path. You led me from theories about life to life itself. You pulled aside the veils from the social shams. You were light in my darkness, but now I, too, see the light. And I am very happy, only . . ." he hesitated painfully, and in his eyes fear leaped large. "Only the persecution. I harm no one. Why will they not let me alone? But it is not that. It is the nature of the persecution. I shouldn't mind if they cut my flesh with stripes, or burned me at the stake, or crucified me head—downward. But it is the asylum that frightens me. Think of it! Of me—in an asylum for the insane! It is revolting. I saw some of the cases at the sanitarium. They were violent. My blood chills when I think of it. And to be imprisoned for the rest of my life amid scenes of screaming madness! No! no! Not that! Not that!"

It was pitiful. His hands shook, his whole body quivered and shrank away from the picture he had conjured. But the next moment he was calm.

"Forgive me," he said simply. "It is my wretched nerves. And if the Master's work leads there, so be it. Who am I to complain?"

I felt like crying aloud as I looked at him: "Great Bishop! O hero! God's hero!"

As the evening wore on we learned more of his doings.

"I sold my house—my houses, rather," he said, "all my other possessions. I knew I must do it secretly, else they would have taken everything away from me. That would have been terrible. I often marvel these days at the immense quantity of potatoes two or three hundred thousand dollars will buy, or bread, or meat, or coal and kindling." He turned to Ernest. "You are right, young man. Labor is dreadfully underpaid. I never did a bit of work in my life, except to appeal aesthetically to Pharisees—I thought I was preaching the message—and yet I was worth half a million dollars. I never knew what half a million dollars meant until I realized how much potatoes and bread and butter and meat it could buy. And then I realized something more. I realized that all those potatoes and that bread and butter and meat were mine, and that I had not worked to make them. Then it was clear to me, some one else had worked and made them and been robbed of them. And when I came down amongst the poor I found those who had been robbed and who were hungry and wretched because they had been robbed."

We drew him back to his narrative.

"The money? I have it deposited in many different banks under different names. It can never be taken away from me, because it can never be found. And it is so good, that money. It buys so much food. I never knew before what money was good for."

"I wish we could get some of it for the propaganda," Ernest said wistfully. "It would do immense good."

"Do you think so?" the Bishop said. "I do not have much faith in politics. In fact, I am afraid I do not understand politics."

Ernest was delicate in such matters. He did not repeat his suggestion, though he knew only too well the sore straits the Socialist Party was in through lack of money.

"I sleep in cheap lodging houses," the Bishop went on. "But I am afraid, and never stay long in one place. Also, I rent two rooms in workingmen's houses in different quarters of the city. It is a great extravagance, I know, but it is necessary. I make up for it in part by doing my own cooking, though sometimes I get something to eat in cheap coffee-houses. And I have made a discovery. Tamales* are very good when the air grows chilly late at night. Only they are so expensive. But I have discovered a place where I can get three for ten cents. They are not so good as the others, but they are very warming.

A Mexican dish, referred to occasionally in the literature of the times. It is supposed that it was warmly seasoned. No recipe of it has come down to us.

"And so I have at last found my work in the world, thanks to you, young man. It is the Master's work." He looked at me, and his eyes twinkled. "You caught me feeding his lambs, you know. And of course you will all keep my secret."

He spoke carelessly enough, but there was real fear behind the speech. He promised to call upon us again. But a week later we read in the newspaper of the sad case of Bishop Morehouse, who had been committed to the Napa Asylum and for whom there were still hopes held out. In vain we tried to see him, to have his case reconsidered or investigated. Nor could we learn anything about him except the reiterated statements that slight hopes were still held for his recovery.

"Christ told the rich young man to sell all he had," Ernest said bitterly. "The Bishop obeyed Christ's injunction and got locked up in a madhouse. Times have changed since Christ's day. A rich man to-day who gives all he has to the poor is crazy. There is no discussion. Society has spoken."

CHAPTER XIII. THE GENERAL STRIKE

Of course Ernest was elected to Congress in the great socialist landslide that took place in the fall of 1912. One great factor that helped to swell the socialist vote was the destruction of Hearst.* This the Plutocracy found an easy task. It cost Hearst eighteen million dollars a year to run his various papers, and this sum, and more, he got back from the middle class in payment for advertising. The source of his financial strength lay wholly in the middle class. The trusts did not advertise.** To destroy Hearst, all that was necessary was to take away from him his advertising.

*William Randolph Hearst—a young California millionaire who became the most powerful newspaper owner in the country. His newspapers were published in all the large cities, and they appealed to the perishing middle class and to the proletariat. So large was his following that he managed to take possession of the empty shell of the old Democratic Party. He occupied an anomalous position, preaching an emasculated socialism combined with a nondescript sort of petty bourgeois capitalism. It was oil and water, and there was no hope for him, though for a short period he was a source of serious apprehension to the Plutocrats.

** The cost of advertising was amazing in those helter-skelter times. Only the small capitalists competed, and *therefore they did the advertising. There being no*

competition where there was a trust, there was no need for

the trusts to advertise.

The whole middle class had not yet been exterminated. The sturdy skeleton of it remained; but it was without power. The small manufacturers and small business men who still survived were at the complete mercy of the Plutocracy. They had no economic nor political souls of their own. When the fiat of the Plutocracy went forth, they withdrew their advertisements from the Hearst papers.

Hearst made a gallant fight. He brought his papers out at a loss of a million and a half each month. He continued to publish the advertisements for which he no longer received pay. Again the fiat of the Plutocracy went forth, and the small business men and manufacturers swamped him with a flood of notices that he must discontinue running their old advertisements. Hearst persisted. Injunctions were served on him. Still he persisted. He received six months' imprisonment for contempt of court in disobeying the injunctions, while he was bankrupted by countless damage suits. He had no chance. The Plutocracy had passed sentence on him. The courts were in the hands of the Plutocracy to carry the sentence out. And with Hearst crashed also to destruction the Democratic Party that he had so recently captured.

With the destruction of Hearst and the Democratic Party, there were only two paths for his following to take. One was into the Socialist Party; the other was into the Republican Party. Then it was that we socialists reaped the fruit of Hearst's pseudo-socialistic preaching; for the great Majority of his followers came over to us.

The expropriation of the farmers that took place at this time would also have swelled our vote had it not been for the brief and futile rise of the Grange Party. Ernest and the socialist leaders fought fiercely to capture the farmers; but the destruction of the socialist press and publishing houses constituted too great a handicap, while the mouth-to-mouth propaganda had not yet been perfected. So it was that politicians like Mr. Calvin, who were themselves farmers long since expropriated, captured the farmers and threw their political strength away in a vain campaign.

"The poor farmers," Ernest once laughed savagely; "the trusts have them both coming and going."

And that was really the situation. The seven great trusts, working together, had pooled their enormous surpluses and made a farm trust. The railroads, controlling rates, and the bankers and stock exchange gamesters, controlling prices, had long since bled the farmers into indebtedness. The bankers, and all the trusts for that matter, had likewise long since loaned colossal amounts of money to the farmers. The farmers were in the net. All that remained to be done was the drawing in of the net. This the farm trust proceeded to do.

The hard times of 1912 had already caused a frightful slump in the farm markets. Prices were now deliberately pressed down to bankruptcy, while the railroads, with extortionate rates, broke the back of the farmer-camel. Thus the farmers were compelled to borrow more and more, while they were prevented from paying back old loans. Then ensued the great foreclosing of mortgages and enforced collection of notes. The farmers simply surrendered the land to the farm trust. There was nothing else for them to do. And having surrendered the land, the farmers next went to work for the farm trust, becoming managers, superintendents, foremen, and common laborers. They worked for wages. They became villeins, in short—serfs bound to the soil by a living wage. They could not leave their masters, for their masters composed the Plutocracy. They could not go to the cities, for there, also, the Plutocracy was in control. They had but one alternative,—to leave the soil and become vagrants, in brief, to starve. And even there they were frustrated, for stringent vagrancy laws were passed and rigidly enforced.

Of course, here and there, farmers, and even whole communities of farmers, escaped expropriation by virtue of exceptional conditions. But they were merely strays and did not count, and they were gathered in anyway during the following year.*

* The destruction of the Roman yeomanry proceeded far less rapidly than the destruction of the American farmers and small capitalists. There was momentum in the twentieth century, while there was practically none in ancient Rome.

Numbers of the farmers, impelled by an insane lust for the soil, and willing to show what beasts they could become, tried to escape expropriation by withdrawing from any and all market-dealing. They sold nothing. They bought nothing. Among themselves a primitive barter began to spring up. Their privation and hardships were terrible, but they persisted. It became quite a movement, in fact. The manner in which they were beaten was unique and logical and simple. The Plutocracy, by virtue of its possession of the government, raised their taxes. It was the weak joint in their armor. Neither buying nor selling, they had no money, and in the end their land was sold to pay the taxes.

Thus it was that in the fall of 1912 the socialist leaders, with the exception of Ernest, decided that the end of capitalism had come. What of the hard times and the consequent vast army of the unemployed; what of the destruction of the farmers and the middle class; and what of the decisive defeat administered all along the line to the labor unions; the socialists were really justified in believing that the end of capitalism had come and in themselves throwing down the gauntlet to the Plutocracy.

Alas, how we underestimated the strength of the enemy! Everywhere the socialists proclaimed their coming victory at the ballot-box, while, in unmistakable terms, they stated the situation. The Plutocracy accepted the challenge. It was the Plutocracy, weighing and balancing, that defeated us by dividing our strength. It was the Plutocracy, through its secret agents, that raised the cry that socialism was sacrilegious and atheistic; it was the Plutocracy that whipped the churches, and especially the Catholic Church, into line, and robbed us of a portion of the labor vote. And it was the Plutocracy, through its secret agents of course, that encouraged the Grange Party and even spread it to the cities into the ranks of the dying middle class.

Nevertheless the socialist landslide occurred. But, instead of a sweeping victory with chief executive officers and majorities in all legislative bodies, we found ourselves in the minority. It is true, we elected fifty Congressmen; but when they took their seats in the spring of 1913, they found themselves without power of any sort. Yet they were more fortunate than the Grangers, who captured a dozen state governments, and who, in the spring, were not permitted to take possession of the captured offices. The incumbents refused to retire, and the courts were in the hands of the Oligarchy. But this is too far in advance of events. I have yet to tell of the stirring times of the winter of 1912.

The hard times at home had caused an immense decrease in consumption. Labor, out of work, had no wages with which to buy. The result was that the Plutocracy found a greater surplus than ever on its hands. This surplus it was compelled to dispose of abroad, and, what of its colossal plans, it needed money. Because of its strenuous efforts to dispose of the surplus in the world market, the Plutocracy clashed with Germany. Economic clashes were usually succeeded by wars, and this particular clash was no exception. The great German war-lord prepared, and so did the United States prepare.

The war-cloud hovered dark and ominous. The stage was set for a world-catastrophe, for in all the world were hard times, labor troubles, perishing middle classes, armies of unemployed, clashes of economic interests in the world-market, and mutterings and rumblings of the socialist revolution.*

* For a long time these mutterings and rumblings had been heard. As far back as 1906 A.D., Lord Avebury, an Englishman, uttered the following in the House of Lords: "The unrest in Europe, the spread of socialism, and the ominous rise of Anarchism, are warnings to the governments and the ruling classes that the condition of the working classes in Europe is becoming intolerable, and that if a revolution is to be avoided some steps must be taken to increase wages, reduce the hours of labor, and lower the prices of the necessaries of life." The Wall Street Journal, a stock gamesters' publication, in commenting upon Lord Avebury's speech, said: "These words were spoken by an aristocrat and a member of the most conservative body in all Europe. That gives them all the more significance. They contain more valuable political economy than is to be found in most of the books. They sound a note of warning. Take heed, gentlemen of the war and navy departments!"

At the same time, Sydney Brooks, writing in America, in Harper's Weekly, said: "You will not hear the socialists mentioned in Washington. Why should you? The politicians are always the last people in this country to see what is

182

going on under their noses. They will jeer at me when I

prophesy, and prophesy with the utmost confidence, that at

the next presidential election the socialists will poll over

a million votes."

The Oligarchy wanted the war with Germany. And it wanted the war for a dozen reasons. In the juggling of events such a war would cause, in the reshuffling of the international cards and the making of new treaties and alliances, the Oligarchy had much to gain. And, furthermore, the war would consume many national surpluses, reduce the armies of unemployed that menaced all countries, and give the Oligarchy a breathing space in which to perfect its plans and carry them out. Such a war would virtually put the Oligarchy in possession of the world-market. Also, such a war would create a large standing army that need never be disbanded, while in the minds of the people would be substituted the issue, "America versus Germany," in place of "Socialism versus Oligarchy."

And truly the war would have done all these things had it not been for the socialists. A secret meeting of the Western leaders was held in our four tiny rooms in Pell Street. Here was first considered the stand the socialists were to take. It was not the first time we had put our foot down upon war,* but it was the first time we had done so in the United States. After our secret meeting we got in touch with the national organization, and soon our code cables were passing back and forth across the Atlantic between us and the International Bureau.

* It was at the very beginning of the twentieth century

A.D., that the international organization of the socialists

finally formulated their long-maturing policy on war.

Epitomized their doctrine was: "Why should the workingmen of one country fight with the workingmen of another country for the benefit of their capitalist masters?"

On May 21, 1905 A.D., when war threatened between Austria and Italy, the socialists of Italy, Austria, and Hungary held a conference at Trieste, and threatened a general strike of the workingmen of both countries in case war was declared. This was repeated the following year, when the "Morocco Affair" threatened to involve France, Germany, and England.

The German socialists were ready to act with us. There were over five million of them, many of them in the standing army, and, in addition, they were on friendly terms with the labor unions. In both countries the socialists came out in bold declaration against the war and threatened the general strike. And in the meantime they made preparation for the general strike. Furthermore, the revolutionary parties in all countries gave public utterance to the socialist principle of international peace that must be preserved at all hazards, even to the extent of revolt and revolution at home.

The general strike was the one great victory we American socialists won. On the 4th of December the American minister was withdrawn from the German capital. That night a German fleet made a dash on Honolulu, sinking three American cruisers and a revenue cutter, and bombarding the city. Next day both Germany and the United States declared war, and within an hour the socialists called the general strike in both countries.

For the first time the German war-lord faced the men of his empire who made his empire go. Without them he could not run his empire. The novelty of the situation lay in that their revolt was passive. They did not fight. They did nothing. And by doing nothing they tied their war-lord's hands. He would have asked for nothing better than an opportunity to loose his war-dogs on his rebellious proletariat. But this was denied him. He could not loose his war-dogs. Neither could he mobilize his army to go forth to war, nor could he punish his recalcitrant subjects. Not a wheel moved in his empire. Not a train ran, not a telegraphic message went over the wires, for the telegraphers and railroad men had ceased work along with the rest of the population.

And as it was in Germany, so it was in the United States. At last organized labor had learned its lesson. Beaten decisively on its own chosen field, it had abandoned that field and come over to the political field of the socialists; for the general strike was a political strike. Besides, organized labor had been so badly beaten that it did not care. It joined in the general strike out of sheer desperation. The workers threw down their tools and left their tasks by the millions. Especially notable were the machinists. Their heads were bloody, their organization had apparently been destroyed, yet out they came, along with their allies in the metal-working trades.

Even the common laborers and all unorganized labor ceased work. The strike had tied everything up so that nobody could work. Besides, the women proved to be the strongest promoters of the strike. They set their faces against the war. They did not want their men to go forth to die. Then, also, the idea of the general strike caught the mood of the people. It struck their sense of humor. The idea was infectious. The children struck in all the schools, and such teachers as came, went home again from deserted class rooms. The general strike took the form of a great national picnic. And the idea of the solidarity of labor, so evidenced, appealed to the imagination of all. And, finally, there was no danger to be incurred by the colossal frolic. When everybody was guilty, how was anybody to be punished?

The United States was paralyzed. No one knew what was happening. There were no newspapers, no letters, no despatches. Every community was as completely isolated as though ten thousand miles of primeval wilderness stretched between it and the rest of the world. For that matter, the world had ceased to exist. And for a week this state of affairs was maintained.

In San Francisco we did not know what was happening even across the bay in Oakland or Berkeley. The effect on one's sensibilities was weird, depressing. It seemed as though some great cosmic thing lay dead. The pulse of the land had ceased to beat. Of a truth the nation had died. There were no wagons rumbling on the streets, no factory whistles, no hum of electricity in the air, no passing of street cars, no cries of news-boys—nothing but persons who at rare intervals went by like furtive ghosts, themselves oppressed and made unreal by the silence.

And during that week of silence the Oligarchy was taught its lesson. And well it learned the lesson. The general strike was a warning. It should never occur again. The Oligarchy would see to that.

At the end of the week, as had been prearranged, the telegraphers of Germany and the United States returned to their posts. Through them the socialist leaders of both countries presented their ultimatum to the rulers. The war should be called off, or the general strike would continue. It did not take long to come to an understanding. The war was declared off, and the populations of both countries returned to their tasks.

It was this renewal of peace that brought about the alliance between Germany and the United States. In reality, this was an alliance between the Emperor and the Oligarchy, for the purpose of meeting their common foe, the revolutionary proletariat of both countries. And it was this alliance that the Oligarchy afterward so treacherously broke when the German socialists rose and drove the war-lord from his throne. It was the very thing the Oligarchy had played for—the destruction of its great rival in the world-market. With the German Emperor out of the way, Germany would have no surplus to sell abroad. By the very nature of the socialist state, the German population would consume all that it produced. Of course, it would trade abroad certain things it produced for things it did not produce; but this would be quite different from an unconsumable surplus.

"I'll wager the Oligarchy finds justification," Ernest said, when its treachery to the German Emperor became known. "As usual, the Oligarchy will believe it has done right."

And sure enough. The Oligarchy's public defence for the act was that it had done it for the sake of the American people whose interests it was looking out for. It had flung its hated rival out of the world-market and enabled us to dispose of our surplus in that market.

"And the howling folly of it is that we are so helpless that such idiots really are managing our interests," was Ernest's comment. "They have enabled us to sell more abroad, which means that we'll be compelled to consume less at home."

CHAPTER XIV. THE BEGINNING OF THE END

As early as January, 1913, Ernest saw the true trend of affairs, but he could not get his brother leaders to see the vision of the Iron Heel that had arisen in his brain. They were too confident. Events were rushing too rapidly to culmination. A crisis had come in world affairs. The American Oligarchy was practically in possession of the world-market, and scores of countries were flung out of that market with unconsumable and unsalable surpluses on their hands. For such countries nothing remained but reorganization. They could not continue their method of producing surpluses. The capitalistic system, so far as they were concerned, had hopelessly broken down.

The reorganization of these countries took the form of revolution. It was a time of confusion and violence. Everywhere institutions and governments were crashing. Everywhere, with the exception of two or three countries, the erstwhile capitalist masters fought bitterly for their possessions. But the governments were taken away from them by the militant proletariat. At last was being realized Karl Marx's classic: "The knell of private capitalist property sounds. The expropriators are expropriated." And as fast as capitalistic governments crashed, cooperative commonwealths arose in their place.

"Why does the United States lag behind?"; "Get busy, you American revolutionists!"; "What's the matter with America?"—were the messages sent to us by our successful comrades in other lands. But we could not keep up. The Oligarchy stood in the way. Its bulk, like that of some huge monster, blocked our path.

"Wait till we take office in the spring," we answered. "Then you'll see."

Behind this lay our secret. We had won over the Grangers, and in the spring a dozen states would pass into their hands by virtue of the elections of the preceding fall. At once would be instituted a dozen cooperative commonwealth states. After that, the rest would be easy.

"But what if the Grangers fail to get possession?" Ernest demanded. And his comrades called him a calamity howler.

But this failure to get possession was not the chief danger that Ernest had in mind. What he foresaw was the defection of the great labor unions and the rise of the castes.

"Ghent has taught the oligarchs how to do it," Ernest said. "I'll wager they've made a text-book out of his 'Benevolent Feudalism.'"*

> *"Our Benevolent Feudalism," a book published in 1902 A.D., by W. J. Ghent. It has always been insisted that Ghent put the idea of the Oligarchy into the minds of the great capitalists. This belief persists throughout the literature of the three centuries of the Iron Heel, and even in the literature of the first century of the Brotherhood of Man. To-day we know better, but our knowledge does not overcome the fact that Ghent remains the most abused innocent man in all history.

Never shall I forget the night when, after a hot discussion with half a dozen labor leaders, Ernest turned to me and said quietly: "That settles it. The Iron Heel has won. The end is in sight."

This little conference in our home was unofficial; but Ernest, like the rest of his comrades, was working for assurances from the labor leaders that they would call out their men in the next general strike. O'Connor, the president of the Association of Machinists, had been foremost of the six leaders present in refusing to give such assurance.

"You have seen that you were beaten soundly at your old tactics of strike and boycott," Ernest urged.

O'Connor and the others nodded their heads.

"And you saw what a general strike would do," Ernest went on. "We stopped the war with Germany. Never was there so fine a display of the solidarity and the power of labor. Labor can and will rule the world. If you continue to stand with us, we'll put an end to the reign of capitalism. It is your only hope. And what is more, you know it. There is no other way out. No matter what you do under your old tactics, you are doomed to defeat, if for no other reason because the masters control the courts." *

*As a sample of the decisions of the courts adverse to labor, the following instances are given. In the coal-mining regions the employment of children was notorious. In 1905 A.D., labor succeeded in getting a law passed in Pennsylvania providing that proof of the age of the child and of certain educational qualifications must accompany the oath of the parent. This was promptly declared unconstitutional by the Luzerne County Court, on the ground that it violated the Fourteenth Amendment in that it discriminated between individuals of the same class—namely, children above fourteen years of age and children below. The state court sustained the decision. The New York Court of Special Sessions, in 1905 A.D., declared unconstitutional the law prohibiting minors and women from working in factories after nine o'clock at night, the ground taken being that such a law was "class legislation." Again, the

*bakers of that time were terribly overworked. The New York
Legislature passed a law restricting work in bakeries to ten
hours a day. In 1906 A.D., the Supreme Court of the United
States declared this law to be unconstitutional. In part
the decision read: "There is no reasonable ground for
interfering with the liberty of persons or the right of free
contract by determining the hours of labor in the occupation
of a baker."*

"You run ahead too fast," O'Connor answered. "You don't know all the ways out. There is another way out. We know what we're about. We're sick of strikes. They've got us beaten that way to a frazzle. But I don't think we'll ever need to call our men out again."

"What is your way out?" Ernest demanded bluntly.

O'Connor laughed and shook his head. "I can tell you this much: We've not been asleep. And we're not dreaming now."

"There's nothing to be afraid of, or ashamed of, I hope," Ernest challenged.

"I guess we know our business best," was the retort.

"It's a dark business, from the way you hide it," Ernest said with growing anger.

"We've paid for our experience in sweat and blood, and we've earned all that's coming to us," was the reply. "Charity begins at home."

"If you're afraid to tell me your way out, I'll tell it to you." Ernest's blood was up. "You're going in for grab-sharing. You've made terms with the enemy, that's what you've done. You've sold out the cause of labor, of all labor. You are leaving the battle-field like cowards."

"I'm not saying anything," O'Connor answered sullenly. "Only I guess we know what's best for us a little bit better than you do."

"And you don't care a cent for what is best for the rest of labor. You kick it into the ditch."

"I'm not saying anything," O'Connor replied, "except that I'm president of the Machinists' Association, and it's my business to consider the interests of the men I represent, that's all."

And then, when the labor leaders had left, Ernest, with the calmness of defeat, outlined to me the course of events to come.

"The socialists used to foretell with joy," he said, "the coming of the day when organized labor, defeated on the industrial field, would come over on to the political field. Well, the Iron Heel has defeated the labor unions on the industrial field and driven them over to the political field; and instead of this being joyful for us, it will be a source of grief. The Iron Heel learned its lesson. We showed it our power in the general strike. It has taken steps to prevent another general strike."

"But how?" I asked.

"Simply by subsidizing the great unions. They won't join in the next general strike. Therefore it won't be a general strike."

"But the Iron Heel can't maintain so costly a programme forever," I objected.

"Oh, it hasn't subsidized all of the unions. That's not necessary. Here is what is going to happen. Wages are going to be advanced and hours shortened in the railroad unions, the iron and steel workers unions, and the engineer and machinist unions. In these unions more favorable conditions will continue to prevail. Membership in these unions will become like seats in Paradise."

"Still I don't see," I objected. "What is to become of the other unions? There are far more unions outside of this combination than in it."

"The other unions will be ground out of existence—all of them. For, don't you see, the railway men, machinists and engineers, iron and steel workers, do all of the vitally essential work in our machine civilization. Assured of their faithfulness, the Iron Heel can snap its fingers at all the rest of labor. Iron, steel, coal, machinery, and transportation constitute the backbone of the whole industrial fabric."

"But coal?" I queried. "There are nearly a million coal miners."

They are practically unskilled labor. They will not count. Their wages will go down and their hours will increase. They will be slaves like all the rest of us, and they will become about the most bestial of all of us. They will be compelled to work, just as the farmers are compelled to work now for the masters who robbed them of their land. And the same with all the other unions outside the combination. Watch them wobble and go to pieces, and their members become slaves driven to toil by empty stomachs and the law of the land.

"Do you know what will happen to Farley* and his strike-breakers? I'll tell you. Strike-breaking as an occupation will cease. There won't be any more strikes. In place of strikes will be slave revolts. Farley and his gang will be promoted to slave-driving. Oh, it won't be called that; it will be called enforcing the law of the land that compels the laborers to work. It simply prolongs the fight, this treachery of the big unions. Heaven only knows now where and when the Revolution will triumph."

* James Farley—a notorious strike-breaker of the period. A man more courageous than ethical, and of undeniable ability. He rose high under the rule of the Iron Heel and finally was translated into the oligarch class. He was assassinated in 1932 by Sarah Jenkins, whose husband, thirty years before, had been killed by Farley's strike-breakers.

"But with such a powerful combination as the Oligarchy and the big unions, is there any reason to believe that the Revolution will ever triumph?" I queried. "May not the combination endure forever?"

He shook his head. "One of our generalizations is that every system founded upon class and caste contains within itself the germs of its own decay. When a system is founded upon class, how can caste be prevented? The Iron Heel will not be able to prevent it, and in the end caste will destroy the Iron Heel. The oligarchs have already developed caste among themselves; but wait until the favored unions develop caste. The Iron Heel will use all its power to prevent it, but it will fail.

"In the favored unions are the flower of the American workingmen. They are strong, efficient men. They have become members of those unions through competition for place. Every fit workman in the United States will be possessed by the ambition to become a member of the favored unions. The Oligarchy will encourage such ambition and the consequent competition. Thus will the strong men, who might else be revolutionists, be won away and their strength used to bolster the Oligarchy.

"On the other hand, the labor castes, the members of the favored unions, will strive to make their organizations into close corporations. And they will succeed. Membership in the labor castes will become hereditary. Sons will succeed fathers, and there will be no inflow of new strength from that eternal reservoir of strength, the common people. This will mean deterioration of the labor castes, and in the end they will become weaker and weaker. At the same time, as an institution, they will become temporarily all-powerful. They will be like the guards of the palace in old Rome, and there will be palace revolutions whereby the labor castes will seize the reins of power. And there will be counter-palace revolutions of the oligarchs, and sometimes the one, and sometimes the other, will be in power. And through it all the inevitable caste-weakening will go on, so that in the end the common people will come into their own."

This foreshadowing of a slow social evolution was made when Ernest was first depressed by the defection of the great unions. I never agreed with him in it, and I disagree now, as I write these lines, more heartily than ever; for even now, though Ernest is gone, we are on the verge of the revolt that will sweep all oligarchies away. Yet I have here given Ernest's prophecy because it was his prophecy. In spite of his belief in it, he worked like a giant against it, and he, more than any man, has made possible the revolt that even now waits the signal to burst forth.*

Everhard's social foresight was remarkable. As clearly as in the light of past events, he saw the defection of the favored unions, the rise and the slow decay of the labor castes, and the struggle between the decaying oligarchs and labor castes for control of the great governmental machine.

"But if the Oligarchy persists," I asked him that evening, "what will become of the great surpluses that will fall to its share every year?"

"The surpluses will have to be expended somehow," he answered; "and trust the oligarchs to find a way. Magnificent roads will be built. There will be great achievements in science, and especially in art. When the oligarchs have completely mastered the people, they will have time to spare for other things. They will become worshippers of beauty. They will become art-lovers. And under their direction and generously rewarded, will toil the artists. The result will be great art; for no longer, as up to yesterday, will the artists pander to the bourgeois taste of the middle class. It will be great art, I tell you, and wonder cities will arise that will make tawdry and cheap the cities of old time. And in these cities will the oligarchs dwell and worship beauty.*

** We cannot but marvel at Everhard's foresight. Before ever
the thought of wonder cities like Ardis and Asgard entered
the minds of the oligarchs, Everhard saw those cities and
the inevitable necessity for their creation.*

"Thus will the surplus be constantly expended while labor does the work. The building of these great works and cities will give a starvation ration to millions of common laborers, for the enormous bulk of the surplus will compel an equally enormous expenditure, and the oligarchs will build for a thousand years—ay, for ten thousand years. They will build as the Egyptians and the Babylonians never dreamed of building; and when the oligarchs have passed away, their great roads and their wonder cities will remain for the brotherhood of labor to tread upon and dwell within.*

** And since that day of prophecy, have passed away the three
centuries of the Iron Heel and the four centuries of the
Brotherhood of Man, and to-day we tread the roads and dwell
in the cities that the oligarchs built. It is true, we are
even now building still more wonderful wonder cities, but
the wonder cities of the oligarchs endure, and I write these
lines in Ardis, one of the most wonderful of them all.*

"These things the oligarchs will do because they cannot help doing them. These great works will be the form their expenditure of the surplus will take, and in the same way that the ruling classes of Egypt of long ago expended the surplus they robbed from the people by the building of temples and pyramids. Under the oligarchs will flourish, not a priest class, but an artist class. And in place of the merchant class of bourgeoisie will be the labor castes. And beneath will be the abyss, wherein will fester and starve and rot, and ever renew itself, the common people, the great bulk of the population. And in the end, who knows in what day, the common people will rise up out of the abyss; the labor castes and the Oligarchy will crumble away; and then, at last, after the travail of the centuries, will it be the day of the common man. I had thought to see that day; but now I know that I shall never see it."

He paused and looked at me, and added:

"Social evolution is exasperatingly slow, isn't it, sweetheart?"

My arms were about him, and his head was on my breast.

"Sing me to sleep," he murmured whimsically. "I have had a visioning, and I wish to forget."

CHAPTER XV. LAST DAYS

It was near the end of January, 1913, that the changed attitude of the Oligarchy toward the favored unions was made public. The newspapers published information of an unprecedented rise in wages and shortening of hours for the railroad employees, the iron and steel workers, and the engineers and machinists. But the whole truth was not told. The oligarchs did not dare permit the telling of the whole truth. In reality, the wages had been raised much higher, and the privileges were correspondingly greater. All this was secret, but secrets will out. Members of the favored unions told their wives, and the wives gossiped, and soon all the labor world knew what had happened.

It was merely the logical development of what in the nineteenth century had been known as grab-sharing. In the industrial warfare of that time, profit-sharing had been tried. That is, the capitalists had striven to placate the workers by interesting them financially in their work. But profit-sharing, as a system, was ridiculous and impossible. Profit-sharing could be successful only in isolated cases in the midst of a system of industrial strife; for if all labor and all capital shared profits, the same conditions would obtain as did obtain when there was no profit-sharing.

So, out of the unpractical idea of profit-sharing, arose the practical idea of grab-sharing. "Give us more pay and charge it to the public," was the slogan of the strong unions.* And here and there this selfish policy worked successfully. In charging it to the public, it was charged to the great mass of unorganized labor and of weakly organized labor. These workers actually paid the increased wages of their stronger brothers who were members of unions that were labor monopolies. This idea, as I say, was merely carried to its logical conclusion, on a large scale, by the combination of the oligarchs and the favored unions.

All the railroad unions entered into this combination with the oligarchs, and it is of interest to note that the first definite application of the policy of profit-grabbing was made by a railroad union in the nineteenth century A.D., namely, the Brotherhood of Locomotive Engineers. P. M. Arthur was for twenty years Grand Chief of the Brotherhood. After the strike on the Pennsylvania Railroad in 1877, he broached a scheme to have the Locomotive Engineers make terms with the railroads and to "go it alone" so far as the rest of the labor unions were concerned. This scheme was eminently successful. It was as successful as it was selfish, and out of it was coined the word "arthurization," to denote grab-sharing on the part of labor unions. This word "arthurization" has long puzzled the etymologists, but its derivation, I hope, is now made clear.

As soon as the secret of the defection of the favored unions leaked out, there were rumblings and mutterings in the labor world. Next, the favored unions withdrew from the international organizations and broke off all affiliations. Then came trouble and violence. The members of the favored unions were branded as traitors, and in saloons and brothels, on the streets and at work, and, in fact, everywhere, they were assaulted by the comrades they had so treacherously deserted.

Countless heads were broken, and there were many killed. No member of the favored unions was safe. They gathered together in bands in order to go to work or to return from work. They walked always in the middle of the street. On the sidewalk they were liable to have their skulls crushed by bricks and cobblestones thrown from windows and house-tops. They were permitted to carry weapons, and the authorities aided them in every way. Their persecutors were sentenced to long terms in prison, where they were harshly treated; while no man, not a member of the favored unions, was permitted to carry weapons. Violation of this law was made a high misdemeanor and punished accordingly.

Outraged labor continued to wreak vengeance on the traitors. Caste lines formed automatically. The children of the traitors were persecuted by the children of the workers who had been betrayed, until it was impossible for the former to play on the streets or to attend the public schools. Also, the wives and families of the traitors were ostracized, while the corner groceryman who sold provisions to them was boycotted.

As a result, driven back upon themselves from every side, the traitors and their families became clannish. Finding it impossible to dwell in safety in the midst of the betrayed proletariat, they moved into new localities inhabited by themselves alone. In this they were favored by the oligarchs. Good dwellings, modern and sanitary, were built for them, surrounded by spacious yards, and separated here and there by parks and playgrounds. Their children attended schools especially built for them, and in these schools manual training and applied science were specialized upon. Thus, and unavoidably, at the very beginning, out of this segregation arose caste. The members of the favored unions became the aristocracy of labor. They were set apart from the rest of labor. They were better housed, better clothed, better fed, better treated. They were grab-sharing with a vengeance.

In the meantime, the rest of the working class was more harshly treated. Many little privileges were taken away from it, while its wages and its standard of living steadily sank down. Incidentally, its public schools deteriorated, and education slowly ceased to be compulsory. The increase in the younger generation of children who could not read nor write was perilous.

The capture of the world-market by the United States had disrupted the rest of the world. Institutions and governments were everywhere crashing or transforming. Germany, Italy, France, Australia, and New Zealand were busy forming cooperative commonwealths. The British Empire was falling apart. England's hands were full. In India revolt was in full swing. The cry in all Asia was, "Asia for the Asiatics!" And behind this cry was Japan, ever urging and aiding the yellow and brown races against the white. And while Japan dreamed of continental empire and strove to realize the dream, she suppressed her own proletarian revolution. It was a simple war of the castes, Coolie versus Samurai, and the coolie socialists were executed by tens of thousands. Forty thousand were killed in the street-fighting of Tokio and in the futile assault on the Mikado's palace. Kobe was a shambles; the slaughter of the cotton operatives by machine-guns became classic as the most terrific execution ever achieved by modern war machines. Most savage of all was the Japanese Oligarchy that arose. Japan dominated the East, and took to herself the whole Asiatic portion of the world-market, with the exception of India.

England managed to crush her own proletarian revolution and to hold on to India, though she was brought to the verge of exhaustion. Also, she was compelled to let her great colonies slip away from her. So it was that the socialists succeeded in making Australia and New Zealand into cooperative commonwealths. And it was for the same reason that Canada was lost to the mother country. But Canada crushed her own socialist revolution, being aided in this by the Iron Heel. At the same time, the Iron Heel helped Mexico and Cuba to put down revolt. The result was that the Iron Heel was firmly established in the New World. It had welded into one compact political mass the whole of North America from the Panama Canal to the Arctic Ocean.

And England, at the sacrifice of her great colonies, had succeeded only in retaining India. But this was no more than temporary. The struggle with Japan and the rest of Asia for India was merely delayed. England was destined shortly to lose India, while behind that event loomed the struggle between a united Asia and the world.

And while all the world was torn with conflict, we of the United States were not placid and peaceful. The defection of the great unions had prevented our proletarian revolt, but violence was everywhere. In addition to the labor troubles, and the discontent of the farmers and of the remnant of the middle class, a religious revival had blazed up. An offshoot of the Seventh Day Adventists sprang into sudden prominence, proclaiming the end of the world.

"Confusion thrice confounded!" Ernest cried. "How can we hope for solidarity with all these cross purposes and conflicts?"

And truly the religious revival assumed formidable proportions. The people, what of their wretchedness, and of their disappointment in all things earthly, were ripe and eager for a heaven where industrial tyrants entered no more than camels passed through needle-eyes. Wild-eyed itinerant preachers swarmed over the land; and despite the prohibition of the civil authorities, and the persecution for disobedience, the flames of religious frenzy were fanned by countless camp-meetings.

It was the last days, they claimed, the beginning of the end of the world. The four winds had been loosed. God had stirred the nations to strife. It was a time of visions and miracles, while seers and prophetesses were legion. The people ceased work by hundreds of thousands and fled to the mountains, there to await the imminent coming of God and the rising of the hundred and forty and four thousand to heaven. But in the meantime God did not come, and they starved to death in great numbers. In their desperation they ravaged the farms for food, and the consequent tumult and anarchy in the country districts but increased the woes of the poor expropriated farmers.

Also, the farms and warehouses were the property of the Iron Heel. Armies of troops were put into the field, and the fanatics were herded back at the bayonet point to their tasks in the cities. There they broke out in ever recurring mobs and riots. Their leaders were executed for sedition or confined in madhouses. Those who were executed went to their deaths with all the gladness of martyrs. It was a time of madness. The unrest spread. In the swamps and deserts and waste places, from Florida to Alaska, the small groups of Indians that survived were dancing ghost dances and waiting the coming of a Messiah of their own.

And through it all, with a serenity and certitude that was terrifying, continued to rise the form of that monster of the ages, the Oligarchy. With iron hand and iron heel it mastered the surging millions, out of confusion brought order, out of the very chaos wrought its own foundation and structure.

"Just wait till we get in," the Grangers said—Calvin said it to us in our Pell Street quarters. "Look at the states we've captured. With you socialists to back us, we'll make them sing another song when we take office."

"The millions of the discontented and the impoverished are ours," the socialists said. "The Grangers have come over to us, the farmers, the middle class, and the laborers. The capitalist system will fall to pieces. In another month we send fifty men to Congress. Two years hence every office will be ours, from the President down to the local dog-catcher."

To all of which Ernest would shake his head and say:

"How many rifles have you got? Do you know where you can get plenty of lead? When it comes to powder, chemical mixtures are better than mechanical mixtures, you take my word."

CHAPTER XVI. THE END

When it came time for Ernest and me to go to Washington, father did not accompany us. He had become enamoured of proletarian life. He looked upon our slum neighborhood as a great sociological laboratory, and he had embarked upon an apparently endless orgy of investigation. He chummed with the laborers, and was an intimate in scores of homes. Also, he worked at odd jobs, and the work was play as well as learned investigation, for he delighted in it and was always returning home with copious notes and bubbling over with new adventures. He was the perfect scientist.

There was no need for his working at all, because Ernest managed to earn enough from his translating to take care of the three of us. But father insisted on pursuing his favorite phantom, and a protean phantom it was, judging from the jobs he worked at. I shall never forget the evening he brought home his street pedler's outfit of shoe-laces and suspenders, nor the time I went into the little corner grocery to make some purchase and had him wait on me. After that I was not surprised when he tended bar for a week in the saloon across the street. He worked as a night watchman, hawked potatoes on the street, pasted labels in a cannery warehouse, was utility man in a paper-box factory, and water-carrier for a street railway construction gang, and even joined the Dishwashers' Union just before it fell to pieces.

I think the Bishop's example, so far as wearing apparel was concerned, must have fascinated father, for he wore the cheap cotton shirt of the laborer and the overalls with the narrow strap about the hips. Yet one habit remained to him from the old life; he always dressed for dinner, or supper, rather.

I could be happy anywhere with Ernest; and father's happiness in our changed circumstances rounded out my own happiness.

"When I was a boy," father said, "I was very curious. I wanted to know why things were and how they came to pass. That was why I became a physicist. The life in me to-day is just as curious as it was in my boyhood, and it's the being curious that makes life worth living."

Sometimes he ventured north of Market Street into the shopping and theatre district, where he sold papers, ran errands, and opened cabs. There, one day, closing a cab, he encountered Mr. Wickson. In high glee father described the incident to us that evening.

"Wickson looked at me sharply when I closed the door on him, and muttered, 'Well, I'll be damned.' Just like that he said it, 'Well, I'll be damned.' His face turned red and he was so confused that he forgot to tip me. But he must have recovered himself quickly, for the cab hadn't gone fifty feet before it turned around and came back. He leaned out of the door.

"'Look here, Professor,' he said, 'this is too much. What can I do for you?'

"'I closed the cab door for you,' I answered. 'According to common custom you might give me a dime.'

"'Bother that!' he snorted. 'I mean something substantial.'

"He was certainly serious—a twinge of ossified conscience or something; and so I considered with grave deliberation for a moment.

"His face was quite expectant when I began my answer, but you should have seen it when I finished.

"'You might give me back my home,' I said, 'and my stock in the Sierra Mills.'"

Father paused.

"What did he say?" I questioned eagerly.

"What could he say? He said nothing. But I said. 'I hope you are happy.' He looked at me curiously. 'Tell me, are you happy?'" I asked.

"He ordered the cabman to drive on, and went away swearing horribly. And he didn't give me the dime, much less the home and stock; so you see, my dear, your father's street-arab career is beset with disappointments."

And so it was that father kept on at our Pell Street quarters, while Ernest and I went to Washington. Except for the final consummation, the old order had passed away, and the final consummation was nearer than I dreamed. Contrary to our expectation, no obstacles were raised to prevent the socialist Congressmen from taking their seats. Everything went smoothly, and I laughed at Ernest when he looked upon the very smoothness as something ominous.

We found our socialist comrades confident, optimistic of their strength and of the things they would accomplish. A few Grangers who had been elected to Congress increased our strength, and an elaborate programme of what was to be done was prepared by the united forces. In all of which Ernest joined loyally and energetically, though he could not forbear, now and again, from saying, apropos of nothing in particular, "When it comes to powder, chemical mixtures are better than mechanical mixtures, you take my word."

The trouble arose first with the Grangers in the various states they had captured at the last election. There were a dozen of these states, but the Grangers who had been elected were not permitted to take office. The incumbents refused to get out. It was very simple. They merely charged illegality in the elections and wrapped up the whole situation in the interminable red tape of the law. The Grangers were powerless. The courts were in the hands of their enemies.

This was the moment of danger. If the cheated Grangers became violent, all was lost. How we socialists worked to hold them back! There were days and nights when Ernest never closed his eyes in sleep. The big leaders of the Grangers saw the peril and were with us to a man. But it was all of no avail. The Oligarchy wanted violence, and it set its agents-provocateurs to work. Without discussion, it was the agents-provocateurs who caused the Peasant Revolt.

In a dozen states the revolt flared up. The expropriated farmers took forcible possession of the state governments. Of course this was unconstitutional, and of course the United States put its soldiers into the field. Everywhere the agents-provocateurs urged the people on. These emissaries of the Iron Heel disguised themselves as artisans, farmers, and farm laborers. In Sacramento, the capital of California, the Grangers had succeeded in maintaining order. Thousands of secret agents were rushed to the devoted city. In mobs composed wholly of themselves, they fired and looted buildings and factories. They worked the people up until they joined them in the pillage. Liquor in large quantities was distributed among the slum classes further to inflame their minds. And then, when all was ready, appeared upon the scene the soldiers of the United States, who were, in reality, the soldiers of the Iron Heel. Eleven thousand men, women, and children were shot down on the streets of Sacramento or murdered in their houses. The national government took possession of the state government, and all was over for California.

And as with California, so elsewhere. Every Granger state was ravaged with violence and washed in blood. First, disorder was precipitated by the secret agents and the Black Hundreds, then the troops were called out. Rioting and mob-rule reigned throughout the rural districts. Day and night the smoke of burning farms, warehouses, villages, and cities filled the sky. Dynamite appeared. Railroad bridges and tunnels were blown up and trains were wrecked. The poor farmers were shot and hanged in great numbers. Reprisals were bitter, and many plutocrats and army officers were murdered. Blood and vengeance were in men's hearts. The regular troops fought the farmers as savagely as had they been Indians. And the regular troops had cause. Twenty-eight hundred of them had been annihilated in a tremendous series of dynamite explosions in Oregon, and in a similar manner, a number of train loads, at different times and places, had been destroyed. So it was that the regular troops fought for their lives as well as did the farmers.

As for the militia, the militia law of 1903 was put into effect, and the workers of one state were compelled, under pain of death, to shoot down their comrade-workers in other states. Of course, the militia law did not work smoothly at first. Many militia officers were murdered, and many militiamen were executed by drumhead court martial. Ernest's prophecy was strikingly fulfilled in the cases of Mr. Kowalt and Mr. Asmunsen. Both were eligible for the militia, and both were drafted to serve in the punitive expedition that was despatched from California against the farmers of Missouri. Mr. Kowalt and Mr. Asmunsen refused to serve. They were given short shrift. Drumhead court martial was their portion, and military execution their end. They were shot with their backs to the firing squad.

Many young men fled into the mountains to escape serving in the militia. There they became outlaws, and it was not until more peaceful times that they received their punishment. It was drastic. The government issued a proclamation for all law-abiding citizens to come in from the mountains for a period of three months. When the proclaimed date arrived, half a million soldiers were sent into the mountainous districts everywhere. There was no investigation, no trial. Wherever a man was encountered, he was shot down on the spot. The troops operated on the basis that no man not an outlaw remained in the mountains. Some bands, in strong positions, fought gallantly, but in the end every deserter from the militia met death.

A more immediate lesson, however, was impressed on the minds of the people by the punishment meted out to the Kansas militia. The great Kansas Mutiny occurred at the very beginning of military operations against the Grangers. Six thousand of the militia mutinied. They had been for several weeks very turbulent and sullen, and for that reason had been kept in camp. Their open mutiny, however, was without doubt precipitated by the agents-provocateurs.

On the night of the 22d of April they arose and murdered their officers, only a small remnant of the latter escaping. This was beyond the scheme of the Iron Heel, for the agents-provocateurs had done their work too well. But everything was grist to the Iron Heel. It had prepared for the outbreak, and the killing of so many officers gave it justification for what followed. As by magic, forty thousand soldiers of the regular army surrounded the malcontents. It was a trap. The wretched militiamen found that their machine-guns had been tampered with, and that the cartridges from the captured magazines did not fit their rifles. They hoisted the white flag of surrender, but it was ignored. There were no survivors. The entire six thousand were annihilated. Common shell and shrapnel were thrown in upon them from a distance, and, when, in their desperation, they charged the encircling lines, they were mowed down by the machine-guns. I talked with an eye-witness, and he said that the nearest any militiaman approached the machine-guns was a hundred and fifty yards. The earth was carpeted with the slain, and a final charge of cavalry, with trampling of horses' hoofs, revolvers, and sabres, crushed the wounded into the ground.

Simultaneously with the destruction of the Grangers came the revolt of the coal miners. It was the expiring effort of organized labor. Three-quarters of a million of miners went out on strike. But they were too widely scattered over the country to advantage from their own strength. They were segregated in their own districts and beaten into submission. This was the first great slave-drive. Pocock* won his spurs as a slave-driver and earned the undying hatred of the proletariat. Countless attempts were made upon his life, but he seemed to bear a charmed existence. It was he who was responsible for the introduction of the Russian passport system among the miners, and the denial of their right of removal from one part of the country to another.

* Albert Pocock, another of the notorious strike-breakers of earlier years, who, to the day of his death, successfully held all the coal-miners of the country to their task. He was succeeded by his son, Lewis Pocock, and for five generations this remarkable line of slave-drivers handled the coal mines. The elder Pocock, known as Pocock I., has been described as follows: "A long, lean head, semicircled by a fringe of brown and gray hair, with big cheek-bones and a heavy chin, . . . a pale face, lustreless gray eyes, a metallic voice, and a languid manner." He was born of humble parents, and began his career as a bartender. He next became a private detective for a street railway

corporation, and by successive steps developed into a

professional strikebreaker. Pocock V., the last of the line,

was blown up in a pump-house by a bomb during a petty revolt

of the miners in the Indian Territory. This occurred in 2073

A.D.

In the meantime, the socialists held firm. While the Grangers expired in flame and blood, and organized labor was disrupted, the socialists held their peace and perfected their secret organization. In vain the Grangers pleaded with us. We rightly contended that any revolt on our part was virtually suicide for the whole Revolution. The Iron Heel, at first dubious about dealing with the entire proletariat at one time, had found the work easier than it had expected, and would have asked nothing better than an uprising on our part. But we avoided the issue, in spite of the fact that agents-provocateurs swarmed in our midst. In those early days, the agents of the Iron Heel were clumsy in their methods. They had much to learn and in the meantime our Fighting Groups weeded them out. It was bitter, bloody work, but we were fighting for life and for the Revolution, and we had to fight the enemy with its own weapons. Yet we were fair. No agent of the Iron Heel was executed without a trial. We may have made mistakes, but if so, very rarely. The bravest, and the most combative and self-sacrificing of our comrades went into the Fighting Groups. Once, after ten years had passed, Ernest made a calculation from figures furnished by the chiefs of the Fighting Groups, and his conclusion was that the average life of a man or woman after becoming a member was five years. The comrades of the Fighting Groups were heroes all, and the peculiar thing about it was that they were opposed to the taking of life. They violated their own natures, yet they loved liberty and knew of no sacrifice too great to make for the Cause.*

These Fighting groups were modelled somewhat after the Fighting Organization of the Russian Revolution, and, despite the unceasing efforts of the Iron Heel, these groups persisted throughout the three centuries of its existence. Composed of men and women actuated by lofty purpose and unafraid to die, the Fighting Groups exercised tremendous influence and tempered the savage brutality of the rulers. Not alone was their work confined to unseen warfare with the secret agents of the Oligarchy. The oligarchs themselves were compelled to listen to the decrees of the Groups, and often, when they disobeyed, were punished by death—and likewise with the subordinates of the oligarchs, with the officers of the army and the leaders of the labor castes.

Stern justice was meted out by these organized avengers, but most remarkable was their passionless and judicial procedure. There were no snap judgments. When a man was captured he was given fair trial and opportunity for defence. Of necessity, many men were tried and condemned by proxy, as in the case of General Lampton. This occurred in 2138 A.D. Possibly the most bloodthirsty and malignant of all the mercenaries that ever served the Iron Heel, he was informed by the Fighting Groups that they had tried him,

211

found him guilty, and condemned him to death—and this,
after three warnings for him to cease from his ferocious
treatment of the proletariat. After his condemnation he
surrounded himself with a myriad protective devices. Years
passed, and in vain the Fighting Groups strove to execute
their decree. Comrade after comrade, men and women, failed
in their attempts, and were cruelly executed by the
Oligarchy. It was the case of General Lampton that revived
crucifixion as a legal method of execution. But in the end
the condemned man found his executioner in the form of a
slender girl of seventeen, Madeline Provence, who, to
accomplish her purpose, served two years in his palace as a
seamstress to the household. She died in solitary
confinement after horrible and prolonged torture; but to-day
she stands in imperishable bronze in the Pantheon of
Brotherhood in the wonder city of Serles.

We, who by personal experience know nothing of bloodshed,
must not judge harshly the heroes of the Fighting Groups.
They gave up their lives for humanity, no sacrifice was too
great for them to accomplish, while inexorable necessity
compelled them to bloody expression in an age of blood. The
Fighting Groups constituted the one thorn in the side of the

Iron Heel that the Iron Heel could never remove. Everhard
was the father of this curious army, and its accomplishments
and successful persistence for three hundred years bear
witness to the wisdom with which he organized and the solid
foundation he laid for the succeeding generations to build
upon. In some respects, despite his great economic and
sociological contributions, and his work as a general leader
in the Revolution, his organization of the Fighting Groups
must be regarded as his greatest achievement.

The task we set ourselves was threefold. First, the weeding out from our circles of the secret agents of the Oligarchy. Second, the organizing of the Fighting Groups, and outside of them, of the general secret organization of the Revolution. And third, the introduction of our own secret agents into every branch of the Oligarchy—into the labor castes and especially among the telegraphers and secretaries and clerks, into the army, the agents-provocateurs, and the slave-drivers. It was slow work, and perilous, and often were our efforts rewarded with costly failures.

The Iron Heel had triumphed in open warfare, but we held our own in the new warfare, strange and awful and subterranean, that we instituted. All was unseen, much was unguessed; the blind fought the blind; and yet through it all was order, purpose, control. We permeated the entire organization of the Iron Heel with our agents, while our own organization was permeated with the agents of the Iron Heel. It was warfare dark and devious, replete with intrigue and conspiracy, plot and counterplot. And behind all, ever menacing, was death, violent and terrible. Men and women disappeared, our nearest and dearest comrades. We saw them to-day. To-morrow they were gone; we never saw them again, and we knew that they had died.

There was no trust, no confidence anywhere. The man who plotted beside us, for all we knew, might be an agent of the Iron Heel. We mined the organization of the Iron Heel with our secret agents, and the Iron Heel countermined with its secret agents inside its own organization. And it was the same with our organization. And despite the absence of confidence and trust we were compelled to base our every effort on confidence and trust. Often were we betrayed. Men were weak. The Iron Heel could offer money, leisure, the joys and pleasures that waited in the repose of the wonder cities. We could offer nothing but the satisfaction of being faithful to a noble ideal. As for the rest, the wages of those who were loyal were unceasing peril, torture, and death.

Men were weak, I say, and because of their weakness we were compelled to make the only other reward that was within our power. It was the reward of death. Out of necessity we had to punish our traitors. For every man who betrayed us, from one to a dozen faithful avengers were loosed upon his heels. We might fail to carry out our decrees against our enemies, such as the Pococks, for instance; but the one thing we could not afford to fail in was the punishment of our own traitors. Comrades turned traitor by permission, in order to win to the wonder cities and there execute our sentences on the real traitors. In fact, so terrible did we make ourselves, that it became a greater peril to betray us than to remain loyal to us.

The Revolution took on largely the character of religion. We worshipped at the shrine of the Revolution, which was the shrine of liberty. It was the divine flashing through us. Men and women devoted their lives to the Cause, and new-born babes were sealed to it as of old they had been sealed to the service of God. We were lovers of Humanity.

CHAPTER XVII. THE SCARLET LIVERY

With the destruction of the Granger states, the Grangers in Congress disappeared. They were being tried for high treason, and their places were taken by the creatures of the Iron Heel. The socialists were in a pitiful minority, and they knew that their end was near. Congress and the Senate were empty pretences, farces. Public questions were gravely debated and passed upon according to the old forms, while in reality all that was done was to give the stamp of constitutional procedure to the mandates of the Oligarchy.

Ernest was in the thick of the fight when the end came. It was in the debate on the bill to assist the unemployed. The hard times of the preceding year had thrust great masses of the proletariat beneath the starvation line, and the continued and wide-reaching disorder had but sunk them deeper. Millions of people were starving, while the oligarchs and their supporters were surfeiting on the surplus.* We called these wretched people the people of the abyss,** and it was to alleviate their awful suffering that the socialists had introduced the unemployed bill. But this was not to the fancy of the Iron Heel. In its own way it was preparing to set these millions to work, but the way was not our way, wherefore it had issued its orders that our bill should be voted down. Ernest and his fellows knew that their effort was futile, but they were tired of the suspense. They wanted something to happen. They were accomplishing nothing, and the best they hoped for was the putting of an end to the legislative farce in which they were unwilling players. They knew not what end would come, but they never anticipated a more disastrous end than the one that did come.

The same conditions obtained in the nineteenth century A.D. under British rule in India. The natives died of starvation by the million, while their rulers robbed them of the fruits of their toil and expended it on magnificent pageants and mumbo-jumbo fooleries. Perforce, in this enlightened age, we have much to blush for in the acts of our ancestors. Our only consolation is philosophic. We must accept the capitalistic stage in social evolution as about on a par with the earlier monkey stage. The human had to pass through those stages in its rise from the mire and slime of low organic life. It was inevitable that much of the mire and slime should cling and be not easily shaken off.

** The people of the abyss—this phrase was struck out by the genius of H. G. Wells in the late nineteenth century A.D. Wells was a sociological seer, sane and normal as well as warm human. Many fragments of his work have come down to us, while two of his greatest achievements, "Anticipations" and "Mankind in the Making," have come down intact. Before the oligarchs, and before Everhard, Wells speculated upon the building of the wonder cities, though in his writings they are referred to as "pleasure cities."

I sat in the gallery that day. We all knew that something terrible was imminent. It was in the air, and its presence was made visible by the armed soldiers drawn up in lines in the corridors, and by the officers grouped in the entrances to the House itself. The Oligarchy was about to strike. Ernest was speaking. He was describing the sufferings of the unemployed, as if with the wild idea of in some way touching their hearts and consciences; but the Republican and Democratic members sneered and jeered at him, and there was uproar and confusion. Ernest abruptly changed front.

"I know nothing that I may say can influence you," he said. "You have no souls to be influenced. You are spineless, flaccid things. You pompously call yourselves Republicans and Democrats. There is no Republican Party. There is no Democratic Party. There are no Republicans nor Democrats in this House. You are lick-spittlers and panderers, the creatures of the Plutocracy. You talk verbosely in antiquated terminology of your love of liberty, and all the while you wear the scarlet livery of the Iron Heel."

Here the shouting and the cries of "Order! order!" drowned his voice, and he stood disdainfully till the din had somewhat subsided. He waved his hand to include all of them, turned to his own comrades, and said:

"Listen to the bellowing of the well-fed beasts."

Pandemonium broke out again. The Speaker rapped for order and glanced expectantly at the officers in the doorways. There were cries of "Sedition!" and a great, rotund New York member began shouting "Anarchist!" at Ernest. And Ernest was not pleasant to look at. Every fighting fibre of him was quivering, and his face was the face of a fighting animal, withal he was cool and collected.

"Remember," he said, in a voice that made itself heard above the din, "that as you show mercy now to the proletariat, some day will that same proletariat show mercy to you."

The cries of "Sedition!" and "Anarchist!" redoubled.

"I know that you will not vote for this bill," Ernest went on. "You have received the command from your masters to vote against it. And yet you call me anarchist. You, who have destroyed the government of the people, and who shamelessly flaunt your scarlet shame in public places, call me anarchist. I do not believe in hell-fire and brimstone; but in moments like this I regret my unbelief. Nay, in moments like this I almost do believe. Surely there must be a hell, for in no less place could it be possible for you to receive punishment adequate to your crimes. So long as you exist, there is a vital need for hell-fire in the Cosmos."

There was movement in the doorways. Ernest, the Speaker, all the members turned to see.

"Why do you not call your soldiers in, Mr. Speaker, and bid them do their work?" Ernest demanded. "They should carry out your plan with expedition."

"There are other plans afoot," was the retort. "That is why the soldiers are present."

"Our plans, I suppose," Ernest sneered. "Assassination or something kindred."

But at the word "assassination" the uproar broke out again. Ernest could not make himself heard, but he remained on his feet waiting for a lull. And then it happened. From my place in the gallery I saw nothing except the flash of the explosion. The roar of it filled my ears and I saw Ernest reeling and falling in a swirl of smoke, and the soldiers rushing up all the aisles. His comrades were on their feet, wild with anger, capable of any violence. But Ernest steadied himself for a moment, and waved his arms for silence.

"It is a plot!" his voice rang out in warning to his comrades. "Do nothing, or you will be destroyed."

Then he slowly sank down, and the soldiers reached him. The next moment soldiers were clearing the galleries and I saw no more.

Though he was my husband, I was not permitted to get to him. When I announced who I was, I was promptly placed under arrest. And at the same time were arrested all socialist Congressmen in Washington, including the unfortunate Simpson, who lay ill with typhoid fever in his hotel.

The trial was prompt and brief. The men were foredoomed. The wonder was that Ernest was not executed. This was a blunder on the part of the Oligarchy, and a costly one. But the Oligarchy was too confident in those days. It was drunk with success, and little did it dream that that small handful of heroes had within them the power to rock it to its foundations. To-morrow, when the Great Revolt breaks out and all the world resounds with the tramp, tramp of the millions, the Oligarchy, will realize, and too late, how mightily that band of heroes has grown.*

*Avis Everhard took for granted that her narrative would be read in her own day, and so omits to mention the outcome of the trial for high treason. Many other similar disconcerting omissions will be noticed in the Manuscript. Fifty-two socialist Congressmen were tried, and all were found guilty. Strange to relate, not one received the death sentence. Everhard and eleven others, among whom were Theodore Donnelson and Matthew Kent, received life imprisonment. The remaining forty received sentences varying from thirty to forty-five years; while Arthur Simpson, referred to in the Manuscript as being ill of typhoid fever at the time of the explosion, received only fifteen years. It is the tradition that he died of starvation in solitary confinement, and this harsh treatment is explained as having been caused by his uncompromising stubbornness and his fiery and tactless hatred for all men that served the despotism. He died in Cabanas in Cuba, where three of his comrades were also confined. The fifty-

two socialist Congressmen were confined in military

fortresses scattered all over the United States. Thus, Du

Bois and Woods were held in Porto Rico, while Everhard and

Merryweather were placed in Alcatraz, an island in San

Francisco Bay that had already seen long service as a

military prison.

As a revolutionist myself, as one on the inside who knew the hopes and fears and secret plans of the revolutionists, I am fitted to answer, as very few are, the charge that they were guilty of exploding the bomb in Congress. And I can say flatly, without qualification or doubt of any sort, that the socialists, in Congress and out, had no hand in the affair. Who threw the bomb we do not know, but the one thing we are absolutely sure of is that we did not throw it.

On the other hand, there is evidence to show that the Iron Heel was responsible for the act. Of course, we cannot prove this. Our conclusion is merely presumptive. But here are such facts as we do know. It had been reported to the Speaker of the House, by secret-service agents of the government, that the Socialist Congressmen were about to resort to terroristic tactics, and that they had decided upon the day when their tactics would go into effect. This day was the very day of the explosion. Wherefore the Capitol had been packed with troops in anticipation. Since we knew nothing about the bomb, and since a bomb actually was exploded, and since the authorities had prepared in advance for the explosion, it is only fair to conclude that the Iron Heel did know. Furthermore, we charge that the Iron Heel was guilty of the outrage, and that the Iron Heel planned and perpetrated the outrage for the purpose of foisting the guilt on our shoulders and so bringing about our destruction.

From the Speaker the warning leaked out to all the creatures in the House that wore the scarlet livery. They knew, while Ernest was speaking, that some violent act was to be committed. And to do them justice, they honestly believed that the act was to be committed by the socialists. At the trial, and still with honest belief, several testified to having seen Ernest prepare to throw the bomb, and that it exploded prematurely. Of course they saw nothing of the sort. In the fevered imagination of fear they thought they saw, that was all.

As Ernest said at the trial: "Does it stand to reason, if I were going to throw a bomb, that I should elect to throw a feeble little squib like the one that was thrown? There wasn't enough powder in it. It made a lot of smoke, but hurt no one except me. It exploded right at my feet, and yet it did not kill me. Believe me, when I get to throwing bombs, I'll do damage. There'll be more than smoke in my petards."

In return it was argued by the prosecution that the weakness of the bomb was a blunder on the part of the socialists, just as its premature explosion, caused by Ernest's losing his nerve and dropping it, was a blunder. And to clinch the argument, there were the several Congressmen who testified to having seen Ernest fumble and drop the bomb.

As for ourselves, not one of us knew how the bomb was thrown. Ernest told me that the fraction of an instant before it exploded he both heard and saw it strike at his feet. He testified to this at the trial, but no one believed him. Besides, the whole thing, in popular slang, was "cooked up." The Iron Heel had made up its mind to destroy us, and there was no withstanding it.

There is a saying that truth will out. I have come to doubt that saying. Nineteen years have elapsed, and despite our untiring efforts, we have failed to find the man who really did throw the bomb. Undoubtedly he was some emissary of the Iron Heel, but he has escaped detection. We have never got the slightest clew to his identity. And now, at this late date, nothing remains but for the affair to take its place among the mysteries of history.*

*Avis Everhard would have had to live for many generations
ere she could have seen the clearing up of this particular

mystery. A little less than a hundred years ago, and a little more than six hundred years after the death, the confession of Pervaise was discovered in the secret archives of the Vatican. It is perhaps well to tell a little something about this obscure document, which, in the main, is of interest to the historian only.

Pervaise was an American, of French descent, who in 1913 A.D., was lying in the Tombs Prison, New York City, awaiting trial for murder. From his confession we learn that he was not a criminal. He was warm-blooded, passionate, emotional. In an insane fit of jealousy he killed his wife—a very common act in those times. Pervaise was mastered by the fear of death, all of which is recounted at length in his confession. To escape death he would have done anything, and the police agents prepared him by assuring him that he could not possibly escape conviction of murder in the first degree when his trial came off. In those days, murder in the first degree was a capital offense. The guilty man or woman was placed in a specially constructed death-chair, and, under the supervision of competent physicians, was destroyed by a current of electricity. This was called electrocution, and it was very popular during that period.

*Anaesthesia, as a mode of compulsory death, was not
introduced until later.*

*This man, good at heart but with a ferocious animalism close
at the surface of his being, lying in jail and expectant of
nothing less than death, was prevailed upon by the agents of
the Iron Heel to throw the bomb in the House of
Representatives. In his confession he states explicitly
that he was informed that the bomb was to be a feeble thing
and that no lives would be lost. This is directly in line
with the fact that the bomb was lightly charged, and that
its explosion at Everhard's feet was not deadly.*

*Pervaise was smuggled into one of the galleries ostensibly
closed for repairs. He was to select the moment for the
throwing of the bomb, and he naively confesses that in his
interest in Everhard's tirade and the general commotion
raised thereby, he nearly forgot his mission.*

*Not only was he released from prison in reward for his deed,
but he was granted an income for life. This he did not long
enjoy. In 1914 A.D., in September, he was stricken with
rheumatism of the heart and lived for three days. It was*

then that he sent for the Catholic priest, Father Peter Durban, and to him made confession. So important did it seem to the priest, that he had the confession taken down in writing and sworn to. What happened after this we can only surmise. The document was certainly important enough to find its way to Rome. Powerful influences must have been brought to bear, hence its suppression. For centuries no hint of its existence reached the world. It was not until in the last century that Lorbia, the brilliant Italian scholar, stumbled upon it quite by chance during his researches in the Vatican.

There is to-day no doubt whatever that the Iron Heel was responsible for the bomb that exploded in the House of Representatives in 1913 A.D. Even though the Pervaise confession had never come to light, no reasonable doubt could obtain; for the act in question, that sent fifty-two Congressmen to prison, was on a par with countless other acts committed by the oligarchs, and, before them, by the capitalists.

There is the classic instance of the ferocious and wanton judicial murder of the innocent and so-called Haymarket

224

Anarchists in Chicago in the penultimate decade of the nineteenth century A.D. In a category by itself is the deliberate burning and destruction of capitalist property by the capitalists themselves. For such destruction of property innocent men were frequently punished—"railroaded" in the parlance of the times.

In the labor troubles of the first decade of the twentieth century A.D., between the capitalists and the Western Federation of Miners, similar but more bloody tactics were employed. The railroad station at Independence was blown up by the agents of the capitalists. Thirteen men were killed, and many more were wounded. And then the capitalists, controlling the legislative and judicial machinery of the state of Colorado, charged the miners with the crime and came very near to convicting them. Romaines, one of the tools in this affair, like Pervaise, was lying in jail in another state, Kansas, awaiting trial, when he was approached by the agents of the capitalists. But, unlike Pervaise the confession of Romaines was made public in his own time.

Then, during this same period, there was the case of Moyer and Haywood, two strong, fearless leaders of labor. One was president and the other was secretary of the Western Federation of Miners. The ex-governor of Idaho had been mysteriously murdered. The crime, at the time, was openly charged to the mine owners by the socialists and miners. Nevertheless, in violation of the national and state constitutions, and by means of conspiracy on the parts of the governors of Idaho and Colorado, Moyer and Haywood were kidnapped, thrown into jail, and charged with the murder. It was this instance that provoked from Eugene V. Debs, national leader of the American socialists at the time, the following words: "The labor leaders that cannot be bribed nor bullied, must be ambushed and murdered. The only crime of Moyer and Haywood is that they have been unswervingly true to the working class. The capitalists have stolen our country, debauched our politics, defiled our judiciary, and ridden over us rough-shod, and now they propose to murder those who will not abjectly surrender to their brutal dominion. The governors of Colorado and Idaho are but executing the mandates of their masters, the Plutocracy. The issue is the Workers versus the Plutocracy. If they strike the first violent blow, we will strike the last."

CHAPTER XVIII. IN THE SHADOW OF SONOMA

Of myself, during this period, there is not much to say. For six months I was kept in prison, though charged with no crime. I was a suspect—a word of fear that all revolutionists were soon to come to know. But our own nascent secret service was beginning to work. By the end of my second month in prison, one of the jailers made himself known as a revolutionist in touch with the organization. Several weeks later, Joseph Parkhurst, the prison doctor who had just been appointed, proved himself to be a member of one of the Fighting Groups.

Thus, throughout the organization of the Oligarchy, our own organization, weblike and spidery, was insinuating itself. And so I was kept in touch with all that was happening in the world without. And furthermore, every one of our imprisoned leaders was in contact with brave comrades who masqueraded in the livery of the Iron Heel. Though Ernest lay in prison three thousand miles away, on the Pacific Coast, I was in unbroken communication with him, and our letters passed regularly back and forth.

The leaders, in prison and out, were able to discuss and direct the campaign. It would have been possible, within a few months, to have effected the escape of some of them; but since imprisonment proved no bar to our activities, it was decided to avoid anything premature. Fifty-two Congressmen were in prison, and fully three hundred more of our leaders. It was planned that they should be delivered simultaneously. If part of them escaped, the vigilance of the oligarchs might be aroused so as to prevent the escape of the remainder. On the other hand, it was held that a simultaneous jail-delivery all over the land would have immense psychological influence on the proletariat. It would show our strength and give confidence.

So it was arranged, when I was released at the end of six months, that I was to disappear and prepare a secure hiding-place for Ernest. To disappear was in itself no easy thing. No sooner did I get my freedom than my footsteps began to be dogged by the spies of the Iron Heel. It was necessary that they should be thrown off the track, and that I should win to California. It is laughable, the way this was accomplished.

Already the passport system, modelled on the Russian, was developing. I dared not cross the continent in my own character. It was necessary that I should be completely lost if ever I was to see Ernest again, for by trailing me after he escaped, he would be caught once more. Again, I could not disguise myself as a proletarian and travel. There remained the disguise of a member of the Oligarchy. While the arch-oligarchs were no more than a handful, there were myriads of lesser ones of the type, say, of Mr. Wickson—men, worth a few millions, who were adherents of the arch-oligarchs. The wives and daughters of these lesser oligarchs were legion, and it was decided that I should assume the disguise of such a one. A few years later this would have been impossible, because the passport system was to become so perfect that no man, woman, nor child in all the land was unregistered and unaccounted for in his or her movements.

When the time was ripe, the spies were thrown off my track. An hour later Avis Everhard was no more. At that time one Felice Van Verdighan, accompanied by two maids and a lap-dog, with another maid for the lap-dog,* entered a drawing-room on a Pullman,** and a few minutes later was speeding west.

---

*This ridiculous picture well illustrates the heartless conduct of the masters. While people starved, lap-dogs were waited upon by maids. This was a serious masquerade on the part of Avis Everhard. Life and death and the Cause were in the issue; therefore the picture must be accepted as a true picture. It affords a striking commentary of the times.

**Pullman—the designation of the more luxurious railway cars of the period and so named from the inventor.

The three maids who accompanied me were revolutionists. Two were members of the Fighting Groups, and the third, Grace Holbrook, entered a group the following year, and six months later was executed by the Iron Heel. She it was who waited upon the dog. Of the other two, Bertha Stole disappeared twelve years later, while Anna Roylston still lives and plays an increasingly important part in the Revolution.*

> * *Despite continual and almost inconceivable hazards, Anna*
>
> *Roylston lived to the royal age of ninety-one. As the*
>
> *Pococks defied the executioners of the Fighting Groups, so*
>
> *she defied the executioners of the Iron Heel. She bore a*
>
> *charmed life and prospered amid dangers and alarms. She*
>
> *herself was an executioner for the Fighting Groups, and,*
>
> *known as the Red Virgin, she became one of the inspired*
>
> *figures of the Revolution. When she was an old woman of*
>
> *sixty-nine she shot "Bloody" Halcliffe down in the midst of*
>
> *his armed escort and got away unscathed. In the end she*
>
> *died peaceably of old age in a secret refuge of the*
>
> *revolutionists in the Ozark mountains.*

Without adventure we crossed the United States to California. When the train stopped at Sixteenth Street Station, in Oakland, we alighted, and there Felice Van Verdighan, with her two maids, her lap-dog, and her lap-dog's maid, disappeared forever. The maids, guided by trusty comrades, were led away. Other comrades took charge of me. Within half an hour after leaving the train I was on board a small fishing boat and out on the waters of San Francisco Bay. The winds baffled, and we drifted aimlessly the greater part of the night. But I saw the lights of Alcatraz where Ernest lay, and found comfort in the thought of nearness to him. By dawn, what with the rowing of the fishermen, we made the Marin Islands. Here we lay in hiding all day, and on the following night, swept on by a flood tide and a fresh wind, we crossed San Pablo Bay in two hours and ran up Petaluma Creek.

Here horses were ready and another comrade, and without delay we were away through the starlight. To the north I could see the loom of Sonoma Mountain, toward which we rode. We left the old town of Sonoma to the right and rode up a canyon that lay between outlying buttresses of the mountain. The wagon-road became a wood-road, the wood-road became a cow-path, and the cow-path dwindled away and ceased among the upland pastures. Straight over Sonoma Mountain we rode. It was the safest route. There was no one to mark our passing.

Dawn caught us on the northern brow, and in the gray light we dropped down through chaparral into redwood canyons deep and warm with the breath of passing summer. It was old country to me that I knew and loved, and soon I became the guide. The hiding-place was mine. I had selected it. We let down the bars and crossed an upland meadow. Next, we went over a low, oak-covered ridge and descended into a smaller meadow. Again we climbed a ridge, this time riding under red-limbed madronos and manzanitas of deeper red. The first rays of the sun streamed upon our backs as we climbed. A flight of quail thrummed off through the thickets. A big jackrabbit crossed our path, leaping swiftly and silently like a deer. And then a deer, a many-pronged buck, the sun flashing red-gold from neck and shoulders, cleared the crest of the ridge before us and was gone.

We followed in his wake a space, then dropped down a zigzag trail that he disdained into a group of noble redwoods that stood about a pool of water murky with minerals from the mountain side. I knew every inch of the way. Once a writer friend of mine had owned the ranch; but he, too, had become a revolutionist, though more disastrously than I, for he was already dead and gone, and none knew where nor how. He alone, in the days he had lived, knew the secret of the hiding-place for which I was bound. He had bought the ranch for beauty, and paid a round price for it, much to the disgust of the local farmers. He used to tell with great glee how they were wont to shake their heads mournfully at the price, to accomplish ponderously a bit of mental arithmetic, and then to say, "But you can't make six per cent on it."

But he was dead now, nor did the ranch descend to his children. Of all men, it was now the property of Mr. Wickson, who owned the whole eastern and northern slopes of Sonoma Mountain, running from the Spreckels estate to the divide of Bennett Valley. Out of it he had made a magnificent deer-park, where, over thousands of acres of sweet slopes and glades and canyons, the deer ran almost in primitive wildness. The people who had owned the soil had been driven away. A state home for the feeble-minded had also been demolished to make room for the deer.

To cap it all, Wickson's hunting lodge was a quarter of a mile from my hiding-place. This, instead of being a danger, was an added security. We were sheltered under the very aegis of one of the minor oligarchs. Suspicion, by the nature of the situation, was turned aside. The last place in the world the spies of the Iron Heel would dream of looking for me, and for Ernest when he joined me, was Wickson's deer-park.

We tied our horses among the redwoods at the pool. From a cache behind a hollow rotting log my companion brought out a variety of things,—a fifty-pound sack of flour, tinned foods of all sorts, cooking utensils, blankets, a canvas tarpaulin, books and writing material, a great bundle of letters, a five-gallon can of kerosene, an oil stove, and, last and most important, a large coil of stout rope. So large was the supply of things that a number of trips would be necessary to carry them to the refuge.

But the refuge was very near. Taking the rope and leading the way, I passed through a glade of tangled vines and bushes that ran between two wooded knolls. The glade ended abruptly at the steep bank of a stream. It was a little stream, rising from springs, and the hottest summer never dried it up. On every hand were tall wooded knolls, a group of them, with all the seeming of having been flung there from some careless Titan's hand. There was no bed-rock in them. They rose from their bases hundreds of feet, and they were composed of red volcanic earth, the famous wine-soil of Sonoma. Through these the tiny stream had cut its deep and precipitous channel.

It was quite a scramble down to the stream bed, and, once on the bed, we went down stream perhaps for a hundred feet. And then we came to the great hole. There was no warning of the existence of the hole, nor was it a hole in the common sense of the word. One crawled through tight-locked briers and branches, and found oneself on the very edge, peering out and down through a green screen. A couple of hundred feet in length and width, it was half of that in depth. Possibly because of some fault that had occurred when the knolls were flung together, and certainly helped by freakish erosion, the hole had been scooped out in the course of centuries by the wash of water. Nowhere did the raw earth appear. All was garmented by vegetation, from tiny maiden-hair and gold-back ferns to mighty redwood and Douglas spruces. These great trees even sprang out from the walls of the hole. Some leaned over at angles as great as forty-five degrees, though the majority towered straight up from the soft and almost perpendicular earth walls.

It was a perfect hiding-place. No one ever came there, not even the village boys of Glen Ellen. Had this hole existed in the bed of a canyon a mile long, or several miles long, it would have been well known. But this was no canyon. From beginning to end the length of the stream was no more than five hundred yards. Three hundred yards above the hole the stream took its rise in a spring at the foot of a flat meadow. A hundred yards below the hole the stream ran out into open country, joining the main stream and flowing across rolling and grass-covered land.

My companion took a turn of the rope around a tree, and with me fast on the other end lowered away. In no time I was on the bottom. And in but a short while he had carried all the articles from the cache and lowered them down to me. He hauled the rope up and hid it, and before he went away called down to me a cheerful parting.

Before I go on I want to say a word for this comrade, John Carlson, a humble figure of the Revolution, one of the countless faithful ones in the ranks. He worked for Wickson, in the stables near the hunting lodge. In fact, it was on Wickson's horses that we had ridden over Sonoma Mountain. For nearly twenty years now John Carlson has been custodian of the refuge. No thought of disloyalty, I am sure, has ever entered his mind during all that time. To betray his trust would have been in his mind a thing undreamed. He was phlegmatic, stolid to such a degree that one could not but wonder how the Revolution had any meaning to him at all. And yet love of freedom glowed sombrely and steadily in his dim soul. In ways it was indeed good that he was not flighty and imaginative. He never lost his head. He could obey orders, and he was neither curious nor garrulous. Once I asked how it was that he was a revolutionist.

"When I was a young man I was a soldier," was his answer. "It was in Germany. There all young men must be in the army. So I was in the army. There was another soldier there, a young man, too. His father was what you call an agitator, and his father was in jail for lese majesty—what you call speaking the truth about the Emperor. And the young man, the son, talked with me much about people, and work, and the robbery of the people by the capitalists. He made me see things in new ways, and I became a socialist. His talk was very true and good, and I have never forgotten. When I came to the United States I hunted up the socialists. I became a member of a section— that was in the day of the S. L. P. Then later, when the split came, I joined the local of the S. P. I was working in a livery stable in San Francisco then. That was before the Earthquake. I have paid my dues for twenty-two years. I am yet a member, and I yet pay my dues, though it is very secret now. I will always pay my dues, and when the cooperative commonwealth comes, I will be glad."

Left to myself, I proceeded to cook breakfast on the oil stove and to prepare my home. Often, in the early morning, or in the evening after dark, Carlson would steal down to the refuge and work for a couple of hours. At first my home was the tarpaulin. Later, a small tent was put up. And still later, when we became assured of the perfect security of the place, a small house was erected. This house was completely hidden from any chance eye that might peer down from the edge of the hole. The lush vegetation of that sheltered spot make a natural shield. Also, the house was built against the perpendicular wall; and in the wall itself, shored by strong timbers, well drained and ventilated, we excavated two small rooms. Oh, believe me, we had many comforts. When Biedenbach, the German terrorist, hid with us some time later, he installed a smoke-consuming device that enabled us to sit by crackling wood fires on winter nights.

And here I must say a word for that gentle-souled terrorist, than whom there is no comrade in the Revolution more fearfully misunderstood. Comrade Biedenbach did not betray the Cause. Nor was he executed by the comrades as is commonly supposed. This canard was circulated by the creatures of the Oligarchy. Comrade Biedenbach was absent-minded, forgetful. He was shot by one of our lookouts at the cave-refuge at Carmel, through failure on his part to remember the secret signals. It was all a sad mistake. And that he betrayed his Fighting Group is an absolute lie. No truer, more loyal man ever labored for the Cause.*

> *Search as we may through all the material of those times that has come down to us, we can find no clew to the Biedenbach here referred to. No mention is made of him anywhere save in the Everhard Manuscript.*

For nineteen years now the refuge that I selected had been almost continuously occupied, and in all that time, with one exception, it has never been discovered by an outsider. And yet it was only a quarter of a mile from Wickson's hunting-lodge, and a short mile from the village of Glen Ellen. I was able, always, to hear the morning and evening trains arrive and depart, and I used to set my watch by the whistle at the brickyards.*

* If the curious traveller will turn south from Glen Ellen, he will find himself on a boulevard that is identical with the old country road seven centuries ago. A quarter of a mile from Glen Ellen, after the second bridge is passed, to the right will be noticed a barranca that runs like a scar across the rolling land toward a group of wooded knolls. The barranca is the site of the ancient right of way that in the time of private property in land ran across the holding of one Chauvet, a French pioneer of California who came from his native country in the fabled days of gold. The wooded knolls are the same knolls referred to by Avis Everhard.

The Great Earthquake of 2368 A.D. broke off the side of one of these knolls and toppled it into the hole where the Everhards made their refuge. Since the finding of the Manuscript excavations have been made, and the house, the two cave rooms, and all the accumulated rubbish of long occupancy have been brought to light. Many valuable relics have been found, among which, curious to relate, is the smoke-consuming device of Biedenbach's mentioned in the narrative. Students interested in such matters should read the brochure of Arnold Bentham soon to be published.

A mile northwest from the wooded knolls brings one to the site of Wake Robin Lodge at the junction of Wild-Water and

Sonoma Creeks. It may be noticed, in passing, that Wild-Water was originally called Graham Creek and was so named on the early local maps. But the later name sticks. It was at Wake Robin Lodge that Avis Everhard later lived for short periods, when, disguised as an agent-provocateur of the Iron Heel, she was enabled to play with impunity her part among men and events. The official permission to occupy Wake Robin Lodge is still on the records, signed by no less a man than Wickson, the minor oligarch of the Manuscript.

CHAPTER XIX. TRANSFORMATION

"You must make yourself over again," Ernest wrote to me. "You must cease to be. You must become another woman—and not merely in the clothes you wear, but inside your skin under the clothes. You must make yourself over again so that even I would not know you—your voice, your gestures, your mannerisms, your carriage, your walk, everything."

This command I obeyed. Every day I practised for hours in burying forever the old Avis Everhard beneath the skin of another woman whom I may call my other self. It was only by long practice that such results could be obtained. In the mere detail of voice intonation I practised almost perpetually till the voice of my new self became fixed, automatic. It was this automatic assumption of a role that was considered imperative. One must become so adept as to deceive oneself. It was like learning a new language, say the French. At first speech in French is self-conscious, a matter of the will. The student thinks in English and then transmutes into French, or reads in French but transmutes into English before he can understand. Then later, becoming firmly grounded, automatic, the student reads, writes, and THINKS in French, without any recourse to English at all.

And so with our disguises. It was necessary for us to practise until our assumed roles became real; until to be our original selves would require a watchful and strong exercise of will. Of course, at first, much was mere blundering experiment. We were creating a new art, and we had much to discover. But the work was going on everywhere; masters in the art were developing, and a fund of tricks and expedients was being accumulated. This fund became a sort of text-book that was passed on, a part of the curriculum, as it were, of the school of Revolution.*

---

* Disguise did become a veritable art during that period.

The revolutionists maintained schools of acting in all their refuges. They scorned accessories, such as wigs and beards, false eyebrows, and such aids of the theatrical actors. The game of revolution was a game of life and death, and mere accessories were traps. Disguise had to be fundamental, intrinsic, part and parcel of one's being, second nature. The Red Virgin is reported to have been one of the most adept in the art, to which must be ascribed her long and successful career.

It was at this time that my father disappeared. His letters, which had come to me regularly, ceased. He no longer appeared at our Pell Street quarters. Our comrades sought him everywhere. Through our secret service we ransacked every prison in the land. But he was lost as completely as if the earth had swallowed him up, and to this day no clew to his end has been discovered.*

Disappearance was one of the horrors of the time. As a motif, in song and story, it constantly crops up. It was an inevitable concomitant of the subterranean warfare that raged through those three centuries. This phenomenon was almost as common in the oligarch class and the labor castes, as it was in the ranks of the revolutionists. Without warning, without trace, men and women, and even children, disappeared and were seen no more, their end shrouded in mystery.

Six lonely months I spent in the refuge, but they were not idle months. Our organization went on apace, and there were mountains of work always waiting to be done. Ernest and his fellow-leaders, from their prisons, decided what should be done; and it remained for us on the outside to do it. There was the organization of the mouth-to-mouth propaganda; the organization, with all its ramifications, of our spy system; the establishment of our secret printing-presses; and the establishment of our underground railways, which meant the knitting together of all our myriads of places of refuge, and the formation of new refuges where links were missing in the chains we ran over all the land.

So I say, the work was never done. At the end of six months my loneliness was broken by the arrival of two comrades. They were young girls, brave souls and passionate lovers of liberty: Lora Peterson, who disappeared in 1922, and Kate Bierce, who later married Du Bois,* and who is still with us with eyes lifted to to-morrow's sun, that heralds in the new age.

Du Bois, the present librarian of Ardis, is a lineal descendant of this revolutionary pair.

The two girls arrived in a flurry of excitement, danger, and sudden death. In the crew of the fishing boat that conveyed them across San Pablo Bay was a spy. A creature of the Iron Heel, he had successfully masqueraded as a revolutionist and penetrated deep into the secrets of our organization. Without doubt he was on my trail, for we had long since learned that my disappearance had been cause of deep concern to the secret service of the Oligarchy. Luckily, as the outcome proved, he had not divulged his discoveries to any one. He had evidently delayed reporting, preferring to wait until he had brought things to a successful conclusion by discovering my hiding-place and capturing me. His information died with him. Under some pretext, after the girls had landed at Petaluma Creek and taken to the horses, he managed to get away from the boat.

Part way up Sonoma Mountain, John Carlson let the girls go on, leading his horse, while he went back on foot. His suspicions had been aroused. He captured the spy, and as to what then happened, Carlson gave us a fair idea.

"I fixed him," was Carlson's unimaginative way of describing the affair. "I fixed him," he repeated, while a sombre light burnt in his eyes, and his huge, toil-distorted hands opened and closed eloquently. "He made no noise. I hid him, and tonight I will go back and bury him deep."

During that period I used to marvel at my own metamorphosis. At times it seemed impossible, either that I had ever lived a placid, peaceful life in a college town, or else that I had become a revolutionist inured to scenes of violence and death. One or the other could not be. One was real, the other was a dream, but which was which? Was this present life of a revolutionist, hiding in a hole, a nightmare? or was I a revolutionist who had somewhere, somehow, dreamed that in some former existence I have lived in Berkeley and never known of life more violent than teas and dances, debating societies, and lectures rooms? But then I suppose this was a common experience of all of us who had rallied under the red banner of the brotherhood of man.

I often remembered figures from that other life, and, curiously enough, they appeared and disappeared, now and again, in my new life. There was Bishop Morehouse. In vain we searched for him after our organization had developed. He had been transferred from asylum to asylum. We traced him from the state hospital for the insane at Napa to the one in Stockton, and from there to the one in the Santa Clara Valley called Agnews, and there the trail ceased. There was no record of his death. In some way he must have escaped. Little did I dream of the awful manner in which I was to see him once again—the fleeting glimpse of him in the whirlwind carnage of the Chicago Commune.

Jackson, who had lost his arm in the Sierra Mills and who had been the cause of my own conversion into a revolutionist, I never saw again; but we all knew what he did before he died. He never joined the revolutionists. Embittered by his fate, brooding over his wrongs, he became an anarchist— not a philosophic anarchist, but a mere animal, mad with hate and lust for revenge. And well he revenged himself. Evading the guards, in the nighttime while all were asleep, he blew the Pertonwaithe palace into atoms. Not a soul escaped, not even the guards. And in prison, while awaiting trial, he suffocated himself under his blankets.

Dr. Hammerfield and Dr. Ballingford achieved quite different fates from that of Jackson. They have been faithful to their salt, and they have been correspondingly rewarded with ecclesiastical palaces wherein they dwell at peace with the world. Both are apologists for the Oligarchy. Both have grown very fat. "Dr. Hammerfield," as Ernest once said, "has succeeded in modifying his metaphysics so as to give God's sanction to the Iron Heel, and also to include much worship of beauty and to reduce to an invisible wraith the gaseous vertebrate described by Haeckel—the difference between Dr. Hammerfield and Dr. Ballingford being that the latter has made the God of the oligarchs a little more gaseous and a little less vertebrate."

Peter Donnelly, the scab foreman at the Sierra Mills whom I encountered while investigating the case of Jackson, was a surprise to all of us. In 1918 I was present at a meeting of the 'Frisco Reds. Of all our Fighting Groups this one was the most formidable, ferocious, and merciless. It was really not a part of our organization. Its members were fanatics, madmen. We dared not encourage such a spirit. On the other hand, though they did not belong to us, we remained on friendly terms with them. It was a matter of vital importance that brought me there that night. I, alone in the midst of a score of men, was the only person unmasked. After the business that brought me there was transacted, I was led away by one of them. In a dark passage this guide struck a match, and, holding it close to his face, slipped back his mask. For a moment I gazed upon the passion-wrought features of Peter Donnelly. Then the match went out.

"I just wanted you to know it was me," he said in the darkness. "D'you remember Dallas, the superintendent?"

I nodded at recollection of the vulpine-face superintendent of the Sierra Mills.

"Well, I got him first," Donnelly said with pride. "'Twas after that I joined the Reds."

"But how comes it that you are here?" I queried. "Your wife and children?"

"Dead," he answered. "That's why. No," he went on hastily, "'tis not revenge for them. They died easily in their beds—sickness, you see, one time and another. They tied my arms while they lived. And now that they're gone, 'tis revenge for my blasted manhood I'm after. I was once Peter Donnelly, the scab foreman. But to-night I'm Number 27 of the 'Frisco Reds. Come on now, and I'll get you out of this."

More I heard of him afterward. In his own way he had told the truth when he said all were dead. But one lived, Timothy, and him his father considered dead because he had taken service with the Iron Heel in the Mercenaries.* A member of the 'Frisco Reds pledged himself to twelve annual executions. The penalty for failure was death. A member who failed to complete his number committed suicide. These executions were not haphazard. This group of madmen met frequently and passed wholesale judgments upon offending members and servitors of the Oligarchy. The executions were afterward apportioned by lot.

*In addition to the labor castes, there arose another caste, the military. A standing army of professional soldiers was created, officered by members of the Oligarchy and known as the Mercenaries. This institution took the place of the militia, which had proved impracticable under the new regime. Outside the regular secret service of the Iron Heel, there was further established a secret service of the Mercenaries, this latter forming a connecting link between the police and the military.

In fact, the business that brought me there the night of my visit was such a trial. One of our own comrades, who for years had successfully maintained himself in a clerical position in the local bureau of the secret service of the Iron Heel, had fallen under the ban of the 'Frisco Reds and was being tried. Of course he was not present, and of course his judges did not know that he was one of our men. My mission had been to testify to his identity and loyalty. It may be wondered how we came to know of the affair at all. The explanation is simple. One of our secret agents was a member of the 'Frisco Reds. It was necessary for us to keep an eye on friend as well as foe, and this group of madmen was not too unimportant to escape our surveillance.

But to return to Peter Donnelly and his son. All went well with Donnelly until, in the following year, he found among the sheaf of executions that fell to him the name of Timothy Donnelly. Then it was that that clannishness, which was his to so extraordinary a degree, asserted itself. To save his son, he betrayed his comrades. In this he was partially blocked, but a dozen of the 'Frisco Reds were executed, and the group was well-nigh destroyed. In retaliation, the survivors meted out to Donnelly the death he had earned by his treason.

Nor did Timothy Donnelly long survive. The 'Frisco Reds pledged themselves to his execution. Every effort was made by the Oligarchy to save him. He was transferred from one part of the country to another. Three of the Reds lost their lives in vain efforts to get him. The Group was composed only of men. In the end they fell back on a woman, one of our comrades, and none other than Anna Roylston. Our Inner Circle forbade her, but she had ever a will of her own and disdained discipline. Furthermore, she was a genius and lovable, and we could never discipline her anyway. She is in a class by herself and not amenable to the ordinary standards of the revolutionists.

Despite our refusal to grant permission to do the deed, she went on with it. Now Anna Roylston was a fascinating woman. All she had to do was to beckon a man to her. She broke the hearts of scores of our young comrades, and scores of others she captured, and by their heart-strings led into our organization. Yet she steadfastly refused to marry. She dearly loved children, but she held that a child of her own would claim her from the Cause, and that it was the Cause to which her life was devoted.

It was an easy task for Anna Roylston to win Timothy Donnelly. Her conscience did not trouble her, for at that very time occurred the Nashville Massacre, when the Mercenaries, Donnelly in command, literally murdered eight hundred weavers of that city. But she did not kill Donnelly. She turned him over, a prisoner, to the 'Frisco Reds. This happened only last year, and now she had been renamed. The revolutionists everywhere are calling her the "Red Virgin." *

It was not until the Second Revolt was crushed, that the 'Frisco Reds flourished again. And for two generations the Group flourished. Then an agent of the Iron Heel managed to become a member, penetrated all its secrets, and brought about its total annihilation. This occurred in 2002 A.D. The members were executed one at a time, at intervals of three weeks, and their bodies exposed in the labor-ghetto of San Francisco.

Colonel Ingram and Colonel Van Gilbert are two more familiar figures that I was later to encounter. Colonel Ingram rose high in the Oligarchy and became Minister to Germany. He was cordially detested by the proletariat of both countries. It was in Berlin that I met him, where, as an accredited international spy of the Iron Heel, I was received by him and afforded much assistance. Incidentally, I may state that in my dual role I managed a few important things for the Revolution.

Colonel Van Gilbert became known as "Snarling" Van Gilbert. His important part was played in drafting the new code after the Chicago

Commune. But before that, as trial judge, he had earned sentence of death by his fiendish malignancy. I was one of those that tried him and passed sentence upon him. Anna Roylston carried out the execution.

Still another figure arises out of the old life—Jackson's lawyer. Least of all would I have expected again to meet this man, Joseph Hurd. It was a strange meeting. Late at night, two years after the Chicago Commune, Ernest and I arrived together at the Benton Harbor refuge. This was in Michigan, across the lake from Chicago. We arrived just at the conclusion of the trial of a spy. Sentence of death had been passed, and he was being led away. Such was the scene as we came upon it. The next moment the wretched man had wrenched free from his captors and flung himself at my feet, his arms clutching me about the knees in a vicelike grip as he prayed in a frenzy for mercy. As he turned his agonized face up to me, I recognized him as Joseph Hurd. Of all the terrible things I have witnessed, never have I been so unnerved as by this frantic creature's pleading for life. He was mad for life. It was pitiable. He refused to let go of me, despite the hands of a dozen comrades. And when at last he was dragged shrieking away, I sank down fainting upon the floor. It is far easier to see brave men die than to hear a coward beg for life.*

---

* The Benton Harbor refuge was a catacomb, the entrance of which was cunningly contrived by way of a well. It has been maintained in a fair state of preservation, and the curious visitor may to-day tread its labyrinths to the assembly hall, where, without doubt, occurred the scene described by Avis Everhard. Farther on are the cells where the prisoners were confined, and the death chamber where the executions took place. Beyond is the cemetery—long, winding galleries hewn out of the solid rock, with recesses on either hand, wherein, tier above tier, lie the revolutionists just as they were laid away by their comrades long years agone.

CHAPTER XX. A LOST OLIGARCH

But in remembering the old life I have run ahead of my story into the new life. The wholesale jail delivery did not occur until well along into 1915. Complicated as it was, it was carried through without a hitch, and as a very creditable achievement it cheered us on in our work. From Cuba to California, out of scores of jails, military prisons, and fortresses, in a single night, we delivered fifty-one of our fifty-two Congressmen, and in addition over three hundred other leaders. There was not a single instance of miscarriage. Not only did they escape, but every one of them won to the refuges as planned. The one comrade Congressman we did not get was Arthur Simpson, and he had already died in Cabanas after cruel tortures.

The eighteen months that followed was perhaps the happiest of my life with Ernest. During that time we were never apart. Later, when we went back into the world, we were separated much. Not more impatiently do I await the flame of to-morrow's revolt than did I that night await the coming of Ernest. I had not seen him for so long, and the thought of a possible hitch or error in our plans that would keep him still in his island prison almost drove me mad. The hours passed like ages. I was all alone. Biedenbach, and three young men who had been living in the refuge, were out and over the mountain, heavily armed and prepared for anything. The refuges all over the land were quite empty, I imagine, of comrades that night.

Just as the sky paled with the first warning of dawn, I heard the signal from above and gave the answer. In the darkness I almost embraced Biedenbach, who came down first; but the next moment I was in Ernest's arms. And in that moment, so complete had been my transformation, I discovered it was only by an effort of will that I could be the old Avis Everhard, with the old mannerisms and smiles, phrases and intonations of voice. It was by strong effort only that I was able to maintain my old identity; I could not allow myself to forget for an instant, so automatically imperative had become the new personality I had created.

Once inside the little cabin, I saw Ernest's face in the light. With the exception of the prison pallor, there was no change in him—at least, not much. He was my same lover-husband and hero. And yet there was a certain ascetic lengthening of the lines of his face. But he could well stand it, for it seemed to add a certain nobility of refinement to the riotous excess of life that had always marked his features. He might have been a trifle graver than of yore, but the glint of laughter still was in his eyes. He was twenty pounds lighter, but in splendid physical condition. He had kept up exercise during the whole period of confinement, and his muscles were like iron. In truth, he was in better condition than when he had entered prison. Hours passed before his head touched pillow and I had soothed him off to sleep. But there was no sleep for me. I was too happy, and the fatigue of jail-breaking and riding horseback had not been mine.

While Ernest slept, I changed my dress, arranged my hair differently, and came back to my new automatic self. Then, when Biedenbach and the other comrades awoke, with their aid I concocted a little conspiracy. All was ready, and we were in the cave-room that served for kitchen and dining room when Ernest opened the door and entered. At that moment Biedenbach addressed me as Mary, and I turned and answered him. Then I glanced at Ernest with curious interest, such as any young comrade might betray on seeing for the first time so noted a hero of the Revolution. But Ernest's glance took me in and questioned impatiently past and around the room. The next moment I was being introduced to him as Mary Holmes.

To complete the deception, an extra plate was laid, and when we sat down to table one chair was not occupied. I could have cried with joy as I noted Ernest's increasing uneasiness and impatience. Finally he could stand it no longer.

"Where's my wife?" he demanded bluntly.

"She is still asleep," I answered.

It was the crucial moment. But my voice was a strange voice, and in it he recognized nothing familiar. The meal went on. I talked a great deal, and enthusiastically, as a hero-worshipper might talk, and it was obvious that he was my hero. I rose to a climax of enthusiasm and worship, and, before he could guess my intention, threw my arms around his neck and kissed him on the lips. He held me from him at arm's length and stared about in annoyance and perplexity. The four men greeted him with roars of laughter, and explanations were made. At first he was sceptical. He scrutinized me keenly and was half convinced, then shook his head and would not believe. It was not until I became the old Avis Everhard and whispered secrets in his ear that none knew but he and Avis Everhard, that he accepted me as his really, truly wife.

It was later in the day that he took me in his arms, manifesting great embarrassment and claiming polygamous emotions.

"You are my Avis," he said, "and you are also some one else. You are two women, and therefore you are my harem. At any rate, we are safe now. If the United States becomes too hot for us, why I have qualified for citizenship in Turkey." *

At that time polygamy was still practised in Turkey.

Life became for me very happy in the refuge. It is true, we worked hard and for long hours; but we worked together. We had each other for eighteen precious months, and we were not lonely, for there was always a coming and going of leaders and comrades—strange voices from the under-world of intrigue and revolution, bringing stranger tales of strife and war from all our battle-line. And there was much fun and delight. We were not mere gloomy conspirators. We toiled hard and suffered greatly, filled the gaps in our ranks and went on, and through all the labour and the play and interplay of life and death we found time to laugh and love. There were artists, scientists, scholars, musicians, and poets among us; and in that hole in the ground culture was higher and finer than in the palaces of wonder-cities of the oligarchs. In truth, many of our comrades toiled at making beautiful those same palaces and wonder-cities.*

This is not braggadocio on the part of Avis Everhard. The flower of the artistic and intellectual world were revolutionists. With the exception of a few of the musicians and singers, and of a few of the oligarchs, all the great creators of the period whose names have come down to us, were revolutionists.

Nor were we confined to the refuge itself. Often at night we rode over the mountains for exercise, and we rode on Wickson's horses. If only he knew how many revolutionists his horses have carried! We even went on picnics to isolated spots we knew, where we remained all day, going before daylight and returning after dark. Also, we used Wickson's cream and butter,* and Ernest was not above shooting Wickson's quail and rabbits, and, on occasion, his young bucks.

Even as late as that period, cream and butter were still crudely extracted from cow's milk. The laboratory preparation of foods had not yet begun.

Indeed, it was a safe refuge. I have said that it was discovered only once, and this brings me to the clearing up of the mystery of the disappearance of young Wickson. Now that he is dead, I am free to speak. There was a nook on the bottom of the great hole where the sun shone for several hours and which was hidden from above. Here we had carried many loads of gravel from the creek-bed, so that it was dry and warm, a pleasant basking place; and here, one afternoon, I was drowsing, half asleep, over a volume of Mendenhall.* I was so comfortable and secure that even his flaming lyrics failed to stir me.

* In all the extant literature and documents of that period, continual reference is made to the poems of Rudolph Mendenhall. By his comrades he was called "The Flame." He was undoubtedly a great genius; yet, beyond weird and haunting fragments of his verse, quoted in the writings of others, nothing of his has come down to us. He was executed by the Iron Heel in 1928 A.D.

I was aroused by a clod of earth striking at my feet. Then from above, I heard a sound of scrambling. The next moment a young man, with a final slide down the crumbling wall, alighted at my feet. It was Philip Wickson, though I did not know him at the time. He looked at me coolly and uttered a low whistle of surprise.

"Well," he said; and the next moment, cap in hand, he was saying, "I beg your pardon. I did not expect to find any one here."

I was not so cool. I was still a tyro so far as concerned knowing how to behave in desperate circumstances. Later on, when I was an international spy, I should have been less clumsy, I am sure. As it was, I scrambled to my feet and cried out the danger call.

"Why did you do that?" he asked, looking at me searchingly.

It was evident that he had no suspicion of our presence when making the descent. I recognized this with relief.

"For what purpose do you think I did it?" I countered. I was indeed clumsy in those days.

"I don't know," he answered, shaking his head. "Unless you've got friends about. Anyway, you've got some explanations to make. I don't like the look of it. You are trespassing. This is my father's land, and—"

But at that moment, Biedenbach, every polite and gentle, said from behind him in a low voice, "Hands up, my young sir."

Young Wickson put his hands up first, then turned to confront Biedenbach, who held a thirty-thirty automatic rifle on him. Wickson was imperturbable.

"Oh, ho," he said, "a nest of revolutionists—and quite a hornet's nest it would seem. Well, you won't abide here long, I can tell you."

"Maybe you'll abide here long enough to reconsider that statement," Biedenbach said quietly. "And in the meanwhile I must ask you to come inside with me."

"Inside?" The young man was genuinely astonished. "Have you a catacomb here? I have heard of such things."

"Come and see," Biedenbach answered with his adorable accent.

"But it is unlawful," was the protest.

"Yes, by your law," the terrorist replied significantly. "But by our law, believe me, it is quite lawful. You must accustom yourself to the fact that you are in another world than the one of oppression and brutality in which you have lived."

"There is room for argument there," Wickson muttered.

"Then stay with us and discuss it."

The young fellow laughed and followed his captor into the house. He was led into the inner cave-room, and one of the young comrades left to guard him, while we discussed the situation in the kitchen.

Biedenbach, with tears in his eyes, held that Wickson must die, and was quite relieved when we outvoted him and his horrible proposition. On the other hand, we could not dream of allowing the young oligarch to depart.

"I'll tell you what to do," Ernest said. "We'll keep him and give him an education."

"I bespeak the privilege, then, of enlightening him in jurisprudence," Biedenbach cried.

And so a decision was laughingly reached. We would keep Philip Wickson a prisoner and educate him in our ethics and sociology. But in the meantime there was work to be done. All trace of the young oligarch must be obliterated. There were the marks he had left when descending the crumbling wall of the hole. This task fell to Biedenbach, and, slung on a rope from above, he toiled cunningly for the rest of the day till no sign remained. Back up the canyon from the lip of the hole all marks were likewise removed. Then, at twilight, came John Carlson, who demanded Wickson's shoes.

The young man did not want to give up his shoes, and even offered to fight for them, till he felt the horseshoer's strength in Ernest's hands. Carlson afterward reported several blisters and much grievous loss of skin due to the smallness of the shoes, but he succeeded in doing gallant work with them. Back from the lip of the hole, where ended the young man's obliterated trial, Carlson put on the shoes and walked away to the left. He walked for miles, around knolls, over ridges and through canyons, and finally covered the trail in the running water of a creek-bed. Here he removed the shoes, and, still hiding trail for a distance, at last put on his own shoes. A week later Wickson got back his shoes.

That night the hounds were out, and there was little sleep in the refuge. Next day, time and again, the baying hounds came down the canyon, plunged off to the left on the trail Carlson had made for them, and were lost to ear in the farther canyons high up the mountain. And all the time our men waited in the refuge, weapons in hand—automatic revolvers and rifles, to say nothing of half a dozen infernal machines of Biedenbach's manufacture. A more surprised party of rescuers could not be imagined, had they ventured down into our hiding-place.

I have now given the true disappearance of Philip Wickson, one-time oligarch, and, later, comrade in the Revolution. For we converted him in the end. His mind was fresh and plastic, and by nature he was very ethical. Several months later we rode him, on one of his father's horses, over Sonoma

Mountains to Petaluma Creek and embarked him in a small fishing-launch. By easy stages we smuggled him along our underground railway to the Carmel refuge.

There he remained eight months, at the end of which time, for two reasons, he was loath to leave us. One reason was that he had fallen in love with Anna Roylston, and the other was that he had become one of us. It was not until he became convinced of the hopelessness of his love affair that he acceded to our wishes and went back to his father. Ostensibly an oligarch until his death, he was in reality one of the most valuable of our agents. Often and often has the Iron Heel been dumbfounded by the miscarriage of its plans and operations against us. If it but knew the number of its own members who are our agents, it would understand. Young Wickson never wavered in his loyalty to the Cause. In truth, his very death was incurred by his devotion to duty. In the great storm of 1927, while attending a meeting of our leaders, he contracted the pneumonia of which he died.*

The case of this young man was not unusual. Many young men of the Oligarchy, impelled by sense of right conduct, or their imaginations captured by the glory of the Revolution, ethically or romantically devoted their lives to it. In similar way, many sons of the Russian nobility played their parts in the earlier and protracted revolution in that country.

CHAPTER XXI. THE ROARING ABYSMAL BEAST

During the long period of our stay in the refuge, we were kept closely in touch with what was happening in the world without, and we were learning thoroughly the strength of the Oligarchy with which we were at war. Out of the flux of transition the new institutions were forming more definitely and taking on the appearance and attributes of permanence. The oligarchs had succeeded in devising a governmental machine, as intricate as it was vast, that worked—and this despite all our efforts to clog and hamper.

This was a surprise to many of the revolutionists. They had not conceived it possible. Nevertheless the work of the country went on. The men toiled in the mines and fields—perforce they were no more than slaves. As for the vital industries, everything prospered. The members of the great labor castes were contented and worked on merrily. For the first time in their lives they knew industrial peace. No more were they worried by slack times, strike and lockout, and the union label. They lived in more comfortable homes and in delightful cities of their own—delightful compared with the slums and ghettos in which they had formerly dwelt. They had better food to eat, less hours of labor, more holidays, and a greater amount and variety of interests and pleasures. And for their less fortunate brothers and sisters, the unfavored laborers, the driven people of the abyss, they cared nothing. An age of selfishness was dawning upon mankind. And yet this is not altogether true. The labor castes were honeycombed by our agents—men whose eyes saw, beyond the belly-need, the radiant figure of liberty and brotherhood.

Another great institution that had taken form and was working smoothly was the Mercenaries. This body of soldiers had been evolved out of the old regular army and was now a million strong, to say nothing of the colonial forces. The Mercenaries constituted a race apart. They dwelt in cities of their own which were practically self-governed, and they were granted many privileges. By them a large portion of the perplexing surplus was consumed. They were losing all touch and sympathy with the rest of the people, and, in fact, were developing their own class morality and consciousness. And yet we had thousands of our agents among them.*

* The Mercenaries, in the last days of the Iron Heel, played an important role. They constituted the balance of power in the struggles between the labor castes and the oligarchs, and now to one side and now to the other, threw their strength according to the play of intrigue and conspiracy.

The oligarchs themselves were going through a remarkable and, it must be confessed, unexpected development. As a class, they disciplined themselves. Every member had his work to do in the world, and this work he was compelled to do. There were no more idle-rich young men. Their strength was used to give united strength to the Oligarchy. They served as leaders of troops and as lieutenants and captains of industry. They found careers in applied science, and many of them became great engineers. They went into the multitudinous divisions of the government, took service in the colonial possessions, and by tens of thousands went into the various secret services. They were, I may say, apprenticed to education, to art, to the church, to science, to literature; and in those fields they served the important function of moulding the thought-processes of the nation in the direction of the perpetuity of the Oligarchy.

They were taught, and later they in turn taught, that what they were doing was right. They assimilated the aristocratic idea from the moment they began, as children, to receive impressions of the world. The aristocratic idea was woven into the making of them until it became bone of them and flesh of them. They looked upon themselves as wild-animal trainers, rulers of beasts. From beneath their feet rose always the subterranean rumbles of revolt. Violent death ever stalked in their midst; bomb and knife and bullet were looked upon as so many fangs of the roaring abysmal beast they must dominate if humanity were to persist. They were the saviours of humanity, and they regarded themselves as heroic and sacrificing laborers for the highest good.

They, as a class, believed that they alone maintained civilization. It was their belief that if ever they weakened, the great beast would ingulf them and everything of beauty and wonder and joy and good in its cavernous and slime-dripping maw. Without them, anarchy would reign and humanity would drop backward into the primitive night out of which it had so painfully emerged. The horrid picture of anarchy was held always before their child's eyes until they, in turn, obsessed by this cultivated fear, held the picture of anarchy before the eyes of the children that followed them. This was the beast to be stamped upon, and the highest duty of the aristocrat was to stamp upon it. In short, they alone, by their unremitting toil and sacrifice, stood between weak humanity and the all-devouring beast; and they believed it, firmly believed it.

I cannot lay too great stress upon this high ethical righteousness of the whole oligarch class. This has been the strength of the Iron Heel, and too many of the comrades have been slow or loath to realize it. Many of them have ascribed the strength of the Iron Heel to its system of reward and punishment. This is a mistake. Heaven and hell may be the prime factors of zeal in the religion of a fanatic; but for the great majority of the religious, heaven and hell are incidental to right and wrong. Love of the right, desire for the right, unhappiness with anything less than the right—in short, right conduct, is the prime factor of religion. And so with the Oligarchy. Prisons, banishment and degradation, honors and palaces and wonder-cities, are all incidental. The great driving force of the oligarchs is the belief that they are doing right. Never mind the exceptions, and never mind the oppression and injustice in which the Iron Heel was conceived. All is granted. The point is that the strength of the Oligarchy today lies in its satisfied conception of its own righteousness.*

* Out of the ethical incoherency and inconsistency of capitalism, the oligarchs emerged with a new ethics, coherent and definite, sharp and severe as steel, the most absurd and unscientific and at the same time the most potent ever possessed by any tyrant class. The oligarchs believed their ethics, in spite of the fact that biology and evolution gave them the lie; and, because of their faith, for three centuries they were able to hold back the mighty tide of human progress—a spectacle, profound, tremendous, puzzling to the metaphysical moralist, and one that to the materialist is the cause of many doubts and reconsiderations.

For that matter, the strength of the Revolution, during these frightful twenty years, has resided in nothing else than the sense of righteousness. In no other way can be explained our sacrifices and martyrdoms. For no other reason did Rudolph Mendenhall flame out his soul for the Cause and sing his wild swan-song that last night of life. For no other reason did Hurlbert die under torture, refusing to the last to betray his comrades. For no other reason has Anna Roylston refused blessed motherhood. For no other reason has John Carlson been the faithful and unrewarded custodian of the Glen Ellen Refuge. It does not matter, young or old, man or woman, high or low, genius or clod, go where one will among the comrades of the Revolution, the motor-force will be found to be a great and abiding desire for the right.

But I have run away from my narrative. Ernest and I well understood, before we left the refuge, how the strength of the Iron Heel was developing.

The labor castes, the Mercenaries, and the great hordes of secret agents and police of various sorts were all pledged to the Oligarchy. In the main, and ignoring the loss of liberty, they were better off than they had been. On the other hand, the great helpless mass of the population, the people of the abyss, was sinking into a brutish apathy of content with misery. Whenever strong proletarians asserted their strength in the midst of the mass, they were drawn away from the mass by the oligarchs and given better conditions by being made members of the labor castes or of the Mercenaries. Thus discontent was lulled and the proletariat robbed of its natural leaders.

The condition of the people of the abyss was pitiable. Common school education, so far as they were concerned, had ceased. They lived like beasts in great squalid labor-ghettos, festering in misery and degradation. All their old liberties were gone. They were labor-slaves. Choice of work was denied them. Likewise was denied them the right to move from place to place, or the right to bear or possess arms. They were not land serfs like the farmers. They were machine-serfs and labor-serfs. When unusual needs arose for them, such as the building of the great highways and air-lines, of canals, tunnels, subways, and fortifications, levies were made on the labor-ghettos, and tens of thousands of serfs, willy-nilly, were transported to the scene of operations. Great armies of them are toiling now at the building of Ardis, housed in wretched barracks where family life cannot exist, and where decency is displaced by dull bestiality. In all truth, there in the labor-ghettos is the roaring abysmal beast the oligarchs fear so dreadfully—but it is the beast of their own making. In it they will not let the ape and tiger die.

And just now the word has gone forth that new levies are being imposed for the building of Asgard, the projected wonder-city that will far exceed Ardis when the latter is completed.* We of the Revolution will go on with that great work, but it will not be done by the miserable serfs. The walls and towers and shafts of that fair city will arise to the sound of singing, and into its beauty and wonder will be woven, not sighs and groans, but music and laughter.

Ardis was completed in 1942 A.D., Asgard was not completed until 1984 A.D. It was fifty-two years in the building, during which time a permanent army of half a million serfs was employed. At times these numbers swelled to over a million—without any account being taken of the hundreds of thousands of the labor castes and the artists.

Ernest was madly impatient to be out in the world and doing, for our ill-fated First Revolt, that had miscarried in the Chicago Commune, was ripening fast. Yet he possessed his soul with patience, and during this time of his torment, when Hadly, who had been brought for the purpose from Illinois, made him over into another man* he revolved great plans in his head for the organization of the learned proletariat, and for the maintenance of at least the rudiments of education amongst the people of the abyss—all this of course in the event of the First Revolt being a failure.

Among the Revolutionists were many surgeons, and in vivisection they attained marvellous proficiency. In Avis Everhard's words, they could literally make a man over. To them the elimination of scars and disfigurements was a trivial detail. They changed the features with such microscopic care that no traces were left of their handiwork. The nose was a favorite organ to work upon. Skin-grafting and hair-transplanting were among their commonest devices. The changes in expression they accomplished were wizard-like. Eyes and eyebrows, lips, mouths, and ears, were radically altered. By cunning operations on tongue, throat, larynx, and nasal cavities a man's whole enunciation and manner of speech could be changed. Desperate times give need for desperate remedies, and the surgeons of the Revolution rose to the need. Among other things, they could increase an adult's stature by as much as four or five inches and decrease it by one or two inches. What they did is to-day a lost art. We have no need for it.

It was not until January, 1917, that we left the refuge. All had been arranged. We took our place at once as agents-provocateurs in the scheme of the Iron Heel. I was supposed to be Ernest's sister. By oligarchs and comrades on the inside who were high in authority, place had been made for us, we were in possession of all necessary documents, and our pasts were accounted for. With help on the inside, this was not difficult, for in that shadow-world of secret service identity was nebulous. Like ghosts the agents came and went, obeying commands, fulfilling duties, following clews, making their reports often to officers they never saw or cooperating with other agents they had never seen before and would never see again.

CHAPTER XXII. THE CHICAGO COMMUNE

As agents-provocateurs, not alone were we able to travel a great deal, but our very work threw us in contact with the proletariat and with our comrades, the revolutionists. Thus we were in both camps at the same time, ostensibly serving the Iron Heel and secretly working with all our might for the Cause. There were many of us in the various secret services of the Oligarchy, and despite the shakings-up and reorganizations the secret services have undergone, they have never been able to weed all of us out.

Ernest had largely planned the First Revolt, and the date set had been somewhere early in the spring of 1918. In the fall of 1917 we were not ready; much remained to be done, and when the Revolt was precipitated, of course it was doomed to failure. The plot of necessity was frightfully intricate, and anything premature was sure to destroy it. This the Iron Heel foresaw and laid its schemes accordingly.

We had planned to strike our first blow at the nervous system of the Oligarchy. The latter had remembered the general strike, and had guarded against the defection of the telegraphers by installing wireless stations, in the control of the Mercenaries. We, in turn, had countered this move. When the signal was given, from every refuge, all over the land, and from the cities, and towns, and barracks, devoted comrades were to go forth and blow up the wireless stations. Thus at the first shock would the Iron Heel be brought to earth and lie practically dismembered.

At the same moment, other comrades were to blow up the bridges and tunnels and disrupt the whole network of railroads. Still further, other groups of comrades, at the signal, were to seize the officers of the Mercenaries and the police, as well as all Oligarchs of unusual ability or who held executive positions. Thus would the leaders of the enemy be removed from the field of the local battles that would inevitably be fought all over the land.

Many things were to occur simultaneously when the signal went forth. The Canadian and Mexican patriots, who were far stronger than the Iron Heel dreamed, were to duplicate our tactics. Then there were comrades (these were the women, for the men would be busy elsewhere) who were to post the proclamations from our secret presses. Those of us in the higher employ of the Iron Heel were to proceed immediately to make confusion and anarchy in all our departments. Inside the Mercenaries were thousands of our comrades. Their work was to blow up the magazines and to destroy the delicate mechanism of all the war machinery. In the cities of the Mercenaries and of the labor castes similar programmes of disruption were to be carried out.

In short, a sudden, colossal, stunning blow was to be struck. Before the paralyzed Oligarchy could recover itself, its end would have come. It would have meant terrible times and great loss of life, but no revolutionist hesitates at such things. Why, we even depended much, in our plan, on the unorganized people of the abyss. They were to be loosed on the palaces and cities of the masters. Never mind the destruction of life and property. Let the abysmal brute roar and the police and Mercenaries slay. The abysmal brute would roar anyway, and the police and Mercenaries would slay anyway. It would merely mean that various dangers to us were harmlessly destroying one another. In the meantime we would be doing our own work, largely unhampered, and gaining control of all the machinery of society.

Such was our plan, every detail of which had to be worked out in secret, and, as the day drew near, communicated to more and more comrades. This was the danger point, the stretching of the conspiracy. But that danger-point was never reached. Through its spy-system the Iron Heel got wind of the Revolt and prepared to teach us another of its bloody lessons. Chicago was the devoted city selected for the instruction, and well were we instructed.

Chicago* was the ripest of all—Chicago which of old time was the city of blood and which was to earn anew its name. There the revolutionary spirit was strong. Too many bitter strikes had been curbed there in the days of capitalism for the workers to forget and forgive. Even the labor castes of the city were alive with revolt. Too many heads had been broken in the early strikes. Despite their changed and favorable conditions, their hatred for the master class had not died. This spirit had infected the Mercenaries, of which three regiments in particular were ready to come over to us en masse.

* Chicago was the industrial inferno of the nineteenth century A.D. A curious anecdote has come down to us of John Burns, a great English labor leader and one time member of the British Cabinet. In Chicago, while on a visit to the United States, he was asked by a newspaper reporter for his opinion of that city. "Chicago," he answered, "is a pocket edition of hell." Some time later, as he was going aboard his steamer to sail to England, he was approached by another reporter, who wanted to know if he had changed his opinion of Chicago. "Yes, I have," was his reply. "My present opinion is that hell is a pocket edition of Chicago."

Chicago had always been the storm-centre of the conflict between labor and capital, a city of street-battles and violent death, with a class-conscious capitalist organization and a class-conscious workman organization, where, in the old days, the very school-teachers were formed into labor unions and affiliated with the hod-carriers and brick-layers in the American Federation of Labor. And Chicago became the storm-centre of the premature First Revolt.

The trouble was precipitated by the Iron Heel. It was cleverly done. The whole population, including the favored labor castes, was given a course of outrageous treatment. Promises and agreements were broken, and most drastic punishments visited upon even petty offenders. The people of the abyss were tormented out of their apathy. In fact, the Iron Heel was preparing to make the abysmal beast roar. And hand in hand with this, in all precautionary measures in Chicago, the Iron Heel was inconceivably careless. Discipline was relaxed among the Mercenaries that remained, while many regiments had been withdrawn and sent to various parts of the country.

It did not take long to carry out this programme—only several weeks. We of the Revolution caught vague rumors of the state of affairs, but had nothing definite enough for an understanding. In fact, we thought it was a spontaneous spirit of revolt that would require careful curbing on our part, and never dreamed that it was deliberately manufactured—and it had been manufactured so secretly, from the very innermost circle of the Iron Heel, that we had got no inkling. The counter-plot was an able achievement, and ably carried out.

I was in New York when I received the order to proceed immediately to Chicago. The man who gave me the order was one of the oligarchs, I could tell that by his speech, though I did not know his name nor see his face. His instructions were too clear for me to make a mistake. Plainly I read between the lines that our plot had been discovered, that we had been countermined. The explosion was ready for the flash of powder, and countless agents of the Iron Heel, including me, either on the ground or being sent there, were to supply that flash. I flatter myself that I maintained my composure under the keen eye of the oligarch, but my heart was beating madly. I could almost have shrieked and flown at his throat with my naked hands before his final, cold-blooded instructions were given.

Once out of his presence, I calculated the time. I had just the moments to spare, if I were lucky, to get in touch with some local leader before catching my train. Guarding against being trailed, I made a rush of it for the Emergency Hospital. Luck was with me, and I gained access at once to comrade Galvin, the surgeon-in-chief. I started to gasp out my information, but he stopped me.

"I already know," he said quietly, though his Irish eyes were flashing. "I knew what you had come for. I got the word fifteen minutes ago, and I have already passed it along. Everything shall be done here to keep the comrades quiet. Chicago is to be sacrificed, but it shall be Chicago alone."

"Have you tried to get word to Chicago?" I asked.

He shook his head. "No telegraphic communication. Chicago is shut off. It's going to be hell there."

He paused a moment, and I saw his white hands clinch. Then he burst out:

"By God! I wish I were going to be there!"

"There is yet a chance to stop it," I said, "if nothing happens to the train and I can get there in time. Or if some of the other secret-service comrades who have learned the truth can get there in time."

"You on the inside were caught napping this time," he said.

I nodded my head humbly.

"It was very secret," I answered. "Only the inner chiefs could have known up to to-day. We haven't yet penetrated that far, so we couldn't escape being kept in the dark. If only Ernest were here. Maybe he is in Chicago now, and all is well."

Dr. Galvin shook his head. "The last news I heard of him was that he had been sent to Boston or New Haven. This secret service for the enemy must hamper him a lot, but it's better than lying in a refuge."

I started to go, and Galvin wrung my hand.

"Keep a stout heart," were his parting words. "What if the First Revolt is lost? There will be a second, and we will be wiser then. Good-by and good luck. I don't know whether I'll ever see you again. It's going to be hell there, but I'd give ten years of my life for your chance to be in it."

The Twentieth Century* left New York at six in the evening, and was supposed to arrive at Chicago at seven next morning. But it lost time that night. We were running behind another train. Among the travellers in my Pullman was comrade Hartman, like myself in the secret service of the Iron Heel. He it was who told me of the train that immediately preceded us. It was an exact duplicate of our train, though it contained no passengers. The idea was that the empty train should receive the disaster were an attempt made to blow up the Twentieth Century. For that matter there were very few people on the train—only a baker's dozen in our car.

This was reputed to be the fastest train in the world

then. It was quite a famous train.

"There must be some big men on board," Hartman concluded. "I noticed a private car on the rear."

Night had fallen when we made our first change of engine, and I walked down the platform for a breath of fresh air and to see what I could see. Through the windows of the private car I caught a glimpse of three men whom I recognized. Hartman was right. One of the men was General Altendorff; and the other two were Mason and Vanderbold, the brains of the inner circle of the Oligarchy's secret service.

It was a quiet moonlight night, but I tossed restlessly and could not sleep. At five in the morning I dressed and abandoned my bed.

I asked the maid in the dressing-room how late the train was, and she told me two hours. She was a mulatto woman, and I noticed that her face was haggard, with great circles under the eyes, while the eyes themselves were wide with some haunting fear.

"What is the matter?" I asked.

"Nothing, miss; I didn't sleep well, I guess," was her reply.

I looked at her closely, and tried her with one of our signals. She responded, and I made sure of her.

"Something terrible is going to happen in Chicago," she said. "There's that fake* train in front of us. That and the troop-trains have made us late."

False.

"Troop-trains?" I queried.

She nodded her head. "The line is thick with them. We've been passing them all night. And they're all heading for Chicago. And bringing them over the air-line—that means business.

"I've a lover in Chicago," she added apologetically. "He's one of us, and he's in the Mercenaries, and I'm afraid for him."

Poor girl. Her lover was in one of the three disloyal regiments.

Hartman and I had breakfast together in the dining car, and I forced myself to eat. The sky had clouded, and the train rushed on like a sullen thunderbolt through the gray pall of advancing day. The very negroes that waited on us knew that something terrible was impending. Oppression sat heavily upon them; the lightness of their natures had ebbed out of them; they were slack and absent-minded in their service, and they whispered gloomily to one another in the far end of the car next to the kitchen. Hartman was hopeless over the situation.

"What can we do?" he demanded for the twentieth time, with a helpless shrug of the shoulders.

He pointed out of the window. "See, all is ready. You can depend upon it that they're holding them like this, thirty or forty miles outside the city, on every road."

He had reference to troop-trains on the side-track. The soldiers were cooking their breakfasts over fires built on the ground beside the track, and they looked up curiously at us as we thundered past without slackening our terrific speed.

All was quiet as we entered Chicago. It was evident nothing had happened yet. In the suburbs the morning papers came on board the train. There was nothing in them, and yet there was much in them for those skilled in reading between the lines that it was intended the ordinary reader should read into the text. The fine hand of the Iron Heel was apparent in every column. Glimmerings of weakness in the armor of the Oligarchy were given. Of course, there was nothing definite. It was intended that the reader should feel his way to these glimmerings. It was cleverly done. As fiction, those morning papers of October 27th were masterpieces.

The local news was missing. This in itself was a masterstroke. It shrouded Chicago in mystery, and it suggested to the average Chicago reader that the Oligarchy did not dare give the local news. Hints that were untrue, of course, were given of insubordination all over the land, crudely disguised with complacent references to punitive measures to be taken. There were reports of numerous wireless stations that had been blown up, with heavy rewards offered for the detection of the perpetrators. Of course no wireless stations had been blown up. Many similar outrages, that dovetailed with the plot of the revolutionists, were given. The impression to be made on the minds of the Chicago comrades was that the general Revolt was beginning, albeit with a confusing miscarriage in many details. It was impossible for one uninformed to escape the vague yet certain feeling that all the land was ripe for the revolt that had already begun to break out.

It was reported that the defection of the Mercenaries in California had become so serious that half a dozen regiments had been disbanded and broken, and that their members with their families had been driven from their own city and on into the labor-ghettos. And the California Mercenaries were in reality the most faithful of all to their salt! But how was Chicago, shut off from the rest of the world, to know? Then there was a ragged telegram describing an outbreak of the populace in New York City, in which the labor castes were joining, concluding with the statement (intended to be accepted as a bluff*) that the troops had the situation in hand.

Jack London

A lie.

And as the oligarchs had done with the morning papers, so had they done in a thousand other ways. These we learned afterward, as, for example, the secret messages of the oligarchs, sent with the express purpose of leaking to the ears of the revolutionists, that had come over the wires, now and again, during the first part of the night.

"I guess the Iron Heel won't need our services," Hartman remarked, putting down the paper he had been reading, when the train pulled into the central depot. "They wasted their time sending us here. Their plans have evidently prospered better than they expected. Hell will break loose any second now."

He turned and looked down the train as we alighted.

"I thought so," he muttered. "They dropped that private car when the papers came aboard."

Hartman was hopelessly depressed. I tried to cheer him up, but he ignored my effort and suddenly began talking very hurriedly, in a low voice, as we passed through the station. At first I could not understand.

"I have not been sure," he was saying, "and I have told no one. I have been working on it for weeks, and I cannot make sure. Watch out for Knowlton. I suspect him. He knows the secrets of a score of our refuges. He carries the lives of hundreds of us in his hands, and I think he is a traitor. It's more a feeling on my part than anything else. But I thought I marked a change in him a short while back. There is the danger that he has sold us out, or is going to sell us out. I am almost sure of it. I wouldn't whisper my suspicions to a soul, but, somehow, I don't think I'll leave Chicago alive. Keep your eye on Knowlton. Trap him. Find out. I don't know anything more. It is only an intuition, and so far I have failed to find the slightest clew." We were just stepping out upon the sidewalk. "Remember," Hartman concluded earnestly. "Keep your eyes upon Knowlton."

And Hartman was right. Before a month went by Knowlton paid for his treason with his life. He was formally executed by the comrades in Milwaukee.

All was quiet on the streets—too quiet. Chicago lay dead. There was no roar and rumble of traffic. There were not even cabs on the streets. The surface cars and the elevated were not running. Only occasionally, on the sidewalks, were there stray pedestrians, and these pedestrians did not loiter. They went their ways with great haste and definiteness, withal there was a curious indecision in their movements, as though they expected the buildings to topple over on them or the sidewalks to sink under their feet or fly up in the air. A few gamins, however, were around, in their eyes a suppressed eagerness in anticipation of wonderful and exciting things to happen.

From somewhere, far to the south, the dull sound of an explosion came to our ears. That was all. Then quiet again, though the gamins had startled and listened, like young deer, at the sound. The doorways to all the buildings were closed; the shutters to the shops were up. But there were many police and watchmen in evidence, and now and again automobile patrols of the Mercenaries slipped swiftly past.

Hartman and I agreed that it was useless to report ourselves to the local chiefs of the secret service. Our failure so to report would be excused, we knew, in the light of subsequent events. So we headed for the great labor-ghetto on the South Side in the hope of getting in contact with some of the comrades. Too late! We knew it. But we could not stand still and do nothing in those ghastly, silent streets. Where was Ernest? I was wondering. What was happening in the cities of the labor castes and Mercenaries? In the fortresses?

As if in answer, a great screaming roar went up, dim with distance, punctuated with detonation after detonation.

"It's the fortresses," Hartman said. "God pity those three regiments!"

At a crossing we noticed, in the direction of the stockyards, a gigantic pillar of smoke. At the next crossing several similar smoke pillars were rising skyward in the direction of the West Side. Over the city of the Mercenaries we saw a great captive war-balloon that burst even as we looked at it, and fell in flaming wreckage toward the earth. There was no clew to that tragedy of the air. We could not determine whether the balloon had been manned by comrades or enemies. A vague sound came to our ears, like the bubbling of a gigantic caldron a long way off, and Hartman said it was machine-guns and automatic rifles.

And still we walked in immediate quietude. Nothing was happening where we were. The police and the automobile patrols went by, and once half a dozen fire-engines, returning evidently from some conflagration. A question was called to the fireman by an officer in an automobile, and we heard one shout in reply: "No water! They've blown up the mains!"

"We've smashed the water supply," Hartman cried excitedly to me. "If we can do all this in a premature, isolated, abortive attempt, what can't we do in a concerted, ripened effort all over the land?"

The automobile containing the officer who had asked the question darted on. Suddenly there was a deafening roar. The machine, with its human freight, lifted in an upburst of smoke, and sank down a mass of wreckage and death.

Hartman was jubilant. "Well done! well done!" he was repeating, over and over, in a whisper. "The proletariat gets its lesson to-day, but it gives one, too."

Police were running for the spot. Also, another patrol machine had halted. As for myself, I was in a daze. The suddenness of it was stunning. How had it happened? I knew not how, and yet I had been looking directly at it. So dazed was I for the moment that I was scarcely aware of the fact that we were being held up by the police. I abruptly saw that a policeman was in the act of shooting Hartman. But Hartman was cool and was giving the proper passwords. I saw the levelled revolver hesitate, then sink down, and heard the disgusted grunt of the policeman. He was very angry, and was cursing the whole secret service. It was always in the way, he was averring, while Hartman was talking back to him and with fitting secret-service pride explaining to him the clumsiness of the police.

The next moment I knew how it had happened. There was quite a group about the wreck, and two men were just lifting up the wounded officer to carry him to the other machine. A panic seized all of them, and they scattered in every direction, running in blind terror, the wounded officer, roughly dropped, being left behind. The cursing policeman alongside of me also ran, and Hartman and I ran, too, we knew not why, obsessed with the same blind terror to get away from that particular spot.

Nothing really happened then, but everything was explained. The flying men were sheepishly coming back, but all the while their eyes were raised apprehensively to the many-windowed, lofty buildings that towered like the sheer walls of a canyon on each side of the street. From one of those countless windows the bomb had been thrown, but which window? There had been no second bomb, only a fear of one.

Thereafter we looked with speculative comprehension at the windows. Any of them contained possible death. Each building was a possible ambuscade. This was warfare in that modern jungle, a great city. Every street was a canyon, every building a mountain. We had not changed much from primitive man, despite the war automobiles that were sliding by.

Turning a corner, we came upon a woman. She was lying on the pavement, in a pool of blood. Hartman bent over and examined her. As for myself, I turned deathly sick. I was to see many dead that day, but the total carnage was not to affect me as did this first forlorn body lying there at my feet abandoned on the pavement. "Shot in the breast," was Hartman's report. Clasped in the hollow of her arm, as a child might be clasped, was a bundle of printed matter. Even in death she seemed loath to part with that which had caused her death; for when Hartman had succeeded in withdrawing the bundle, we found that it consisted of large printed sheets, the proclamations of the revolutionists.

"A comrade," I said.

But Hartman only cursed the Iron Heel, and we passed on. Often we were halted by the police and patrols, but our passwords enabled us to proceed. No more bombs fell from the windows, the last pedestrians seemed to have vanished from the streets, and our immediate quietude grew more profound; though the gigantic caldron continued to bubble in the distance, dull roars of explosions came to us from all directions, and the smoke-pillars were towering more ominously in the heavens.

CHAPTER XXIII. THE PEOPLE OF THE ABYSS

Suddenly a change came over the face of things. A tingle of excitement ran along the air. Automobiles fled past, two, three, a dozen, and from them warnings were shouted to us. One of the machines swerved wildly at high speed half a block down, and the next moment, already left well behind it, the pavement was torn into a great hole by a bursting bomb. We saw the police disappearing down the cross-streets on the run, and knew that something terrible was coming. We could hear the rising roar of it.

"Our brave comrades are coming," Hartman said.

We could see the front of their column filling the street from gutter to gutter, as the last war-automobile fled past. The machine stopped for a moment just abreast of us. A soldier leaped from it, carrying something carefully in his hands. This, with the same care, he deposited in the gutter. Then he leaped back to his seat and the machine dashed on, took the turn at the corner, and was gone from sight. Hartman ran to the gutter and stooped over the object.

"Keep back," he warned me.

I could see he was working rapidly with his hands. When he returned to me the sweat was heavy on his forehead.

"I disconnected it," he said, "and just in the nick of time. The soldier was clumsy. He intended it for our comrades, but he didn't give it enough time. It would have exploded prematurely. Now it won't explode at all."

Everything was happening rapidly now. Across the street and half a block down, high up in a building, I could see heads peering out. I had just pointed them out to Hartman, when a sheet of flame and smoke ran along that portion of the face of the building where the heads had appeared, and the air was shaken by the explosion. In places the stone facing of the building was torn away, exposing the iron construction beneath. The next moment similar sheets of flame and smoke smote the front of the building across the street opposite it. Between the explosions we could hear the rattle of the automatic pistols and rifles. For several minutes this mid-air battle continued, then died out. It was patent that our comrades were in one building, that Mercenaries were in the other, and that they were fighting across the street. But we could not tell which was which—which building contained our comrades and which the Mercenaries.

By this time the column on the street was almost on us. As the front of it passed under the warring buildings, both went into action again—one building dropping bombs into the street, being attacked from across the street, and in return replying to that attack. Thus we learned which building was held by our comrades, and they did good work, saving those in the street from the bombs of the enemy.

Hartman gripped my arm and dragged me into a wide entrance.

"They're not our comrades," he shouted in my ear.

The inner doors to the entrance were locked and bolted. We could not escape. The next moment the front of the column went by. It was not a column, but a mob, an awful river that filled the street, the people of the abyss, mad with drink and wrong, up at last and roaring for the blood of their masters. I had seen the people of the abyss before, gone through its ghettos, and thought I knew it; but I found that I was now looking on it for the first time. Dumb apathy had vanished. It was now dynamic—a fascinating spectacle of dread. It surged past my vision in concrete waves of wrath, snarling and growling, carnivorous, drunk with whiskey from pillaged warehouses, drunk with hatred, drunk with lust for blood—men, women, and children, in rags and tatters, dim ferocious intelligences with all the godlike blotted from their features and all the fiendlike stamped in, apes and tigers, anaemic consumptives and great hairy beasts of burden, wan faces from which vampire society had sucked the juice of life, bloated forms swollen with physical grossness and corruption, withered hags and death's-heads bearded like patriarchs, festering youth and festering age, faces of fiends, crooked, twisted, misshapen monsters blasted with the ravages of disease and all the horrors of chronic innutrition—the refuse and the scum of life, a raging, screaming, screeching, demoniacal horde.

And why not? The people of the abyss had nothing to lose but the misery and pain of living. And to gain?—nothing, save one final, awful glut of vengeance. And as I looked the thought came to me that in that rushing stream of human lava were men, comrades and heroes, whose mission had been to rouse the abysmal beast and to keep the enemy occupied in coping with it.

And now a strange thing happened to me. A transformation came over me. The fear of death, for myself and for others, left me. I was strangely exalted, another being in another life. Nothing mattered. The Cause for this one time was lost, but the Cause would be here to-morrow, the same Cause, ever fresh and ever burning. And thereafter, in the orgy of horror that raged through the succeeding hours, I was able to take a calm interest. Death meant nothing, life meant nothing. I was an interested spectator of events, and, sometimes swept on by the rush, was myself a curious participant. For my mind had leaped to a star-cool altitude and grasped a passionless transvaluation of values. Had it not done this, I know that I should have died.

Half a mile of the mob had swept by when we were discovered. A woman in fantastic rags, with cheeks cavernously hollow and with narrow black eyes like burning gimlets, caught a glimpse of Hartman and me. She let out a shrill shriek and bore in upon us. A section of the mob tore itself loose and surged in after her. I can see her now, as I write these lines, a leap in advance, her gray hair flying in thin tangled strings, the blood dripping down her forehead from some wound in the scalp, in her right hand a hatchet, her left hand, lean and wrinkled, a yellow talon, gripping the air convulsively. Hartman sprang in front of me. This was no time for explanations. We were well dressed, and that was enough. His fist shot out, striking the woman between her burning eyes. The impact of the blow drove her backward, but she struck the wall of her on-coming fellows and bounced forward again, dazed and helpless, the brandished hatchet falling feebly on Hartman's shoulder.

The next moment I knew not what was happening. I was overborne by the crowd. The confined space was filled with shrieks and yells and curses. Blows were falling on me. Hands were ripping and tearing at my flesh and garments. I felt that I was being torn to pieces. I was being borne down, suffocated. Some strong hand gripped my shoulder in the thick of the press and was dragging fiercely at me. Between pain and pressure I fainted. Hartman never came out of that entrance. He had shielded me and received the first brunt of the attack. This had saved me, for the jam had quickly become too dense for anything more than the mad gripping and tearing of hands.

I came to in the midst of wild movement. All about me was the same movement. I had been caught up in a monstrous flood that was sweeping me I knew not whither. Fresh air was on my cheek and biting sweetly in my lungs. Faint and dizzy, I was vaguely aware of a strong arm around my body under the arms, and half-lifting me and dragging me along. Feebly my own limbs were helping me. In front of me I could see the moving back of a man's coat. It had been slit from top to bottom along the centre seam, and it pulsed rhythmically, the slit opening and closing regularly with every leap of the wearer. This phenomenon fascinated me for a time, while my senses were coming back to me. Next I became aware of stinging cheeks and nose, and could feel blood dripping on my face. My hat was gone. My hair was down and flying, and from the stinging of the scalp I managed to recollect a hand in the press of the entrance that had torn at my hair. My chest and arms were bruised and aching in a score of places.

My brain grew clearer, and I turned as I ran and looked at the man who was holding me up. He it was who had dragged me out and saved me. He noticed my movement.

"It's all right!" he shouted hoarsely. "I knew you on the instant."

I failed to recognize him, but before I could speak I trod upon something that was alive and that squirmed under my foot. I was swept on by those behind and could not look down and see, and yet I knew that it was a woman who had fallen and who was being trampled into the pavement by thousands of successive feet.

"It's all right," he repeated. "I'm Garthwaite."

He was bearded and gaunt and dirty, but I succeeded in remembering him as the stalwart youth that had spent several months in our Glen Ellen refuge three years before. He passed me the signals of the Iron Heel's secret service, in token that he, too, was in its employ.

"I'll get you out of this as soon as I can get a chance," he assured me. "But watch your footing. On your life don't stumble and go down."

All things happened abruptly on that day, and with an abruptness that was sickening the mob checked itself. I came in violent collision with a large woman in front of me (the man with the split coat had vanished), while those behind collided against me. A devilish pandemonium reigned,—shrieks, curses, and cries of death, while above all rose the churning rattle of machine-guns and the put-a-put, put-a-put of rifles. At first I could make out nothing. People were falling about me right and left. The woman in front doubled up and went down, her hands on her abdomen in a frenzied clutch. A man was quivering against my legs in a death-struggle.

It came to me that we were at the head of the column. Half a mile of it had disappeared—where or how I never learned. To this day I do not know what became of that half-mile of humanity—whether it was blotted out by some frightful bolt of war, whether it was scattered and destroyed piecemeal, or whether it escaped. But there we were, at the head of the column instead of in its middle, and we were being swept out of life by a torrent of shrieking lead.

As soon as death had thinned the jam, Garthwaite, still grasping my arm, led a rush of survivors into the wide entrance of an office building. Here, at the rear, against the doors, we were pressed by a panting, gasping mass of creatures. For some time we remained in this position without a change in the situation.

"I did it beautifully," Garthwaite was lamenting to me. "Ran you right into a trap. We had a gambler's chance in the street, but in here there is no chance at all. It's all over but the shouting. Vive la Revolution!"

Then, what he expected, began. The Mercenaries were killing without quarter. At first, the surge back upon us was crushing, but as the killing continued the pressure was eased. The dead and dying went down and made room. Garthwaite put his mouth to my ear and shouted, but in the frightful din I could not catch what he said. He did not wait. He seized me and threw me down. Next he dragged a dying woman over on top of me, and, with much squeezing and shoving, crawled in beside me and partly over me. A mound of dead and dying began to pile up over us, and over this mound, pawing and moaning, crept those that still survived. But these, too, soon ceased, and a semi-silence settled down, broken by groans and sobs and sounds of strangulation.

I should have been crushed had it not been for Garthwaite. As it was, it seemed inconceivable that I could bear the weight I did and live. And yet, outside of pain, the only feeling I possessed was one of curiosity. How was it going to end? What would death be like? Thus did I receive my red baptism in that Chicago shambles. Prior to that, death to me had been a theory; but ever afterward death has been a simple fact that does not matter, it is so easy.

But the Mercenaries were not content with what they had done. They invaded the entrance, killing the wounded and searching out the unhurt that, like ourselves, were playing dead. I remember one man they dragged out of a heap, who pleaded abjectly until a revolver shot cut him short. Then there was a woman who charged from a heap, snarling and shooting. She fired six shots before they got her, though what damage she did we could not know. We could follow these tragedies only by the sound. Every little while flurries like this occurred, each flurry culminating in the revolver shot that put an end to it. In the intervals we could hear the soldiers talking and swearing as they rummaged among the carcasses, urged on by their officers to hurry up.

At last they went to work on our heap, and we could feel the pressure diminish as they dragged away the dead and wounded. Garthwaite began uttering aloud the signals. At first he was not heard. Then he raised his voice.

"Listen to that," we heard a soldier say. And next the sharp voice of an officer. "Hold on there! Careful as you go!"

Oh, that first breath of air as we were dragged out! Garthwaite did the talking at first, but I was compelled to undergo a brief examination to prove service with the Iron Heel.

"Agents-provocateurs all right," was the officer's conclusion. He was a beardless young fellow, a cadet, evidently, of some great oligarch family.

"It's a hell of a job," Garthwaite grumbled. "I'm going to try and resign and get into the army. You fellows have a snap."

"You've earned it," was the young officer's answer. "I've got some pull, and I'll see if it can be managed. I can tell them how I found you."

He took Garthwaite's name and number, then turned to me.

"And you?"

"Oh, I'm going to be married," I answered lightly, "and then I'll be out of it all."

And so we talked, while the killing of the wounded went on. It is all a dream, now, as I look back on it; but at the time it was the most natural thing in the world. Garthwaite and the young officer fell into an animated conversation over the difference between so-called modern warfare and the present street-fighting and sky-scraper fighting that was taking place all over the city. I followed them intently, fixing up my hair at the same time and pinning together my torn skirts. And all the time the killing of the wounded went on. Sometimes the revolver shots drowned the voices of Garthwaite and the officer, and they were compelled to repeat what they had been saying.

I lived through three days of the Chicago Commune, and the vastness of it and of the slaughter may be imagined when I say that in all that time I saw practically nothing outside the killing of the people of the abyss and the mid-air fighting between sky-scrapers. I really saw nothing of the heroic work done by the comrades. I could hear the explosions of their mines and bombs, and see the smoke of their conflagrations, and that was all. The mid-air part of one great deed I saw, however, and that was the balloon attacks made by our comrades on the fortresses. That was on the second day. The three disloyal regiments had been destroyed in the fortresses to the last man. The fortresses were crowded with Mercenaries, the wind blew in the right direction, and up went our balloons from one of the office buildings in the city.

Now Biedenbach, after he left Glen Ellen, had invented a most powerful explosive—"expedite" he called it. This was the weapon the balloons used. They were only hot-air balloons, clumsily and hastily made, but they did the work. I saw it all from the top of an office building. The first balloon missed the fortresses completely and disappeared into the country; but we learned about it afterward. Burton and O'Sullivan were in it. As they were descending they swept across a railroad directly over a troop-train that was heading at full speed for Chicago. They dropped their whole supply of expedite upon the locomotive. The resulting wreck tied the line up for days. And the best of it was that, released from the weight of expedite, the balloon shot up into the air and did not come down for half a dozen miles, both heroes escaping unharmed.

The second balloon was a failure. Its flight was lame. It floated too low and was shot full of holes before it could reach the fortresses. Herford and Guinness were in it, and they were blown to pieces along with the field into which they fell. Biedenbach was in despair—we heard all about it afterward—and he went up alone in the third balloon. He, too, made a low flight, but he was in luck, for they failed seriously to puncture his balloon. I can see it now as I did then, from the lofty top of the building—that inflated bag drifting along the air, and that tiny speck of a man clinging on beneath. I could not see the fortress, but those on the roof with me said he was directly over it. I did not see the expedite fall when he cut it loose. But I did see the balloon suddenly leap up into the sky. An appreciable time after that the great column of the explosion towered in the air, and after that, in turn, I heard the roar of it. Biedenbach the gentle had destroyed a fortress. Two other balloons followed at the same time. One was blown to pieces in the air, the expedite exploding, and the shock of it disrupted the second balloon, which fell prettily into the remaining fortress. It couldn't have been better planned, though the two comrades in it sacrificed their lives.

But to return to the people of the abyss. My experiences were confined to them. They raged and slaughtered and destroyed all over the city proper, and were in turn destroyed; but never once did they succeed in reaching the city of the oligarchs over on the west side. The oligarchs had protected themselves well. No matter what destruction was wreaked in the heart of the city, they, and their womenkind and children, were to escape hurt. I am told that their children played in the parks during those terrible days and that their favorite game was an imitation of their elders stamping upon the proletariat.

But the Mercenaries found it no easy task to cope with the people of the abyss and at the same time fight with the comrades. Chicago was true to her traditions, and though a generation of revolutionists was wiped out, it took along with it pretty close to a generation of its enemies. Of course, the Iron Heel kept the figures secret, but, at a very conservative estimate, at least one hundred and thirty thousand Mercenaries were slain. But the comrades had no chance. Instead of the whole country being hand in hand in revolt, they were all alone, and the total strength of the Oligarchy could have been directed against them if necessary. As it was, hour after hour, day after day, in endless train-loads, by hundreds of thousands, the Mercenaries were hurled into Chicago.

And there were so many of the people of the abyss! Tiring of the slaughter, a great herding movement was begun by the soldiers, the intent of which was to drive the street mobs, like cattle, into Lake Michigan. It was at the beginning of this movement that Garthwaite and I had encountered the young officer. This herding movement was practically a failure, thanks to the splendid work of the comrades. Instead of the great host the Mercenaries had hoped to gather together, they succeeded in driving no more than forty thousand of the wretches into the lake. Time and again, when a mob of them was well in hand and being driven along the streets to the water, the comrades would create a diversion, and the mob would escape through the consequent hole torn in the encircling net.

Garthwaite and I saw an example of this shortly after meeting with the young officer. The mob of which we had been a part, and which had been put in retreat, was prevented from escaping to the south and east by strong bodies of troops. The troops we had fallen in with had held it back on the west. The only outlet was north, and north it went toward the lake, driven on from east and west and south by machine-gun fire and automatics. Whether it divined that it was being driven toward the lake, or whether it was merely a blind squirm of the monster, I do not know; but at any rate the mob took a cross street to the west, turned down the next street, and came back upon its track, heading south toward the great ghetto.

Garthwaite and I at that time were trying to make our way westward to get out of the territory of street-fighting, and we were caught right in the thick of it again. As we came to the corner we saw the howling mob bearing down upon us. Garthwaite seized my arm and we were just starting to run, when he dragged me back from in front of the wheels of half a dozen war automobiles, equipped with machine-guns, that were rushing for the spot. Behind them came the soldiers with their automatic rifles. By the time they took position, the mob was upon them, and it looked as though they would be overwhelmed before they could get into action.

Here and there a soldier was discharging his rifle, but this scattered fire had no effect in checking the mob. On it came, bellowing with brute rage. It seemed the machine-guns could not get started. The automobiles on which they were mounted blocked the street, compelling the soldiers to find positions in, between, and on the sidewalks. More and more soldiers were arriving, and in the jam we were unable to get away. Garthwaite held me by the arm, and we pressed close against the front of a building.

The mob was no more than twenty-five feet away when the machine-guns opened up; but before that flaming sheet of death nothing could live. The mob came on, but it could not advance. It piled up in a heap, a mound, a huge and growing wave of dead and dying. Those behind urged on, and the column, from gutter to gutter, telescoped upon itself. Wounded creatures, men and women, were vomited over the top of that awful wave and fell squirming down the face of it till they threshed about under the automobiles and against the legs of the soldiers. The latter bayoneted the struggling wretches, though one I saw who gained his feet and flew at a soldier's throat with his teeth. Together they went down, soldier and slave, into the welter.

The firing ceased. The work was done. The mob had been stopped in its wild attempt to break through. Orders were being given to clear the wheels of the war-machines. They could not advance over that wave of dead, and the idea was to run them down the cross street. The soldiers were dragging the bodies away from the wheels when it happened. We learned afterward how it happened. A block distant a hundred of our comrades had been holding a building. Across roofs and through buildings they made their way, till they found themselves looking down upon the close-packed soldiers. Then it was counter-massacre.

Without warning, a shower of bombs fell from the top of the building. The automobiles were blown to fragments, along with many soldiers. We, with the survivors, swept back in mad retreat. Half a block down another building opened fire on us. As the soldiers had carpeted the street with dead slaves, so, in turn, did they themselves become carpet. Garthwaite and I bore charmed lives. As we had done before, so again we sought shelter in an entrance. But he was not to be caught napping this time. As the roar of the bombs died away, he began peering out.

"The mob's coming back!" he called to me. "We've got to get out of this!"

We fled, hand in hand, down the bloody pavement, slipping and sliding, and making for the corner. Down the cross street we could see a few soldiers still running. Nothing was happening to them. The way was clear. So we paused a moment and looked back. The mob came on slowly. It was busy arming itself with the rifles of the slain and killing the wounded. We saw the end of the young officer who had rescued us. He painfully lifted himself on his elbow and turned loose with his automatic pistol.

"There goes my chance of promotion," Garthwaite laughed, as a woman bore down on the wounded man, brandishing a butcher's cleaver. "Come on. It's the wrong direction, but we'll get out somehow."

And we fled eastward through the quiet streets, prepared at every cross street for anything to happen. To the south a monster conflagration was filling the sky, and we knew that the great ghetto was burning. At last I sank down on the sidewalk. I was exhausted and could go no farther. I was bruised and sore and aching in every limb; yet I could not escape smiling at Garthwaite, who was rolling a cigarette and saying:

"I know I'm making a mess of rescuing you, but I can't get head nor tail of the situation. It's all a mess. Every time we try to break out, something happens and we're turned back. We're only a couple of blocks now from where I got you out of that entrance. Friend and foe are all mixed up. It's chaos. You can't tell who is in those darned buildings. Try to find out, and you get a bomb on your head. Try to go peaceably on your way, and you run into a mob and are killed by machine-guns, or you run into the Mercenaries and are killed by your own comrades from a roof. And on the top of it all the mob comes along and kills you, too."

He shook his head dolefully, lighted his cigarette, and sat down beside me.

"And I'm that hungry," he added, "I could eat cobblestones."

The next moment he was on his feet again and out in the street prying up a cobblestone. He came back with it and assaulted the window of a store behind us.

"It's ground floor and no good," he explained as he helped me through the hole he had made; "but it's the best we can do. You get a nap and I'll reconnoitre. I'll finish this rescue all right, but I want time, time, lots of it— and something to eat."

It was a harness store we found ourselves in, and he fixed me up a couch of horse blankets in the private office well to the rear. To add to my wretchedness a splitting headache was coming on, and I was only too glad to close my eyes and try to sleep.

"I'll be back," were his parting words. "I don't hope to get an auto, but I'll surely bring some grub,* anyway."

* *Food.*

And that was the last I saw of Garthwaite for three years. Instead of coming back, he was carried away to a hospital with a bullet through his lungs and another through the fleshy part of his neck.

CHAPTER XXIV. NIGHTMARE

I had not closed my eyes the night before on the Twentieth Century, and what of that and of my exhaustion I slept soundly. When I first awoke, it was night. Garthwaite had not returned. I had lost my watch and had no idea of the time. As I lay with my eyes closed, I heard the same dull sound of distant explosions. The inferno was still raging. I crept through the store to the front. The reflection from the sky of vast conflagrations made the street almost as light as day. One could have read the finest print with ease. From several blocks away came the crackle of small hand-bombs and the churning of machine-guns, and from a long way off came a long series of heavy explosions. I crept back to my horse blankets and slept again.

When next I awoke, a sickly yellow light was filtering in on me. It was dawn of the second day. I crept to the front of the store. A smoke pall, shot through with lurid gleams, filled the sky. Down the opposite side of the street tottered a wretched slave. One hand he held tightly against his side, and behind him he left a bloody trail. His eyes roved everywhere, and they were filled with apprehension and dread. Once he looked straight across at me, and in his face was all the dumb pathos of the wounded and hunted animal. He saw me, but there was no kinship between us, and with him, at least, no sympathy of understanding; for he cowered perceptibly and dragged himself on. He could expect no aid in all God's world. He was a helot in the great hunt of helots that the masters were making. All he could hope for, all he sought, was some hole to crawl away in and hide like any animal. The sharp clang of a passing ambulance at the corner gave him a start. Ambulances were not for such as he. With a groan of pain he threw himself into a doorway. A minute later he was out again and desperately hobbling on.

I went back to my horse blankets and waited an hour for Garthwaite. My headache had not gone away. On the contrary, it was increasing. It was by an effort of will only that I was able to open my eyes and look at objects. And with the opening of my eyes and the looking came intolerable torment. Also, a great pulse was beating in my brain. Weak and reeling, I went out through the broken window and down the street, seeking to escape, instinctively and gropingly, from the awful shambles. And thereafter I lived nightmare. My memory of what happened in the succeeding hours is the memory one would have of nightmare. Many events are focussed sharply on my brain, but between these indelible pictures I retain are intervals of unconsciousness. What occurred in those intervals I know not, and never shall know.

I remember stumbling at the corner over the legs of a man. It was the poor hunted wretch that had dragged himself past my hiding-place. How distinctly do I remember his poor, pitiful, gnarled hands as he lay there on the pavement—hands that were more hoof and claw than hands, all twisted and distorted by the toil of all his days, with on the palms a horny growth of callous a half inch thick. And as I picked myself up and started on, I looked into the face of the thing and saw that it still lived; for the eyes, dimly intelligent, were looking at me and seeing me.

After that came a kindly blank. I knew nothing, saw nothing, merely tottered on in my quest for safety. My next nightmare vision was a quiet street of the dead. I came upon it abruptly, as a wanderer in the country would come upon a flowing stream. Only this stream I gazed upon did not flow. It was congealed in death. From pavement to pavement, and covering the sidewalks, it lay there, spread out quite evenly, with only here and there a lump or mound of bodies to break the surface. Poor driven people of the abyss, hunted helots—they lay there as the rabbits in California after a drive.* Up the street and down I looked. There was no movement, no sound. The quiet buildings looked down upon the scene from their many windows. And once, and once only, I saw an arm that moved in that dead stream. I swear I saw it move, with a strange writhing gesture of agony, and with it lifted a head, gory with nameless horror, that gibbered at me and then lay down again and moved no more.

* In those days, so sparsely populated was the land that

wild animals often became pests. In California the custom

of rabbit-driving obtained. On a given day all the farmers

in a locality would assemble and sweep across the country in

converging lines, driving the rabbits by scores of thousands

into a prepared enclosure, where they were clubbed to death

by men and boys.

I remember another street, with quiet buildings on either side, and the panic that smote me into consciousness as again I saw the people of the abyss, but this time in a stream that flowed and came on. And then I saw there was nothing to fear. The stream moved slowly, while from it arose groans and lamentations, cursings, babblings of senility, hysteria, and insanity; for these were the very young and the very old, the feeble and the sick, the helpless and the hopeless, all the wreckage of the ghetto. The burning of the great ghetto on the South Side had driven them forth into the inferno of the street-fighting, and whither they wended and whatever became of them I did not know and never learned.*

* It was long a question of debate, whether the burning of

the South Side ghetto was accidental, or whether it was done

by the Mercenaries; but it is definitely settled now that

the ghetto was fired by the Mercenaries under orders from

their chiefs.

I have faint memories of breaking a window and hiding in some shop to escape a street mob that was pursued by soldiers. Also, a bomb burst near me, once, in some still street, where, look as I would, up and down, I could see no human being. But my next sharp recollection begins with the crack of a rifle and an abrupt becoming aware that I am being fired at by a soldier in an automobile. The shot missed, and the next moment I was screaming and motioning the signals. My memory of riding in the automobile is very hazy, though this ride, in turn, is broken by one vivid picture. The crack of the rifle of the soldier sitting beside me made me open my eyes, and I saw George Milford, whom I had known in the Pell Street days, sinking slowly down to the sidewalk. Even as he sank the soldier fired again, and Milford doubled in, then flung his body out, and fell sprawling. The soldier chuckled, and the automobile sped on.

The next I knew after that I was awakened out of a sound sleep by a man who walked up and down close beside me. His face was drawn and strained, and the sweat rolled down his nose from his forehead. One hand was clutched tightly against his chest by the other hand, and blood dripped down upon the floor as he walked. He wore the uniform of the Mercenaries. From without, as through thick walls, came the muffled roar of bursting bombs. I was in some building that was locked in combat with some other building.

A surgeon came in to dress the wounded soldier, and I learned that it was two in the afternoon. My headache was no better, and the surgeon paused from his work long enough to give me a powerful drug that would depress the heart and bring relief. I slept again, and the next I knew I was on top of the building. The immediate fighting had ceased, and I was watching the balloon attack on the fortresses. Some one had an arm around me and I was leaning close against him. It came to me quite as a matter of course that this was Ernest, and I found myself wondering how he had got his hair and eyebrows so badly singed.

It was by the merest chance that we had found each other in that terrible city. He had had no idea that I had left New York, and, coming through the room where I lay asleep, could not at first believe that it was I. Little more I saw of the Chicago Commune. After watching the balloon attack, Ernest took me down into the heart of the building, where I slept the afternoon out and the night. The third day we spent in the building, and on the fourth, Ernest having got permission and an automobile from the authorities, we left Chicago.

My headache was gone, but, body and soul, I was very tired. I lay back against Ernest in the automobile, and with apathetic eyes watched the soldiers trying to get the machine out of the city. Fighting was still going on, but only in isolated localities. Here and there whole districts were still in possession of the comrades, but such districts were surrounded and guarded by heavy bodies of troops. In a hundred segregated traps were the comrades thus held while the work of subjugating them went on. Subjugation meant death, for no quarter was given, and they fought heroically to the last man.*

*Numbers of the buildings held out over a week, while one held out eleven days. Each building had to be stormed like a fort, and the Mercenaries fought their way upward floor by floor. It was deadly fighting. Quarter was neither given nor taken, and in the fighting the revolutionists had the advantage of being above. While the revolutionists were wiped out, the loss was not one-sided. The proud Chicago proletariat lived up to its ancient boast. For as many of itself as were killed, it killed that many of the enemy.

Whenever we approached such localities, the guards turned us back and sent us around. Once, the only way past two strong positions of the comrades was through a burnt section that lay between. From either side we could hear the rattle and roar of war, while the automobile picked its way through smoking ruins and tottering walls. Often the streets were blocked by mountains of debris that compelled us to go around. We were in a labyrinth of ruin, and our progress was slow.

The stockyards (ghetto, plant, and everything) were smouldering ruins. Far off to the right a wide smoke haze dimmed the sky,—the town of Pullman, the soldier chauffeur told us, or what had been the town of Pullman, for it was utterly destroyed. He had driven the machine out there, with despatches, on the afternoon of the third day. Some of the heaviest fighting had occurred there, he said, many of the streets being rendered impassable by the heaps of the dead.

Swinging around the shattered walls of a building, in the stockyards district, the automobile was stopped by a wave of dead. It was for all the world like a wave tossed up by the sea. It was patent to us what had happened. As the mob charged past the corner, it had been swept, at right angles and point-blank range, by the machine-guns drawn up on the cross street. But disaster had come to the soldiers. A chance bomb must have exploded among them, for the mob, checked until its dead and dying formed the wave, had white-capped and flung forward its foam of living, fighting slaves. Soldiers and slaves lay together, torn and mangled, around and over the wreckage of the automobiles and guns.

Ernest sprang out. A familiar pair of shoulders in a cotton shirt and a familiar fringe of white hair had caught his eye. I did not watch him, and it was not until he was back beside me and we were speeding on that he said:

"It was Bishop Morehouse."

Soon we were in the green country, and I took one last glance back at the smoke-filled sky. Faint and far came the low thud of an explosion. Then I turned my face against Ernest's breast and wept softly for the Cause that was lost. Ernest's arm about me was eloquent with love.

"For this time lost, dear heart," he said, "but not forever. We have learned. To-morrow the Cause will rise again, strong with wisdom and discipline."

The automobile drew up at a railroad station. Here we would catch a train to New York. As we waited on the platform, three trains thundered past, bound west to Chicago. They were crowded with ragged, unskilled laborers, people of the abyss.

"Slave-levies for the rebuilding of Chicago," Ernest said. "You see, the Chicago slaves are all killed."

CHAPTER XXV. THE TERRORISTS

It was not until Ernest and I were back in New York, and after weeks had elapsed, that we were able to comprehend thoroughly the full sweep of the disaster that had befallen the Cause. The situation was bitter and bloody. In many places, scattered over the country, slave revolts and massacres had occurred. The roll of the martyrs increased mightily. Countless executions took place everywhere. The mountains and waste regions were filled with outlaws and refugees who were being hunted down mercilessly. Our own refuges were packed with comrades who had prices on their heads. Through information furnished by its spies, scores of our refuges were raided by the soldiers of the Iron Heel.

Many of the comrades were disheartened, and they retaliated with terroristic tactics. The set-back to their hopes made them despairing and desperate. Many terrorist organizations unaffiliated with us sprang into existence and caused us much trouble.* These misguided people sacrificed their own lives wantonly, very often made our own plans go astray, and retarded our organization.

* *The annals of this short-lived era of despair make bloody reading. Revenge was the ruling motive, and the members of the terroristic organizations were careless of their own lives and hopeless about the future. The Danites, taking their name from the avenging angels of the Mormon mythology, sprang up in the mountains of the Great West and spread over the Pacific Coast from Panama to Alaska. The Valkyries were women. They were the most terrible of all. No woman was*

eligible for membership who had not lost near relatives at the hands of the Oligarchy. They were guilty of torturing their prisoners to death. Another famous organization of women was The Widows of War. A companion organization to the Valkyries was the Berserkers. These men placed no value whatever upon their own lives, and it was they who totally destroyed the great Mercenary city of Bellona along with its population of over a hundred thousand souls. The Bedlamites and the Helldamites were twin slave organizations, while a new religious sect that did not flourish long was called The Wrath of God. Among others, to show the whimsicality of their deadly seriousness, may be mentioned the following: The Bleeding Hearts, Sons of the Morning, the Morning Stars, The Flamingoes, The Triple Triangles, The Three Bars, The Rubonics, The Vindicators, The Comanches, and the Erebusites.

And through it all moved the Iron Heel, impassive and deliberate, shaking up the whole fabric of the social structure in its search for the comrades, combing out the Mercenaries, the labor castes, and all its secret services, punishing without mercy and without malice, suffering in silence all retaliations that were made upon it, and filling the gaps in its fighting line as fast as they appeared. And hand in hand with this, Ernest and the other leaders were hard at work reorganizing the forces of the Revolution. The magnitude of the task may be understood when it is taken into.*

* This is the end of the Everhard Manuscript. It breaks off abruptly in the middle of a sentence. She must have received warning of the coming of the Mercenaries, for she had time safely to hide the Manuscript before she fled or was captured. It is to be regretted that she did not live to complete her narrative, for then, undoubtedly, would have been cleared away the mystery that has shrouded for seven centuries the execution of Ernest Everhard.

SOUTH SEA TALES

THE HOUSE OF MAPUHI

Despite the heavy clumsiness of her lines, the Aorai handled easily in the light breeze, and her captain ran her well in before he hove to just outside the suck of the surf. The atoll of Hikueru lay low on the water, a circle of pounded coral sand a hundred yards wide, twenty miles in circumference, and from three to five feet above high-water mark. On the bottom of the huge and glassy lagoon was much pearl shell, and from the deck of the schooner, across the slender ring of the atoll, the divers could be seen at work. But the lagoon had no entrance for even a trading schooner. With a favoring breeze cutters could win in through the tortuous and shallow channel, but the schooners lay off and on outside and sent in their small boats.

The Aorai swung out a boat smartly, into which sprang half a dozen brown-skinned sailors clad only in scarlet loincloths. They took the oars, while in the stern sheets, at the steering sweep, stood a young man garbed in the tropic white that marks the European. The golden strain of Polynesia betrayed itself in the sun-gilt of his fair skin and cast up golden sheens and lights through the glimmering blue of his eyes. Raoul he was, Alexandre Raoul, youngest son of Marie Raoul, the wealthy quarter-caste, who owned and managed half a dozen trading schooners similar to the Aorai. Across an eddy just outside the entrance, and in and through and over a boiling tide-rip, the boat fought its way to the mirrored calm of the lagoon. Young Raoul leaped out upon the white sand and shook hands with a tall native. The man's chest and shoulders were magnificent, but the stump of a right arm, beyond the flesh of which the age-whitened bone projected several inches, attested the encounter with a shark that had put an end to his diving days and made him a fawner and an intriguer for small favors.

"Have you heard, Alec?" were his first words. "Mapuhi has found a pearl—such a pearl. Never was there one like it ever fished up in Hikueru, nor in all the Paumotus, nor in all the world. Buy it from him. He has it now. And remember that I told you first. He is a fool and you can get it cheap. Have you any tobacco?"

Straight up the beach to a shack under a pandanus tree Raoul headed. He was his mother's supercargo, and his business was to comb all the Paumotus for the wealth of copra, shell, and pearls that they yielded up.

He was a young supercargo, it was his second voyage in such capacity, and he suffered much secret worry from his lack of experience in pricing pearls. But when Mapuhi exposed the pearl to his sight he managed to suppress the startle it gave him, and to maintain a careless, commercial expression on his face. For the pearl had struck him a blow. It was large as a pigeon egg, a perfect sphere, of a whiteness that reflected opalescent lights from all colors about it. It was alive. Never had he seen anything like it. When Mapuhi dropped it into his hand he was surprised by the weight of it. That showed that it was a good pearl. He examined it closely, through a pocket magnifying glass. It was without flaw or blemish. The purity of it seemed almost to melt into the atmosphere out of his hand. In the shade it was softly luminous, gleaming like a tender moon. So translucently white was it, that when he dropped it into a glass of water he had difficulty in finding it. So straight and swiftly had it sunk to the bottom that he knew its weight was excellent.

"Well, what do you want for it?" he asked, with a fine assumption of nonchalance.

"I want—" Mapuhi began, and behind him, framing his own dark face, the dark faces of two women and a girl nodded concurrence in what he wanted. Their heads were bent forward, they were animated by a suppressed eagerness, their eyes flashed avariciously.

"I want a house," Mapuhi went on. "It must have a roof of galvanized iron and an octagon-drop-clock. It must be six fathoms long with a porch all around. A big room must be in the centre, with a round table in the middle of it and the octagon-drop-clock on the wall. There must be four bedrooms, two on each side of the big room, and in each bedroom must be an iron bed, two chairs, and a washstand. And back of the house must be a kitchen, a good kitchen, with pots and pans and a stove. And you must build the house on my island, which is Fakarava."

"Is that all?" Raoul asked incredulously.

"There must be a sewing machine," spoke up Tefara, Mapuhi's wife.

"Not forgetting the octagon-drop-clock," added Nauri, Mapuhi's mother.

"Yes, that is all," said Mapuhi.

Young Raoul laughed. He laughed long and heartily. But while he laughed he secretly performed problems in mental arithmetic. He had never built a house in his life, and his notions concerning house building were hazy. While he laughed, he calculated the cost of the voyage to Tahiti for materials, of the materials themselves, of the voyage back again to Fakarava, and the cost of landing the materials and of building the house. It would come to four thousand French dollars, allowing a margin for safety—four thousand French dollars were equivalent to twenty thousand francs. It was impossible. How was he to know the value of such a pearl? Twenty thousand francs was a lot of money—and of his mother's money at that.

"Mapuhi," he said, "you are a big fool. Set a money price."

But Mapuhi shook his head, and the three heads behind him shook with his.

"I want the house," he said. "It must be six fathoms long with a porch all around—"

"Yes, yes," Raoul interrupted. "I know all about your house, but it won't do. I'll give you a thousand Chili dollars."

The four heads chorused a silent negative.

"And a hundred Chili dollars in trade."

"I want the house," Mapuhi began.

"What good will the house do you?" Raoul demanded. "The first hurricane that comes along will wash it away. You ought to know."

"Captain Raffy says it looks like a hurricane right now."

"Not on Fakarava," said Mapuhi. "The land is much higher there. On this island, yes. Any hurricane can sweep Hikueru. I will have the house on Fakarava. It must be six fathoms long with a porch all around—"

And Raoul listened again to the tale of the house. Several hours he spent in the endeavor to hammer the house obsession out of Mapuhi's mind; but Mapuhi's mother and wife, and Ngakura, Mapuhi's daughter, bolstered him in his resolve for the house. Through the open doorway, while he listened for the twentieth time to the detailed description of the house that was wanted, Raoul saw his schooner's second boat draw up on the beach. The sailors rested on the oars, advertising haste to be gone. The first mate of the Aorai sprang ashore, exchanged a word with the one-armed native, then hurried toward Raoul. The day grew suddenly dark, as a squall obscured the face of the sun. Across the lagoon Raoul could see approaching the ominous line of the puff of wind.

"Captain Raffy says you've got to get to hell outa here," was the mate's greeting. "If there's any shell, we've got to run the risk of picking it up later on—so he says. The barometer's dropped to twenty-nine-seventy."

The gust of wind struck the pandanus tree overhead and tore through the palms beyond, flinging half a dozen ripe cocoanuts with heavy thuds to the ground. Then came the rain out of the distance, advancing with the roar of a gale of wind and causing the water of the lagoon to smoke in driven windrows. The sharp rattle of the first drops was on the leaves when Raoul sprang to his feet.

"A thousand Chili dollars, cash down, Mapuhi," he said. "And two hundred Chili dollars in trade."

"I want a house—" the other began.

"Mapuhi!" Raoul yelled, in order to make himself heard. "You are a fool!"

He flung out of the house, and, side by side with the mate, fought his way down the beach toward the boat. They could not see the boat. The tropic rain sheeted about them so that they could see only the beach under their feet and the spiteful little waves from the lagoon that snapped and bit at the sand. A figure appeared through the deluge. It was Huru-Huru, the man with the one arm.

"Did you get the pearl?" he yelled in Raoul's ear.

"Mapuhi is a fool!" was the answering yell, and the next moment they were lost to each other in the descending water.

Half an hour later, Huru-Huru, watching from the seaward side of the atoll, saw the two boats hoisted in and the Aorai pointing her nose out to sea. And near her, just come in from the sea on the wings of the squall, he saw another schooner hove to and dropping a boat into the water. He knew her. It was the OROHENA, owned by Toriki, the half-caste trader, who served as his own supercargo and who doubtlessly was even then in the stern sheets of the boat. Huru-Huru chuckled. He knew that Mapuhi owed Toriki for trade goods advanced the year before.

The squall had passed. The hot sun was blazing down, and the lagoon was once more a mirror. But the air was sticky like mucilage, and the weight of it seemed to burden the lungs and make breathing difficult.

"Have you heard the news, Toriki?" Huru-Huru asked. "Mapuhi has found a pearl. Never was there a pearl like it ever fished up in Hikueru, nor anywhere in the Paumotus, nor anywhere in all the world. Mapuhi is a fool. Besides, he owes you money. Remember that I told you first. Have you any tobacco?"

And to the grass shack of Mapuhi went Toriki. He was a masterful man, withal a fairly stupid one. Carelessly he glanced at the wonderful pearl— glanced for a moment only; and carelessly he dropped it into his pocket.

"You are lucky," he said. "It is a nice pearl. I will give you credit on the books."

"I want a house," Mapuhi began, in consternation. "It must be six fathoms—"

"Six fathoms your grandmother!" was the trader's retort. "You want to pay up your debts, that's what you want. You owed me twelve hundred dollars Chili. Very well; you owe them no longer. The amount is squared. Besides, I will give you credit for two hundred Chili. If, when I get to Tahiti, the pearl sells well, I will give you credit for another hundred—that will make three hundred. But mind, only if the pearl sells well. I may even lose money on it."

Mapuhi folded his arms in sorrow and sat with bowed head. He had been robbed of his pearl. In place of the house, he had paid a debt. There was nothing to show for the pearl.

"You are a fool," said Tefara.

"You are a fool," said Nauri, his mother. "Why did you let the pearl into his hand?"

"What was I to do?" Mapuhi protested. "I owed him the money. He knew I had the pearl. You heard him yourself ask to see it. I had not told him. He knew. Somebody else told him. And I owed him the money."

"Mapuhi is a fool," mimicked Ngakura.

She was twelve years old and did not know any better. Mapuhi relieved his feelings by sending her reeling from a box on the ear; while Tefara and Nauri burst into tears and continued to upbraid him after the manner of women.

Huru-Huru, watching on the beach, saw a third schooner that he knew heave to outside the entrance and drop a boat. It was the Hira, well named, for she was owned by Levy, the German Jew, the greatest pearl buyer of them all, and, as was well known, Hira was the Tahitian god of fishermen and thieves.

"Have you heard the news?" Huru-Huru asked, as Levy, a fat man with massive asymmetrical features, stepped out upon the beach. "Mapuhi has found a pearl. There was never a pearl like it in Hikueru, in all the Paumotus, in all the world. Mapuhi is a fool. He has sold it to Toriki for fourteen hundred Chili—I listened outside and heard. Toriki is likewise a fool. You can buy it from him cheap. Remember that I told you first. Have you any tobacco?"

"Where is Toriki?"

"In the house of Captain Lynch, drinking absinthe. He has been there an hour."

And while Levy and Toriki drank absinthe and chaffered over the pearl, Huru-Huru listened and heard the stupendous price of twenty-five thousand francs agreed upon.

It was at this time that both the OROHENA and the Hira, running in close to the shore, began firing guns and signalling frantically. The three men stepped outside in time to see the two schooners go hastily about and head off shore, dropping mainsails and flying jibs on the run in the teeth of the squall that heeled them far over on the whitened water. Then the rain blotted them out.

"They'll be back after it's over," said Toriki. "We'd better be getting out of here."

"I reckon the glass has fallen some more," said Captain Lynch.

He was a white-bearded sea-captain, too old for service, who had learned that the only way to live on comfortable terms with his asthma was on Hikueru. He went inside to look at the barometer.

"Great God!" they heard him exclaim, and rushed in to join him at staring at a dial, which marked twenty-nine-twenty.

Again they came out, this time anxiously to consult sea and sky. The squall had cleared away, but the sky remained overcast. The two schooners, under all sail and joined by a third, could be seen making back. A veer in the wind induced them to slack off sheets, and five minutes afterward a sudden veer from the opposite quarter caught all three schooners aback, and those on shore could see the boom-tackles being slacked away or cast off on the jump. The sound of the surf was loud, hollow, and menacing, and a heavy swell was setting in. A terrible sheet of lightning burst before their eyes, illuminating the dark day, and the thunder rolled wildly about them.

Toriki and Levy broke into a run for their boats, the latter ambling along like a panic-stricken hippopotamus. As their two boats swept out the entrance, they passed the boat of the Aorai coming in. In the stern sheets, encouraging the rowers, was Raoul. Unable to shake the vision of the pearl from his mind, he was returning to accept Mapuhi's price of a house.

He landed on the beach in the midst of a driving thunder squall that was so dense that he collided with Huru-Huru before he saw him.

"Too late," yelled Huru-Huru. "Mapuhi sold it to Toriki for fourteen hundred Chili, and Toriki sold it to Levy for twenty-five thousand francs. And Levy will sell it in France for a hundred thousand francs. Have you any tobacco?"

Raoul felt relieved. His troubles about the pearl were over. He need not worry any more, even if he had not got the pearl. But he did not believe Huru-Huru. Mapuhi might well have sold it for fourteen hundred Chili, but that Levy, who knew pearls, should have paid twenty-five thousand francs was too wide a stretch. Raoul decided to interview Captain Lynch on the subject, but when he arrived at that ancient mariner's house, he found him looking wide-eyed at the barometer.

"What do you read it?" Captain Lynch asked anxiously, rubbing his spectacles and staring again at the instrument.

"Twenty-nine-ten," said Raoul. "I have never seen it so low before."

"I should say not!" snorted the captain. "Fifty years boy and man on all the seas, and I've never seen it go down to that. Listen!"

They stood for a moment, while the surf rumbled and shook the house. Then they went outside. The squall had passed. They could see the Aorai lying becalmed a mile away and pitching and tossing madly in the tremendous seas that rolled in stately procession down out of the northeast and flung themselves furiously upon the coral shore. One of the sailors from the boat pointed at the mouth of the passage and shook his head. Raoul looked and saw a white anarchy of foam and surge.

"I guess I'll stay with you tonight, Captain," he said; then turned to the sailor and told him to haul the boat out and to find shelter for himself and fellows.

"Twenty-nine flat," Captain Lynch reported, coming out from another look at the barometer, a chair in his hand.

He sat down and stared at the spectacle of the sea. The sun came out, increasing the sultriness of the day, while the dead calm still held. The seas continued to increase in magnitude.

"What makes that sea is what gets me," Raoul muttered petulantly.

"There is no wind, yet look at it, look at that fellow there!"

Miles in length, carrying tens of thousands of tons in weight, its impact shook the frail atoll like an earthquake. Captain Lynch was startled.

"Gracious!" he bellowed, half rising from his chair, then sinking back.

"But there is no wind," Raoul persisted. "I could understand it if there was wind along with it."

"You'll get the wind soon enough without worryin' for it," was the grim reply.

The two men sat on in silence. The sweat stood out on their skin in myriads of tiny drops that ran together, forming blotches of moisture, which, in turn, coalesced into rivulets that dripped to the ground. They panted for breath, the old man's efforts being especially painful. A sea swept up the beach, licking around the trunks of the cocoanuts and subsiding almost at their feet.

"Way past high water mark," Captain Lynch remarked; "and I've been here eleven years." He looked at his watch. "It is three o'clock."

A man and woman, at their heels a motley following of brats and curs, trailed disconsolately by. They came to a halt beyond the house, and, after much irresolution, sat down in the sand. A few minutes later another family trailed in from the opposite direction, the men and women carrying a heterogeneous assortment of possessions. And soon several hundred persons of all ages and sexes were congregated about the captain's dwelling. He called to one new arrival, a woman with a nursing babe in her arms, and in answer received the information that her house had just been swept into the lagoon.

This was the highest spot of land in miles, and already, in many places on either hand, the great seas were making a clean breach of the slender ring of the atoll and surging into the lagoon. Twenty miles around stretched the ring of the atoll, and in no place was it more than fifty fathoms wide. It was the height of the diving season, and from all the islands around, even as far as Tahiti, the natives had gathered.

"There are twelve hundred men, women, and children here," said Captain Lynch. "I wonder how many will be here tomorrow morning."

"But why don't it blow?—that's what I want to know," Raoul demanded.

"Don't worry, young man, don't worry; you'll get your troubles fast enough."

Even as Captain Lynch spoke, a great watery mass smote the atoll.

The sea water churned about them three inches deep under the chairs. A low wail of fear went up from the many women. The children, with clasped hands, stared at the immense rollers and cried piteously. Chickens and cats, wading perturbedly in the water, as by common consent, with flight and scramble took refuge on the roof of the captain's house. A Paumotan, with a litter of new-born puppies in a basket, climbed into a cocoanut tree and twenty feet above the ground made the basket fast. The mother floundered about in the water beneath, whining and yelping.

And still the sun shone brightly and the dead calm continued. They sat and watched the seas and the insane pitching of the Aorai. Captain Lynch gazed at the huge mountains of water sweeping in until he could gaze no more. He covered his face with his hands to shut out the sight; then went into the house.

"Twenty-eight-sixty," he said quietly when he returned.

In his arm was a coil of small rope. He cut it into two-fathom lengths, giving one to Raoul and, retaining one for himself, distributed the remainder among the women with the advice to pick out a tree and climb.

A light air began to blow out of the northeast, and the fan of it on his cheek seemed to cheer Raoul up. He could see the Aorai trimming her sheets and heading off shore, and he regretted that he was not on her. She would get away at any rate, but as for the atoll—A sea breached across, almost sweeping him off his feet, and he selected a tree. Then he remembered the barometer and ran back to the house. He encountered Captain Lynch on the same errand and together they went in.

"Twenty-eight-twenty," said the old mariner. "It's going to be fair hell around here—what was that?"

The air seemed filled with the rush of something. The house quivered and vibrated, and they heard the thrumming of a mighty note of sound. The windows rattled. Two panes crashed; a draught of wind tore in, striking them and making them stagger. The door opposite banged shut, shattering the latch. The white door knob crumbled in fragments to the floor. The room's walls bulged like a gas balloon in the process of sudden inflation. Then came a new sound like the rattle of musketry, as the spray from a sea struck the wall of the house. Captain Lynch looked at his watch. It was four o'clock. He put on a coat of pilot cloth, unhooked the barometer, and stowed it away in a capacious pocket. Again a sea struck the house, with a heavy thud, and the light building tilted, twisted, quarter around on its foundation, and sank down, its floor at an angle of ten degrees.

Raoul went out first. The wind caught him and whirled him away. He noted that it had hauled around to the east. With a great effort he threw himself on the sand, crouching and holding his own. Captain Lynch, driven like a wisp of straw, sprawled over him. Two of the Aorai's sailors, leaving a cocoanut tree to which they had been clinging, came to their aid, leaning against the wind at impossible angles and fighting and clawing every inch of the way.

The old man's joints were stiff and he could not climb, so the sailors, by means of short ends of rope tied together, hoisted him up the trunk, a few feet at a time, till they could make him fast, at the top of the tree, fifty feet from the ground. Raoul passed his length of rope around the base of an adjacent tree and stood looking on. The wind was frightful. He had never dreamed it could blow so hard. A sea breached across the atoll, wetting him to the knees ere it subsided into the lagoon. The sun had disappeared, and a lead-colored twilight settled down. A few drops of rain, driving horizontally, struck him. The impact was like that of leaden pellets. A splash of salt spray struck his face. It was like the slap of a man's hand. His cheeks stung, and involuntary tears of pain were in his smarting eyes. Several hundred natives had taken to the trees, and he could have laughed at the bunches of human fruit clustering in the tops. Then, being Tahitian-born, he doubled his body at the waist, clasped the trunk of his tree with his hands, pressed the soles of his feet against the near surface of the trunk, and began to walk up the tree. At the top he found two women, two children, and a man. One little girl clasped a housecat in her arms.

From his eyrie he waved his hand to Captain Lynch, and that doughty patriarch waved back. Raoul was appalled at the sky. It had approached much nearer—in fact, it seemed just over his head; and it had turned from lead to black. Many people were still on the ground grouped about the bases of the trees and holding on. Several such clusters were praying, and in one the Mormon missionary was exhorting. A weird sound, rhythmical, faint as the faintest chirp of a far cricket, enduring but for a moment, but in the moment suggesting to him vaguely the thought of heaven and celestial music, came to his ear. He glanced about him and saw, at the base of another tree, a large cluster of people holding on by ropes and by one another. He could see their faces working and their lips moving in unison. No sound came to him, but he knew that they were singing hymns.

Still the wind continued to blow harder. By no conscious process could he measure it, for it had long since passed beyond all his experience of wind; but he knew somehow, nevertheless, that it was blowing harder. Not far away a tree was uprooted, flinging its load of human beings to the ground. A sea washed across the strip of sand, and they were gone. Things were happening quickly. He saw a brown shoulder and a black head silhouetted against the churning white of the lagoon. The next instant that, too, had vanished. Other trees were going, falling and criss-crossing like matches. He was amazed at the power of the wind. His own tree was swaying perilously, one woman was wailing and clutching the little girl, who in turn still hung on to the cat.

The man, holding the other child, touched Raoul's arm and pointed. He looked and saw the Mormon church careering drunkenly a hundred feet away. It had been torn from its foundations, and wind and sea were heaving and shoving it toward the lagoon. A frightful wall of water caught it, tilted it, and flung it against half a dozen cocoanut trees. The bunches of human fruit fell like ripe cocoanuts. The subsiding wave showed them on the ground, some lying motionless, others squirming and writhing. They reminded him strangely of ants. He was not shocked. He had risen above horror. Quite as a matter of course he noted the succeeding wave sweep the sand clean of the human wreckage. A third wave, more colossal than any he had yet seen, hurled the church into the lagoon, where it floated off into the obscurity to leeward, half-submerged, reminding him for all the world of a Noah's ark.

He looked for Captain Lynch's house, and was surprised to find it gone. Things certainly were happening quickly. He noticed that many of the people in the trees that still held had descended to the ground. The wind had yet again increased. His own tree showed that. It no longer swayed or bent over and back. Instead, it remained practically stationary, curved in a rigid angle from the wind and merely vibrating. But the vibration was sickening. It was like that of a tuning-fork or the tongue of a jew's-harp. It was the rapidity of the vibration that made it so bad. Even though its roots held, it could not stand the strain for long. Something would have to break.

Ah, there was one that had gone. He had not seen it go, but there it stood, the remnant, broken off half-way up the trunk. One did not know what happened unless he saw it. The mere crashing of trees and wails of human despair occupied no place in that mighty volume of sound. He chanced to be looking in Captain Lynch's direction when it happened. He saw the trunk of the tree, half-way up, splinter and part without noise. The head of the tree, with three sailors of the Aorai and the old captain sailed off over the lagoon. It did not fall to the ground, but drove through the air like a piece of chaff. For a hundred yards he followed its flight, when it struck the water. He strained his eyes, and was sure that he saw Captain Lynch wave farewell.

Raoul did not wait for anything more. He touched the native and made signs to descend to the ground. The man was willing, but his women were paralyzed from terror, and he elected to remain with them. Raoul passed his rope around the tree and slid down. A rush of salt water went over his head. He held his breath and clung desperately to the rope. The water subsided, and in the shelter of the trunk he breathed once more. He fastened the rope more securely, and then was put under by another sea. One of the women slid down and joined him, the native remaining by the other woman, the two children, and the cat.

The supercargo had noticed how the groups clinging at the bases of the other trees continually diminished. Now he saw the process work out alongside him. It required all his strength to hold on, and the woman who had joined him was growing weaker. Each time he emerged from a sea he was surprised to find himself still there, and next, surprised to find the woman still there. At last he emerged to find himself alone. He looked up. The top of the tree had gone as well. At half its original height, a splintered end vibrated. He was safe. The roots still held, while the tree had been shorn of its windage. He began to climb up. He was so weak that he went slowly, and sea after sea caught him before he was above them. Then he tied himself to the trunk and stiffened his soul to face the night and he knew not what.

He felt very lonely in the darkness. At times it seemed to him that it was the end of the world and that he was the last one left alive. Still the wind increased. Hour after hour it increased. By what he calculated was eleven o'clock, the wind had become unbelievable. It was a horrible, monstrous thing, a screaming fury, a wall that smote and passed on but that continued to smite and pass on—a wall without end. It seemed to him that he had become light and ethereal; that it was he that was in motion; that he was being driven with inconceivable velocity through unending solidness. The wind was no longer air in motion. It had become substantial as water or quicksilver. He had a feeling that he could reach into it and tear it out in chunks as one might do with the meat in the carcass of a steer; that he could seize hold of the wind and hang on to it as a man might hang on to the face of a cliff.

The wind strangled him. He could not face it and breathe, for it rushed in through his mouth and nostrils, distending his lungs like bladders. At such moments it seemed to him that his body was being packed and swollen with solid earth. Only by pressing his lips to the trunk of the tree could he breathe. Also, the ceaseless impact of the wind exhausted him. Body and brain became wearied. He no longer observed, no longer thought, and was but semiconscious. One idea constituted his consciousness: SO THIS WAS A HURRICANE. That one idea persisted irregularly. It was like a feeble flame that flickered occasionally. From a state of stupor he would return to it—SO THIS WAS A HURRICANE. Then he would go off into another stupor.

The height of the hurricane endured from eleven at night till three in the morning, and it was at eleven that the tree in which clung Mapuhi and his women snapped off. Mapuhi rose to the surface of the lagoon, still clutching his daughter Ngakura. Only a South Sea islander could have lived in such a driving smother. The pandanus tree, to which he attached himself, turned over and over in the froth and churn; and it was only by holding on at times and waiting, and at other times shifting his grips rapidly, that he was able to get his head and Ngakura's to the surface at intervals sufficiently near together to keep the breath in them. But the air was mostly water, what with flying spray and sheeted rain that poured along at right angles to the perpendicular.

It was ten miles across the lagoon to the farther ring of sand. Here, tossing tree trunks, timbers, wrecks of cutters, and wreckage of houses, killed nine out of ten of the miserable beings who survived the passage of the lagoon. Half-drowned, exhausted, they were hurled into this mad mortar of the elements and battered into formless flesh. But Mapuhi was fortunate. His chance was the one in ten; it fell to him by the freakage of fate. He emerged upon the sand, bleeding from a score of wounds.

Ngakura's left arm was broken; the fingers of her right hand were crushed; and cheek and forehead were laid open to the bone. He clutched a tree that yet stood, and clung on, holding the girl and sobbing for air, while the waters of the lagoon washed by knee-high and at times waist-high.

At three in the morning the backbone of the hurricane broke. By five no more than a stiff breeze was blowing. And by six it was dead calm and the sun was shining. The sea had gone down. On the yet restless edge of the lagoon, Mapuhi saw the broken bodies of those that had failed in the landing. Undoubtedly Tefara and Nauri were among them. He went along the beach examining them, and came upon his wife, lying half in and half out of the water. He sat down and wept, making harsh animal noises after the manner of primitive grief. Then she stirred uneasily, and groaned. He looked more closely. Not only was she alive, but she was uninjured. She was merely sleeping. Hers also had been the one chance in ten.

Of the twelve hundred alive the night before but three hundred remained. The Mormon missionary and a gendarme made the census. The lagoon was cluttered with corpses. Not a house nor a hut was standing. In the whole atoll not two stones remained one upon another. One in fifty of the cocoanut palms still stood, and they were wrecks, while on not one of them remained a single nut.

There was no fresh water. The shallow wells that caught the surface seepage of the rain were filled with salt. Out of the lagoon a few soaked bags of flour were recovered. The survivors cut the hearts out of the fallen cocoanut trees and ate them. Here and there they crawled into tiny hutches, made by hollowing out the sand and covering over with fragments of metal roofing. The missionary made a crude still, but he could not distill water for three hundred persons. By the end of the second day, Raoul, taking a bath in the lagoon, discovered that his thirst was somewhat relieved. He cried out the news, and thereupon three hundred men, women, and children could have been seen, standing up to their necks in the lagoon and trying to drink water in through their skins. Their dead floated about them, or were stepped upon where they still lay upon the bottom. On the third day the people buried their dead and sat down to wait for the rescue steamers.

In the meantime, Nauri, torn from her family by the hurricane, had been swept away on an adventure of her own. Clinging to a rough plank that wounded and bruised her and that filled her body with splinters, she was thrown clear over the atoll and carried away to sea. Here, under the amazing buffets of mountains of water, she lost her plank. She was an old woman nearly sixty; but she was Paumotan-born, and she had never been out of sight of the sea in her life. Swimming in the darkness, strangling, suffocating, fighting for air, she was struck a heavy blow on the shoulder by a cocoanut. On the instant her plan was formed, and she seized the nut. In the next hour she captured seven more. Tied together, they formed a life-buoy that preserved her life while at the same time it threatened to pound her to a jelly. She was a fat woman, and she bruised easily; but she had had experience of hurricanes, and while she prayed to her shark god for protection from sharks, she waited for the wind to break. But at three o'clock she was in such a stupor that she did not know. Nor did she know at six o'clock when the dead calm settled down. She was shocked into consciousness when she was thrown upon the sand. She dug in with raw and bleeding hands and feet and clawed against the backwash until she was beyond the reach of the waves.

She knew where she was. This land could be no other than the tiny islet of Takokota. It had no lagoon. No one lived upon it.

Hikueru was fifteen miles away. She could not see Hikueru, but she knew that it lay to the south. The days went by, and she lived on the cocoanuts that had kept her afloat. They supplied her with drinking water and with food. But she did not drink all she wanted, nor eat all she wanted. Rescue was problematical. She saw the smoke of the rescue steamers on the horizon, but what steamer could be expected to come to lonely, uninhabited Takokota?

From the first she was tormented by corpses. The sea persisted in flinging them upon her bit of sand, and she persisted, until her strength failed, in thrusting them back into the sea where the sharks tore at them and devoured them. When her strength failed, the bodies festooned her beach with ghastly horror, and she withdrew from them as far as she could, which was not far.

By the tenth day her last cocoanut was gone, and she was shrivelling from thirst. She dragged herself along the sand, looking for cocoanuts. It was strange that so many bodies floated up, and no nuts. Surely, there were more cocoanuts afloat than dead men! She gave up at last, and lay exhausted. The end had come. Nothing remained but to wait for death.

Coming out of a stupor, she became slowly aware that she was gazing at a patch of sandy-red hair on the head of a corpse. The sea flung the body toward her, then drew it back. It turned over, and she saw that it had no face. Yet there was something familiar about that patch of sandy-red hair. An hour passed. She did not exert herself to make the identification. She was waiting to die, and it mattered little to her what man that thing of horror once might have been.

But at the end of the hour she sat up slowly and stared at the corpse. An unusually large wave had thrown it beyond the reach of the lesser waves. Yes, she was right; that patch of red hair could belong to but one man in the Paumotus. It was Levy, the German Jew, the man who had bought the pearl and carried it away on the Hira. Well, one thing was evident: The Hira had been lost. The pearl buyer's god of fishermen and thieves had gone back on him.

She crawled down to the dead man. His shirt had been torn away, and she could see the leather money belt about his waist. She held her breath and tugged at the buckles. They gave easier than she had expected, and she crawled hurriedly away across the sand, dragging the belt after her. Pocket after pocket she unbuckled in the belt and found empty. Where could he have put it? In the last pocket of all she found it, the first and only pearl he had bought on the voyage. She crawled a few feet farther, to escape the pestilence of the belt, and examined the pearl. It was the one Mapuhi had found and been robbed of by Toriki. She weighed it in her hand and rolled it back and forth caressingly. But in it she saw no intrinsic beauty. What she did see was the house Mapuhi and Tefara and she had builded so carefully in their minds. Each time she looked at the pearl she saw the house in all its details, including the octagon-drop-clock on the wall. That was something to live for.

She tore a strip from her ahu and tied the pearl securely about her neck. Then she went on along the beach, panting and groaning, but resolutely seeking for cocoanuts. Quickly she found one, and, as she glanced around, a second. She broke one, drinking its water, which was mildewy, and eating the last particle of the meat. A little later she found a shattered dugout. Its outrigger was gone, but she was hopeful, and, before the day was out, she found the outrigger. Every find was an augury. The pearl was a talisman. Late in the afternoon she saw a wooden box floating low in the water. When she dragged it out on the beach its contents rattled, and inside she found ten tins of salmon. She opened one by hammering it on the canoe. When a leak was started, she drained the tin. After that she spent several hours in extracting the salmon, hammering and squeezing it out a morsel at a time.

Eight days longer she waited for rescue. In the meantime she fastened the outrigger back on the canoe, using for lashings all the cocoanut fibre she could find, and also what remained of her ahu. The canoe was badly cracked, and she could not make it water-tight; but a calabash made from a cocoanut she stored on board for a bailer. She was hard put for a paddle. With a piece of tin she sawed off all her hair close to the scalp. Out of the hair she braided a cord; and by means of the cord she lashed a three-foot piece of broom handle to a board from the salmon case.

She gnawed wedges with her teeth and with them wedged the lashing.

On the eighteenth day, at midnight, she launched the canoe through the surf and started back for Hikueru. She was an old woman. Hardship had stripped her fat from her till scarcely more than bones and skin and a few stringy muscles remained. The canoe was large and should have been paddled by three strong men.

But she did it alone, with a make-shift paddle. Also, the canoe leaked badly, and one-third of her time was devoted to bailing. By clear daylight she looked vainly for Hikueru. Astern, Takokota had sunk beneath the sea rim. The sun blazed down on her nakedness, compelling her body to surrender its moisture. Two tins of salmon were left, and in the course of the day she battered holes in them and drained the liquid. She had no time to waste in extracting the meat. A current was setting to the westward, she made westing whether she made southing or not.

In the early afternoon, standing upright in the canoe, she sighted Hikueru. Its wealth of cocoanut palms was gone. Only here and there, at wide intervals, could she see the ragged remnants of trees. The sight cheered her. She was nearer than she had thought. The current was setting her to the westward. She bore up against it and paddled on. The wedges in the paddle lashing worked loose, and she lost much time, at frequent intervals, in driving them tight. Then there was the bailing. One hour in three she had to cease paddling in order to bail. And all the time she drifted to the westward.

By sunset Hikueru bore southeast from her, three miles away. There was a full moon, and by eight o'clock the land was due east and two miles away. She struggled on for another hour, but the land was as far away as ever. She was in the main grip of the current; the canoe was too large; the paddle was too inadequate; and too much of her time and strength was wasted in bailing. Besides, she was very weak and growing weaker. Despite her efforts, the canoe was drifting off to the westward.

She breathed a prayer to her shark god, slipped over the side, and began to swim. She was actually refreshed by the water, and quickly left the canoe astern. At the end of an hour the land was perceptibly nearer. Then came her fright. Right before her eyes, not twenty feet away, a large fin cut the water. She swam steadily toward it, and slowly it glided away, curving off toward the right and circling around her. She kept her eyes on the fin and swam on. When the fin disappeared, she lay face downward in the water and watched. When the fin reappeared she resumed her swimming. The monster was lazy—she could see that. Without doubt he had been well fed since the hurricane. Had he been very hungry, she knew he would not have hesitated from making a dash for her. He was fifteen feet long, and one bite, she knew, could cut her in half.

But she did not have any time to waste on him. Whether she swam or not, the current drew away from the land just the same. A half hour went by, and the shark began to grow bolder. Seeing no harm in her he drew closer, in narrowing circles, cocking his eyes at her impudently as he slid past. Sooner or later, she knew well enough, he would get up sufficient courage to dash at her. She resolved to play first. It was a desperate act she meditated. She was an old woman, alone in the sea and weak from starvation and hardship; and yet she, in the face of this sea tiger, must anticipate his dash by herself dashing at him. She swam on, waiting her chance. At last he passed languidly by, barely eight feet away. She rushed at him suddenly, feigning that she was attacking him. He gave a wild flirt of his tail as he fled away, and his sandpaper hide, striking her, took off her skin from elbow to shoulder. He swam rapidly, in a widening circle, and at last disappeared.

In the hole in the sand, covered over by fragments of metal roofing, Mapuhi and Tefara lay disputing.

"If you had done as I said," charged Tefara, for the thousandth time, "and hidden the pearl and told no one, you would have it now."

"But Huru-Huru was with me when I opened the shell—have I not told you so times and times and times without end?"

"And now we shall have no house. Raoul told me today that if you had not sold the pearl to Toriki—"

"I did not sell it. Toriki robbed me."

"—that if you had not sold the pearl, he would give you five thousand French dollars, which is ten thousand Chili."

"He has been talking to his mother," Mapuhi explained. "She has an eye for a pearl."

"And now the pearl is lost," Tefara complained.

"It paid my debt with Toriki. That is twelve hundred I have made, anyway."

"Toriki is dead," she cried. "They have heard no word of his schooner. She was lost along with the Aorai and the Hira. Will Toriki pay you the three hundred credit he promised? No, because Toriki is dead. And had you found no pearl, would you today owe Toriki the twelve hundred? No, because Toriki is dead, and you cannot pay dead men."

"But Levy did not pay Toriki," Mapuhi said. "He gave him a piece of paper that was good for the money in Papeete; and now Levy is dead and cannot pay; and Toriki is dead and the paper lost with him, and the pearl is lost with Levy. You are right, Tefara. I have lost the pearl, and got nothing for it. Now let us sleep."

He held up his hand suddenly and listened. From without came a noise, as of one who breathed heavily and with pain. A hand fumbled against the mat that served for a door.

"Who is there?" Mapuhi cried.

"Nauri," came the answer. "Can you tell me where is my son, Mapuhi?"

Tefara screamed and gripped her husband's arm.

"A ghost!" she chattered. "A ghost!"

Mapuhi's face was a ghastly yellow. He clung weakly to his wife.

"Good woman," he said in faltering tones, striving to disguise his vice, "I know your son well. He is living on the east side of the lagoon."

From without came the sound of a sigh. Mapuhi began to feel elated. He had fooled the ghost.

"But where do you come from, old woman?" he asked.

"From the sea," was the dejected answer.

"I knew it! I knew it!" screamed Tefara, rocking to and fro.

"Since when has Tefara bedded in a strange house?" came Nauri's voice through the matting.

Mapuhi looked fear and reproach at his wife. It was her voice that had betrayed them.

"And since when has Mapuhi, my son, denied his old mother?" the voice went on.

"No, no, I have not—Mapuhi has not denied you," he cried. "I am not Mapuhi. He is on the east end of the lagoon, I tell you."

Ngakura sat up in bed and began to cry. The matting started to shake.

"What are you doing?" Mapuhi demanded.

"I am coming in," said the voice of Nauri.

One end of the matting lifted. Tefara tried to dive under the blankets, but Mapuhi held on to her. He had to hold on to something. Together, struggling with each other, with shivering bodies and chattering teeth, they gazed with protruding eyes at the lifting mat. They saw Nauri, dripping with sea water, without her ahu, creep in. They rolled over backward from her and fought for Ngakura's blanket with which to cover their heads.

"You might give your old mother a drink of water," the ghost said plaintively.

"Give her a drink of water," Tefara commanded in a shaking voice.

"Give her a drink of water," Mapuhi passed on the command to Ngakura.

And together they kicked out Ngakura from under the blanket. A minute later, peeping, Mapuhi saw the ghost drinking. When it reached out a shaking hand and laid it on his, he felt the weight of it and was convinced that it was no ghost. Then he emerged, dragging Tefara after him, and in a few minutes all were listening to Nauri's tale. And when she told of Levy, and dropped the pearl into Tefara's hand, even she was reconciled to the reality of her mother-in-law.

"In the morning," said Tefara, "you will sell the pearl to Raoul for five thousand French."

"The house?" objected Nauri.

"He will build the house," Tefara answered. "He ways it will cost four thousand French. Also will he give one thousand French in credit, which is two thousand Chili."

"And it will be six fathoms long?" Nauri queried.

"Ay," answered Mapuhi, "six fathoms."

"And in the middle room will be the octagon-drop-clock?"

"Ay, and the round table as well."

"Then give me something to eat, for I am hungry," said Nauri, complacently. "And after that we will sleep, for I am weary. And tomorrow we will have more talk about the house before we sell the pearl. It will be better if we take the thousand French in cash. Money is ever better than credit in buying goods from the traders."

THE WHALE TOOTH

It was in the early days in Fiji, when John Starhurst arose in the mission house at Rewa Village and announced his intention of carrying the gospel throughout all Viti Levu. Now Viti Levu means the "Great Land," it being the largest island in a group composed of many large islands, to say nothing of hundreds of small ones. Here and there on the coasts, living by most precarious tenure, was a sprinkling of missionaries, traders, bêche-de-mer fishers, and whaleship deserters. The smoke of the hot ovens arose under their windows, and the bodies of the slain were dragged by their doors on the way to the feasting.

The Lotu, or the Worship, was progressing slowly, and, often, in crablike fashion. Chiefs, who announced themselves Christians and were welcomed into the body of the chapel, had a distressing habit of backsliding in order to partake of the flesh of some favorite enemy. Eat or be eaten had been the law of the land; and eat or be eaten promised to remain the law of the land for a long time to come. There were chiefs, such as Tanoa, Tuiveikoso, and Tuikilakila, who had literally eaten hundreds of their fellow men. But among these gluttons Ra Undreundre ranked highest. Ra Undreundre lived at Takiraki. He kept a register of his gustatory exploits. A row of stones outside his house marked the bodies he had eaten. This row was two hundred and thirty paces long, and the stones in it numbered eight hundred and seventy-two. Each stone represented a body. The row of stones might have been longer, had not Ra Undreundre unfortunately received a spear in the small of his back in a bush skirmish on Somo Somo and been served up on the table of Naungavuli, whose mediocre string of stones numbered only forty-eight.

The hard-worked, fever-stricken missionaries stuck doggedly to their task, at times despairing, and looking forward for some special manifestation, some outburst of Pentecostal fire that would bring a glorious harvest of souls. But cannibal Fiji had remained obdurate. The frizzle-headed man-eaters were loath to leave their fleshpots so long as the harvest of human carcases was plentiful. Sometimes, when the harvest was too plentiful, they imposed on the missionaries by letting the word slip out that on such a day there would be a killing and a barbecue. Promptly the missionaries would buy the lives of the victims with stick tobacco, fathoms of calico, and quarts of trade beads. Natheless the chiefs drove a handsome trade in thus disposing of their surplus live meat. Also, they could always go out and catch more.

It was at this juncture that John Starhurst proclaimed that he would carry the Gospel from coast to coast of the Great Land, and that he would begin by penetrating the mountain fastnesses of the headwaters of the Rewa River. His words were received with consternation.

The native teachers wept softly. His two fellow missionaries strove to dissuade him. The King of Rewa warned him that the mountain dwellers would surely kai-kai him—kai-kai meaning "to eat"—and that he, the King of Rewa, having become Lotu, would be put to the necessity of going to war with the mountain dwellers. That he could not conquer them he was perfectly aware. That they might come down the river and sack Rewa Village he was likewise perfectly aware. But what was he to do? If John Starhurst persisted in going out and being eaten, there would be a war that would cost hundreds of lives.

Later in the day a deputation of Rewa chiefs waited upon John Starhurst. He heard them patiently, and argued patiently with them, though he abated not a whit from his purpose. To his fellow missionaries he explained that he was not bent upon martyrdom; that the call had come for him to carry the Gospel into Viti Levu, and that he was merely obeying the Lord's wish.

To the traders who came and objected most strenuously of all, he said: "Your objections are valueless. They consist merely of the damage that may be done your businesses. You are interested in making money, but I am interested in saving souls. The heathen of this dark land must be saved."

John Starhurst was not a fanatic. He would have been the first man to deny the imputation. He was eminently sane and practical.

He was sure that his mission would result in good, and he had private visions of igniting the Pentecostal spark in the souls of the mountaineers and of inaugurating a revival that would sweep down out of the mountains and across the length and breadth of the Great Land from sea to sea and to the isles in the midst of the sea. There were no wild lights in his mild gray eyes, but only calm resolution and an unfaltering trust in the Higher Power that was guiding him.

One man only he found who approved of his project, and that was Ra Vatu, who secretly encouraged him and offered to lend him guides to the first foothills. John Starhurst, in turn, was greatly pleased by Ra Vatu's conduct. From an incorrigible heathen, with a heart as black as his practices, Ra Vatu was beginning to emanate light. He even spoke of becoming Lotu. True, three years before he had expressed a similar intention, and would have entered the church had not John Starhurst entered objection to his bringing his four wives along with him. Ra Vatu had had economic and ethical objections to monogamy. Besides, the missionary's hair-splitting objection had offended him; and, to prove that he was a free agent and a man of honor, he had swung his huge war club over Starhurst's head. Starhurst had escaped by rushing in under the club and holding on to him until help arrived. But all that was now forgiven and forgotten. Ra Vatu was coming into the church, not merely as a converted heathen, but as a converted polygamist as well. He was only waiting, he assured Starhurst, until his oldest wife, who was very sick, should die.

John Starhurst journeyed up the sluggish Rewa in one of Ra Vatu's canoes. This canoe was to carry him for two days, when, the head of navigation reached, it would return. Far in the distance, lifted into the sky, could be seen the great smoky mountains that marked the backbone of the Great Land. All day John Starhurst gazed at them with eager yearning.

Sometimes he prayed silently. At other times he was joined in prayer by Narau, a native teacher, who for seven years had been Lotu, ever since the day he had been saved from the hot oven by Dr. James Ellery Brown at the trifling expense of one hundred sticks of tobacco, two cotton blankets, and a large bottle of painkiller. At the last moment, after twenty hours of solitary supplication and prayer, Narau's ears had heard the call to go forth with John Starhurst on the mission to the mountains.

"Master, I will surely go with thee," he had announced.

John Starhurst had hailed him with sober delight. Truly, the Lord was with him thus to spur on so broken-spirited a creature as Narau.

"I am indeed without spirit, the weakest of the Lord's vessels," Narau explained, the first day in the canoe.

"You should have faith, stronger faith," the missionary chided him.

Another canoe journeyed up the Rewa that day. But it journeyed an hour astern, and it took care not to be seen. This canoe was also the property of Ra Vatu. In it was Erirola, Ra Vatu's first cousin and trusted henchman; and in the small basket that never left his hand was a whale tooth. It was a magnificent tooth, fully six inches long, beautifully proportioned, the ivory turned yellow and purple with age. This tooth was likewise the property of Ra Vatu; and in Fiji, when such a tooth goes forth, things usually happen. For this is the virtue of the whale tooth: Whoever accepts it cannot refuse the request that may accompany it or follow it. The request may be anything from a human life to a tribal alliance, and no Fijian is so dead to honor as to deny the request when once the tooth has been accepted. Sometimes the request hangs fire, or the fulfilment is delayed, with untoward consequences.

High up the Rewa, at the village of a chief, Mongondro by name, John Starhurst rested at the end of the second day of the journey. In the morning, attended by Narau, he expected to start on foot for the smoky mountains that were now green and velvety with nearness. Mongondro was a sweet-tempered, mild-mannered little old chief, short-sighted and afflicted with elephantiasis, and no longer inclined toward the turbulence of war. He received the missionary with warm hospitality, gave him food from his own table, and even discussed religious matters with him. Mongondro was of an inquiring bent of mind, and pleased John Starhurst greatly by asking him to account for the existence and beginning of things. When the missionary had finished his summary of the Creation according to Genesis, he saw that Mongondro was deeply affected. The little old chief smoked silently for some time. Then he took the pipe from his mouth and shook his head sadly.

"It cannot be," he said. "I, Mongondro, in my youth, was a good workman with the adze. Yet three months did it take me to make a canoe—a small canoe, a very small canoe. And you say that all this land and water was made by one man—"

"Nay, was made by one God, the only true God," the missionary interrupted.

"It is the same thing," Mongondro went on, "that all the land and all the water, the trees, the fish, and bush and mountains, the sun, the moon, and the stars, were made in six days! No, no. I tell you that in my youth I was an able man, yet did it require me three months for one small canoe. It is a story to frighten children with; but no man can believe it."

"I am a man," the missionary said.

"True, you are a man. But it is not given to my dark understanding to know what you believe."

"I tell you, I do believe that everything was made in six days."

"So you say, so you say," the old cannibal murmured soothingly.

It was not until after John Starhurst and Narau had gone off to bed that Erirola crept into the chief's house, and, after diplomatic speech, handed the whale tooth to Mongondro.

The old chief held the tooth in his hands for a long time. It was a beautiful tooth, and he yearned for it. Also, he divined the request that must accompany it. "No, no; whale teeth were beautiful," and his mouth watered for it, but he passed it back to Erirola with many apologies.

In the early dawn John Starhurst was afoot, striding along the bush trail in his big leather boots, at his heels the faithful Narau, himself at the heels of a naked guide lent him by Mongondro to show the way to the next village, which was reached by midday. Here a new guide showed the way. A mile in the rear plodded Erirola, the whale tooth in the basket slung on his shoulder.

For two days more he brought up the missionary's rear, offering the tooth to the village chiefs. But village after village refused the tooth. It followed so quickly the missionary's advent that they divined the request that would be made, and would have none of it.

They were getting deep into the mountains, and Erirola took a secret trail, cut in ahead of the missionary, and reached the stronghold of the Buli of Gatoka. Now the Buli was unaware of John Starhurst's imminent arrival. Also, the tooth was beautiful—an extraordinary specimen, while the coloring of it was of the rarest order. The tooth was presented publicly. The Buli of Gatoka, seated on his best mat, surrounded by his chief men, three busy fly-brushers at his back, deigned to receive from the hand of his herald the whale tooth presented by Ra Vatu and carried into the mountains by his cousin, Erirola. A clapping of hands went up at the acceptance of the present, the assembled headman, heralds, and fly-brushers crying aloud in chorus:

"A! woi! woi! woi! A! woi! woi! woi! woi! A tabua levu! woi! woi! A mudua, mudua, mudua!'

"Soon will come a man, a white man," Erirola began, after the proper pause. "He is a missionary man, and he will come today. Ra Vatu is pleased to desire his boots. He wishes to present them to his good friend, Mongondro, and it is in his mind to send them with the feet along in them, for Mongondro is an old man and his teeth are not good. Be sure, O Buli, that the feet go along in the boots. As for the rest of him, it may stop here."

The delight in the whale tooth faded out of the Buli's eyes, and he glanced about him dubiously. Yet had he already accepted the tooth.

"A little thing like a missionary does not matter," Erirola prompted.

"No, a little thing like a missionary does not matter," the Buli answered, himself again. "Mongondro shall have the boots. Go, you young men, some three or four of you, and meet the missionary on the trail. Be sure you bring back the boots as well."

"It is too late," said Erirola. "Listen! He comes now."

Breaking through the thicket of brush, John Starhurst, with Narau close on his heels, strode upon the scene. The famous boots, having filled in wading the stream, squirted fine jets of water at every step. Starhurst looked about him with flashing eyes. Upborne by an unwavering trust, untouched by doubt or fear, he exulted in all he saw. He knew that since the beginning of time he was the first white man ever to tread the mountain stronghold of Gatoka.

The grass houses clung to the steep mountain side or overhung the rushing Rewa. On either side towered a mighty precipice. At the best, three hours of sunlight penetrated that narrow gorge. No cocoanuts nor bananas were to be seen, though dense, tropic vegetation overran everything, dripping in airy festoons from the sheer lips of the precipices and running riot in all the crannied ledges. At the far end of the gorge the Rewa leaped eight hundred feet in a single span, while the atmosphere of the rock fortress pulsed to the rhythmic thunder of the fall.

From the Buli's house, John Starhurst saw emerging the Buli and his followers.

"I bring you good tidings," was the missionary's greeting.

"Who has sent you?" the Buli rejoined quietly.

"God."

"It is a new name in Viti Levu," the Buli grinned. "Of what islands, villages, or passes may he be chief?"

"He is the chief over all islands, all villages, all passes," John Starhurst answered solemnly. "He is the Lord over heaven and earth, and I am come to bring His word to you."

"Has he sent whale teeth?" was the insolent query.

"No, but more precious than whale teeth is the—"

"It is the custom, between chiefs, to send whale teeth," the Buli interrupted.

"Your chief is either a niggard, or you are a fool, to come empty-handed into the mountains. Behold, a more generous than you is before you."

So saying, he showed the whale tooth he had received from Erirola.

Narau groaned.

"It is the whale tooth of Ra Vatu," he whispered to Starhurst. "I know it well. Now are we undone."

"A gracious thing," the missionary answered, passing his hand through his long beard and adjusting his glasses. "Ra Vatu has arranged that we should be well received."

But Narau groaned again, and backed away from the heels he had dogged so faithfully.

"Ra Vatu is soon to become Lotu," Starhurst explained, "and I have come bringing the Lotu to you."

"I want none of your Lotu," said the Buli, proudly. "And it is in my mind that you will be clubbed this day."

The Buli nodded to one of his big mountaineers, who stepped forward, swinging a club. Narau bolted into the nearest house, seeking to hide among the woman and mats; but John Starhurst sprang in under the club and threw his arms around his executioner's neck. From this point of vantage he proceeded to argue. He was arguing for his life, and he knew it; but he was neither excited nor afraid.

"It would be an evil thing for you to kill me," he told the man. "I have done you no wrong, nor have I done the Buli wrong."

So well did he cling to the neck of the one man that they dared not strike with their clubs. And he continued to cling and to dispute for his life with those who clamored for his death.

"I am John Starhurst," he went on calmly. "I have labored in Fiji for three years, and I have done it for no profit. I am here among you for good. Why should any man kill me? To kill me will not profit any man."

The Buli stole a look at the whale tooth. He was well paid for the deed.

The missionary was surrounded by a mass of naked savages, all struggling to get at him. The death song, which is the song of the oven, was raised, and his expostulations could no longer be heard. But so cunningly did he twine and wreathe his body about his captor's that the death blow could not be struck. Erirola smiled, and the Buli grew angry.

"Away with you!" he cried. "A nice story to go back to the coast—a dozen of you and one missionary, without weapons, weak as a woman, overcoming all of you."

"Wait, O Buli," John Starhurst called out from the thick of the scuffle, "and I will overcome even you. For my weapons are Truth and Right, and no man can withstand them."

"Come to me, then," the Buli answered, "for my weapon is only a poor miserable club, and, as you say, it cannot withstand you."

The group separated from him, and John Starhurst stood alone, facing the Buli, who was leaning on an enormous, knotted warclub.

"Come to me, missionary man, and overcome me," the Buli challenged.

"Even so will I come to you and overcome you," John Starhurst made answer, first wiping his spectacles and settling them properly, then beginning his advance.

The Buli raised the club and waited.

"In the first place, my death will profit you nothing," began the argument.

"I leave the answer to my club," was the Buli's reply.

And to every point he made the same reply, at the same time watching the missionary closely in order to forestall that cunning run-in under the lifted club. Then, and for the first time, John Starhurst knew that his death was at hand. He made no attempt to run in. Bareheaded, he stood in the sun and prayed aloud—the mysterious figure of the inevitable white man, who, with Bible, bullet, or rum bottle, has confronted the amazed savage in his every stronghold. Even so stood John Starhurst in the rock fortress of the Buli of Gatoka.

"Forgive them, for they know not what they do," he prayed. "O Lord! Have mercy upon Fiji. Have compassion for Fiji. O Jehovah, hear us for His sake, Thy Son, whom Thou didst give that through Him all men might also become Thy children. From Thee we came, and our mind is that to Thee we may return. The land is dark, O Lord, the land is dark. But Thou art mighty to save. Reach out Thy hand, O Lord, and save Fiji, poor cannibal Fiji."

The Buli grew impatient.

"Now will I answer thee," he muttered, at the same time swinging his club with both hands.

Narau, hiding among the women and the mats, heard the impact of the blow and shuddered. Then the death song arose, and he knew his beloved missionary's body was being dragged to the oven as he heard the words:

"Drag me gently. Drag me gently."

"For I am the champion of my land."

"Give thanks! Give thanks! Give thanks!"

Next, a single voice arose out of the din, asking:

"Where is the brave man?"

A hundred voices bellowed the answer:

"Gone to be dragged into the oven and cooked."

"Where is the coward?" the single voice demanded.

"Gone to report!" the hundred voices bellowed back. "Gone to report! Gone to report!"

Narau groaned in anguish of spirit. The words of the old song were true. He was the coward, and nothing remained to him but to go and report.

MAUKI

He weighed one hundred and ten pounds. His hair was kinky and negroid, and he was black. He was peculiarly black. He was neither blue-black nor purple-black, but plum-black. His name was Mauki, and he was the son of a chief. He had three tambos. Tambo is Melanesian for taboo, and is first cousin to that Polynesian word. Mauki's three tambos were as follows: First, he must never shake hands with a woman, nor have a woman's hand touch him or any of his personal belongings; secondly, he must never eat clams nor any food from a fire in which clams had been cooked; thirdly, he must never touch a crocodile, nor travel in a canoe that carried any part of a crocodile even if as large as a tooth.

Of a different black were his teeth, which were deep black, or, perhaps better, LAMP-black. They had been made so in a single night, by his mother, who had compressed about them a powdered mineral which was dug from the landslide back of Port Adams. Port Adams is a salt-water village on Malaita, and Malaita is the most savage island in the Solomons—so savage that no traders or planters have yet gained a foothold on it; while, from the time of the earliest bêche-de-mer fishers and sandalwood traders down to the latest labor recruiters equipped with automatic rifles and gasolene engines, scores of white adventurers have been passed out by tomahawks and soft-nosed Snider bullets. So Malaita remains today, in the twentieth century, the stamping ground of the labor recruiters, who farm its coasts for laborers who engage and contract themselves to toil on the plantations of the neighboring and more civilized islands for a wage of thirty dollars a year. The natives of those neighboring and more civilized islands have themselves become too civilized to work on plantations.

Mauki's ears were pierced, not in one place, nor two places, but in a couple of dozen places. In one of the smaller holes he carried a clay pipe. The larger holes were too large for such use. The bowl of the pipe would have fallen through. In fact, in the largest hole in each ear he habitually wore round wooden plugs that were an even four inches in diameter. Roughly speaking, the circumference of said holes was twelve and one-half inches. Mauki was catholic in his tastes. In the various smaller holes he carried such things as empty rifle cartridges, horseshoe nails, copper screws, pieces of string, braids of sennit, strips of green leaf, and, in the cool of the day, scarlet hibiscus flowers. From which it will be seen that pockets were not necessary to his well-being. Besides, pockets were impossible, for his only wearing apparel consisted of a piece of calico several inches wide. A pocket knife he wore in his hair, the blade snapped down on a kinky lock. His most prized possession was the handle of a china cup, which he suspended from a ring of turtle-shell, which, in turn, was passed through the partition-cartilage of his nose.

But in spite of embellishments, Mauki had a nice face. It was really a pretty face, viewed by any standard, and for a Melanesian it was a remarkably good-looking face. Its one fault was its lack of strength. It was softly effeminate, almost girlish. The features were small, regular, and delicate. The chin was weak, and the mouth was weak. There was no strength nor character in the jaws, forehead, and nose. In the eyes only could be caught any hint of the unknown quantities that were so large a part of his make-up and that other persons could not understand. These unknown quantities were pluck, pertinacity, fearlessness, imagination, and cunning; and when they found expression in some consistent and striking action, those about him were astounded.

Mauki's father was chief over the village at Port Adams, and thus, by birth a salt-water man, Mauki was half amphibian. He knew the way of the fishes and oysters, and the reef was an open book to him. Canoes, also, he knew. He learned to swim when he was a year old. At seven years he could hold his breath a full minute and swim straight down to bottom through thirty feet of water. And at seven years he was stolen by the bushmen, who cannot even swim and who are afraid of salt water. Thereafter Mauki saw the sea only from a distance, through rifts in the jungle and from open spaces on the high mountain sides. He became the slave of old Fanfoa, head chief over a score of scattered bush-villages on the range-lips of Malaita, the smoke of which, on calm mornings, is about the only evidence the seafaring white men have of the teeming interior population. For the whites do not penetrate Malaita. They tried it once, in the days when the search was on for gold, but they always left their heads behind to grin from the smoky rafters of the bushmen's huts.

When Mauki was a young man of seventeen, Fanfoa got out of tobacco. He got dreadfully out of tobacco. It was hard times in all his villages. He had been guilty of a mistake. Suo was a harbor so small that a large schooner could not swing at anchor in it. It was surrounded by mangroves that overhung the deep water. It was a trap, and into the trap sailed two white men in a small ketch. They were after recruits, and they possessed much tobacco and trade goods, to say nothing of three rifles and plenty of ammunition. Now there were no salt-water men living at Suo, and it was there that the bushmen could come down to the sea. The ketch did a splendid traffic. It signed on twenty recruits the first day. Even old Fanfoa signed on. And that same day the score of new recruits chopped off the two white men's head, killed the boat's crew, and burned the ketch. Thereafter, and for three months, there was tobacco and trade goods in plenty and to spare in all the bush villages. Then came the man-of-war that threw shells for miles into the hills, frightening the people out of their villages and into the deeper bush. Next the man-of-war sent landing parties ashore. The villages were all burned, along with the tobacco and trade stuff.

The cocoanuts and bananas were chopped down, the taro gardens uprooted, and the pigs and chickens killed.

It taught Fanfoa a lesson, but in the meantime he was out of tobacco. Also, his young men were too frightened to sign on with the recruiting vessels. That was why Fanfoa ordered his slave, Mauki, to be carried down and signed on for half a case of tobacco advance, along with knives, axes, calico, and beads, which he would pay for with his toil on the plantations. Mauki was sorely frightened when they brought him on board the schooner. He was a lamb led to the slaughter. White men were ferocious creatures. They had to be, or else they would not make a practice of venturing along the Malaita coast and into all harbors, two on a schooner, when each schooner carried from fifteen to twenty blacks as boat's crew, and often as high as sixty or seventy black recruits. In addition to this, there was always the danger of the shore population, the sudden attack and the cutting off of the schooner and all hands. Truly, white men must be terrible. Besides, they were possessed of such devil-devils—rifles that shot very rapidly many times, things of iron and brass that made the schooners go when there was no wind, and boxes that talked and laughed just as men talked and laughed.

Ay, and he had heard of one white man whose particular devil-devil was so powerful that he could take out all his teeth and put them back at will.

Down into the cabin they took Mauki. On deck, the one white man kept guard with two revolvers in his belt. In the cabin the other white man sat with a book before him, in which he inscribed strange marks and lines. He looked at Mauki as though he had been a pig or a fowl, glanced under the hollows of his arms, and wrote in the book. Then he held out the writing stick and Mauki just barely touched it with his hand, in so doing pledging himself to toil for three years on the plantations of the Moongleam Soap Company. It was not explained to him that the will of the ferocious white men would be used to enforce the pledge, and that, behind all, for the same use, was all the power and all the warships of Great Britain.

Other blacks there were on board, from unheard-of far places, and when the white man spoke to them, they tore the long feather from Mauki's hair, cut that same hair short, and wrapped about his waist a lava-lava of bright yellow calico.

After many days on the schooner, and after beholding more land and islands than he had ever dreamed of, he was landed on New Georgia, and put to work in the field clearing jungle and cutting cane grass. For the first time he knew what work was. Even as a slave to Fanfoa he had not worked like this. And he did not like work. It was up at dawn and in at dark, on two meals a day. And the food was tiresome. For weeks at a time they were given nothing but sweet potatoes to eat, and for weeks at a time it would be nothing but rice. He cut out the cocoanut from the shells day after day; and for long days and weeks he fed the fires that smoked the copra, till his eyes got sore and he was set to felling trees. He was a good axe-man, and later he was put in the bridge-building gang. Once, he was punished by being put in the road-building gang. At times he served as boat's crew in the whale boats, when they brought in copra from distant beaches or when the white men went out to dynamite fish.

Among other things he learned beche-de-mer English, with which he could talk with all white men, and with all recruits who otherwise would have talked in a thousand different dialects. Also, he learned certain things about the white men, principally that they kept their word. If they told a boy he was going to receive a stick of tobacco, he got it. If they told a boy they would knock seven bells out of him if he did a certain thing, when he did that thing, seven bells invariably were knocked out of him. Mauki did not know what seven bells were, but they occurred in beche-de-mer, and he imagined them to be the blood and teeth that sometimes accompanied the process of knocking out seven bells. One other thing he learned: no boy was struck or punished unless he did wrong. Even when the white men were drunk, as they were frequently, they never struck unless a rule had been broken.

Mauki did not like the plantation. He hated work, and he was the son of a chief. Furthermore, it was ten years since he had been stolen from Port Adams by Fanfoa, and he was homesick. He was even homesick for the slavery under Fanfoa. So he ran away. He struck back into the bush, with the idea of working southward to the beach and stealing a canoe in which to go home to Port Adams.

But the fever got him, and he was captured and brought back more dead than alive.

A second time he ran away, in the company of two Malaita boys. They got down the coast twenty miles, and were hidden in the hut of a Malaita freeman, who dwelt in that village. But in the dead of night two white men came, who were not afraid of all the village people and who knocked seven bells out of the three runaways, tied them like pigs, and tossed them into the whale boat. But the man in whose house they had hidden—seven times seven bells must have been knocked out of him from the way the hair, skin, and teeth flew, and he was discouraged for the rest of his natural life from harboring runaway laborers.

For a year Mauki toiled on. Then he was made a house-boy, and had good food and easy times, with light work in keeping the house clean and serving the white men with whiskey and beer at all hours of the day and most hours of the night. He liked it, but he liked Port Adams more. He had two years longer to serve, but two years were too long for him in the throes of homesickness. He had grown wiser with his year of service, and, being now a house-boy, he had opportunity. He had the cleaning of the rifles, and he knew where the key to the store room was hung. He planned to escape, and one night ten Malaita boys and one boy from San Cristoval sneaked from the barracks and dragged one of the whale boats down to the beach. It was Mauki who supplied the key that opened the padlock on the boat, and it was Mauki who equipped the boat with a dozen Winchesters, an immense amount of ammunition, a case of dynamite with detonators and fuse, and ten cases of tobacco.

The northwest monsoon was blowing, and they fled south in the night time, hiding by day on detached and uninhabited islets, or dragging their whale boat into the bush on the large islands. Thus they gained Guadalcanar, skirted halfway along it, and crossed the Indispensable Straits to Florida Island. It was here that they killed the San Cristoval boy, saving his head and cooking and eating the rest of him. The Malaita coast was only twenty miles away, but the last night a strong current and baffling winds prevented them from gaining across. Daylight found them still several miles from their goal. But daylight brought a cutter, in which were two white men, who were not afraid of eleven Malaita men armed with twelve rifles. Mauki and his companions were carried back to Tulagi, where lived the great white master of all the white men. And the great white master held a court, after which, one by one, the runaways were tied up and given twenty lashes each, and sentenced to a fine of fifteen dollars. They were sent back to New Georgia, where the white men knocked seven bells out of them all around and put them to work. But Mauki was no longer house-boy. He was put in the road-making gang. The fine of fifteen dollars had been paid by the white men from whom he had run away, and he was told that he would have to work it out, which meant six months' additional toil. Further, his share of the stolen tobacco earned him another year of toil.

Port Adams was now three years and a half away, so he stole a canoe one night, hid on the islets in Manning Straits, passed through the Straits, and began working along the eastern coast of Ysabel, only to be captured, two-thirds of the way along, by the white men on Meringe Lagoon. After a week, he escaped from them and took to the bush. There were no bush natives on Ysabel, only salt-water men, who were all Christians. The white men put up a reward of five-hundred sticks of tobacco, and every time Mauki ventured down to the sea to steal a canoe he was chased by the salt-water men. Four months of this passed, when, the reward having been raised to a thousand sticks, he was caught and sent back to New Georgia and the road-building gang. Now a thousand sticks are worth fifty dollars, and Mauki had to pay the reward himself, which required a year and eight months' labor. So Port Adams was now five years away.

His homesickness was greater than ever, and it did not appeal to him to settle down and be good, work out his four years, and go home. The next time, he was caught in the very act of running away. His case was brought before Mr. Haveby, the island manager of the Moongleam Soap Company, who adjudged him an incorrigible. The Company had plantations on the Santa Cruz Islands, hundreds of miles across the sea, and there it sent its Solomon Islands' incorrigibles. And there Mauki was sent, though he never arrived. The schooner stopped at Santa Anna, and in the night Mauki swam ashore, where he stole two rifles and a case of tobacco from the trader and got away in a canoe to Cristoval. Malaita was now to the north, fifty or sixty miles away. But when he attempted the passage, he was caught by a light gale and driven back to Santa Anna, where the trader clapped him in irons and held him against the return of the schooner from Santa Cruz. The two rifles the trader recovered, but the case of tobacco was charged up to Mauki at the rate of another year. The sum of years he now owed the Company was six.

On the way back to New Georgia, the schooner dropped anchor in Marau Sound, which lies at the southeastern extremity of Guadalcanar. Mauki swam ashore with handcuffs on his wrists and got away to the bush. The schooner went on, but the Moongleam trader ashore offered a thousand sticks, and to him Mauki was brought by the bushmen with a year and eight months tacked on to his account. Again, and before the schooner called in, he got away, this time in a whale boat accompanied by a case of the trader's tobacco. But a northwest gale wrecked him upon Ugi, where the Christian natives stole his tobacco and turned him over to the Moongleam trader who resided there. The tobacco the natives stole meant another year for him, and the tale was now eight years and a half.

"We'll send him to Lord Howe," said Mr. Haveby. "Bunster is there, and we'll let them settle it between them. It will be a case, I imagine, of Mauki getting Bunster, or Bunster getting Mauki, and good riddance in either event."

If one leaves Meringe Lagoon, on Ysabel, and steers a course due north, magnetic, at the end of one hundred and fifty miles he will lift the pounded coral beaches of Lord Howe above the sea. Lord Howe is a ring of land some one hundred and fifty miles in circumference, several hundred yards wide at its widest, and towering in places to a height of ten feet above sea level. Inside this ring of sand is a mighty lagoon studded with coral patches. Lord Howe belongs to the Solomons neither geographically nor ethnologically. It is an atoll, while the Solomons are high islands; and its people and language are Polynesian, while the inhabitants of the Solomons are Melanesian.

Lord Howe has been populated by the westward Polynesian drift which continues to this day, big outrigger canoes being washed upon its beaches by the southeast trade. That there has been a slight Melanesian drift in the period of the northwest monsoon, is also evident.

Nobody ever comes to Lord Howe, or Ontong-Java as it is sometimes called. Thomas Cook & Son do not sell tickets to it, and tourists do not dream of its existence. Not even a white missionary has landed on its shore. Its five thousand natives are as peaceable as they are primitive. Yet they were not always peaceable. The Sailing Directions speak of them as hostile and treacherous. But the men who compile the Sailing Directions have never heard of the change that was worked in the hearts of the inhabitants, who, not many years ago, cut off a big bark and killed all hands with the exception of the second mate. The survivor carried the news to his brothers. The captains of three trading schooners returned with him to Lord Howe. They sailed their vessels right into the lagoon and proceeded to preach the white man's gospel that only white men shall kill white men and that the lesser breeds must keep hands off. The schooners sailed up and down the lagoon, harrying and destroying. There was no escape from the narrow sand-circle, no bush to which to flee. The men were shot down at sight, and there was no avoiding being sighted. The villages were burned, the canoes smashed, the chickens and pigs killed, and the precious cocoanut trees chopped down. For a month this continued, when the schooner sailed away; but the fear of the white man had been seared into the souls of the islanders and never again were they rash enough to harm one.

Max Bunster was the one white man on Lord Howe, trading in the pay of the ubiquitous Moongleam Soap Company. And the Company billeted him on Lord Howe, because, next to getting rid of him, it was the most out-of-the-way place to be found. That the Company did not get rid of him was due to the difficulty of finding another man to take his place. He was a strapping big German, with something wrong in his brain. Semi-madness would be a charitable statement of his condition. He was a bully and a coward, and a thrice-bigger savage than any savage on the island.

Being a coward, his brutality was of the cowardly order. When he first went into the Company's employ, he was stationed on Savo. When a consumptive colonial was sent to take his place, he beat him up with his fists and sent him off a wreck in the schooner that brought him.

Mr. Haveby next selected a young Yorkshire giant to relieve Bunster. The Yorkshire man had a reputation as a bruiser and preferred fighting to eating. But Bunster wouldn't fight. He was a regular little lamb—for ten days, at the end of which time the Yorkshire man was prostrated by a combined attack of dysentery and fever. Then Bunster went for him, among other things getting him down and jumping on him a score or so of times. Afraid of what would happen when his victim recovered. Bunster fled away in a cutter to Guvutu, where he signalized himself by beating up a young Englishman already crippled by a Boer bullet through both hips.

Then it was that Mr. Haveby sent Bunster to Lord Howe, the falling-off place. He celebrated his landing by mopping up half a case of gin and by thrashing the elderly and wheezy mate of the schooner which had brought him. When the schooner departed, he called the kanakas down to the beach and challenged them to throw him in a wrestling bout, promising a case of tobacco to the one who succeeded. Three kanakas he threw, but was promptly thrown by a fourth, who, instead of receiving the tobacco, got a bullet through his lungs.

And so began Bunster's reign on Lord Howe. Three thousand people lived in the principal village; but it was deserted, even in broad day, when he passed through. Men, women, and children fled before him. Even the dogs and pigs got out of the way, while the king was not above hiding under a mat. The two prime ministers lived in terror of Bunster, who never discussed any moot subject, but struck out with his fists instead.

And to Lord Howe came Mauki, to toil for Bunster for eight long years and a half. There was no escaping from Lord Howe. For better or worse, Bunster and he were tied together. Bunster weighed two hundred pounds. Mauki weighed one hundred and ten. Bunster was a degenerate brute. But Mauki was a primitive savage. While both had wills and ways of their own.

Mauki had no idea of the sort of master he was to work for. He had had no warnings, and he had concluded as a matter of course that Bunster would be like other white men, a drinker of much whiskey, a ruler and a lawgiver who always kept his word and who never struck a boy undeserved. Bunster had the advantage. He knew all about Mauki, and gloated over the coming into possession of him. The last cook was suffering from a broken arm and a dislocated shoulder, so Bunster made Mauki cook and general house-boy.

And Mauki soon learned that there were white men and white men. On the very day the schooner departed he was ordered to buy a chicken from Samisee, the native Tongan missionary. But Samisee had sailed across the lagoon and would not be back for three days. Mauki returned with the information. He climbed the steep stairway (the house stood on piles twelve feet above the sand), and entered the living room to report. The trader demanded the chicken. Mauki opened his mouth to explain the missionary's absence. But Bunster did not care for explanations. He struck out with his fist. The blow caught Mauki on the mouth and lifted him into the air. Clear through the doorway he flew, across the narrow veranda, breaking the top railing, and down to the ground.

His lips were a contused, shapeless mass, and his mouth was full of blood and broken teeth.

"That'll teach you that back talk don't go with me," the trader shouted, purple with rage, peering down at him over the broken railing.

Mauki had never met a white man like this, and he resolved to walk small and never offend. He saw the boat boys knocked about, and one of them put in irons for three days with nothing to eat for the crime of breaking a rowlock while pulling. Then, too, he heard the gossip of the village and learned why Bunster had taken a third wife—by force, as was well known. The first and second wives lay in the graveyard, under the white coral sand, with slabs of coral rock at head and feet. They had died, it was said, from beatings he had given them. The third wife was certainly ill-used, as Mauki could see for himself.

But there was no way by which to avoid offending the white man who seemed offended with life. When Mauki kept silent, he was struck and called a sullen brute. When he spoke, he was struck for giving back talk. When he was grave, Bunster accused him of plotting and gave him a thrashing in advance; and when he strove to be cheerful and to smile, he was charged with sneering at his lord and master and given a taste of stick. Bunster was a devil.

The village would have done for him, had it not remembered the lesson of the three schooners. It might have done for him anyway, if there had been a bush to which to flee. As it was, the murder of the white men, of any white man, would bring a man-of-war that would kill the offenders and chop down the precious cocoanut trees. Then there were the boat boys, with minds fully made up to drown him by accident at the first opportunity to capsize the cutter. Only Bunster saw to it that the boat did not capsize.

341

Mauki was of a different breed, and escape being impossible while Bunster lived, he was resolved to get the white man. The trouble was that he could never find a chance. Bunster was always on guard. Day and night his revolvers were ready to hand. He permitted nobody to pass behind his back, as Mauki learned after having been knocked down several times. Bunster knew that he had more to fear from the good-natured, even sweet-faced, Malaita boy than from the entire population of Lord Howe; and it gave added zest to the programme of torment he was carrying out. And Mauki walked small, accepted his punishments, and waited.

All other white men had respected his tambos, but not so Bunster.

Mauki's weekly allowance of tobacco was two sticks. Bunster passed them to his woman and ordered Mauki to receive them from her hand. But this could not be, and Mauki went without his tobacco. In the same way he was made to miss many a meal, and to go hungry many a day. He was ordered to make chowder out of the big clams that grew in the lagoon. This he could not do, for clams were tambo. Six times in succession he refused to touch the clams, and six times he was knocked senseless. Bunster knew that the boy would die first, but called his refusal mutiny, and would have killed him had there been another cook to take his place.

One of the trader's favorite tricks was to catch Mauki's kinky locks and bat his head against the wall. Another trick was to catch Mauki unawares and thrust the live end of a cigar against his flesh. This Bunster called vaccination, and Mauki was vaccinated a number of times a week. Once, in a rage, Bunster ripped the cup handle from Mauki's nose, tearing the hole clear out of the cartilage.

"Oh, what a mug!" was his comment, when he surveyed the damage he had wrought.

The skin of a shark is like sandpaper, but the skin of a ray fish is like a rasp. In the South Seas the natives use it as a wood file in smoothing down canoes and paddles. Bunster had a mitten made of ray fish skin. The first time he tried it on Mauki, with one sweep of the hand it fetched the skin off his back from neck to armpit. Bunster was delighted. He gave his wife a taste of the mitten, and tried it out thoroughly on the boat boys. The prime ministers came in for a stroke each, and they had to grin and take it for a joke.

"Laugh, damn you, laugh!" was the cue he gave.

Mauki came in for the largest share of the mitten. Never a day passed without a caress from it. There were times when the loss of so much cuticle kept him awake at night, and often the half-healed surface was raked raw afresh by the facetious Mr. Bunster. Mauki continued his patient wait, secure in the knowledge that sooner or later his time would come. And he knew just what he was going to do, down to the smallest detail, when the time did come.

One morning Bunster got up in a mood for knocking seven bells out of the universe. He began on Mauki, and wound up on Mauki, in the interval knocking down his wife and hammering all the boat boys. At breakfast he called the coffee slops and threw the scalding contents of the cup into Mauki's face. By ten o'clock Bunster was shivering with ague, and half an hour later he was burning with fever. It was no ordinary attack. It quickly became pernicious, and developed into black-water fever. The days passed, and he grew weaker and weaker, never leaving his bed. Mauki waited and watched, the while his skin grew intact once more. He ordered the boys to beach the cutter, scrub her bottom, and give her a general overhauling. They thought the order emanated from Bunster, and they obeyed. But Bunster at the time was lying unconscious and giving no orders. This was Mauki's chance, but still he waited.

When the worst was past, and Bunster lay convalescent and conscious, but weak as a baby, Mauki packed his few trinkets, including the china cup handle, into his trade box. Then he went over to the village and interviewed the king and his two prime ministers.

"This fella Bunster, him good fella you like too much?" he asked.

They explained in one voice that they liked the trader not at all. The ministers poured forth a recital of all the indignities and wrongs that had been heaped upon them. The king broke down and wept. Mauki interrupted rudely.

"You savve me—me big fella marster my country. You no like 'm this fella white marster. Me no like 'm. Plenty good you put hundred cocoanut, two hundred cocoanut, three hundred cocoanut along cutter. Him finish, you go sleep 'm good fella. Altogether kanaka sleep m good fella. Bime by big fella noise along house, you no savve hear 'm that fella noise. You altogether sleep strong fella too much."

In like manner Mauki interviewed the boat boys. Then he ordered Bunster's wife to return to her family house. Had she refused, he would have been in a quandary, for his tambo would not have permitted him to lay hands on her.

The house deserted, he entered the sleeping room, where the trader lay in a doze. Mauki first removed the revolvers, then placed the ray fish mitten on his hand. Bunster's first warning was a stroke of the mitten that removed the skin the full length of his nose.

"Good fella, eh?" Mauki grinned, between two strokes, one of which swept the forehead bare and the other of which cleaned off one side of his face. "Laugh, damn you, laugh."

Mauki did his work throughly, and the kanakas, hiding in their houses, heard the "big fella noise" that Bunster made and continued to make for an hour or more.

When Mauki was done, he carried the boat compass and all the rifles and ammunition down to the cutter, which he proceeded to ballast with cases of tobacco. It was while engaged in this that a hideous, skinless thing came out of the house and ran screaming down the beach till it fell in the sand and mowed and gibbered under the scorching sun. Mauki looked toward it and hesitated. Then he went over and removed the head, which he wrapped in a mat and stowed in the stern locker of the cutter.

So soundly did the kanakas sleep through that long hot day that they did not see the cutter run out through the passage and head south, close-hauled on the southeast trade. Nor was the cutter ever sighted on that long tack to the shores of Ysabel, and during the tedious head-beat from there to

Malaita. He landed at Port Adams with a wealth of rifles and tobacco such as no one man had ever possessed before. But he did not stop there. He had taken a white man's head, and only the bush could shelter him. So back he went to the bush villages, where he shot old Fanfoa and half a dozen of the chief men, and made himself the chief over all the villages. When his father died, Mauki's brother ruled in Port Adams, and joined together, salt-water men and bushmen, the resulting combination was the strongest of the ten score fighting tribes of Malaita.

More than his fear of the British government was Mauki's fear of the all-powerful Moongleam Soap Company; and one day a message came up to him in the bush, reminding him that he owed the Company eight and one-half years of labor. He sent back a favorable answer, and then appeared the inevitable white man, the captain of the schooner, the only white man during Mauki's reign, who ventured the bush and came out alive. This man not only came out, but he brought with him seven hundred and fifty dollars in gold sovereigns—the money price of eight years and a half of labor plus the cost price of certain rifles and cases of tobacco.

Mauki no longer weighs one hundred and ten pounds. His stomach is three times its former girth, and he has four wives. He has many other things—rifles and revolvers, the handle of a china cup, and an excellent collection of bushmen's heads. But more precious than the entire collection is another head, perfectly dried and cured, with sandy hair and a yellowish beard, which is kept wrapped in the finest of fibre lava-lavas. When Mauki goes to war with villages beyond his realm, he invariably gets out this head, and alone in his grass palace, contemplates it long and solemnly. At such times the hush of death falls on the village, and not even a pickaninny dares make a noise. The head is esteemed the most powerful devil-devil on Malaita, and to the possession of it is ascribed all of Mauki's greatness.

"YAH! YAH! YAH!"

He was a whiskey-guzzling Scotchman, and he downed his whiskey neat, beginning with his first tot punctually at six in the morning, and thereafter repeating it at regular intervals throughout the day till bedtime, which was usually midnight. He slept but five hours out of the twenty-four, and for the remaining nineteen hours he was quietly and decently drunk. During the eight weeks I spent with him on Oolong Atoll, I never saw him draw a sober breath. In fact, his sleep was so short that he never had time to sober up. It was the most beautiful and orderly perennial drunk I have ever observed.

McAllister was his name. He was an old man, and very shaky on his pins. His hand trembled as with a palsy, especially noticeable when he poured his whiskey, though I never knew him to spill a drop. He had been twenty-eight years in Melanesia, ranging from German New Guinea to the German Solomons, and so thoroughly had he become identified with that portion of the world, that he habitually spoke in that bastard lingo called "bech-de-mer." Thus, in conversation with me, SUN HE COME UP meant sunrise; KAI-KAI HE STOP meant that dinner was served; and BELLY BELONG ME WALK ABOUT meant that he was sick at his stomach. He was a small man, and a withered one, burned inside and outside by ardent spirits and ardent sun. He was a cinder, a bit of a clinker of a man, a little animated clinker, not yet quite cold, that moved stiffly and by starts and jerks like an automaton. A gust of wind would have blown him away. He weighed ninety pounds.

But the immense thing about him was the power with which he ruled. Oolong Atoll was one hundred and forty miles in circumference. One steered by compass course in its lagoon. It was populated by five thousand Polynesians, all strapping men and women, many of them standing six feet in height and weighing a couple of hundred pounds. Oolong was two hundred and fifty miles from the nearest land. Twice a year a little schooner called to collect copra. The one white man on Oolong was McAllister, petty trader and unintermittent guzzler; and he ruled Oolong and its six thousand savages with an iron hand. He said come, and they came, go, and they went. They never questioned his will nor judgment. He was cantankerous as only an aged Scotchman can be, and interfered continually in their personal affairs. When Nugu, the king's daughter, wanted to marry Haunau from the other end of the atoll, her father said yes; but McAllister said no, and the marriage never came off. When the king wanted to buy a certain islet in the lagoon from the chief priest, McAllister said no. The king was in debt to the Company to the tune of 180,000 cocoanuts, and until that was paid he was not to spend a single cocoanut on anything else.

And yet the king and his people did not love McAllister. In truth, they hated him horribly, and, to my knowledge, the whole population, with the priests at the head, tried vainly for three months to pray him to death. The devil-devils they sent after him were awe-inspiring, but since McAllister did not believe in devil-devils, they were without power over him. With drunken Scotchmen all signs fail. They gathered up scraps of food which had touched his lips, an empty whiskey bottle, a cocoanut from which he had drunk, and even his spittle, and performed all kinds of deviltries over them. But McAllister lived on. His health was superb. He never caught fever; nor coughs nor colds; dysentery passed him by; and the malignant ulcers and vile skin diseases that attack blacks and whites alike in that climate never fastened upon him. He must have been so saturated with alcohol as to defy the lodgment of germs. I used to imagine them falling to the ground in showers of microscopic cinders as fast as they entered his whiskey-sodden aura. No one loved him, not even germs, while he loved only whiskey, and still he lived.

I was puzzled. I could not understand six thousand natives putting up with that withered shrimp of a tyrant. It was a miracle that he had not died suddenly long since. Unlike the cowardly Melanesians, the people were high-stomached and warlike. In the big graveyard, at head and feet of the graves, were relics of past sanguinary history—blubber-spades, rusty old bayonets and cutlasses, copper bolts, rudder-irons, harpoons, bomb guns, bricks that could have come from nowhere but a whaler's trying-out furnace, and old brass pieces of the sixteenth century that verified the traditions of the early Spanish navigators. Ship after ship had come to grief on Oolong. Not thirty years before, the whaler BLENNERDALE, running into the lagoon for repair, had been cut off with all hands. In similar fashion had the crew of the GASKET, a sandalwood trader, perished. There was a big French bark, the TOULON, becalmed off the atoll, which the islanders boarded after a sharp tussle and wrecked in the Lipau Passage, the captain and a handful of sailors escaping in the longboat. Then there were the Spanish pieces, which told of the loss of one of the early explorers. All this, of the vessels named, is a matter of history, and is to be found in the SOUTH PACIFIC SAILING DIRECTORY. But that there was other history, unwritten, I was yet to learn. In the meantime I puzzled why six thousand primitive savages let one degenerate Scotch despot live.

One hot afternoon McAllister and I sat on the veranda looking out over the lagoon, with all its wonder of jeweled colors. At our backs, across the hundred yards of palm-studded sand, the outer surf roared on the reef. It was dreadfully warm. We were in four degree south latitude and the sun was directly overhead, having crossed the Line a few days before on its journey south. There was no wind—not even a catspaw. The season of the southeast trade was drawing to an early close, and the northwest monsoon had not yet begun to blow.

"They can't dance worth a damn," said McAllister.

I had happened to mention that the Polynesian dances were superior to the Papuan, and this McAllister had denied, for no other reason than his cantankerousness. But it was too hot to argue, and I said nothing. Besides, I had never seen the Oolong people dance.

"I'll prove it to you," he announced, beckoning to the black New Hanover boy, a labor recruit, who served as cook and general house servant. "Hey, you, boy, you tell 'm one fella king come along me."

The boy departed, and back came the prime minister, perturbed, ill at ease, and garrulous with apologetic explanation. In short, the king slept, and was not to be disturbed.

"King he plenty strong fella sleep," was his final sentence.

McAllister was in such a rage that the prime minister incontinently fled, to return with the king himself. They were a magnificent pair, the king especially, who must have been all of six feet three inches in height. His features had the eagle-like quality that is so frequently found in those of the North American Indian. He had been molded and born to rule. His eyes flashed as he listened, but right meekly he obeyed McAllister's command to fetch a couple of hundred of the best dancers, male and female, in the village. And dance they did, for two mortal hours, under that broiling sun. They did not love him for it, and little he cared, in the end dismissing them with abuse and sneers.

The abject servility of those magnificent savages was terrifying. How could it be? What was the secret of his rule? More and more I puzzled as the days went by, and though I observed perpetual examples of his undisputed sovereignty, never a clew was there as to how it was.

One day I happened to speak of my disappointment in failing to trade for a beautiful pair of orange cowries. The pair was worth five pounds in Sydney if it was worth a cent. I had offered two hundred sticks of tobacco to the owner, who had held out for three hundred. When I casually mentioned the situation, McAllister immediately sent for the man, took the shells from him, and turned them over to me. Fifty sticks were all he permitted me to pay for them. The man accepted the tobacco and seemed overjoyed at getting off so easily. As for me, I resolved to keep a bridle on my tongue in the future. And still I mulled over the secret of McAllister's power. I even went to the extent of asking him directly, but all he did was to cock one eye, look wise, and take another drink.

One night I was out fishing in the lagoon with Oti, the man who had been mulcted of the cowries. Privily, I had made up to him an additional hundred and fifty sticks, and he had come to regard me with a respect that was almost veneration, which was curious, seeing that he was an old man, twice my age at least.

"What name you fella kanaka all the same pickaninny?" I began on him. "This fella trader he one fella. You fella kanaka plenty fella too much. You fella kanaka just like 'm dog—plenty fright along that fella trader. He no eat you, fella. He no get 'm teeth along him. What name you too much fright?"

"S'pose plenty fella kanaka kill 'm?" he asked.

"He die," I retorted. "You fella kanaka kill 'm plenty fella white man long time before. What name you fright this fella white man?"

"Yes, we kill 'm plenty," was his answer. "My word! Any amount! Long time before. One time, me young fella too much, one big fella ship he stop outside. Wind he no blow. Plenty fella kanaka we get 'm canoe, plenty fella canoe, we go catch 'm that fella ship. My word—we catch 'm big fella fight. Two, three white men shoot like hell. We no fright. We come alongside, we go up side, plenty fella, maybe I think fifty-ten (five hundred). One fella white Mary (woman) belong that fella ship. Never before I see 'm white Mary. Bime by plenty white man finish. One fella skipper he no die. Five fella, six fella white man no die. Skipper he sing out. Some fella white man he fight. Some fella white man he lower away boat. After that, all together over the side they go. Skipper he sling white Mary down. After that they washee (row) strong fella plenty too much. Father belong me, that time he strong fella. He throw 'm one fella spear. That fella spear he go in one side that white Mary. He no stop. My word, he go out other side that fella Mary. She finish. Me no fright. Plenty kanaka too much no fright."

Old Oti's pride had been touched, for he suddenly stripped down his lava-lava and showed me the unmistakable scar of a bullet. Before I could speak, his line ran out suddenly. He checked it and attempted to haul in, but found that the fish had run around a coral branch. Casting a look of reproach at me for having beguiled him from his watchfulness, he went over the side, feet first, turning over after he got under and following his line down to bottom. The water was ten fathoms. I leaned over and watched the play of his feet, growing dim and dimmer, as they stirred the wan phosphorescence into ghostly fires. Ten fathoms—sixty feet—it was nothing to him, an old man, compared with the value of a hook and line. After what seemed five minutes, though it could not have been more than a minute, I saw him flaming whitely upward. He broke surface and dropped a ten pound rock cod into the canoe, the line and hook intact, the latter still fast in the fish's mouth.

"It may be," I said remorselessly. "You no fright long ago. You plenty fright now along that fella trader."

"Yes, plenty fright," he confessed, with an air of dismissing the subject. For half an hour we pulled up our lines and flung them out in silence. Then small fish-sharks began to bite, and after losing a hook apiece, we hauled in and waited for the sharks to go their way.

"I speak you true," Oti broke into speech, "then you savve we fright now."

I lighted up my pipe and waited, and the story that Oti told me in atrocious bech-de-mer I here turn into proper English. Otherwise, in spirit and order of narrative, the tale is as it fell from Oti's lips.

"It was after that that we were very proud. We had fought many times with the strange white men who live upon the sea, and always we had beaten them. A few of us were killed, but what was that compared with the stores of wealth of a thousand thousand kinds that we found on the ships? And then one day, maybe twenty years ago, or twenty-five, there came a schooner right through the passage and into the lagoon. It was a large schooner with three masts. She had five white men and maybe forty boat's crew, black fellows from New Guinea and New Britain; and she had come to fish beche-de-mer. She lay at anchor across the lagoon from here, at Pauloo, and her boats scattered out everywhere, making camps on the beaches where they cured the beche-de-mer. This made them weak by dividing them, for those who fished here and those on the schooner at Pauloo were fifty miles apart, and there were others farther away still.

"Our king and headmen held council, and I was one in the canoe that paddled all afternoon and all night across the lagoon, bringing word to the people of Pauloo that in the morning we would attack the fishing camps at the one time and that it was for them to take the schooner. We who brought the word were tired with the paddling, but we took part in the attack. On the schooner were two white men, the skipper and the second mate, with half a dozen black boys. The skipper with three boys we caught on shore and killed, but first eight of us the skipper killed with his two revolvers. We fought close together, you see, at hand grapples.

351

"The noise of our fighting told the mate what was happening, and he put food and water and a sail in the small dingy, which was so small that it was no more than twelve feet long. We came down upon the schooner, a thousand men, covering the lagoon with our canoes. Also, we were blowing conch shells, singing war songs, and striking the sides of the canoes with our paddles. What chance had one white man and three black boys against us? No chance at all, and the mate knew it.

"White men are hell. I have watched them much, and I am an old man now, and I understand at last why the white men have taken to themselves all the islands in the sea. It is because they are hell. Here are you in the canoe with me. You are hardly more than a boy. You are not wise, for each day I tell you many things you do not know. When I was a little pickaninny, I knew more about fish and the ways of fish than you know now. I am an old man, but I swim down to the bottom of the lagoon, and you cannot follow me. What are you good for, anyway? I do not know, except to fight. I have never seen you fight, yet I know that you are like your brothers and that you will fight like hell. Also, you are a fool, like your brothers. You do not know when you are beaten. You will fight until you die, and then it will be too late to know that you are beaten.

"Now behold what this mate did. As we came down upon him, covering the sea and blowing our conches, he put off from the schooner in the small boat, along with the three black boys, and rowed for the passage. There again he was a fool, for no wise man would put out to sea in so small a boat. The sides of it were not four inches above the water. Twenty canoes went after him, filled with two hundred young men. We paddled five fathoms while his black boys were rowing one fathom. He had no chance, but he was a fool. He stood up in the boat with a rifle, and he shot many times. He was not a good shot, but as we drew close many of us were wounded and killed. But still he had no chance.

"I remember that all the time he was smoking a cigar. When we were forty feet away and coming fast, he dropped the rifle, lighted a stick of dynamite with the cigar, and threw it at us. He lighted another and another, and threw them at us very rapidly, many of them. I know now that he must have split the ends of the fuses and stuck in match heads, because they lighted so quickly. Also, the fuses were very short. Sometimes the dynamite sticks went off in the air, but most of them went off in the canoes. And each time they went off in a canoe, that canoe was finished. Of the twenty canoes, the half were smashed to pieces. The canoe I was in was so smashed, and likewise the two men who sat next to me. The dynamite fell between them. The other canoes turned and ran away. Then that mate yelled, Yah! Yah! Yah!' at us. Also he went at us again with his rifle, so that many were killed through the back as they fled away. And all the time the black boys in the boat went on rowing. You see, I told you true, that mate was hell.

"Nor was that all. Before he left the schooner, he set her on fire, and fixed up all the powder and dynamite so that it would go off at one time. There were hundreds of us on board, trying to put out the fire, heaving up water from overside, when the schooner blew up. So that all we had fought for was lost to us, besides many more of us being killed. Sometimes, even now, in my old age, I have bad dreams in which I hear that mate yell, Yah! Yah! Yah!' In a voice of thunder he yells, Yah! Yah! Yah!' But all those in the fishing camps were killed.

"The mate went out of the passage in his little boat, and that was the end of him we made sure, for how could so small a boat, with four men in it, live on the ocean? A month went by, and then, one morning, between two rain squalls, a schooner sailed in through our passage and dropped anchor before the village. The king and the headmen made big talk, and it was agreed that we would take the schooner in two or three days. In the meantime, as it was our custom always to appear friendly, we went off to her in canoes, bringing strings of cocoanuts, fowls, and pigs, to trade. But when we were alongside, many canoes of us, the men on board began to shoot us with rifles, and as we paddled away I saw the mate who had gone to sea in the little boat spring upon the rail and dance and yell, Yah! Yah! Yah!'

"That afternoon they landed from the schooner in three small boats filled with white men. They went right through the village, shooting every man they saw. Also they shot the fowls and pigs. We who were not killed got away in canoes and paddled out into the lagoon. Looking back, we could see all the houses on fire. Late in the afternoon we saw many canoes coming from Nihi, which is the village near the Nihi Passage in the northeast. They were all that were left, and like us their village had been burned by a second schooner that had come through Nihi Passage.

"We stood on in the darkness to the westward for Pauloo, but in the middle of the night we heard women wailing and then we ran into a big fleet of canoes. They were all that were left of Pauloo, which likewise was in ashes, for a third schooner had come in through the Pauloo Passage. You see, that mate, with his black boys, had not been drowned. He had made the Solomon Islands, and there told his brothers of what we had done in Oolong. And all his brothers had said they would come and punish us, and there they were in the three schooners, and our three villages were wiped out.

"And what was there for us to do? In the morning the two schooners from windward sailed down upon us in the middle of the lagoon. The trade wind was blowing fresh, and by scores of canoes they ran us down. And the rifles never ceased talking. We scattered like flying fish before the bonita, and there were so many of us that we escaped by thousands, this way and that, to the islands on the rim of the atoll.

"And thereafter the schooners hunted us up and down the lagoon. In the nighttime we slipped past them. But the next day, or in two days or three days, the schooners would be coming back, hunting us toward the other end of the lagoon. And so it went. We no longer counted nor remembered our dead. True, we were many and they were few. But what could we do? I was in one of the twenty canoes filled with men who were not afraid to die. We attacked the smallest schooner. They shot us down in heaps. They threw dynamite into the canoes, and when the dynamite gave out, they threw hot water down upon us. And the rifles never ceased talking. And those whose canoes were smashed were shot as they swam away. And the mate danced up and down upon the cabin top and yelled, 'Yah! Yah! Yah!'"

"Every house on every smallest island was burned. Not a pig nor a fowl was left alive. Our wells were defiled with the bodies of the slain, or else heaped high with coral rock. We were twenty-five thousand on Oolong before the three schooners came. Today we are five thousand. After the schooners left, we were but three thousand, as you shall see.

"At last the three schooners grew tired of chasing us back and forth. So they went, the three of them, to Nihi, in the northeast. And then they drove us steadily to the west. Their nine boats were in the water as well. They beat up every island as they moved along. They drove us, drove us, drove us day by day. And every night the three schooners and the nine boats made a chain of watchfulness that stretched across the lagoon from rim to rim, so that we could not escape back.

"They could not drive us forever that way, for the lagoon was only so large, and at last all of us that yet lived were driven upon the last sand bank to the west. Beyond lay the open sea. There were ten thousand of us, and we covered the sand bank from the lagoon edge to the pounding surf on the other side. No one could lie down. There was no room. We stood hip to hip and shoulder to shoulder. Two days they kept us there, and the mate would climb up in the rigging to mock us and yell, Yah! Yah! Yah!' till we were well sorry that we had ever harmed him or his schooner a month before. We had no food, and we stood on our feet two days and nights. The little babies died, and the old and weak died, and the wounded died. And worst of all, we had no water to quench our thirst, and for two days the sun beat down on us, and there was no shade. Many men and women waded out into the ocean and were drowned, the surf casting their bodies back on the beach. And there came a pest of flies. Some men swam to the sides of the schooners, but they were shot to the last one. And we that lived were very sorry that in our pride we tried to take the schooner with the three masts that came to fish for beche-de-mer.

"On the morning of the third day came the skippers of the three schooners and that mate in a small boat. They carried rifles, all of them, and revolvers, and they made talk. It was only that they were weary of killing us that they had stopped, they told us. And we told them that we were sorry, that never again would we harm a white man, and in token of our submission we poured sand upon our heads. And all the women and children set up a great wailing for water, so that for some time no man could make himself heard. Then we were told our punishment. We must fill the three schooners with copra and beche-de-mer. And we agreed, for we wanted water, and our hearts were broken, and we knew that we were children at fighting when we fought with white men who fight like hell. And when all the talk was finished, the mate stood up and mocked us, and yelled, Yah! Yah! Yah!' After that we paddled away in our canoes and sought water.

"And for weeks we toiled at catching beche-de-mer and curing it, in gathering the cocoanuts and turning them into copra. By day and night the smoke rose in clouds from all the beaches of all the islands of Oolong as we paid the penalty of our wrongdoing. For in those days of death it was burned clearly on all our brains that it was very wrong to harm a white man.

"By and by, the schooners full of copra and beche-de-mer and our trees empty of cocoanuts, the three skippers and that mate called us all together for a big talk. And they said they were very glad that we had learned our lesson, and we said for the ten-thousandth time that we were sorry and that we would not do it again. Also, we poured sand upon our heads. Then the skippers said that it was all very well, but just to show us that they did not forget us, they would send a devil-devil that we would never forget and that we would always remember any time we might feel like harming a white man. After that the mate mocked us one more time and yelled, Yah! Yah! Yah!' Then six of our men, whom we thought long dead, were put ashore from one of the schooners, and the schooners hoisted their sails and ran out through the passage for the Solomons.

"The six men who were put ashore were the first to catch the devil-devil the skippers sent back after us."

"A great sickness came," I interrupted, for I recognized the trick. The schooner had had measles on board, and the six prisoners had been deliberately exposed to it.

"Yes, a great sickness," Oti went on. "It was a powerful devil-devil. The oldest man had never heard of the like. Those of our priests that yet lived we killed because they could not overcome the devil-devil. The sickness spread. I have said that there were ten thousand of us that stood hip to hip and shoulder to shoulder on the sandbank. When the sickness left us, there were three thousand yet alive. Also, having made all our cocoanuts into copra, there was a famine.

"That fella trader," Oti concluded, "he like 'm that much dirt. He like 'm clam he die KAI-KAI (meat) he stop, stink 'm any amount. He like 'm one fella dog, one sick fella dog plenty fleas stop along him. We no fright along that fella trader. We fright because he white man. We savve plenty too much no good kill white man. That one fella sick dog trader he plenty brother stop along him, white men like 'm you fight like hell. We no fright that damn trader. Some time he made kanaka plenty cross along him and kanaka want 'm kill m, kanaka he think devil-devil and kanaka he hear that fella mate sing out, Yah! Yah! Yah!' and kanaka no kill 'm."

Oti baited his hook with a piece of squid, which he tore with his teeth from the live and squirming monster, and hook and bait sank in white flames to the bottom.

"Shark walk about he finish," he said. "I think we catch 'm plenty fella fish."

His line jerked savagely. He pulled it in rapidly, hand under hand, and landed a big gasping rock cod in the bottom of the canoe.

"Sun he come up, I make 'm that dam fella trader one present big fella fish," said Oti.

THE HEATHEN

I met him first in a hurricane; and though we had gone through the hurricane on the same schooner, it was not until the schooner had gone to pieces under us that I first laid eyes on him. Without doubt I had seen him with the rest of the kanaka crew on board, but I had not consciously been aware of his existence, for the Petite Jeanne was rather overcrowded. In addition to her eight or ten kanaka seamen, her white captain, mate, and supercargo, and her six cabin passengers, she sailed from Rangiroa with something like eighty-five deck passengers—Paumotans and Tahitians, men, women, and children each with a trade box, to say nothing of sleeping mats, blankets, and clothes bundles.

The pearling season in the Paumotus was over, and all hands were returning to Tahiti. The six of us cabin passengers were pearl buyers. Two were Americans, one was Ah Choon (the whitest Chinese I have ever known), one was a German, one was a Polish Jew, and I completed the half dozen.

It had been a prosperous season. Not one of us had cause for complaint, nor one of the eighty-five deck passengers either. All had done well, and all were looking forward to a rest-off and a good time in Papeete.

Of course, the Petite Jeanne was overloaded. She was only seventy tons, and she had no right to carry a tithe of the mob she had on board. Beneath her hatches she was crammed and jammed with pearl shell and copra. Even the trade room was packed full with shell. It was a miracle that the sailors could work her. There was no moving about the decks. They simply climbed back and forth along the rails.

In the night time they walked upon the sleepers, who carpeted the deck, I'll swear, two deep. Oh! And there were pigs and chickens on deck, and sacks of yams, while every conceivable place was festooned with strings of drinking cocoanuts and bunches of bananas. On both sides, between the fore and main shrouds, guys had been stretched, just low enough for the foreboom to swing clear; and from each of these guys at least fifty bunches of bananas were suspended.

It promised to be a messy passage, even if we did make it in the two or three days that would have been required if the southeast trades had been blowing fresh. But they weren't blowing fresh. After the first five hours the trade died away in a dozen or so gasping fans. The calm continued all that night and the next day—one of those glaring, glassy, calms, when the very thought of opening one's eyes to look at it is sufficient to cause a headache.

The second day a man died—an Easter Islander, one of the best divers that season in the lagoon. Smallpox—that is what it was; though how smallpox could come on board, when there had been no known cases ashore when we left Rangiroa, is beyond me. There it was, though—smallpox, a man dead, and three others down on their backs.

There was nothing to be done. We could not segregate the sick, nor could we care for them. We were packed like sardines. There was nothing to do but rot and die—that is, there was nothing to do after the night that followed the first death. On that night, the mate, the supercargo, the Polish Jew, and four native divers sneaked away in the large whale boat. They were never heard of again. In the morning the captain promptly scuttled the remaining boats, and there we were.

That day there were two deaths; the following day three; then it jumped to eight. It was curious to see how we took it. The natives, for instance, fell into a condition of dumb, stolid fear. The captain—Oudouse, his name was, a Frenchman—became very nervous and voluble. He actually got the twitches. He was a large fleshy man, weighing at least two hundred pounds, and he quickly became a faithful representation of a quivering jelly-mountain of fat.

The German, the two Americans, and myself bought up all the Scotch whiskey, and proceeded to stay drunk. The theory was beautiful—namely, if we kept ourselves soaked in alcohol, every smallpox germ that came into contact with us would immediately be scorched to a cinder. And the theory worked, though I must confess that neither Captain Oudouse nor Ah Choon were attacked by the disease either. The Frenchman did not drink at all, while Ah Choon restricted himself to one drink daily.

It was a pretty time. The sun, going into northern declination, was straight overhead. There was no wind, except for frequent squalls, which blew fiercely for from five minutes to half an hour, and wound up by deluging us with rain. After each squall, the awful sun would come out, drawing clouds of steam from the soaked decks.

The steam was not nice. It was the vapor of death, freighted with millions and millions of germs. We always took another drink when we saw it going up from the dead and dying, and usually we took two or three more drinks, mixing them exceptionally stiff. Also, we made it a rule to take an additional several each time they hove the dead over to the sharks that swarmed about us.

We had a week of it, and then the whiskey gave out. It is just as well, or I shouldn't be alive now. It took a sober man to pull through what followed, as you will agree when I mention the little fact that only two men did pull through. The other man was the heathen—at least, that was what I heard Captain Oudouse call him at the moment I first became aware of the heathen's existence. But to come back.

It was at the end of the week, with the whiskey gone, and the pearl buyers sober, that I happened to glance at the barometer that hung in the cabin companionway. Its normal register in the Paumotus was 29.90, and it was quite customary to see it vacillate between 29.85 and 30.00, or even 30.05; but to see it as I saw it, down to 29.62, was sufficient to sober the most drunken pearl buyer that ever incinerated smallpox microbes in Scotch whiskey.

I called Captain Oudouse's attention to it, only to be informed that he had watched it going down for several hours. There was little to do, but that little he did very well, considering the circumstances. He took off the light sails, shortened right down to storm canvas, spread life lines, and waited for the wind. His mistake lay in what he did after the wind came. He hove to on the port tack, which was the right thing to do south of the Equator, if—and there was the rub—IF one were NOT in the direct path of the hurricane.

We were in the direct path. I could see that by the steady increase of the wind and the equally steady fall of the barometer. I wanted him to turn and run with the wind on the port quarter until the barometer ceased falling, and then to heave to. We argued till he was reduced to hysteria, but budge he would not. The worst of it was that I could not get the rest of the pearl buyers to back me up. Who was I, anyway, to know more about the sea and its ways than a properly qualified captain? was what was in their minds, I knew.

Of course, the sea rose with the wind frightfully; and I shall never forget the first three seas the Petite Jeanne shipped. She had fallen off, as vessels do at times when hove to, and the first sea made a clean breach. The life lines were only for the strong and well, and little good were they even for them when the women and children, the bananas and cocoanuts, the pigs and trade boxes, the sick and the dying, were swept along in a solid, screeching, groaning mass.

The second sea filled the Petite Jeanne's decks flush with the rails; and, as her stern sank down and her bow tossed skyward, all the miserable dunnage of life and luggage poured aft. It was a human torrent. They came head first, feet first, sidewise, rolling over and over, twisting, squirming, writhing, and crumpling up. Now and again one caught a grip on a stanchion or a rope; but the weight of the bodies behind tore such grips loose.

One man I noticed fetch up, head on and square on, with the starboard bitt. His head cracked like an egg. I saw what was coming, sprang on top of the cabin, and from there into the mainsail itself. Ah Choon and one of the Americans tried to follow me, but I was one jump ahead of them. The American was swept away and over the stern like a piece of chaff. Ah Choon caught a spoke of the wheel, and swung in behind it. But a strapping Raratonga vahine (woman)—she must have weighed two hundred and fifty— brought up against him, and got an arm around his neck. He clutched the kanaka steersman with his other hand; and just at that moment the schooner flung down to starboard.

The rush of bodies and sea that was coming along the port runway between the cabin and the rail turned abruptly and poured to starboard. Away they went—vahine, Ah Choon, and steersman; and I swear I saw Ah Choon grin at me with philosophic resignation as he cleared the rail and went under.

The third sea—the biggest of the three—did not do so much damage. By the time it arrived nearly everybody was in the rigging. On deck perhaps a dozen gasping, half-drowned, and half-stunned wretches were rolling about or attempting to crawl into safety. They went by the board, as did the wreckage of the two remaining boats. The other pearl buyers and myself, between seas, managed to get about fifteen women and children into the cabin, and battened down. Little good it did the poor creatures in the end.

Wind? Out of all my experience I could not have believed it possible for the wind to blow as it did. There is no describing it. How can one describe a nightmare? It was the same way with that wind. It tore the clothes off our bodies. I say TORE THEM OFF, and I mean it. I am not asking you to believe it. I am merely telling something that I saw and felt. There are times when I do not believe it myself. I went through it, and that is enough. One could not face that wind and live. It was a monstrous thing, and the most monstrous thing about it was that it increased and continued to increase.

Imagine countless millions and billions of tons of sand. Imagine this sand tearing along at ninety, a hundred, a hundred and twenty, or any other number of miles per hour. Imagine, further, this sand to be invisible, impalpable, yet to retain all the weight and density of sand. Do all this, and you may get a vague inkling of what that wind was like.

Perhaps sand is not the right comparison. Consider it mud, invisible, impalpable, but heavy as mud. Nay, it goes beyond that. Consider every molecule of air to be a mudbank in itself. Then try to imagine the multitudinous impact of mudbanks. No; it is beyond me. Language may be adequate to express the ordinary conditions of life, but it cannot possibly express any of the conditions of so enormous a blast of wind. It would have been better had I stuck by my original intention of not attempting a description.

I will say this much: The sea, which had risen at first, was beaten down by that wind. More: it seemed as if the whole ocean had been sucked up in the maw of the hurricane, and hurled on through that portion of space which previously had been occupied by the air.

Of course, our canvas had gone long before. But Captain Oudouse had on the Petite Jeanne something I had never before seen on a South Sea schooner—a sea anchor. It was a conical canvas bag, the mouth of which was kept open by a huge loop of iron. The sea anchor was bridled something like a kite, so that it bit into the water as a kite bites into the air, but with a difference. The sea anchor remained just under the surface of the ocean in a perpendicular position. A long line, in turn, connected it with the schooner. As a result, the Petite Jeanne rode bow on to the wind and to what sea there was.

The situation really would have been favorable had we not been in the path of the storm. True, the wind itself tore our canvas out of the gaskets, jerked out our topmasts, and made a raffle of our running gear, but still we would have come through nicely had we not been square in front of the advancing storm center. That was what fixed us. I was in a state of stunned, numbed, paralyzed collapse from enduring the impact of the wind, and I think I was just about ready to give up and die when the center smote us. The blow we received was an absolute lull. There was not a breath of air. The effect on one was sickening.

Remember that for hours we had been at terrific muscular tension, withstanding the awful pressure of that wind. And then, suddenly, the pressure was removed. I know that I felt as though I was about to expand, to fly apart in all directions. It seemed as if every atom composing my body was repelling every other atom and was on the verge of rushing off irresistibly into space. But that lasted only for a moment. Destruction was upon us.

In the absence of the wind and pressure the sea rose. It jumped, it leaped, it soared straight toward the clouds. Remember, from every point of the compass that inconceivable wind was blowing in toward the center of calm. The result was that the seas sprang up from every point of the compass. There was no wind to check them. They popped up like corks released from the bottom of a pail of water. There was no system to them, no stability. They were hollow, maniacal seas. They were eighty feet high at the least. They were not seas at all. They resembled no sea a man had ever seen.

363

They were splashes, monstrous splashes—that is all. Splashes that were eighty feet high. Eighty! They were more than eighty. They went over our mastheads. They were spouts, explosions. They were drunken. They fell anywhere, anyhow. They jostled one another; they collided. They rushed together and collapsed upon one another, or fell apart like a thousand waterfalls all at once. It was no ocean any man had ever dreamed of, that hurricane center. It was confusion thrice confounded. It was anarchy. It was a hell pit of sea water gone mad.

The Petite Jeanne? I don't know. The heathen told me afterwards that he did not know. She was literally torn apart, ripped wide open, beaten into a pulp, smashed into kindling wood, annihilated. When I came to I was in the water, swimming automatically, though I was about two-thirds drowned. How I got there I had no recollection. I remembered seeing the Petite Jeanne fly to pieces at what must have been the instant that my own consciousness was buffeted out of me. But there I was, with nothing to do but make the best of it, and in that best there was little promise. The wind was blowing again, the sea was much smaller and more regular, and I knew that I had passed through the center. Fortunately, there were no sharks about. The hurricane had dissipated the ravenous horde that had surrounded the death ship and fed off the dead.

It was about midday when the Petite Jeanne went to pieces, and it must have been two hours afterwards when I picked up with one of her hatch covers. Thick rain was driving at the time; and it was the merest chance that flung me and the hatch cover together. A short length of line was trailing from the rope handle; and I knew that I was good for a day, at least, if the sharks did not return. Three hours later, possibly a little longer, sticking close to the cover, and with closed eyes, concentrating my whole soul upon the task of breathing in enough air to keep me going and at the same time of avoiding breathing in enough water to drown me, it seemed to me that I heard voices. The rain had ceased, and wind and sea were easing marvelously. Not twenty feet away from me, on another hatch cover were Captain Oudouse and the heathen. They were fighting over the possession of the cover—at least, the Frenchman was. "Paien noir!" I heard him scream, and at the same time I saw him kick the kanaka.

Now, Captain Oudouse had lost all his clothes, except his shoes, and they were heavy brogans. It was a cruel blow, for it caught the heathen on the mouth and the point of the chin, half stunning him. I looked for him to retaliate, but he contented himself with swimming about forlornly a safe ten feet away. Whenever a fling of the sea threw him closer, the Frenchman, hanging on with his hands, kicked out at him with both feet. Also, at the moment of delivering each kick, he called the kanaka a black heathen.

"For two centimes I'd come over there and drown you, you white beast!" I yelled.

The only reason I did not go was that I felt too tired. The very thought of the effort to swim over was nauseating. So I called to the kanaka to come to me, and proceeded to share the hatch cover with him. Otoo, he told me his name was (pronounced o-to-o); also, he told me that he was a native of Bora Bora, the most westerly of the Society Group. As I learned afterward, he had got the hatch cover first, and, after some time, encountering Captain Oudouse, had offered to share it with him, and had been kicked off for his pains.

And that was how Otoo and I first came together. He was no fighter. He was all sweetness and gentleness, a love creature, though he stood nearly six feet tall and was muscled like a gladiator. He was no fighter, but he was also no coward. He had the heart of a lion; and in the years that followed I have seen him run risks that I would never dream of taking. What I mean is that while he was no fighter, and while he always avoided precipitating a row, he never ran away from trouble when it started. And it was "Ware shoal!" when once Otoo went into action. I shall never forget what he did to Bill King. It occurred in German Samoa. Bill King was hailed the champion heavyweight of the American Navy. He was a big brute of a man, a veritable gorilla, one of those hard-hitting, rough-housing chaps, and clever with his fists as well. He picked the quarrel, and he kicked Otoo twice and struck him once before Otoo felt it to be necessary to fight. I don't think it lasted four minutes, at the end of which time Bill King was the unhappy possessor of four broken ribs, a broken forearm, and a dislocated shoulder blade. Otoo knew nothing of scientific boxing. He was merely a manhandler; and Bill King was something like three months in recovering from the bit of manhandling he received that afternoon on Apia beach.

But I am running ahead of my yarn. We shared the hatch cover between us. We took turn and turn about, one lying flat on the cover and resting, while the other, submerged to the neck, merely held on with his hands. For two days and nights, spell and spell, on the cover and in the water, we drifted over the ocean. Towards the last I was delirious most of the time; and there were times, too, when I heard Otoo babbling and raving in his native tongue. Our continuous immersion prevented us from dying of thirst, though the sea water and the sunshine gave us the prettiest imaginable combination of salt pickle and sunburn.

In the end, Otoo saved my life; for I came to lying on the beach twenty feet from the water, sheltered from the sun by a couple of cocoanut leaves. No one but Otoo could have dragged me there and stuck up the leaves for shade. He was lying beside me. I went off again; and the next time I came round, it was cool and starry night, and Otoo was pressing a drinking cocoanut to my lips.

We were the sole survivors of the Petite Jeanne. Captain Oudouse must have succumbed to exhaustion, for several days later his hatch cover drifted ashore without him. Otoo and I lived with the natives of the atoll for a week, when we were rescued by the French cruiser and taken to Tahiti. In the meantime, however, we had performed the ceremony of exchanging names. In the South Seas such a ceremony binds two men closer together than blood brothership. The initiative had been mine; and Otoo was rapturously delighted when I suggested it.

"It is well," he said, in Tahitian. "For we have been mates together for two days on the lips of Death."

"But death stuttered," I smiled.

"It was a brave deed you did, master," he replied, "and Death was not vile enough to speak."

"Why do you 'master' me?" I demanded, with a show of hurt feelings. "We have exchanged names. To you I am Otoo. To me you are Charley. And between you and me, forever and forever, you shall be Charley, and I shall be

Otoo. It is the way of the custom. And when we die, if it does happen that we live again somewhere beyond the stars and the sky, still shall you be Charley to me, and I Otoo to you."

"Yes, master," he answered, his eyes luminous and soft with joy.

"There you go!" I cried indignantly.

"What does it matter what my lips utter?" he argued. "They are only my lips. But I shall think Otoo always. Whenever I think of myself, I shall think of you. Whenever men call me by name, I shall think of you. And beyond the sky and beyond the stars, always and forever, you shall be Otoo to me. Is it well, master?"

I hid my smile, and answered that it was well.

We parted at Papeete. I remained ashore to recuperate; and he went on in a cutter to his own island, Bora Bora. Six weeks later he was back. I was surprised, for he had told me of his wife, and said that he was returning to her, and would give over sailing on far voyages.

"Where do you go, master?" he asked, after our first greetings.

I shrugged my shoulders. It was a hard question.

"All the world," was my answer—"all the world, all the sea, and all the islands that are in the sea."

"I will go with you," he said simply. "My wife is dead."

I never had a brother; but from what I have seen of other men's brothers, I doubt if any man ever had a brother that was to him what Otoo was to me. He was brother and father and mother as well. And this I know: I lived a straighter and better man because of Otoo. I cared little for other men, but I had to live straight in Otoo's eyes. Because of him I dared not tarnish myself. He made me his ideal, compounding me, I fear, chiefly out of his own love and worship and there were times when I stood close to the steep pitch of hell, and would have taken the plunge had not the thought of Otoo restrained me. His pride in me entered into me, until it became one of the major rules in my personal code to do nothing that would diminish that pride of his.

Naturally, I did not learn right away what his feelings were toward me. He never criticized, never censured; and slowly the exalted place I held in his eyes dawned upon me, and slowly I grew to comprehend the hurt I could inflict upon him by being anything less than my best.

For seventeen years we were together; for seventeen years he was at my shoulder, watching while I slept, nursing me through fever and wounds—ay, and receiving wounds in fighting for me. He signed on the same ships with me; and together we ranged the Pacific from Hawaii to Sydney Head, and from Torres Straits to the Galapagos. We blackbirded from the New Hebrides and the Line Islands over to the westward clear through the Louisades, New Britain, New Ireland, and New Hanover. We were wrecked three times—in the Gilberts, in the Santa Cruz group, and in the Fijis. And we traded and salved wherever a dollar promised in the way of pearl and pearl shell, copra, beche-de-mer, hawkbill turtle shell, and stranded wrecks.

It began in Papeete, immediately after his announcement that he was going with me over all the sea, and the islands in the midst thereof. There was a club in those days in Papeete, where the pearlers, traders, captains, and riffraff of South Sea adventurers forgathered. The play ran high, and the drink ran high; and I am very much afraid that I kept later hours than were becoming or proper. No matter what the hour was when I left the club, there was Otoo waiting to see me safely home.

At first I smiled; next I chided him. Then I told him flatly that I stood in need of no wet-nursing. After that I did not see him when I came out of the club. Quite by accident, a week or so later, I discovered that he still saw me home, lurking across the street among the shadows of the mango trees. What could I do? I know what I did do.

Insensibly I began to keep better hours. On wet and stormy nights, in the thick of the folly and the fun, the thought would persist in coming to me of Otoo keeping his dreary vigil under the dripping mangoes. Truly, he made a better man of me. Yet he was not strait-laced. And he knew nothing of common Christian morality. All the people on Bora Bora were Christians; but he was a heathen, the only unbeliever on the island, a gross materialist, who believed that when he died he was dead. He believed merely in fair play and square dealing. Petty meanness, in his code, was almost as serious as wanton homicide; and I do believe that he respected a murderer more than a man given to small practices.

Concerning me, personally, he objected to my doing anything that was hurtful to me. Gambling was all right. He was an ardent gambler himself. But late hours, he explained, were bad for one's health. He had seen men who did not take care of themselves die of fever. He was no teetotaler, and welcomed a stiff nip any time when it was wet work in the boats. On the other hand, he believed in liquor in moderation. He had seen many men killed or disgraced by square-face or Scotch.

Otoo had my welfare always at heart. He thought ahead for me, weighed my plans, and took a greater interest in them than I did myself. At first, when I was unaware of this interest of his in my affairs, he had to divine my intentions, as, for instance, at Papeete, when I contemplated going partners with a knavish fellow-countryman on a guano venture. I did not know he was a knave. Nor did any white man in Papeete. Neither did Otoo know, but he saw how thick we were getting, and found out for me, and without my asking him. Native sailors from the ends of the seas knock about on the beach in Tahiti; and Otoo, suspicious merely, went among them till he had gathered sufficient data to justify his suspicions. Oh, it was a nice history, that of Randolph Waters. I couldn't believe it when Otoo first narrated it; but when I sheeted it home to Waters he gave in without a murmur, and got away on the first steamer to Aukland.

At first, I am free to confess, I couldn't help resenting Otoo's poking his nose into my business. But I knew that he was wholly unselfish; and soon I had to acknowledge his wisdom and discretion. He had his eyes open always to my main chance, and he was both keen-sighted and far-sighted. In time he became my counselor, until he knew more of my business than I did myself. He really had my interest at heart more than I did. Mine was the magnificent carelessness of youth, for I preferred romance to dollars, and adventure to a comfortable billet with all night in. So it was well that I had some one to look out for me. I know that if it had not been for Otoo, I should not be here today.

Of numerous instances, let me give one. I had had some experience in blackbirding before I went pearling in the Paumotus. Otoo and I were on the beach in Samoa—we really were on the beach and hard aground—when my chance came to go as recruiter on a blackbird brig. Otoo signed on before the mast; and for the next half-dozen years, in as many ships, we knocked about the wildest portions of Melanesia. Otoo saw to it that he always pulled stroke-oar in my boat. Our custom in recruiting labor was to land the recruiter on the beach. The covering boat always lay on its oars several hundred feet off shore, while the recruiter's boat, also lying on its oars, kept afloat on the edge of the beach. When I landed with my trade goods, leaving my steering sweep apeak, Otoo left his stroke position and came into the stern sheets, where a Winchester lay ready to hand under a flap of canvas. The boat's crew was also armed, the Sniders concealed under canvas flaps that ran the length of the gunwales.

While I was busy arguing and persuading the woolly-headed cannibals to come and labor on the Queensland plantations Otoo kept watch. And often and often his low voice warned me of suspicious actions and impending treachery. Sometimes it was the quick shot from his rifle, knocking a nigger over, that was the first warning I received. And in my rush to the boat his hand was always there to jerk me flying aboard. Once, I remember, on SANTA ANNA, the boat grounded just as the trouble began. The covering boat was dashing to our assistance, but the several score of savages would have wiped us out before it arrived. Otoo took a flying leap ashore, dug both hands into the trade goods, and scattered tobacco, beads, tomahawks, knives, and calicoes in all directions.

This was too much for the woolly-heads. While they scrambled for the treasures, the boat was shoved clear, and we were aboard and forty feet away. And I got thirty recruits off that very beach in the next four hours.

The particular instance I have in mind was on Malaita, the most savage island in the easterly Solomons. The natives had been remarkably friendly; and how were we to know that the whole village had been taking up a collection for over two years with which to buy a white man's head? The beggars are all head-hunters, and they especially esteem a white man's head. The fellow who captured the head would receive the whole collection. As I say, they appeared very friendly; and on this day I was fully a hundred yards down the beach from the boat. Otoo had cautioned me; and, as usual when I did not heed him, I came to grief.

The first I knew, a cloud of spears sailed out of the mangrove swamp at me. At least a dozen were sticking into me. I started to run, but tripped over one that was fast in my calf, and went down. The woolly-heads made a run for me, each with a long-handled, fantail tomahawk with which to hack off my head. They were so eager for the prize that they got in one another's way. In the confusion, I avoided several hacks by throwing myself right and left on the sand.

Then Otoo arrived—Otoo the manhandler. In some way he had got hold of a heavy war club, and at close quarters it was a far more efficient weapon than a rifle. He was right in the thick of them, so that they could not spear him, while their tomahawks seemed worse than useless. He was fighting for me, and he was in a true Berserker rage. The way he handled that club was amazing.

Their skulls squashed like overripe oranges. It was not until he had driven them back, picked me up in his arms, and started to run, that he received his first wounds. He arrived in the boat with four spear thrusts, got his Winchester, and with it got a man for every shot. Then we pulled aboard the schooner, and doctored up.

Seventeen years we were together. He made me. I should today be a supercargo, a recruiter, or a memory, if it had not been for him.

"You spend your money, and you go out and get more," he said one day. "It is easy to get money now. But when you get old, your money will be spent, and you will not be able to go out and get more. I know, master. I have studied the way of white men. On the beaches are many old men who were young once, and who could get money just like you. Now they are old, and they have nothing, and they wait about for the young men like you to come ashore and buy drinks for them.

"The black boy is a slave on the plantations. He gets twenty dollars a year. He works hard. The overseer does not work hard. He rides a horse and watches the black boy work. He gets twelve hundred dollars a year. I am a sailor on the schooner. I get fifteen dollars a month. That is because I am a good sailor. I work hard. The captain has a double awning, and drinks beer out of long bottles. I have never seen him haul a rope or pull an oar. He gets one hundred and fifty dollars a month. I am a sailor. He is a navigator. Master, I think it would be very good for you to know navigation."

Otoo spurred me on to it. He sailed with me as second mate on my first schooner, and he was far prouder of my command than I was myself. Later on it was:

"The captain is well paid, master; but the ship is in his keeping, and he is never free from the burden. It is the owner who is better paid—the owner who sits ashore with many servants and turns his money over."

"True, but a schooner costs five thousand dollars—an old schooner at that," I objected. "I should be an old man before I saved five thousand dollars."

"There be short ways for white men to make money," he went on, pointing ashore at the cocoanut-fringed beach.

We were in the Solomons at the time, picking up a cargo of ivory nuts along the east coast of Guadalcanar.

"Between this river mouth and the next it is two miles," he said.

"The flat land runs far back. It is worth nothing now. Next year—who knows?—or the year after, men will pay much money for that land. The anchorage is good. Big steamers can lie close up. You can buy the land four miles deep from the old chief for ten thousand sticks of tobacco, ten bottles of square-face, and a Snider, which will cost you, maybe, one hundred dollars. Then you place the deed with the commissioner; and the next year, or the year after, you sell and become the owner of a ship."

I followed his lead, and his words came true, though in three years, instead of two. Next came the grasslands deal on Guadalcanar—twenty thousand acres, on a governmental nine hundred and ninety-nine years' lease at a nominal sum. I owned the lease for precisely ninety days, when I sold it to a company for half a fortune. Always it was Otoo who looked ahead and saw the opportunity. He was responsible for the salving of the Doncaster—bought in at auction for a hundred pounds, and clearing three thousand after every expense was paid. He led me into the Savaii plantation and the cocoa venture on Upolu.

We did not go seafaring so much as in the old days. I was too well off. I married, and my standard of living rose; but Otoo remained the same old-time Otoo, moving about the house or trailing through the office, his wooden pipe in his mouth, a shilling undershirt on his back, and a four-shilling lava-lava about his loins. I could not get him to spend money. There was no way of repaying him except with love, and God knows he got that in full measure from all of us. The children worshipped him; and if he had been spoilable, my wife would surely have been his undoing.

The children! He really was the one who showed them the way of their feet in the world practical. He began by teaching them to walk. He sat up with them when they were sick. One by one, when they were scarcely toddlers, he took them down to the lagoon, and made them into amphibians. He taught them more than I ever knew of the habits of fish and the ways of catching them. In the bush it was the same thing. At seven, Tom knew more woodcraft than I ever dreamed existed. At six, Mary went over the Sliding Rock without a quiver, and I have seen strong men balk at that feat. And when Frank had just turned six he could bring up shillings from the bottom in three fathoms.

"My people in Bora Bora do not like heathen—they are all Christians; and I do not like Bora Bora Christians," he said one day, when I, with the idea of getting him to spend some of the money that was rightfully his, had been trying to persuade him to make a visit to his own island in one of our schooners—a special voyage which I had hoped to make a record breaker in the matter of prodigal expense.

I say one of OUR schooners, though legally at the time they belonged to me. I struggled long with him to enter into partnership.

"We have been partners from the day the Petite Jeanne went down," he said at last. "But if your heart so wishes, then shall we become partners by the law. I have no work to do, yet are my expenses large. I drink and eat and smoke in plenty—it costs much, I know. I do not pay for the playing of billiards, for I play on your table; but still the money goes. Fishing on the reef is only a rich man's pleasure. It is shocking, the cost of hooks and cotton line. Yes; it is necessary that we be partners by the law. I need the money. I shall get it from the head clerk in the office."

So the papers were made out and recorded. A year later I was compelled to complain.

"Charley," said I, "you are a wicked old fraud, a miserly skinflint, a miserable land crab. Behold, your share for the year in all our partnership has been thousands of dollars. The head clerk has given me this paper. It says that in the year you have drawn just eighty-seven dollars and twenty cents."

"Is there any owing me?" he asked anxiously.

"I tell you thousands and thousands," I answered.

His face brightened, as with an immense relief.

"It is well," he said. "See that the head clerk keeps good account of it. When I want it, I shall want it, and there must not be a cent missing."

"If there is," he added fiercely, after a pause, "it must come out of the clerk's wages."

And all the time, as I afterwards learned, his will, drawn up by Carruthers, and making me sole beneficiary, lay in the American consul's safe.

But the end came, as the end must come to all human associations.

It occurred in the Solomons, where our wildest work had been done in the wild young days, and where we were once more—principally on a holiday, incidentally to look after our holdings on Florida Island and to look over the pearling possibilities of the Mboli Pass. We were lying at Savo, having run in to trade for curios.

Now, Savo is alive with sharks. The custom of the woolly-heads of burying their dead in the sea did not tend to discourage the sharks from making the adjacent waters a hangout. It was my luck to be coming aboard in a tiny, overloaded, native canoe, when the thing capsized. There were four woolly-heads and myself in it, or rather, hanging to it. The schooner was a hundred yards away.

I was just hailing for a boat when one of the woolly-heads began to scream. Holding on to the end of the canoe, both he and that portion of the canoe were dragged under several times. Then he loosed his clutch and disappeared. A shark had got him.

The three remaining niggers tried to climb out of the water upon the bottom of the canoe. I yelled and cursed and struck at the nearest with my fist, but it was no use. They were in a blind funk. The canoe could barely have supported one of them. Under the three it upended and rolled sidewise, throwing them back into the water.

I abandoned the canoe and started to swim toward the schooner, expecting to be picked up by the boat before I got there. One of the niggers elected to come with me, and we swam along silently, side by side, now and again putting our faces into the water and peering about for sharks. The screams of the man who stayed by the canoe informed us that he was taken. I was peering into the water when I saw a big shark pass directly beneath me. He was fully sixteen feet in length. I saw the whole thing. He got the woolly-head by the middle, and away he went, the poor devil, head, shoulders, and arms out of the water all the time, screeching in a heart-rending way. He was carried along in this fashion for several hundred feet, when he was dragged beneath the surface.

I swam doggedly on, hoping that that was the last unattached shark. But there was another. Whether it was one that had attacked the natives earlier, or whether it was one that had made a good meal elsewhere, I do not know. At any rate, he was not in such haste as the others. I could not swim so rapidly now, for a large part of my effort was devoted to keeping track of him. I was watching him when he made his first attack. By good luck I got both hands on his nose, and, though his momentum nearly shoved me under, I managed to keep him off. He veered clear, and began circling about again. A second time I escaped him by the same manoeuvre. The third rush was a miss on both sides. He sheered at the moment my hands should have landed on his nose, but his sandpaper hide (I had on a sleeveless undershirt) scraped the skin off one arm from elbow to shoulder.

By this time I was played out, and gave up hope. The schooner was still two hundred feet away. My face was in the water, and I was watching him manoeuvre for another attempt, when I saw a brown body pass between us. It was Otoo.

"Swim for the schooner, master!" he said. And he spoke gayly, as though the affair was a mere lark. "I know sharks. The shark is my brother."

I obeyed, swimming slowly on, while Otoo swam about me, keeping always between me and the shark, foiling his rushes and encouraging me.

"The davit tackle carried away, and they are rigging the falls," he explained, a minute or so later, and then went under to head off another attack.

By the time the schooner was thirty feet away I was about done for. I could scarcely move. They were heaving lines at us from on board, but they continually fell short. The shark, finding that it was receiving no hurt, had become bolder. Several times it nearly got me, but each time Otoo was there just the moment before it was too late. Of course, Otoo could have saved himself any time. But he stuck by me.

"Good-by, Charley! I'm finished!" I just managed to gasp.

I knew that the end had come, and that the next moment I should throw up my hands and go down.

But Otoo laughed in my face, saying:

"I will show you a new trick. I will make that shark feel sick!"

He dropped in behind me, where the shark was preparing to come at me.

"A little more to the left!" he next called out. "There is a line there on the water. To the left, master—to the left!"

I changed my course and struck out blindly. I was by that time barely conscious. As my hand closed on the line I heard an exclamation from on board. I turned and looked. There was no sign of Otoo. The next instant he broke surface. Both hands were off at the wrist, the stumps spouting blood.

"Otoo!" he called softly. And I could see in his gaze the love that thrilled in his voice.

Then, and then only, at the very last of all our years, he called me by that name.

"Good-by, Otoo!" he called.

Then he was dragged under, and I was hauled aboard, where I fainted in the captain's arms.

And so passed Otoo, who saved me and made me a man, and who saved me in the end. We met in the maw of a hurricane, and parted in the maw of a shark, with seventeen intervening years of comradeship, the like of which I dare to assert has never befallen two men, the one brown and the other white. If Jehovah be from His high place watching every sparrow fall, not least in His kingdom shall be Otoo, the one heathen of Bora Bora.

THE TERRIBLE SOLOMONS

There is no gainsaying that the Solomons are a hard-bitten bunch of islands. On the other hand, there are worse places in the world. But to the new chum who has no constitutional understanding of men and life in the rough, the Solomons may indeed prove terrible.

It is true that fever and dysentery are perpetually on the walk-about, that loathsome skin diseases abound, that the air is saturated with a poison that bites into every pore, cut, or abrasion and plants malignant ulcers, and that many strong men who escape dying there return as wrecks to their own countries. It is also true that the natives of the Solomons are a wild lot, with a hearty appetite for human flesh and a fad for collecting human heads. Their highest instinct of sportsmanship is to catch a man with his back turned and to smite him a cunning blow with a tomahawk that severs the spinal column at the base of the brain. It is equally true that on some islands, such as Malaita, the profit and loss account of social intercourse is calculated in homicides. Heads are a medium of exchange, and white heads are extremely valuable. Very often a dozen villages make a jack-pot, which they fatten moon by moon, against the time when some brave warrior presents a white man's head, fresh and gory, and claims the pot.

All the foregoing is quite true, and yet there are white men who have lived in the Solomons a score of years and who feel homesick when they go away from them. A man needs only to be careful—and lucky—to live a long time in the Solomons; but he must also be of the right sort. He must have the hallmark of the inevitable white man stamped upon his soul. He must be inevitable. He must have a certain grand carelessness of odds, a certain colossal self-satisfaction, and a racial egotism that convinces him that one white is better than a thousand niggers every day in the week, and that on Sunday he is able to clean out two thousand niggers. For such are the things that have made the white man inevitable. Oh, and one other thing—the white man who wishes to be inevitable, must not merely despise the lesser breeds and think a lot of himself; he must also fail to be too long on imagination. He must not understand too well the instincts, customs, and mental processes of the blacks, the yellows, and the browns; for it is not in such fashion that the white race has tramped its royal road around the world.

Bertie Arkwright was not inevitable. He was too sensitive, too finely strung, and he possessed too much imagination. The world was too much with him. He projected himself too quiveringly into his environment. Therefore, the last place in the world for him to come was the Solomons. He did not come, expecting to stay. A five weeks' stop-over between steamers, he decided, would satisfy the call of the primitive he felt thrumming the strings of his being. At least, so he told the lady tourists on the MAKEMBO, though in different terms; and they worshipped him as a hero, for they were lady tourists and they would know only the safety of the steamer's deck as she threaded her way through the Solomons.

There was another man on board, of whom the ladies took no notice. He was a little shriveled wisp of a man, with a withered skin the color of mahogany. His name on the passenger list does not matter, but his other name, Captain Malu, was a name for niggers to conjure with, and to scare naughty pickaninnies to righteousness from New Hanover to the New Hebrides. He had farmed savages and savagery, and from fever and hardship, the crack of Sniders and the lash of the overseers, had wrested five millions of money in the form of bêche-de-mer, sandalwood, pearl-shell and turtle-shell, ivory nuts and copra, grasslands, trading stations, and plantations. Captain Malu's little finger, which was broken, had more inevitableness in it than Bertie Arkwright's whole carcass. But then, the lady tourists had nothing by which to judge save appearances, and Bertie certainly was a fine-looking man.

Bertie talked with Captain Malu in the smoking room, confiding to him his intention of seeing life red and bleeding in the Solomons. Captain Malu agreed that the intention was ambitious and honorable. It was not until several days later that he became interested in Bertie, when that young adventurer insisted on showing him an automatic 44-caliber pistol. Bertie explained the mechanism and demonstrated by slipping a loaded magazine up the hollow butt.

"It is so simple," he said. He shot the outer barrel back along the inner one. "That loads it and cocks it, you see. And then all I have to do is pull the trigger, eight times, as fast as I can quiver my finger. See that safety clutch. That's what I like about it. It is safe. It is positively fool-proof." He slipped out the magazine. "You see how safe it is."

As he held it in his hand, the muzzle came in line with Captain Malu's stomach. Captain Malu's blue eyes looked at it unswervingly.

"Would you mind pointing it in some other direction?" he asked.

"It's perfectly safe," Bertie assured him. "I withdrew the magazine. It's not loaded now, you know."

"A gun is always loaded."

"But this one isn't."

"Turn it away just the same."

Captain Malu's voice was flat and metallic and low, but his eyes never left the muzzle until the line of it was drawn past him and away from him.

"I'll bet a fiver it isn't loaded," Bertie proposed warmly.

The other shook his head.

"Then I'll show you."

Bertie started to put the muzzle to his own temple with the evident intention of pulling the trigger.

"Just a second," Captain Malu said quietly, reaching out his hand. "Let me look at it."

He pointed it seaward and pulled the trigger. A heavy explosion followed, instantaneous with the sharp click of the mechanism that flipped a hot and smoking cartridge sidewise along the deck.

Bertie's jaw dropped in amazement.

"I slipped the barrel back once, didn't I?" he explained. "It was silly of me, I must say."

He giggled flabbily, and sat down in a steamer chair. The blood had ebbed from his face, exposing dark circles under his eyes. His hands were trembling and unable to guide the shaking cigarette to his lips. The world was too much with him, and he saw himself with dripping brains prone upon the deck.

"Really," he said, "... really."

"It's a pretty weapon," said Captain Malu, returning the automatic to him.

The Commissioner was on board the Makembo, returning from Sydney, and by his permission a stop was made at Ugi to land a missionary. And at Ugi lay the ketch ARLA, Captain Hansen, skipper. Now the Arla was one of many vessels owned by Captain Malu, and it was at his suggestion and by his invitation that Bertie went aboard the Arla as guest for a four days' recruiting cruise on the coast of Malaita. Thereafter the ARLA would drop him at Reminge Plantation (also owned by Captain Malu), where Bertie could remain for a week, and then be sent over to Tulagi, the seat of government, where he would become the Commissioner's guest. Captain Malu was responsible for two other suggestions, which given, he disappears from this narrative. One was to Captain Hansen, the other to Mr. Harriwell, manager of Reminge Plantation. Both suggestions were similar in tenor, namely, to give Mr. Bertram Arkwright an insight into the rawness and redness of life in the Solomons. Also, it is whispered that Captain Malu mentioned that a case of Scotch would be coincidental with any particularly gorgeous insight Mr. Arkwright might receive.............

"Yes, Swartz always was too pig-headed. You see, he took four of his boat's crew to Tulagi to be flogged—officially, you know—then started back with them in the whaleboat. It was pretty squally, and the boat capsized just outside. Swartz was the only one drowned. Of course, it was an accident."

"Was it? Really?" Bertie asked, only half-interested, staring hard at the black man at the wheel.

Ugi had dropped astern, and the ARLA was sliding along through a summer sea toward the wooded ranges of Malaita. The helmsman who so attracted Bertie's eyes sported a ten penny nail, stuck skewerwise through his nose. About his neck was a string of pants buttons. Thrust through holes in his ears were a can opener, the broken handle of a toothbrush, a clay pipe, the brass wheel of an alarm clock, and several Winchester rifle cartridges.

On his chest, suspended from around his neck hung the half of a china plate. Some forty similarly appareled blacks lay about the deck, fifteen of which were boat's crew, the remainder being fresh labor recruits.

"Of course it was an accident," spoke up the ARLA'S mate, Jacobs, a slender, dark-eyed man who looked more a professor than a sailor. "Johnny Bedip nearly had the same kind of accident. He was bringing back several from a flogging, when they capsized him. But he knew how to swim as well as they, and two of them were drowned. He used a boat stretcher and a revolver. Of course it was an accident."

"Quite common, them accidents," remarked the skipper. "You see that man at the wheel, Mr. Arkwright? He's a man eater. Six months ago, he and the rest of the boat's crew drowned the then captain of the ARLA. They did it on deck, sir, right aft there by the mizzen-traveler."

"The deck was in a shocking state," said the mate.

"Do I understand—?" Bertie began.

"Yes, just that," said Captain Hansen. "It was an accidental drowning."

"But on deck—?"

"Just so. I don't mind telling you, in confidence, of course, that they used an axe."

"This present crew of yours?"

Captain Hansen nodded.

"The other skipper always was too careless," explained the mate. "He but just turned his back, when they let him have it."

382

"We haven't any show down here," was the skipper's complaint. "The government protects a nigger against a white every time. You can't shoot first. You've got to give the nigger first shot, or else the government calls it murder and you go to Fiji. That's why there's so many drowning accidents."

Dinner was called, and Bertie and the skipper went below, leaving the mate to watch on deck.

"Keep an eye out for that black devil, Auiki," was the skipper's parting caution. "I haven't liked his looks for several days."

"Right O," said the mate.

Dinner was part way along, and the skipper was in the middle of his story of the cutting out of the Scottish Chiefs.

"Yes," he was saying, "she was the finest vessel on the coast. But when she missed stays, and before ever she hit the reef, the canoes started for her. There were five white men, a crew of twenty Santa Cruz boys and Samoans, and only the supercargo escaped. Besides, there were sixty recruits. They were all kai-kai'd. Kai-kai?—oh, I beg your pardon. I mean they were eaten. Then there was the James Edwards, a dandy-rigged—"

But at that moment there was a sharp oath from the mate on deck and a chorus of savage cries. A revolver went off three times, and then was heard a loud splash. Captain Hansen had sprung up the companionway on the instant, and Bertie's eyes had been fascinated by a glimpse of him drawing his revolver as he sprang.

Bertie went up more circumspectly, hesitating before he put his head above the companionway slide. But nothing happened. The mate was shaking with excitement, his revolver in his hand. Once he startled, and half-jumped around, as if danger threatened his back.

"One of the natives fell overboard," he was saying, in a queer tense voice. "He couldn't swim."

"Who was it?" the skipper demanded.

"Auiki," was the answer.

"But I say, you know, I heard shots," Bertie said, in trembling eagerness, for he scented adventure, and adventure that was happily over with.

The mate whirled upon him, snarling:

"It's a damned lie. There ain't been a shot fired. The nigger fell overboard."

Captain Hansen regarded Bertie with unblinking, lack-luster eyes.

"I—I thought—" Bertie was beginning.

"Shots?" said Captain Hansen, dreamily. "Shots? Did you hear any shots, Mr. Jacobs?"

"Not a shot," replied Mr. Jacobs.

The skipper looked at his guest triumphantly, and said:

"Evidently an accident. Let us go down, Mr. Arkwright, and finish dinner."

Bertie slept that night in the captain's cabin, a tiny stateroom off the main cabin. The for'ard bulkhead was decorated with a stand of rifles. Over the bunk were three more rifles. Under the bunk was a big drawer, which, when he pulled it out, he found filled with ammunition, dynamite, and several boxes of detonators. He elected to take the settee on the opposite side. Lying conspicuously on the small table, was the Arla's log. Bertie did not know that it had been especially prepared for the occasion by Captain Malu, and he read therein how on September 21, two boat's crew had fallen overboard and been drowned. Bertie read between the lines and knew better. He read how the Arla's whale boat had been bushwhacked at Su'u and had lost three men; of how the skipper discovered the cook stewing human flesh on the galley fire—flesh purchased by the boat's crew ashore in Fui; of how an accidental discharge of dynamite, while signaling, had killed another boat's crew; of night attacks; ports fled from between the dawns; attacks by bushmen in mangrove swamps and by fleets of salt-water men in the larger passages. One item that occurred with monotonous frequency was death by dysentery. He noticed with alarm that two white men had so died—guests, like himself, on the Arla.

"I say, you know," Bertie said next day to Captain Hansen. "I've been glancing through your log."

The skipper displayed quick vexation that the log had been left lying about.

"And all that dysentery, you know, that's all rot, just like the accidental drownings," Bertie continued. "What does dysentery really stand for?"

The skipper openly admired his guest's acumen, stiffened himself to make indignant denial, then gracefully surrendered.

"You see, it's like this, Mr. Arkwright. These islands have got a bad enough name as it is. It's getting harder every day to sign on white men. Suppose a man is killed. The company has to pay through the nose for another man to take the job. But if the man merely dies of sickness, it's all right. The new chums don't mind disease. What they draw the line at is being murdered. I thought the skipper of the Arla had died of dysentery when I took his billet. Then it was too late. I'd signed the contract."

"Besides," said Mr. Jacobs, "there's altogether too many accidental drownings anyway. It don't look right. It's the fault of the government. A white man hasn't a chance to defend himself from the niggers."

"Yes, look at the Princess and that Yankee mate," the skipper took up the tale. "She carried five white men besides a government agent. The captain, the agent, and the supercargo were ashore in the two boats. They were killed to the last man. The mate and boson, with about fifteen of the crew—Samoans and Tongans—were on board. A crowd of niggers came off from shore. First thing the mate knew, the boson and the crew were killed in the first rush. The mate grabbed three cartridge belts and two Winchesters and skinned up to the cross-trees. He was the sole survivor, and you can't blame him for being mad. He pumped one rifle till it got so hot he couldn't hold it, then he pumped the other. The deck was black with niggers. He cleaned them out. He dropped them as they went over the rail, and he dropped them as fast as they picked up their paddles. Then they jumped into the water and started to swim for it, and being mad, he got half a dozen more. And what did he get for it?"

"Seven years in Fiji," snapped the mate.

"The government said he wasn't justified in shooting after they'd taken to the water," the skipper explained.

"And that's why they die of dysentery nowadays," the mate added.

"Just fancy," said Bertie, as he felt a longing for the cruise to be over.

Later on in the day he interviewed the black who had been pointed out to him as a cannibal. This fellow's name was Sumasai. He had spent three years on a Queensland plantation. He had been to Samoa, and Fiji, and Sydney; and as a boat's crew had been on recruiting schooners through New Britain, New Ireland, New Guinea, and the Admiralties. Also, he was a wag, and he had taken a line on his skipper's conduct. Yes, he had eaten many men. How many? He could not remember the tally. Yes, white men, too; they were very good, unless they were sick. He had once eaten a sick one.

"My word!" he cried, at the recollection. "Me sick plenty along him. My belly walk about too much."

Bertie shuddered, and asked about heads. Yes, Sumasai had several hidden ashore, in good condition, sun-dried, and smoke-cured. One was of the captain of a schooner. It had long whiskers. He would sell it for two quid. Black men's heads he would sell for one quid. He had some pickaninny heads, in poor condition, that he would let go for ten bob.

Five minutes afterward, Bertie found himself sitting on the companionway-slide alongside a black with a horrible skin disease. He sheered off, and on inquiry was told that it was leprosy. He hurried below and washed himself with antiseptic soap. He took many antiseptic washes in the course of the day, for every native on board was afflicted with malignant ulcers of one sort or another.

As the Arla drew in to an anchorage in the midst of mangrove swamps, a double row of barbed wire was stretched around above her rail. That looked like business, and when Bertie saw the shore canoes alongside, armed with spears, bows and arrows, and Sniders, he wished more earnestly than ever that the cruise was over.

That evening the natives were slow in leaving the ship at sundown. A number of them checked the mate when he ordered them ashore. "Never mind, I'll fix them," said Captain Hansen, diving below.

When he came back, he showed Bertie a stick of dynamite attached to a fish hook. Now it happens that a paper-wrapped bottle of chlorodyne with a piece of harmless fuse projecting can fool anybody. It fooled Bertie, and it fooled the natives. When Captain Hansen lighted the fuse and hooked the fish hook into the tail end of a native's loin cloth, that native was smitten with so an ardent a desire for the shore that he forgot to shed the loin cloth. He started for'ard, the fuse sizzling and spluttering at his rear, the natives in his path taking headers over the barbed wire at every jump. Bertie was horror-stricken. So was Captain Hansen. He had forgotten his twenty-five recruits, on each of which he had paid thirty shillings advance. They went over the side along with the shore-dwelling folk and followed by him who trailed the sizzling chlorodyne bottle.

Bertie did not see the bottle go off; but the mate opportunely discharging a stick of real dynamite aft where it would harm nobody, Bertie would have sworn in any admiralty court to a nigger blown to flinders. The flight of the twenty-five recruits had actually cost the Arla forty pounds, and, since they had taken to the bush, there was no hope of recovering them. The skipper and his mate proceeded to drown their sorrow in cold tea.

The cold tea was in whiskey bottles, so Bertie did not know it was cold tea they were mopping up. All he knew was that the two men got very drunk and argued eloquently and at length as to whether the exploded nigger should be reported as a case of dysentery or as an accidental drowning. When they snored off to sleep, he was the only white man left, and he kept a perilous watch till dawn, in fear of an attack from shore and an uprising of the crew.

Three more days the Arla spent on the coast, and three more nights the skipper and the mate drank overfondly of cold tea, leaving Bertie to keep the watch. They knew he could be depended upon, while he was equally certain that if he lived, he would report their drunken conduct to Captain Malu. Then the Arla dropped anchor at Reminge Plantation, on Guadalcanar, and

Bertie landed on the beach with a sigh of relief and shook hands with the manager. Mr. Harriwell was ready for him.

"Now you mustn't be alarmed if some of our fellows seem downcast," Mr. Harriwell said, having drawn him aside in confidence. "There's been talk of an outbreak, and two or three suspicious signs I'm willing to admit, but personally I think it's all poppycock."

"How—how many blacks have you on the plantation?" Bertie asked, with a sinking heart.

"We're working four hundred just now," replied Mr. Harriwell, cheerfully; "but the three of us, with you, of course, and the skipper and mate of the Arla, can handle them all right."

Bertie turned to meet one McTavish, the storekeeper, who scarcely acknowledged the introduction, such was his eagerness to present his resignation.

"It being that I'm a married man, Mr. Harriwell, I can't very well afford to remain on longer. Trouble is working up, as plain as the nose on your face. The niggers are going to break out, and there'll be another Hohono horror here."

"What's a Hohono horror?" Bertie asked, after the storekeeper had been persuaded to remain until the end of the month.

"Oh, he means Hohono Plantation, on Ysabel," said the manager. "The niggers killed the five white men ashore, captured the schooner, killed the captain and mate, and escaped in a body to Malaita. But I always said they were careless on Hohono. They won't catch us napping here. Come along, Mr. Arkwright, and see our view from the veranda."

Bertie was too busy wondering how he could get away to Tulagi to the Commissioner's house, to see much of the view. He was still wondering, when a rifle exploded very near to him, behind his back. At the same moment his arm was nearly dislocated, so eagerly did Mr. Harriwell drag him indoors.

"I say, old man, that was a close shave," said the manager, pawing him over to see if he had been hit. "I can't tell you how sorry I am. But it was broad daylight, and I never dreamed."

Bertie was beginning to turn pale.

"They got the other manager that way," McTavish vouchsafed. "And a dashed fine chap he was. Blew his brains out all over the veranda. You noticed that dark stain there between the steps and the door?"

Bertie was ripe for the cocktail which Mr. Harriwell pitched in and compounded for him; but before he could drink it, a man in riding trousers and puttees entered.

"What's the matter now?" the manager asked, after one look at the newcomer's face. "Is the river up again?"

"River be blowed—it's the niggers. Stepped out of the cane grass, not a dozen feet away, and whopped at me. It was a Snider, and he shot from the hip. Now what I want to know is where'd he get that Snider?—Oh, I beg pardon. Glad to know you, Mr. Arkwright."

"Mr. Brown is my assistant," explained Mr. Harriwell. "And now let's have that drink."

"But where'd he get that Snider?" Mr. Brown insisted. "I always objected to keeping those guns on the premises."

"They're still there," Mr. Harriwell said, with a show of heat.

Mr. Brown smiled incredulously.

"Come along and see," said the manager.

Bertie joined the procession into the office, where Mr. Harriwell pointed triumphantly at a big packing case in a dusty corner.

"Well, then where did the beggar get that Snider?" harped Mr. Brown.

But just then McTavish lifted the packing case. The manager started, then tore off the lid. The case was empty. They gazed at one another in horrified silence. Harriwell drooped wearily.

Then McVeigh cursed.

"What I contended all along—the house-boys are not to be trusted."

"It does look serious," Harriwell admitted, "but we'll come through it all right. What the sanguinary niggers need is a shaking up. Will you gentlemen please bring your rifles to dinner, and will you, Mr. Brown, kindly prepare forty or fifty sticks of dynamite. Make the fuses good and short. We'll give them a lesson. And now, gentlemen, dinner is served."

One thing that Bertie detested was rice and curry, so it happened that he alone partook of an inviting omelet. He had quite finished his plate, when Harriwell helped himself to the omelet. One mouthful he tasted, then spat out vociferously.

"That's the second time," McTavish announced ominously.

Harriwell was still hawking and spitting.

"Second time, what?" Bertie quavered.

"Poison," was the answer. "That cook will be hanged yet."

"That's the way the bookkeeper went out at Cape March," Brown spoke up. "Died horribly. They said on the Jessie that they heard him screaming three miles away."

"I'll put the cook in irons," sputtered Harriwell. "Fortunately we discovered it in time."

Bertie sat paralyzed. There was no color in his face. He attempted to speak, but only an inarticulate gurgle resulted. All eyed him anxiously.

"Don't say it, don't say it," McTavish cried in a tense voice.

"Yes, I ate it, plenty of it, a whole plateful!" Bertie cried explosively, like a diver suddenly regaining breath.

The awful silence continued half a minute longer, and he read his fate in their eyes.

"Maybe it wasn't poison after all," said Harriwell, dismally.

"Call in the cook," said Brown.

In came the cook, a grinning black boy, nose-spiked and ear-plugged.

"Here, you, Wi-wi, what name that?" Harriwell bellowed, pointing accusingly at the omelet.

Wi-wi was very naturally frightened and embarrassed.

"Him good fella kai-kai," he murmured apologetically.

"Make him eat it," suggested McTavish. "That's a proper test."

Harriwell filled a spoon with the stuff and jumped for the cook, who fled in panic.

"That settles it," was Brown's solemn pronouncement. "He won't eat it."

"Mr. Brown, will you please go and put the irons on him?" Harriwell turned cheerfully to Bertie. "It's all right, old man, the Commissioner will deal with him, and if you die, depend upon it, he will be hanged."

"Don't think the government'll do it," objected McTavish.

"But gentlemen, gentlemen," Bertie cried. "In the meantime think of me."

Harriwell shrugged his shoulders pityingly.

"Sorry, old man, but it's a native poison, and there are no known antidotes for native poisons. Try and compose yourself and if—"

Two sharp reports of a rifle from without, interrupted the discourse, and Brown, entering, reloaded his rifle and sat down to table.

"The cook's dead," he said. "Fever. A rather sudden attack."

"I was just telling Mr. Arkwright that there are no antidotes for native poisons—"

"Except gin," said Brown.

Harriwell called himself an absent-minded idiot and rushed for the gin bottle.

"Neat, man, neat," he warned Bertie, who gulped down a tumbler two-thirds full of the raw spirits, and coughed and choked from the angry bite of it till the tears ran down his cheeks.

Harriwell took his pulse and temperature, made a show of looking out for him, and doubted that the omelet had been poisoned. Brown and McTavish also doubted; but Bertie discerned an insincere ring in their voices. His appetite had left him, and he took his own pulse stealthily under the table. There was no question but what it was increasing, but he failed to ascribe it to the gin he had taken. McTavish, rifle in hand, went out on the veranda to reconnoiter.

"They're massing up at the cook-house," was his report. "And they've no end of Sniders. My idea is to sneak around on the other side and take them in flank. Strike the first blow, you know. Will you come along, Brown?"

Harriwell ate on steadily, while Bertie discovered that his pulse had leaped up five beats. Nevertheless, he could not help jumping when the rifles began to go off. Above the scattering of Sniders could be heard the pumping of Brown's and McTavish's Winchesters—all against a background of demoniacal screeching and yelling.

"They've got them on the run," Harriwell remarked, as voices and gunshots faded away in the distance.

Scarcely were Brown and McTavish back at the table when the latter reconnoitered.

"They've got dynamite," he said.

"Then let's charge them with dynamite," Harriwell proposed.

Thrusting half a dozen sticks each into their pockets and equipping themselves with lighted cigars, they started for the door. And just then it happened. They blamed McTavish for it afterward, and he admitted that the charge had been a trifle excessive. But at any rate it went off under the house, which lifted up cornerwise and settled back on its foundations. Half the china on the table was shattered, while the eight-day clock stopped. Yelling for vengeance, the three men rushed out into the night, and the bombardment began.

When they returned, there was no Bertie. He had dragged himself away to the office, barricaded himself in, and sunk upon the floor in a gin-soaked nightmare, wherein he died a thousand deaths while the valorous fight went on around him. In the morning, sick and headachey from the gin, he crawled out to find the sun still in the sky and God presumable in heaven, for his hosts were alive and uninjured.

Harriwell pressed him to stay on longer, but Bertie insisted on sailing immediately on the Arla for Tulagi, where, until the following steamer day, he stuck close by the Commissioner's house. There were lady tourists on the outgoing steamer, and Bertie was again a hero, while Captain Malu, as usual, passed unnoticed. But Captain Malu sent back from Sydney two cases of the best Scotch whiskey on the market, for he was not able to make up his mind as to whether it was Captain Hansen or Mr Harriwell who had given Bertie Arkwright the more gorgeous insight into life in the Solomons.

THE INEVITABLE WHITE MAN

"The black will never understand the white, nor the white the black, as long as black is black and white is white."

So said Captain Woodward. We sat in the parlor of Charley Roberts' pub in Apia, drinking long Abu Hameds compounded and shared with us by the aforesaid Charley Roberts, who claimed the recipe direct from Stevens, famous for having invented the Abu Hamed at a time when he was spurred on by Nile thirst—the Stevens who was responsible for "With Kitchener to Kartoun," and who passed out at the siege of Ladysmith.

Captain Woodward, short and squat, elderly, burned by forty years of tropic sun, and with the most beautiful liquid brown eyes I ever saw in a man, spoke from a vast experience. The crisscross of scars on his bald pate bespoke a tomahawk intimacy with the black, and of equal intimacy was the advertisement, front and rear, on the right side of his neck, where an arrow had at one time entered and been pulled clean through. As he explained, he had been in a hurry on that occasion—the arrow impeded his running—and he felt that he could not take the time to break off the head and pull out the shaft the way it had come in. At the present moment he was commander of the SAVAII, the big steamer that recruited labor from the westward for the German plantations on Samoa.

"Half the trouble is the stupidity of the whites," said Roberts, pausing to take a swig from his glass and to curse the Samoan bar-boy in affectionate terms. "If the white man would lay himself out a bit to understand the workings of the black man's mind, most of the messes would be avoided."

"I've seen a few who claimed they understood niggers," Captain Woodward retorted, "and I always took notice that they were the first to be kai-kai'd (eaten). Look at the missionaries in New Guinea and the New Hebrides—the martyr isle of Erromanga and all the rest. Look at the Austrian expedition that was cut to pieces in the Solomons, in the bush of Guadalcanar.

And look at the traders themselves, with a score of years' experience, making their brag that no nigger would ever get them, and whose heads to this day are ornamenting the rafters of the canoe houses. There was old Johnny Simons— twenty-six years on the raw edges of Melanesia, swore he knew the niggers like a book and that they'd never do for him, and he passed out at Marovo Lagoon, New Georgia, had his head sawed off by a black Mary (woman) and an old nigger with only one leg, having left the other leg in the mouth of a shark while diving for dynamited fish. There was Billy Watts, horrible reputation as a nigger killer, a man to scare the devil. I remember lying at Cape Little, New Ireland you know, when the niggers stole half a case of trade-tobacco—cost him about three dollars and a half. In retaliation he turned out, shot six niggers, smashed up their war canoes and burned two villages. And it was at Cape Little, four years afterward, that he was jumped along with fifty Buku boys he had with him fishing bêche-de-mer. In five minutes they were all dead, with the exception of three boys who got away in a canoe. Don't talk to me about understanding the nigger. The white man's mission is to farm the world, and it's a big enough job cut out for him. What time has he got left to understand niggers anyway?"

"Just so," said Roberts. "And somehow it doesn't seem necessary, after all, to understand the niggers. In direct proportion to the white man's stupidity is his success in farming the world—"

"And putting the fear of God into the nigger's heart," Captain Woodward blurted out. "Perhaps you're right, Roberts. Perhaps it's his stupidity that makes him succeed, and surely one phase of his stupidity is his inability to understand the niggers. But there's one thing sure, the white has to run the niggers whether he understands them or not. It's inevitable. It's fate."

"And of course the white man is inevitable—it's the niggers' fate," Roberts broke in. "Tell the white man there's pearl shell in some lagoon infested by ten-thousand howling cannibals, and he'll head there all by his lonely, with half a dozen kanaka divers and a tin alarm clock for chronometer, all packed like sardines on a commodious, five-ton ketch. Whisper that there's a gold strike at the North Pole, and that same inevitable white-skinned creature will set out at once, armed with pick and shovel, a side of bacon, and the latest patent rocker—and what's more, he'll get there. Tip it off to him that there's diamonds on the red-hot ramparts of hell, and Mr. White Man will storm the ramparts and set old Satan himself to pick-and-shovel work. That's what comes of being stupid and inevitable."

"But I wonder what the black man must think of the—the inevitableness," I said.

Captain Woodward broke into quiet laughter. His eyes had a reminiscent gleam.

"I'm just wondering what the niggers of Malu thought and still must be thinking of the one inevitable white man we had on board when we visited them in the DUCHESS," he explained.

Roberts mixed three more Abu Hameds.

"That was twenty years ago. Saxtorph was his name. He was certainly the most stupid man I ever saw, but he was as inevitable as death. There was only one thing that chap could do, and that was shoot. I remember the first time I ran into him—right here in Apia, twenty years ago. That was before your time, Roberts. I was sleeping at Dutch Henry's hotel, down where the market is now. Ever heard of him? He made a tidy stake smuggling arms in to the rebels, sold out his hotel, and was killed in Sydney just six weeks afterward in a saloon row.

"But Saxtorph. One night I'd just got to sleep, when a couple of cats began to sing in the courtyard. It was out of bed and up window, water jug in hand. But just then I heard the window of the next room go up. Two shots were fired, and the window was closed. I fail to impress you with the celerity of the transaction. Ten seconds at the outside. Up went the window, bang bang went the revolver, and down went the window. Whoever it was, he had never stopped to see the effect of his shots. He knew. Do you follow me?—he KNEW. There was no more cat concert, and in the morning there lay the two offenders, stone dead. It was marvelous to me. It still is marvelous. First, it was starlight, and Saxtorph shot without drawing a bead; next, he shot so rapidly that the two reports were like a double report; and finally, he knew he had hit his marks without looking to see.

"Two days afterward he came on board to see me. I was mate, then, on the Duchess, a whacking big one-hundred-and fifty-ton schooner, a blackbirder. And let me tell you that blackbirders were blackbirders in those days. There weren't any government protection for US, either. It was rough work, give and take, if we were finished, and nothing said, and we ran niggers from every south sea island they didn't kick us off from. Well, Saxtorph came on board, John Saxtorph was the name he gave. He was a sandy little man, hair sandy, complexion sandy, and eyes sandy, too. Nothing striking about him. His soul was as neutral as his color scheme. He said he was strapped and wanted to ship on board. Would go cabin boy, cook, supercargo, or common sailor. Didn't know anything about any of the billets, but said that he was willing to learn. I didn't want him, but his shooting had so impressed me that I took him as common sailor, wages three pounds per month.

"He was willing to learn all right, I'll say that much. But he was constitutionally unable to learn anything. He could no more box the compass than I could mix drinks like Roberts here. And as for steering, he gave me my first gray hairs. I never dared risk him at the wheel when we were running in a big sea, while full-and-by and close-and-by were insoluble mysteries. Couldn't ever tell the difference between a sheet and a tackle, simply couldn't. The fore-throat-jig and the jib-jig were all one to him. Tell him to slack off the mainsheet, and before you know it, he'd drop the peak. He fell overboard three times, and he couldn't swim. But he was always cheerful, never seasick, and he was the most willing man I ever knew. He was an uncommunicative soul. Never talked about himself. His history, so far as we were concerned, began the day he signed on the DUCHESS. Where he learned to shoot, the stars alone can tell. He was a Yankee—that much we knew from the twang in his speech. And that was all we ever did know.

"And now we begin to get to the point. We had bad luck in the New Hebrides, only fourteen boys for five weeks, and we ran up before the southeast for the Solomons. Malaita, then as now, was good recruiting ground, and we ran into Malu, on the northwestern corner. There's a shore reef and an outer reef, and a mighty nervous anchorage; but we made it all right and fired off our dynamite as a signal to the niggers to come down and be recruited. In three days we got not a boy. The niggers came off to us in their canoes by hundreds, but they only laughed when we showed them beads and calico and hatchets and talked of the delights of plantation work in Samoa.

"On the fourth day there came a change. Fifty-odd boys signed on and were billeted in the main-hold, with the freedom of the deck, of course. And of course, looking back, this wholesale signing on was suspicious, but at the time we thought some powerful chief had removed the ban against recruiting. The morning of the fifth day our two boats went ashore as usual—one to cover the other, you know, in case of trouble. And, as usual, the fifty niggers on board were on deck, loafing, talking, smoking, and sleeping. Saxtorph and myself, along with four other sailors, were all that were left on board. The two boats were manned with Gilbert Islanders. In the one were the captain, the supercargo, and the recruiter. In the other, which was the covering boat and which lay off shore a hundred yards, was the second mate. Both boats were well-armed, though trouble was little expected.

"Four of the sailors, including Saxtorph, were scraping the poop rail. The fifth sailor, rifle in hand, was standing guard by the water-tank just for'ard of the mainmast. I was for'ard, putting in the finishing licks on a new jaw for the fore-gaff. I was just reaching for my pipe where I had laid it down, when I heard a shot from shore. I straightened up to look. Something struck me on the back of the head, partially stunning me and knocking me to the deck. My first thought was that something had carried away aloft; but even as I went down, and before I struck the deck, I heard the devil's own tattoo of rifles from the boats, and twisting sidewise, I caught a glimpse of the sailor who was standing guard. Two big niggers were holding his arms, and a third nigger from behind was braining him with a tomahawk.

"I can see it now, the water-tank, the mainmast, the gang hanging on to him, the hatchet descending on the back of his head, and all under the blazing sunlight. I was fascinated by that growing vision of death. The tomahawk seemed to take a horribly long time to come down. I saw it land, and the man's legs give under him as he crumpled. The niggers held him up by sheer strength while he was hacked a couple of times more. Then I got two more hacks on the head and decided that I was dead. So did the brute that was hacking me. I was too helpless to move, and I lay there and watched them removing the sentry's head. I must say they did it slick enough. They were old hands at the business.

"The rifle firing from the boats had ceased, and I made no doubt that they were finished off and that the end had come to everything. It was only a matter of moments when they would return for my head. They were evidently taking the heads from the sailors aft. Heads are valuable on Malaita, especially white heads. They have the place of honor in the canoe houses of the salt-water natives. What particular decorative effect the bushmen get out of them I didn't know, but they prize them just as much as the salt-water crowd.

"I had a dim notion of escaping, and I crawled on hands and knees to the winch, where I managed to drag myself to my feet. From there I could look aft and see three heads on top the cabin—the heads of three sailors I had given orders to for months. The niggers saw me standing, and started for me. I reached for my revolver, and found they had taken it. I can't say that I was scared. I've been near to death several times, but it never seemed easier than right then. I was half-stunned, and nothing seemed to matter.

"The leading nigger had armed himself with a cleaver from the galley, and he grimaced like an ape as he prepared to slice me down. But the slice was never made. He went down on the deck all of a heap, and I saw the blood gush from his mouth. In a dim way I heard a rifle go off and continue to go off. Nigger after nigger went down. My senses began to clear, and I noted that there was never a miss. Every time that the rifle went off a nigger dropped. I sat down on deck beside the winch and looked up. Perched in the crosstrees was Saxtorph. How he had managed it I can't imagine, for he had carried up with him two Winchesters and I don't know how many bandoliers of ammunition; and he was now doing the one only thing in this world that he was fitted to do.

"I've seen shooting and slaughter, but I never saw anything like that. I sat by the winch and watched the show. I was weak and faint, and it seemed to be all a dream. Bang, bang, bang, bang, went his rifle, and thud, thud, thud, thud, went the niggers to the deck. It was amazing to see them go down. After their first rush to get me, when about a dozen had dropped, they seemed paralyzed; but he never left off pumping his gun. By this time canoes and the two boats arrived from shore, armed with Sniders, and with Winchesters which they had captured in the boats. The fusillade they let loose on Saxtorph was tremendous. Luckily for him the niggers are only good at close range. They are not used to putting the gun to their shoulders. They wait until they are right on top of a man, and then they shoot from the hip. When his rifle got too hot, Saxtorph changed off. That had been his idea when he carried two rifles up with him.

"The astounding thing was the rapidity of his fire. Also, he never made a miss. If ever anything was inevitable, that man was. It was the swiftness of it that made the slaughter so appalling. The niggers did not have time to think. When they did manage to think, they went over the side in a rush, capsizing the canoes of course. Saxtorph never let up. The water was covered with them, and plump, plump, plump, he dropped his bullets into them. Not a single miss, and I could hear distinctly the thud of every bullet as it buried in human flesh.

"The niggers spread out and headed for the shore, swimming. The water was carpeted with bobbing heads, and I stood up, as in a dream, and watched it all—the bobbing heads and the heads that ceased to bob. Some of the long shots were magnificent. Only one man reached the beach, but as he stood up to wade ashore, Saxtorph got him. It was beautiful. And when a couple of niggers ran down to drag him out of the water, Saxtorph got them, too.

"I thought everything was over then, when I heard the rifle go off again. A nigger had come out of the cabin companion on the run for the rail and gone down in the middle of it. The cabin must have been full of them. I counted twenty. They came up one at a time and jumped for the rail. But they never got there. It reminded me of trapshooting. A black body would pop out of the companion, bang would go Saxtorph's rifle, and down would go the black body. Of course, those below did not know what was happening on deck, so they continued to pop out until the last one was finished off.

"Saxtorph waited a while to make sure, and then came down on deck. He and I were all that were left of the DUCHESS'S complement, and I was pretty well to the bad, while he was helpless now that the shooting was over. Under my direction he washed out my scalp wounds and sewed them up. A big drink of whiskey braced me to make an effort to get out. There was nothing else to do. All the rest were dead. We tried to get up sail, Saxtorph hoisting and I holding the turn. He was once more the stupid lubber. He couldn't hoist worth a cent, and when I fell in a faint, it looked all up with us.

"When I came to, Saxtorph was sitting helplessly on the rail, waiting to ask me what he should do. I told him to overhaul the wounded and see if there were any able to crawl. He gathered together six. One, I remember, had a broken leg; but Saxtorph said his arms were all right. I lay in the shade, brushing the flies off and directing operations, while Saxtorph bossed his hospital gang. I'll be blessed if he didn't make those poor niggers heave at every rope on the pin-rails before he found the halyards. One of them let go the rope in the midst of the hoisting and slipped down to the deck dead; but Saxtorph hammered the others and made them stick by the job. When the fore and main were up, I told him to knock the shackle out of the anchor chain and let her go. I had had myself helped aft to the wheel, where I was going to make a shift at steering. I can't guess how he did it, but instead of knocking the shackle out, down went the second anchor, and there we were doubly moored.

"In the end he managed to knock both shackles out and raise the staysail and jib, and the Duchess filled away for the entrance. Our decks were a spectacle. Dead and dying niggers were everywhere. They were wedged away some of them in the most inconceivable places. The cabin was full of them where they had crawled off the deck and cashed in. I put Saxtorph and his graveyard gang to work heaving them overside, and over they went, the living and the dead. The sharks had fat pickings that day. Of course our four murdered sailors went the same way. Their heads, however, we put in a sack with weights, so that by no chance should they drift on the beach and fall into the hands of the niggers.

"Our five prisoners I decided to use as crew, but they decided otherwise. They watched their opportunity and went over the side. Saxtorph got two in mid-air with his revolver, and would have shot the other three in the water if I hadn't stopped him. I was sick of the slaughter, you see, and besides, they'd helped work the schooner out. But it was mercy thrown away, for the sharks got the three of them.

"I had brain fever or something after we got clear of the land. Anyway, the DUCHESS lay hove to for three weeks, when I pulled myself together and we jogged on with her to Sydney. Anyway those niggers of Malu learned the everlasting lesson that it is not good to monkey with a white man. In their case, Saxtorph was certainly inevitable."

Charley Roberts emitted a long whistle and said:

"Well I should say so. But whatever became of Saxtorph?"

"He drifted into seal hunting and became a crackerjack. For six years he was high line of both the Victoria and San Francisco fleets. The seventh year his schooner was seized in Bering Sea by a Russian cruiser, and all hands, so the talk went, were slammed into the Siberian salt mines. At least I've never heard of him since."

"Farming the world," Roberts muttered. "Farming the world. Well here's to them. Somebody's got to do it—farm the world, I mean."

Captain Woodward rubbed the criss-crosses on his bald head.

"I've done my share of it," he said. "Forty years now. This will be my last trip. Then I'm going home to stay."

"I'll wager the wine you don't," Roberts challenged. "You'll die in the harness, not at home."

Captain Woodward promptly accepted the bet, but personally I think Charley Roberts has the best of it.

THE SEED OF McCOY

The Pyrenees, her iron sides pressed low in the water by her cargo of wheat, rolled sluggishly, and made it easy for the man who was climbing aboard from out a tiny outrigger canoe. As his eyes came level with the rail, so that he could see inboard, it seemed to him that he saw a dim, almost indiscernible haze. It was more like an illusion, like a blurring film that had spread abruptly over his eyes. He felt an inclination to brush it away, and the same instant he thought that he was growing old and that it was time to send to San Francisco for a pair of spectacles.

As he came over the rail he cast a glance aloft at the tall masts, and, next, at the pumps. They were not working. There seemed nothing the matter with the big ship, and he wondered why she had hoisted the signal of distress. He thought of his happy islanders, and hoped it was not disease. Perhaps the ship was short of water or provisions. He shook hands with the captain whose gaunt face and care-worn eyes made no secret of the trouble, whatever it was. At the same moment the newcomer was aware of a faint, indefinable smell. It seemed like that of burnt bread, but different.

He glanced curiously about him. Twenty feet away a weary-faced sailor was calking the deck. As his eyes lingered on the man, he saw suddenly arise from under his hands a faint spiral of haze that curled and twisted and was gone. By now he had reached the deck. His bare feet were pervaded by a dull warmth that quickly penetrated the thick calluses. He knew now the nature of the ship's distress. His eyes roved swiftly forward, where the full crew of weary-faced sailors regarded him eagerly. The glance from his liquid brown eyes swept over them like a benediction, soothing them, rapping them about as in the mantle of a great peace. "How long has she been afire, Captain?" he asked in a voice so gentle and unperturbed that it was as the cooing of a dove.

At first the captain felt the peace and content of it stealing in upon him; then the consciousness of all that he had gone through and was going through smote him, and he was resentful. By what right did this ragged beachcomber, in dungaree trousers and a cotton shirt, suggest such a thing as peace and content to him and his overwrought, exhausted soul? The captain did not reason this; it was the unconscious process of emotion that caused his resentment.

"Fifteen days," he answered shortly. "Who are you?"

"My name is McCoy," came the answer in tones that breathed tenderness and compassion.

"I mean, are you the pilot?"

McCoy passed the benediction of his gaze over the tall, heavy-shouldered man with the haggard, unshaven face who had joined the captain.

"I am as much a pilot as anybody," was McCoy's answer. "We are all pilots here, Captain, and I know every inch of these waters."

But the captain was impatient.

"What I want is some of the authorities. I want to talk with them, and blame quick."

"Then I'll do just as well."

Again that insidious suggestion of peace, and his ship a raging furnace beneath his feet! The captain's eyebrows lifted impatiently and nervously, and his fist clenched as if he were about to strike a blow with it.

"Who in hell are you?" he demanded.

"I am the chief magistrate," was the reply in a voice that was still the softest and gentlest imaginable.

The tall, heavy-shouldered man broke out in a harsh laugh that was partly amusement, but mostly hysterical. Both he and the captain regarded McCoy with incredulity and amazement. That this barefooted beachcomber should possess such high-sounding dignity was inconceivable. His cotton shirt, unbuttoned, exposed a grizzled chest and the fact that there was no undershirt beneath.

A worn straw hat failed to hide the ragged gray hair. Halfway down his chest descended an untrimmed patriarchal beard. In any slop shop, two shillings would have outfitted him complete as he stood before them.

"Any relation to the McCoy of the Bounty?" the captain asked.

"He was my great-grandfather."

"Oh," the captain said, then bethought himself. "My name is Davenport, and this is my first mate, Mr. Konig."

They shook hands.

"And now to business." The captain spoke quickly, the urgency of a great haste pressing his speech. "We've been on fire for over two weeks. She's ready to break all hell loose any moment. That's why I held for Pitcairn. I want to beach her, or scuttle her, and save the hull."

"Then you made a mistake, Captain," said McCoy. "You should have slacked away for Mangareva. There's a beautiful beach there, in a lagoon where the water is like a mill pond."

"But we're here, ain't we?" the first mate demanded. "That's the point. We're here, and we've got to do something."

McCoy shook his head kindly.

"You can do nothing here. There is no beach. There isn't even anchorage."

"Gammon!" said the mate. "Gammon!" he repeated loudly, as the captain signaled him to be more soft spoken. "You can't tell me that sort of stuff. Where d'ye keep your own boats, hey—your schooner, or cutter, or whatever you have? Hey? Answer me that."

McCoy smiled as gently as he spoke. His smile was a caress, an embrace that surrounded the tired mate and sought to draw him into the quietude and rest of McCoy's tranquil soul.

"We have no schooner or cutter," he replied. "And we carry our canoes to the top of the cliff."

"You've got to show me," snorted the mate. "How d'ye get around to the other islands, heh? Tell me that."

"We don't get around. As governor of Pitcairn, I sometimes go. When I was younger, I was away a great deal—sometimes on the trading schooners, but mostly on the missionary brig. But she's gone now, and we depend on passing vessels. Sometimes we have had as high as six calls in one year. At other times, a year, and even longer, has gone by without one passing ship. Yours is the first in seven months."

"And you mean to tell me—" the mate began.

But Captain Davenport interfered.

"Enough of this. We're losing time. What is to be done, Mr. McCoy?"

The old man turned his brown eyes, sweet as a woman's, shoreward, and both captain and mate followed his gaze around from the lonely rock of Pitcairn to the crew clustering forward and waiting anxiously for the announcement of a decision. McCoy did not hurry. He thought smoothly and slowly, step by step, with the certitude of a mind that was never vexed or outraged by life.

"The wind is light now," he said finally. "There is a heavy current setting to the westward."

"That's what made us fetch to leeward," the captain interrupted, desiring to vindicate his seamanship.

"Yes, that is what fetched you to leeward," McCoy went on. "Well, you can't work up against this current today. And if you did, there is no beach. Your ship will be a total loss."

He paused, and captain and mate looked despair at each other.

"But I will tell you what you can do. The breeze will freshen tonight around midnight—see those tails of clouds and that thickness to windward, beyond the point there? That's where she'll come from, out of the southeast, hard. It is three hundred miles to Mangareva. Square away for it. There is a beautiful bed for your ship there."

The mate shook his head.

"Come in to the cabin, and we'll look at the chart," said the captain.

McCoy found a stifling, poisonous atmosphere in the pent cabin. Stray waftures of invisible gases bit his eyes and made them sting. The deck was hotter, almost unbearably hot to his bare feet. The sweat poured out of his body. He looked almost with apprehension about him. This malignant, internal heat was astounding. It was a marvel that the cabin did not burst into flames. He had a feeling as if of being in a huge bake oven where the heat might at any moment increase tremendously and shrivel him up like a blade of grass.

As he lifted one foot and rubbed the hot sole against the leg of his trousers, the mate laughed in a savage, snarling fashion.

"The anteroom of hell," he said. "Hell herself is right down there under your feet."

"It's hot!" McCoy cried involuntarily, mopping his face with a bandana handkerchief.

"Here's Mangareva," the captain said, bending over the table and pointing to a black speck in the midst of the white blankness of the chart. "And here, in between, is another island. Why not run for that?"

McCoy did not look at the chart.

"That's Crescent Island," he answered. "It is uninhabited, and it is only two or three feet above water. Lagoon, but no entrance. No, Mangareva is the nearest place for your purpose."

"Mangareva it is, then," said Captain Davenport, interrupting the mate's growling objection. "Call the crew aft, Mr. Konig."

The sailors obeyed, shuffling wearily along the deck and painfully endeavoring to make haste. Exhaustion was evident in every movement. The cook came out of his galley to hear, and the cabin boy hung about near him.

When Captain Davenport had explained the situation and announced his intention of running for Mangareva, an uproar broke out. Against a background of throaty rumbling arose inarticulate cries of rage, with here and there a distinct curse, or word, or phrase. A shrill Cockney voice soared and dominated for a moment, crying: "Gawd! After bein' in ell for fifteen days—an' now e wants us to sail this floatin' ell to sea again?"

The captain could not control them, but McCoy's gentle presence seemed to rebuke and calm them, and the muttering and cursing died away, until the full crew, save here and there an anxious face directed at the captain, yearned dumbly toward the green clad peaks and beetling coast of Pitcairn.

Soft as a spring zephyr was the voice of McCoy:

"Captain, I thought I heard some of them say they were starving."

"Ay," was the answer, "and so we are. I've had a sea biscuit and a spoonful of salmon in the last two days. We're on whack. You see, when we discovered the fire, we battened down immediately to suffocate the fire. And then we found how little food there was in the pantry. But it was too late. We didn't dare break out the lazarette. Hungry? I'm just as hungry as they are."

He spoke to the men again, and again the throat rumbling and cursing arose, their faces convulsed and animal-like with rage. The second and third mates had joined the captain, standing behind him at the break of the poop. Their faces were set and expressionless; they seemed bored, more than anything else, by this mutiny of the crew. Captain Davenport glanced questioningly at his first mate, and that person merely shrugged his shoulders in token of his helplessness.

"You see," the captain said to McCoy, "you can't compel sailors to leave the safe land and go to sea on a burning vessel. She has been their floating coffin for over two weeks now. They are worked out, and starved out, and they've got enough of her. We'll beat up for Pitcairn."

But the wind was light, the Pyrenees' bottom was foul, and she could not beat up against the strong westerly current. At the end of two hours she had lost three miles. The sailors worked eagerly, as if by main strength they could compel the PYRENEES against the adverse elements. But steadily, port tack and starboard tack, she sagged off to the westward. The captain paced restlessly up and down, pausing occasionally to survey the vagrant smoke wisps and to trace them back to the portions of the deck from which they sprang. The carpenter was engaged constantly in attempting to locate such places, and, when he succeeded, in calking them tighter and tighter.

"Well, what do you think?" the captain finally asked McCoy, who was watching the carpenter with all a child's interest and curiosity in his eyes.

McCoy looked shoreward, where the land was disappearing in the thickening haze.

"I think it would be better to square away for Mangareva. With that breeze that is coming, you'll be there tomorrow evening."

"But what if the fire breaks out? It is liable to do it any moment."

"Have your boats ready in the falls. The same breeze will carry your boats to Mangareva if the ship burns out from under."

Captain Davenport debated for a moment, and then McCoy heard the question he had not wanted to hear, but which he knew was surely coming.

"I have no chart of Mangareva. On the general chart it is only a fly speck. I would not know where to look for the entrance into the lagoon. Will you come along and pilot her in for me?"

McCoy's serenity was unbroken.

"Yes, Captain," he said, with the same quiet unconcern with which he would have accepted an invitation to dinner; "I'll go with you to Mangareva."

Again the crew was called aft, and the captain spoke to them from the break of the poop.

"We've tried to work her up, but you see how we've lost ground. She's setting off in a two-knot current. This gentleman is the Honorable McCoy, Chief Magistrate and Governor of Pitcairn Island. He will come along with us to Mangareva. So you see the situation is not so dangerous. He would not make such an offer if he thought he was going to lose his life. Besides, whatever risk there is, if he of his own free will come on board and take it, we can do no less. What do you say for Mangareva?"

This time there was no uproar. McCoy's presence, the surety and calm that seemed to radiate from him, had had its effect. They conferred with one another in low voices. There was little urging. They were virtually unanimous, and they shoved the Cockney out as their spokesman. That worthy was overwhelmed with consciousness of the heroism of himself and his mates, and with flashing eyes he cried:

"By Gawd! If 'e will, we will!"

The crew mumbled its assent and started forward.

"One moment, Captain," McCoy said, as the other was turning to give orders to the mate. "I must go ashore first."

Mr. Konig was thunderstruck, staring at McCoy as if he were a madman.

"Go ashore!" the captain cried. "What for? It will take you three hours to get there in your canoe."

McCoy measured the distance of the land away, and nodded.

"Yes, it is six now. I won't get ashore till nine. The people cannot be assembled earlier than ten. As the breeze freshens up tonight, you can begin to work up against it, and pick me up at daylight tomorrow morning."

"In the name of reason and common sense," the captain burst forth, "what do you want to assemble the people for? Don't you realize that my ship is burning beneath me?"

McCoy was as placid as a summer sea, and the other's anger produced not the slightest ripple upon it.

"Yes, Captain," he cooed in his dove-like voice. "I do realize that your ship is burning. That is why I am going with you to Mangareva. But I must get permission to go with you. It is our custom. It is an important matter when the governor leaves the island. The people's interests are at stake, and so they have the right to vote their permission or refusal. But they will give it, I know that."

"Are you sure?"

"Quite sure."

"Then if you know they will give it, why bother with getting it? Think of the delay—a whole night."

"It is our custom," was the imperturbable reply. "Also, I am the governor, and I must make arrangements for the conduct of the island during my absence."

"But it is only a twenty-four hour run to Mangareva," the captain objected. "Suppose it took you six times that long to return to windward; that would bring you back by the end of a week."

McCoy smiled his large, benevolent smile.

"Very few vessels come to Pitcairn, and when they do, they are usually from San Francisco or from around the Horn. I shall be fortunate if I get back in six months. I may be away a year, and I may have to go to San Francisco in order to find a vessel that will bring me back. My father once left Pitcairn to be gone three months, and two years passed before he could get back. Then, too, you are short of food. If you have to take to the boats, and the weather comes up bad, you may be days in reaching land. I can bring off two canoe loads of food in the morning. Dried bananas will be best. As the breeze freshens, you beat up against it. The nearer you are, the bigger loads I can bring off. Goodby."

He held out his hand. The captain shook it, and was reluctant to let go. He seemed to cling to it as a drowning sailor clings to a life buoy.

"How do I know you will come back in the morning?" he asked.

"Yes, that's it!" cried the mate. "How do we know but what he's skinning out to save his own hide?"

McCoy did not speak. He looked at them sweetly and benignantly, and it seemed to them that they received a message from his tremendous certitude of soul.

411

The captain released his hand, and, with a last sweeping glance that embraced the crew in its benediction, McCoy went over the rail and descended into his canoe.

The wind freshened, and the Pyrenees, despite the foulness of her bottom, won half a dozen miles away from the westerly current. At daylight, with Pitcairn three miles to windward, Captain Davenport made out two canoes coming off to him. Again McCoy clambered up the side and dropped over the rail to the hot deck. He was followed by many packages of dried bananas, each package wrapped in dry leaves.

"Now, Captain," he said, "swing the yards and drive for dear life. You see, I am no navigator," he explained a few minutes later, as he stood by the captain aft, the latter with gaze wandering from aloft to overside as he estimated the Pyrenees' speed. "You must fetch her to Mangareva. When you have picked up the land, then I will pilot her in. What do you think she is making?"

"Eleven," Captain Davenport answered, with a final glance at the water rushing past.

"Eleven. Let me see, if she keeps up that gait, we'll sight Mangareva between eight and nine o'clock tomorrow morning. I'll have her on the beach by ten or by eleven at latest. And then your troubles will be all over."

It almost seemed to the captain that the blissful moment had already arrived, such was the persuasive convincingness of McCoy.

Captain Davenport had been under the fearful strain of navigating his burning ship for over two weeks, and he was beginning to feel that he had had enough.

A heavier flaw of wind struck the back of his neck and whistled by his ears. He measured the weight of it, and looked quickly overside.

"The wind is making all the time," he announced. "The old girl's doing nearer twelve than eleven right now. If this keeps up, we'll be shortening down tonight."

412

All day the Pyrenees, carrying her load of living fire, tore across the foaming sea. By nightfall, royals and topgallantsails were in, and she flew on into the darkness, with great, crested seas roaring after her. The auspicious wind had had its effect, and fore and aft a visible brightening was apparent. In the second dog-watch some careless soul started a song, and by eight bells the whole crew was singing.

Captain Davenport had his blankets brought up and spread on top the house.

"I've forgotten what sleep is," he explained to McCoy. "I'm all in. But give me a call at any time you think necessary."

At three in the morning he was aroused by a gentle tugging at his arm. He sat up quickly, bracing himself against the skylight, stupid yet from his heavy sleep. The wind was thrumming its war song in the rigging, and a wild sea was buffeting the PYRENEES. Amidships she was wallowing first one rail under and then the other, flooding the waist more often than not. McCoy was shouting something he could not hear. He reached out, clutched the other by the shoulder, and drew him close so that his own ear was close to the other's lips.

"It's three o'clock," came McCoy's voice, still retaining its dovelike quality, but curiously muffled, as if from a long way off. "We've run two hundred and fifty. Crescent Island is only thirty miles away, somewhere there dead ahead. There's no lights on it. If we keep running, we'll pile up, and lose ourselves as well as the ship."

"What d' ye think—heave to?"

"Yes; heave to till daylight. It will only put us back four hours."

So the Pyrenees, with her cargo of fire, was hove to, bitting the teeth of the gale and fighting and smashing the pounding seas. She was a shell, filled with a conflagration, and on the outside of the shell, clinging precariously, the little motes of men, by pull and haul, helped her in the battle.

413

"It is most unusual, this gale," McCoy told the captain, in the lee of the cabin. "By rights there should be no gale at this time of the year. But everything about the weather has been unusual. There has been a stoppage of the trades, and now it's howling right out of the trade quarter." He waved his hand into the darkness, as if his vision could dimly penetrate for hundreds of miles. "It is off to the westward. There is something big making off there somewhere—a hurricane or something. We're lucky to be so far to the eastward. But this is only a little blow," he added. "It can't last. I can tell you that much."

By daylight the gale had eased down to normal. But daylight revealed a new danger. It had come on thick. The sea was covered by a fog, or, rather, by a pearly mist that was fog-like in density, in so far as it obstructed vision, but that was no more than a film on the sea, for the sun shot it through and filled it with a glowing radiance.

The deck of the Pyrenees was making more smoke than on the preceding day, and the cheerfulness of officers and crew had vanished. In the lee of the galley the cabin boy could be heard whimpering. It was his first voyage, and the fear of death was at his heart. The captain wandered about like a lost soul, nervously chewing his mustache, scowling, unable to make up his mind what to do.

"What do you think?" he asked, pausing by the side of McCoy, who was making a breakfast off fried bananas and a mug of water.

McCoy finished the last banana, drained the mug, and looked slowly around. In his eyes was a smile of tenderness as he said:

"Well, Captain, we might as well drive as burn. Your decks are not going to hold out forever. They are hotter this morning. You haven't a pair of shoes I can wear? It is getting uncomfortable for my bare feet."

The Pyrenees shipped two heavy seas as she was swung off and put once more before it, and the first mate expressed a desire to have all that water down in the hold, if only it could be introduced without taking off the hatches. McCoy ducked his head into the binnacle and watched the course set.

"I'd hold her up some more, Captain," he said. "She's been making drift when hove to."

"I've set it to a point higher already," was the answer. "Isn't that enough?"

"I'd make it two points, Captain. This bit of a blow kicked that westerly current ahead faster than you imagine."

Captain Davenport compromised on a point and a half, and then went aloft, accompanied by McCoy and the first mate, to keep a lookout for land. Sail had been made, so that the Pyrenees was doing ten knots. The following sea was dying down rapidly. There was no break in the pearly fog, and by ten o'clock Captain Davenport was growing nervous. All hands were at their stations, ready, at the first warning of land ahead, to spring like fiends to the task of bringing the Pyrenees up on the wind. That land ahead, a surf-washed outer reef, would be perilously close when it revealed itself in such a fog.

Another hour passed. The three watchers aloft stared intently into the pearly radiance. "What if we miss Mangareva?" Captain Davenport asked abruptly.

McCoy, without shifting his gaze, answered softly:

"Why, let her drive, captain. That is all we can do. All the Paumotus are before us. We can drive for a thousand miles through reefs and atolls. We are bound to fetch up somewhere."

"Then drive it is." Captain Davenport evidenced his intention of descending to the deck. "We've missed Mangareva. God knows where the next land is. I wish I'd held her up that other half-point," he confessed a moment later. "This cursed current plays the devil with a navigator."

"The old navigators called the Paumotus the Dangerous Archipelago," McCoy said, when they had regained the poop. "This very current was partly responsible for that name."

"I was talking with a sailor chap in Sydney, once," said Mr. Konig. "He'd been trading in the Paumotus. He told me insurance was eighteen per cent. Is that right?"

McCoy smiled and nodded.

"Except that they don't insure," he explained. "The owners write off twenty per cent of the cost of their schooners each year."

"My God!" Captain Davenport groaned. "That makes the life of a schooner only five years!" He shook his head sadly, murmuring, "Bad waters! Bad waters!"

Again they went into the cabin to consult the big general chart; but the poisonous vapors drove them coughing and gasping on deck.

"Here is Moerenhout Island," Captain Davenport pointed it out on the chart, which he had spread on the house. "It can't be more than a hundred miles to leeward."

"A hundred and ten." McCoy shook his head doubtfully. "It might be done, but it is very difficult. I might beach her, and then again I might put her on the reef. A bad place, a very bad place."

"We'll take the chance," was Captain Davenport's decision, as he set about working out the course.

Sail was shortened early in the afternoon, to avoid running past in the night; and in the second dog-watch the crew manifested its regained cheerfulness. Land was so very near, and their troubles would be over in the morning.

But morning broke clear, with a blazing tropic sun. The southeast trade had swung around to the eastward, and was driving the PYRENEES through the water at an eight-knot clip. Captain Davenport worked up his dead reckoning, allowing generously for drift, and announced Moerenhout Island to be not more than ten miles off. The Pyrenees sailed the ten miles; she sailed ten miles more; and the lookouts at the three mastheads saw naught but the naked, sun-washed sea.

"But the land is there, I tell you," Captain Davenport shouted to them from the poop.

McCoy smiled soothingly, but the captain glared about him like a madman, fetched his sextant, and took a chronometer sight.

"I knew I was right," he almost shouted, when he had worked up the observation. "Twenty-one, fifty-five, south; one-thirty-six, two, west. There you are. We're eight miles to windward yet. What did you make it out, Mr. Konig?"

The first mate glanced at his own figures, and said in a low voice:

"Twenty-one, fifty-five all right; but my longitude's one-thirty-six, forty-eight. That puts us considerably to leeward—"

But Captain Davenport ignored his figures with so contemptuous a silence as to make Mr. Konig grit his teeth and curse savagely under his breath.

"Keep her off," the captain ordered the man at the wheel. "Three points—steady there, as she goes!"

Then he returned to his figures and worked them over. The sweat poured from his face. He chewed his mustache, his lips, and his pencil, staring at the figures as a man might at a ghost. Suddenly, with a fierce, muscular outburst, he crumpled the scribbled paper in his fist and crushed it under foot. Mr. Konig grinned vindictively and turned away, while Captain Davenport leaned against the cabin and for half an hour spoke no word, contenting himself with gazing to leeward with an expression of musing hopelessness on his face.

"Mr. McCoy," he broke silence abruptly. "The chart indicates a group of islands, but not how many, off there to the north'ard, or nor'-nor'westward, about forty miles—the Acteon Islands. What about them?"

"There are four, all low," McCoy answered. "First to the southeast is Matuerui—no people, no entrance to the lagoon. Then comes Tenarunga. There used to be about a dozen people there, but they may be all gone now. Anyway, there is no entrance for a ship—only a boat entrance, with a fathom of water. Vehauga and Teua-raro are the other two. No entrances, no people, very low. There is no bed for the Pyrenees in that group. She would be a total wreck."

"Listen to that!" Captain Davenport was frantic. "No people! No entrances! What in the devil are islands good for?

417

"Well, then," he barked suddenly, like an excited terrier, "the chart gives a whole mess of islands off to the nor'west. What about them? What one has an entrance where I can lay my ship?"

McCoy calmly considered. He did not refer to the chart. All these islands, reefs, shoals, lagoons, entrances, and distances were marked on the chart of his memory. He knew them as the city dweller knows his buildings, streets, and alleys.

"Papakena and Vanavana are off there to the westward, or west-nor'westward a hundred miles and a bit more," he said. "One is uninhabited, and I heard that the people on the other had gone off to Cadmus Island. Anyway, neither lagoon has an entrance. Ahunui is another hundred miles on to the nor'west. No entrance, no people."

"Well, forty miles beyond them are two islands?" Captain Davenport queried, raising his head from the chart.

McCoy shook his head.

"Paros and Manuhungi—no entrances, no people. Nengo-Nengo is forty miles beyond them, in turn, and it has no people and no entrance. But there is Hao Island. It is just the place. The lagoon is thirty miles long and five miles wide. There are plenty of people. You can usually find water. And any ship in the world can go through the entrance."

He ceased and gazed solicitously at Captain Davenport, who, bending over the chart with a pair of dividers in hand, had just emitted a low groan.

"Is there any lagoon with an entrance anywhere nearer than Hao Island?" he asked.

"No, Captain; that is the nearest."

"Well, it's three hundred and forty miles." Captain Davenport was speaking very slowly, with decision. "I won't risk the responsibility of all these lives. I'll wreck her on the Acteons. And she's a good ship, too," he added regretfully, after altering the course, this time making more allowance than ever for the westerly current.

An hour later the sky was overcast. The southeast trade still held, but the ocean was a checker board of squalls.

"We'll be there by one o'clock," Captain Davenport announced confidently. "By two o'clock at the outside. McCoy, you put her ashore on the one where the people are."

The sun did not appear again, nor, at one o'clock, was any land to be seen. Captain Davenport looked astern at the Pyrenees' canting wake.

"Good Lord!" he cried. "An easterly current? Look at that!"

Mr. Konig was incredulous. McCoy was noncommittal, though he said that in the Paumotus there was no reason why it should not be an easterly current. A few minutes later a squall robbed the Pyrenees temporarily of all her wind, and she was left rolling heavily in the trough.

"Where's that deep lead? Over with it, you there!" Captain Davenport held the lead line and watched it sag off to the northeast. "There, look at that! Take hold of it for yourself."

McCoy and the mate tried it, and felt the line thrumming and vibrating savagely to the grip of the tidal stream.

"A four-knot current," said Mr. Konig.

"An easterly current instead of a westerly," said Captain "Davenport, glaring accusingly at McCoy, as if to cast the blame for it upon him.

"That is one of the reasons, Captain, for insurance being eighteen per cent in these waters," McCoy answered cheerfully. "You can never tell. The currents are always changing. There was a man who wrote books, I forget his name, in the yacht Casco. He missed Takaroa by thirty miles and fetched Tikei, all because of the shifting currents. You are up to windward now, and you'd better keep off a few points."

"But how much has this current set me?" the captain demanded irately. "How am I to know how much to keep off?"

"I don't know, Captain," McCoy said with great gentleness.

The wind returned, and the PYRENEES, her deck smoking and shimmering in the bright gray light, ran off dead to leeward. Then she worked back, port tack and starboard tack, crisscrossing her track, combing the sea for the Acteon Islands, which the masthead lookouts failed to sight.

Captain Davenport was beside himself. His rage took the form of sullen silence, and he spent the afternoon in pacing the poop or leaning against the weather shrouds. At nightfall, without even consulting McCoy, he squared away and headed into the northwest. Mr. Konig, surreptitiously consulting chart and binnacle, and McCoy, openly and innocently consulting the binnacle, knew that they were running for Hao Island. By midnight the squalls ceased, and the stars came out. Captain Davenport was cheered by the promise of a clear day.

"I'll get an observation in the morning," he told McCoy, "though what my latitude is, is a puzzler. But I'll use the Sumner method, and settle that. Do you know the Sumner line?"

And thereupon he explained it in detail to McCoy.

The day proved clear, the trade blew steadily out of the east, and the Pyrenees just as steadily logged her nine knots. Both the captain and mate worked out the position on a Sumner line, and agreed, and at noon agreed again, and verified the morning sights by the noon sights.

"Another twenty-four hours and we'll be there," Captain Davenport assured McCoy. "It's a miracle the way the old girl's decks hold out. But they can't last. They can't last. Look at them smoke, more and more every day. Yet it was a tight deck to begin with, fresh-calked in Frisco. I was surprised when the fire first broke out and we battened down. Look at that!"

He broke off to gaze with dropped jaw at a spiral of smoke that coiled and twisted in the lee of the mizzenmast twenty feet above the deck.

"Now, how did that get there?" he demanded indignantly.

Beneath it there was no smoke. Crawling up from the deck, sheltered from the wind by the mast, by some freak it took form and visibility at that height. It writhed away from the mast, and for a moment overhung the captain like some threatening portent. The next moment the wind whisked it away, and the captain's jaw returned to place.

"As I was saying, when we first battened down, I was surprised. It was a tight deck, yet it leaked smoke like a sieve. And we've calked and calked ever since. There must be tremendous pressure underneath to drive so much smoke through."

That afternoon the sky became overcast again, and squally, drizzly weather set in. The wind shifted back and forth between southeast and northeast, and at midnight the Pyrenees was caught aback by a sharp squall from the southwest, from which point the wind continued to blow intermittently.

"We won't make Hao until ten or eleven," Captain Davenport complained at seven in the morning, when the fleeting promise of the sun had been erased by hazy cloud masses in the eastern sky. And the next moment he was plaintively demanding, "And what are the currents doing?"

Lookouts at the mastheads could report no land, and the day passed in drizzling calms and violent squalls. By nightfall a heavy sea began to make from the west. The barometer had fallen to 29.50. There was no wind, and still the ominous sea continued to increase. Soon the Pyrenees was rolling madly in the huge waves that marched in an unending procession from out of the darkness of the west. Sail was shortened as fast as both watches could work, and, when the tired crew had finished, its grumbling and complaining voices, peculiarly animal-like and menacing, could be heard in the darkness. Once the starboard watch was called aft to lash down and make secure, and the men openly advertised their sullenness and unwillingness. Every slow movement was a protest and a threat. The atmosphere was moist and sticky like mucilage, and in the absence of wind all hands seemed to pant and gasp for air. The sweat stood out on faces and bare arms, and Captain Davenport for one, his face more gaunt and care-worn than ever, and his eyes troubled and staring, was oppressed by a feeling of impending calamity.

"It's off to the westward," McCoy said encouragingly. "At worst, we'll be only on the edge of it."

But Captain Davenport refused to be comforted, and by the light of a lantern read up the chapter in his Epitome that related to the strategy of shipmasters in cyclonic storms. From somewhere amidships the silence was broken by a low whimpering from the cabin boy.

"Oh, shut up!" Captain Davenport yelled suddenly and with such force as to startle every man on board and to frighten the offender into a wild wail of terror.

"Mr. Konig," the captain said in a voice that trembled with rage and nerves, "will you kindly step for'ard and stop that brat's mouth with a deck mop?"

But it was McCoy who went forward, and in a few minutes had the boy comforted and asleep.

Shortly before daybreak the first breath of air began to move from out the southeast, increasing swiftly to a stiff and stiffer breeze. All hands were on deck waiting for what might be behind it. "We're all right now, Captain," said McCoy, standing close to his shoulder. "The hurricane is to the west'ard, and we are south of it. This breeze is the in-suck. It won't blow any harder. You can begin to put sail on her."

"But what's the good? Where shall I sail? This is the second day without observations, and we should have sighted Hao Island yesterday morning. Which way does it bear, north, south, east, or what? Tell me that, and I'll make sail in a jiffy."

"I am no navigator, Captain," McCoy said in his mild way.

"I used to think I was one," was the retort, "before I got into these Paumotus."

At midday the cry of "Breakers ahead!" was heard from the lookout. The Pyrenees was kept off, and sail after sail was loosed and sheeted home. The Pyrenees was sliding through the water and fighting a current that threatened to set her down upon the breakers. Officers and men were working like mad, cook and cabin boy, Captain Davenport himself, and McCoy all lending a hand. It was a close shave. It was a low shoal, a bleak and perilous place over which the seas broke unceasingly, where no man could live, and on which not even sea birds could rest. The PYRENEES was swept within a hundred yards of it before the wind carried her clear, and at this moment the panting crew, its work done, burst out in a torrent of curses upon the head of McCoy—of McCoy who had come on board, and proposed the run to Mangareva, and lured them all away from the safety of Pitcairn Island to certain destruction in this baffling and terrible stretch of sea. But McCoy's tranquil soul was undisturbed. He smiled at them with simple and gracious benevolence, and, somehow, the exalted goodness of him seemed to penetrate to their dark and somber souls, shaming them, and from very shame stilling the curses vibrating in their throats.

"Bad waters! Bad waters!" Captain Davenport was murmuring as his ship forged clear; but he broke off abruptly to gaze at the shoal which should have been dead astern, but which was already on the PYRENEES' weather-quarter and working up rapidly to windward.

He sat down and buried his face in his hands. And the first mate saw, and McCoy saw, and the crew saw, what he had seen. South of the shoal an easterly current had set them down upon it; north of the shoal an equally swift westerly current had clutched the ship and was sweeping her away.

"I've heard of these Paumotus before," the captain groaned, lifting his blanched face from his hands. "Captain Moyendale told me about them after losing his ship on them. And I laughed at him behind his back. God forgive me, I laughed at him. What shoal is that?" he broke off, to ask McCoy.

"I don't know, Captain."

"Why don't you know?"

"Because I never saw it before, and because I have never heard of it. I do know that it is not charted. These waters have never been thoroughly surveyed."

"Then you don't know where we are?"

"No more than you do," McCoy said gently.

At four in the afternoon cocoanut trees were sighted, apparently growing out of the water. A little later the low land of an atoll was raised above the sea.

"I know where we are now, Captain." McCoy lowered the glasses from his eyes. "That's Resolution Island. We are forty miles beyond Hao Island, and the wind is in our teeth."

"Get ready to beach her then. Where's the entrance?"

"There's only a canoe passage. But now that we know where we are, we can run for Barclay de Tolley. It is only one hundred and twenty miles from here, due nor'-nor'west. With this breeze we can be there by nine o'clock tomorrow morning."

Captain Davenport consulted the chart and debated with himself.

"If we wreck her here," McCoy added, "we'd have to make the run to Barclay de Tolley in the boats just the same."

The captain gave his orders, and once more the Pyrenees swung off for another run across the inhospitable sea.

And the middle of the next afternoon saw despair and mutiny on her smoking deck. The current had accelerated, the wind had slackened, and the Pyrenees had sagged off to the west. The lookout sighted Barclay de Tolley to the eastward, barely visible from the masthead, and vainly and for hours the PYRENEES tried to beat up to it. Ever, like a mirage, the cocoanut trees hovered on the horizon, visible only from the masthead. From the deck they were hidden by the bulge of the world.

Again Captain Davenport consulted McCoy and the chart. Makemo lay seventy-five miles to the southwest. Its lagoon was thirty miles long, and its entrance was excellent. When Captain Davenport gave his orders, the crew refused duty. They announced that they had had enough of hell fire under their feet. There was the land. What if the ship could not make it? They could make it in the boats. Let her burn, then. Their lives amounted to something to them. They had served faithfully the ship, now they were going to serve themselves.

They sprang to the boats, brushing the second and third mates out of the way, and proceeded to swing the boats out and to prepare to lower away. Captain Davenport and the first mate, revolvers in hand, were advancing to the break of the poop, when McCoy, who had climbed on top of the cabin, began to speak.

He spoke to the sailors, and at the first sound of his dovelike, cooing voice they paused to hear. He extended to them his own ineffable serenity and peace. His soft voice and simple thoughts flowed out to them in a magic stream, soothing them against their wills. Long forgotten things came back to them, and some remembered lullaby songs of childhood and the content and rest of the mother's arm at the end of the day. There was no more trouble, no more danger, no more irk, in all the world. Everything was as it should be, and it was only a matter of course that they should turn their backs upon the land and put to sea once more with hell fire hot beneath their feet.

McCoy spoke simply; but it was not what he spoke. It was his personality that spoke more eloquently than any word he could utter. It was an alchemy of soul occultly subtle and profoundly deep—a mysterious emanation of the spirit, seductive, sweetly humble, and terribly imperious. It was illumination in the dark crypts of their souls, a compulsion of purity and gentleness vastly greater than that which resided in the shining, death-spitting revolvers of the officers.

The men wavered reluctantly where they stood, and those who had loosed the turns made them fast again. Then one, and then another, and then all of them, began to sidle awkwardly away.

McCoy's face was beaming with childlike pleasure as he descended from the top of the cabin. There was no trouble. For that matter there had been no trouble averted. There never had been any trouble, for there was no place for such in the blissful world in which he lived.

"You hypnotized em," Mr. Konig grinned at him, speaking in a low voice.

"Those boys are good," was the answer. "Their hearts are good. They have had a hard time, and they have worked hard, and they will work hard to the end."

Mr. Konig had not time to reply. His voice was ringing out orders, the sailors were springing to obey, and the PYRENEES was paying slowly off from the wind until her bow should point in the direction of Makemo.

The wind was very light, and after sundown almost ceased. It was insufferably warm, and fore and aft men sought vainly to sleep. The deck was too hot to lie upon, and poisonous vapors, oozing through the seams, crept like evil spirits over the ship, stealing into the nostrils and windpipes of the unwary and causing fits of sneezing and coughing. The stars blinked lazily in the dim vault overhead; and the full moon, rising in the east, touched with its light the myriads of wisps and threads and spidery films of smoke that intertwined and writhed and twisted along the deck, over the rails, and up the masts and shrouds.

"Tell me," Captain Davenport said, rubbing his smarting eyes, "what happened with that BOUNTY crowd after they reached Pitcairn? The account I read said they burnt the Bounty, and that they were not discovered until many years later. But what happened in the meantime? I've always been curious to know. They were men with their necks in the rope. There were some native men, too. And then there were women. That made it look like trouble right from the jump."

"There was trouble," McCoy answered. "They were bad men. They quarreled about the women right away. One of the mutineers, Williams, lost his wife. All the women were Tahitian women. His wife fell from the cliffs when hunting sea birds. Then he took the wife of one of the native men away from him. All the native men were made very angry by this, and they killed off nearly all the mutineers. Then the mutineers that escaped killed off all the native men. The women helped. And the natives killed each other. Everybody killed everybody. They were terrible men.

"Timiti was killed by two other natives while they were combing his hair in friendship. The white men had sent them to do it. Then the white men killed them. The wife of Tullaloo killed him in a cave because she wanted a white man for husband. They were very wicked. God had hidden His face from them. At the end of two years all the native men were murdered, and all the white men except four. They were Young, John Adams, McCoy, who was my great-grandfather, and Quintal. He was a very bad man, too. Once, just because his wife did not catch enough fish for him, he bit off her ear."

"They were a bad lot!" Mr. Konig exclaimed.

"Yes, they were very bad," McCoy agreed and went on serenely cooing of the blood and lust of his iniquitous ancestry. "My great-grandfather escaped murder in order to die by his own hand. He made a still and manufactured alcohol from the roots of the ti-plant. Quintal was his chum, and they got drunk together all the time. At last McCoy got delirium tremens, tied a rock to his neck, and jumped into the sea.

"Quintal's wife, the one whose ear he bit off, also got killed by falling from the cliffs. Then Quintal went to Young and demanded his wife, and went to Adams and demanded his wife. Adams and Young were afraid of Quintal. They knew he would kill them. So they killed him, the two of them together, with a hatchet. Then Young died. And that was about all the trouble they had."

"I should say so," Captain Davenport snorted. "There was nobody left to kill."

"You see, God had hidden His face," McCoy said.

By morning no more than a faint air was blowing from the eastward, and, unable to make appreciable southing by it, Captain Davenport hauled up full-and-by on the port track. He was afraid of that terrible westerly current which had cheated him out of so many ports of refuge. All day the calm continued, and all night, while the sailors, on a short ration of dried banana, were grumbling. Also, they were growing weak and complaining of stomach pains caused by the straight banana diet. All day the current swept the PYRENEES to the westward, while there was no wind to bear her south. In the middle of the first dogwatch, cocoanut trees were sighted due south, their tufted heads rising above the water and marking the low-lying atoll beneath.

"That is Taenga Island," McCoy said. "We need a breeze tonight, or else we'll miss Makemo."

"What's become of the southeast trade?" the captain demanded. "Why don't it blow? What's the matter?"

"It is the evaporation from the big lagoons—there are so many of them," McCoy explained. "The evaporation upsets the whole system of trades. It even causes the wind to back up and blow gales from the southwest. This is the Dangerous Archipelago, Captain."

Captain Davenport faced the old man, opened his mouth, and was about to curse, but paused and refrained. McCoy's presence was a rebuke to the blasphemies that stirred in his brain and trembled in his larynx. McCoy's influence had been growing during the many days they had been together. Captain Davenport was an autocrat of the sea, fearing no man, never bridling his tongue, and now he found himself unable to curse in the presence of this old man with the feminine brown eyes and the voice of a dove. When he realized this, Captain Davenport experienced a distinct shock. This old man was merely the seed of McCoy, of McCoy of the BOUNTY, the mutineer fleeing from the hemp that waited him in England, the McCoy who was a power for evil in the early days of blood and lust and violent death on Pitcairn Island.

Captain Davenport was not religious, yet in that moment he felt a mad impulse to cast himself at the other's feet—and to say he knew not what. It was an emotion that so deeply stirred him, rather than a coherent thought, and he was aware in some vague way of his own unworthiness and smallness in the presence of this other man who possessed the simplicity of a child and the gentleness of a woman.

Of course he could not so humble himself before the eyes of his officers and men. And yet the anger that had prompted the blasphemy still raged in him. He suddenly smote the cabin with his clenched hand and cried:

"Look here, old man, I won't be beaten. These Paumotus have cheated and tricked me and made a fool of me. I refuse to be beaten. I am going to drive this ship, and drive and drive and drive clear through the Paumotus to China but what I find a bed for her. If every man deserts, I'll stay by her. I'll show the Paumotus. They can't fool me. She's a good girl, and I'll stick by her as long as there's a plank to stand on. You hear me?"

"And I'll stay with you, Captain," McCoy said.

During the night, light, baffling airs blew out of the south, and the frantic captain, with his cargo of fire, watched and measured his westward drift and went off by himself at times to curse softly so that McCoy should not hear.

Daylight showed more palms growing out of the water to the south.

"That's the leeward point of Makemo," McCoy said. "Katiu is only a few miles to the west. We may make that."

But the current, sucking between the two islands, swept them to the northwest, and at one in the afternoon they saw the palms of Katiu rise above the sea and sink back into the sea again.

A few minutes later, just as the captain had discovered that a new current from the northeast had gripped the Pyrenees, the masthead lookouts raised cocoanut palms in the northwest.

"It is Raraka," said McCoy. "We won't make it without wind. The current is drawing us down to the southwest. But we must watch out. A few miles farther on a current flows north and turns in a circle to the northwest. This will sweep us away from Fakarava, and Fakarava is the place for the Pyrenees to find her bed."

"They can sweep all they da—all they well please," Captain Davenport remarked with heat. "We'll find a bed for her somewhere just the same."

But the situation on the Pyrenees was reaching a culmination. The deck was so hot that it seemed an increase of a few degrees would cause it to burst into flames. In many places even the heavy-soled shoes of the men were no protection, and they were compelled to step lively to avoid scorching their feet. The smoke had increased and grown more acrid. Every man on board was suffering from inflamed eyes, and they coughed and strangled like a crew of tuberculosis patients. In the afternoon the boats were swung out and equipped. The last several packages of dried bananas were stored in them, as well as the instruments of the officers. Captain Davenport even put the chronometer into the longboat, fearing the blowing up of the deck at any moment.

All night this apprehension weighed heavily on all, and in the first morning light, with hollow eyes and ghastly faces, they stared at one another as if in surprise that the Pyrenees still held together and that they still were alive.

Walking rapidly at times, and even occasionally breaking into an undignified hop-skip-and-run, Captain Davenport inspected his ship's deck.

"It is a matter of hours now, if not of minutes," he announced on his return to the poop.

The cry of land came down from the masthead. From the deck the land was invisible, and McCoy went aloft, while the captain took advantage of the opportunity to curse some of the bitterness out of his heart. But the cursing was suddenly stopped by a dark line on the water which he sighted to the northeast. It was not a squall, but a regular breeze—the disrupted trade wind, eight points out of its direction but resuming business once more.

"Hold her up, Captain," McCoy said as soon as he reached the poop. "That's the easterly point of Fakarava, and we'll go in through the passage full-tilt, the wind abeam, and every sail drawing."

At the end of an hour, the cocoanut trees and the low-lying land were visible from the deck. The feeling that the end of the PYRENEES' resistance was imminent weighed heavily on everybody. Captain Davenport had the three boats lowered and dropped short astern, a man in each to keep them apart. The Pyrenees closely skirted the shore, the surf-whitened atoll a bare two cable lengths away.

And a minute later the land parted, exposing a narrow passage and the lagoon beyond, a great mirror, thirty miles in length and a third as broad.

"Now, Captain."

For the last time the yards of the Pyrenees swung around as she obeyed the wheel and headed into the passage. The turns had scarcely been made, and nothing had been coiled down, when the men and mates swept back to the poop in panic terror. Nothing had happened, yet they averred that something was going to happen. They could not tell why. They merely knew that it was about to happen. McCoy started forward to take up his position on the bow in order to con the vessel in; but the captain gripped his arm and whirled him around.

"Do it from here," he said. "That deck's not safe. What's the matter?" he demanded the next instant. "We're standing still."

McCoy smiled.

"You are bucking a seven-knot current, Captain," he said. "That is the way the full ebb runs out of this passage."

At the end of another hour the Pyrenees had scarcely gained her length, but the wind freshened and she began to forge ahead.

"Better get into the boats, some of you," Captain Davenport commanded.

His voice was still ringing, and the men were just beginning to move in obedience, when the amidship deck of the Pyrenees, in a mass of flame and smoke, was flung upward into the sails and rigging, part of it remaining there and the rest falling into the sea. The wind being abeam, was what had saved the men crowded aft. They made a blind rush to gain the boats, but McCoy's voice, carrying its convincing message of vast calm and endless time, stopped them.

"Take it easy," he was saying. "Everything is all right. Pass that boy down somebody, please."

The man at the wheel had forsaken it in a funk, and Captain Davenport had leaped and caught the spokes in time to prevent the ship from yawing in the current and going ashore.

"Better take charge of the boats," he said to Mr. Konig. "Tow one of them short, right under the quarter.... When I go over, it'll be on the jump."

Mr. Konig hesitated, then went over the rail and lowered himself into the boat.

"Keep her off half a point, Captain."

Captain Davenport gave a start. He had thought he had the ship to himself.

"Ay, ay; half a point it is," he answered.

Amidships the Pyrenees was an open flaming furnace, out of which poured an immense volume of smoke which rose high above the masts and completely hid the forward part of the ship. McCoy, in the shelter of the mizzen-shrouds, continued his difficult task of conning the ship through the intricate channel. The fire was working aft along the deck from the seat of explosion, while the soaring tower of canvas on the mainmast went up and vanished in a sheet of flame. Forward, though they could not see them, they knew that the head-sails were still drawing.

"If only she don't burn all her canvas off before she makes inside," the captain groaned.

"She'll make it," McCoy assured him with supreme confidence. "There is plenty of time. She is bound to make it. And once inside, we'll put her before it; that will keep the smoke away from us and hold back the fire from working aft."

A tongue of flame sprang up the mizzen, reached hungrily for the lowest tier of canvas, missed it, and vanished. From aloft a burning shred of rope stuff fell square on the back of Captain Davenport's neck. He acted with the celerity of one stung by a bee as he reached up and brushed the offending fire from his skin.

"How is she heading, Captain?"

"Nor'west by west."

"Keep her west-nor-west."

Captain Davenport put the wheel up and steadied her.

"West by north, Captain."

"West by north she is."

"And now west."

Slowly, point by point, as she entered the lagoon, the PYRENEES described the circle that put her before the wind; and point by point, with all the calm certitude of a thousand years of time to spare, McCoy chanted the changing course.

"Another point, Captain."

"A point it is."

Captain Davenport whirled several spokes over, suddenly reversing and coming back one to check her.

"Steady."

"Steady she is—right on it."

Despite the fact that the wind was now astern, the heat was so intense that Captain Davenport was compelled to steal sidelong glances into the binnacle, letting go the wheel now with one hand, now with the other, to rub or shield his blistering cheeks.

McCoy's beard was crinkling and shriveling and the smell of it, strong in the other's nostrils, compelled him to look toward McCoy with sudden solicitude. Captain Davenport was letting go the spokes alternately with his hands in order to rub their blistering backs against his trousers. Every sail on the mizzenmast vanished in a rush of flame, compelling the two men to crouch and shield their faces.

"Now," said McCoy, stealing a glance ahead at the low shore, "four points up, Captain, and let her drive."

Shreds and patches of burning rope and canvas were falling about them and upon them. The tarry smoke from a smouldering piece of rope at the captain's feet set him off into a violent coughing fit, during which he still clung to the spokes.

The Pyrenees struck, her bow lifted and she ground ahead gently to a stop. A shower of burning fragments, dislodged by the shock, fell about them. The ship moved ahead again and struck a second time. She crushed the fragile coral under her keel, drove on, and struck a third time.

"Hard over," said McCoy. "Hard over?" he questioned gently, a minute later.

"She won't answer," was the reply.

"All right. She is swinging around." McCoy peered over the side. "Soft, white sand. Couldn't ask better. A beautiful bed."

As the Pyrenees swung around her stern away from the wind, a fearful blast of smoke and flame poured aft. Captain Davenport deserted the wheel in blistering agony. He reached the painter of the boat that lay under the quarter, then looked for McCoy, who was standing aside to let him go down.

"You first," the captain cried, gripping him by the shoulder and almost throwing him over the rail. But the flame and smoke were too terrible, and he followed hard after McCoy, both men wriggling on the rope and sliding down into the boat together. A sailor in the bow, without waiting for orders, slashed the painter through with his sheath knife. The oars, poised in readiness, bit into the water, and the boat shot away.

"A beautiful bed, Captain," McCoy murmured, looking back.

"Ay, a beautiful bed, and all thanks to you," was the answer.

The three boats pulled away for the white beach of pounded coral, beyond which, on the edge of a cocoanut grove, could be seen a half dozen grass houses and a score or more of excited natives, gazing wide-eyed at the conflagration that had come to land.

The boats grounded and they stepped out on the white beach.

"And now," said McCoy, "I must see about getting back to Pitcairn."

About Author

John Griffith London (born **John Griffith Chaney**; January 12, 1876 – November 22, 1916) was an American novelist, journalist, and social activist. A pioneer in the world of commercial magazine fiction, he was one of the first writers to become a worldwide celebrity and earn a large fortune from writing. He was also an innovator in the genre that would later become known as science fiction.

His most famous works include The Call of the Wild and White Fang, both set in the Klondike Gold Rush, as well as the short stories "To Build a Fire", "An Odyssey of the North", and "Love of Life". He also wrote about the South Pacific in stories such as "The Pearls of Parlay", and "The Heathen".

London was part of the radical literary group "The Crowd" in San Francisco and a passionate advocate of unionization, workers' rights, socialism, and eugenics. He wrote several works dealing with these topics, such as his dystopian novel The Iron Heel, his non-fiction exposé The People of the Abyss, The War of the Classes, and Before Adam.

Family

Jack London's mother, Flora Wellman, was the fifth and youngest child of Pennsylvania Canal builder Marshall Wellman and his first wife, Eleanor Garrett Jones. Marshall Wellman was descended from Thomas Wellman, an early Puritan settler in the Massachusetts Bay Colony. Flora left Ohio and moved to the Pacific coast when her father remarried after her mother died. In San Francisco, Flora worked as a music teacher and spiritualist, claiming to channel the spirit of a Sauk chief, Black Hawk.

Biographer Clarice Stasz and others believe London's father was astrologer William Chaney. Flora Wellman was living with Chaney in San Francisco when she became pregnant. Whether Wellman and Chaney were legally married is unknown. Stasz notes that in his memoirs, Chaney refers to London's mother Flora Wellman as having been his "wife"; he also cites an advertisement in which Flora called herself "Florence Wellman Chaney".

According to Flora Wellman's account, as recorded in the San Francisco Chronicle of June 4, 1875, Chaney demanded that she have an abortion. When she refused, he disclaimed responsibility for the child. In desperation, she shot herself. She was not seriously wounded, but she was temporarily deranged. After giving birth, Flora turned the baby over for care to Virginia Prentiss, an African-American woman and former slave. She was a major maternal figure throughout London's life. Late in 1876, Flora Wellman married John London, a partially disabled Civil War veteran, and brought her baby John, later known as Jack, to live with the newly married couple. The family moved around the San Francisco Bay Area before settling in Oakland, where London completed public grade school.

In 1897, when he was 21 and a student at the University of California, Berkeley, London searched for and read the newspaper accounts of his mother's suicide attempt and the name of his biological father. He wrote to William Chaney, then living in Chicago. Chaney responded that he could not be London's father because he was impotent; he casually asserted that London's mother had relations with other men and averred that she had slandered him when she said he insisted on an abortion. Chaney concluded by saying that he was more to be pitied than London. London was devastated by his father's letter; in the months following, he quit school at Berkeley and went to the Klondike during the gold rush boom.

Early life

London was born near Third and Brannan Streets in San Francisco. The house burned down in the fire after the 1906 San Francisco earthquake; the California Historical Society placed a plaque at the site in 1953. Although the family was working class, it was not as impoverished as London's later accounts claimed. London was largely self-educated.

In 1885, London found and read Ouida's long Victorian novel Signa. He credited this as the seed of his literary success. In 1886, he went to the Oakland Public Library and found a sympathetic librarian, Ina Coolbrith, who encouraged his learning. (She later became California's first poet laureate and an important figure in the San Francisco literary community).

In 1889, London began working 12 to 18 hours a day at Hickmott's Cannery. Seeking a way out, he borrowed money from his foster mother Virginia Prentiss, bought the sloop Razzle-Dazzle from an oyster pirate named French Frank, and became an oyster pirate himself. In his memoir, John Barleycorn, he claims also to have stolen French Frank's mistress Mamie. After a few months, his sloop became damaged beyond repair. London hired on as a member of the California Fish Patrol.

In 1893, he signed on to the sealing schooner Sophie Sutherland, bound for the coast of Japan. When he returned, the country was in the grip of the panic of '93 and Oakland was swept by labor unrest. After grueling jobs in a jute mill and a street-railway power plant, London joined Coxey's Army and began his career as a tramp. In 1894, he spent 30 days for vagrancy in the Erie County Penitentiary at Buffalo, New York. In The Road, he wrote:

> Man-handling was merely one of the very minor unprintable horrors of the Erie County Pen. I say 'unprintable'; and in justice I must also say undescribable. They were unthinkable to me until I saw them, and I was no spring chicken in the ways of the world and the awful abysses of human degradation. It would take a deep plummet to reach bottom in the Erie County Pen, and I do but skim lightly and facetiously the surface of things as I there saw them.

> —Jack London, The Road

After many experiences as a hobo and a sailor, he returned to Oakland and attended Oakland High School. He contributed a number of articles to the high school's magazine, The Aegis. His first published work was "Typhoon off the Coast of Japan", an account of his sailing experiences.

As a schoolboy, London often studied at Heinold's First and Last Chance Saloon, a port-side bar in Oakland. At 17, he confessed to the bar's owner, John Heinold, his desire to attend university and pursue a career as a writer. Heinold lent London tuition money to attend college.

London desperately wanted to attend the University of California, located in Berkeley. In 1896, after a summer of intense studying to pass certification exams, he was admitted. Financial circumstances forced him to leave in 1897 and he never graduated. No evidence has surfaced that he ever wrote for student publications while studying at Berkeley.

While at Berkeley, London continued to study and spend time at Heinold's saloon, where he was introduced to the sailors and adventurers who would influence his writing. In his autobiographical novel, John Barleycorn, London mentioned the pub's likeness seventeen times. Heinold's was the place where London met Alexander McLean, a captain known for his cruelty at sea. London based his protagonist Wolf Larsen, in the novel The Sea-Wolf, on McLean.

Heinold's First and Last Chance Saloon is now unofficially named Jack London's Rendezvous in his honor.

Gold rush and first success

On July 12, 1897, London (age 21) and his sister's husband Captain Shepard sailed to join the Klondike Gold Rush. This was the setting for some of his first successful stories. London's time in the harsh Klondike, however, was detrimental to his health. Like so many other men who were malnourished in the goldfields, London developed scurvy. His gums became swollen, leading to the loss of his four front teeth. A constant gnawing pain affected his hip and leg muscles, and his face was stricken with marks that always reminded him of the struggles he faced in the Klondike. Father William Judge, "The Saint of Dawson", had a facility in Dawson that provided shelter, food and any available medicine to London and others. His struggles there inspired London's short story, "To Build a Fire" (1902, revised in 1908), which many critics assess as his best.

His landlords in Dawson were mining engineers Marshall Latham Bond and Louis Whitford Bond, educated at Yale and Stanford, respectively. The brothers' father, Judge Hiram Bond, was a wealthy mining investor. The Bonds, especially Hiram, were active Republicans. Marshall Bond's diary mentions friendly sparring with London on political issues as a camp pastime.

London left Oakland with a social conscience and socialist leanings; he returned to become an activist for socialism. He concluded that his only hope of escaping the work "trap" was to get an education and "sell his brains". He saw his writing as a business, his ticket out of poverty, and, he hoped, a means of beating the wealthy at their own game. On returning to California in 1898, London began working to get published, a struggle described in his novel, Martin Eden (serialized in 1908, published in 1909). His first published story since high school was "To the Man On Trail", which has frequently been collected in anthologies. When The Overland Monthly offered him only five dollars for it—and was slow paying—London came close to abandoning his writing career. In his words, "literally and literarily I was saved" when The Black Cat accepted his story "A Thousand Deaths", and paid him $40—the "first money I ever received for a story".

London began his writing career just as new printing technologies enabled lower-cost production of magazines. This resulted in a boom in popular magazines aimed at a wide public audience and a strong market for short fiction. In 1900, he made $2,500 in writing, about $77,000 in today's currency. Among the works he sold to magazines was a short story known as either "Diable" (1902) or "Bâtard" (1904), two editions of the same basic story; London received $141.25 for this story on May 27, 1902. In the text, a cruel French Canadian brutalizes his dog, and the dog retaliates and kills the man. London told some of his critics that man's actions are the main cause of the behavior of their animals, and he would show this in another story, The Call of the Wild.

In early 1903, London sold The Call of the Wild to The Saturday Evening Post for $750, and the book rights to Macmillan for $2,000. Macmillan's promotional campaign propelled it to swift success.

While living at his rented villa on Lake Merritt in Oakland, California, London met poet George Sterling; in time they became best friends. In 1902, Sterling helped London find a home closer to his own in nearby Piedmont. In his letters London addressed Sterling as "Greek", owing to Sterling's aquiline nose and classical profile, and he signed them as "Wolf". London was later to depict Sterling as Russ Brissenden in his autobiographical novel Martin Eden (1910) and as Mark Hall in The Valley of the Moon (1913).

In later life London indulged his wide-ranging interests by accumulating a personal library of 15,000 volumes. He referred to his books as "the tools of my trade".

First marriage (1900–04)

London married Elizabeth "Bessie" Maddern on April 7, 1900, the same day The Son of the Wolf was published. Bess had been part of his circle of friends for a number of years. She was related to stage actresses Minnie Maddern Fiske and Emily Stevens. Stasz says, "Both acknowledged publicly that they were not marrying out of love, but from friendship and a belief that they would produce sturdy children." Kingman says, "they were comfortable together... Jack had made it clear to Bessie that he did not love her, but that he liked her enough to make a successful marriage."

London met Bessie through his friend at Oakland High School, Fred Jacobs; she was Fred's fiancée. Bessie, who tutored at Anderson's University Academy in Alameda California, tutored Jack in preparation for his entrance exams for the University of California at Berkeley in 1896. Jacobs was killed aboard the USAT Scandia in 1897, but Jack and Bessie continued their friendship, which included taking photos and developing the film together. This was the beginning of Jack's passion for photography.

During the marriage, London continued his friendship with Anna Strunsky, co-authoring The Kempton-Wace Letters, an epistolary novel contrasting two philosophies of love. Anna, writing "Dane Kempton's" letters, arguing for a romantic view of marriage, while London, writing "Herbert Wace's" letters, argued for a scientific view, based on Darwinism and eugenics. In the novel, his fictional character contrasted two women he had known.

London's pet name for Bess was "Mother-Girl" and Bess's for London was "Daddy-Boy". Their first child, Joan, was born on January 15, 1901, and their second, Bessie (later called Becky), on October 20, 1902. Both children were born in Piedmont, California. Here London wrote one of his most celebrated works, The Call of the Wild.

While London had pride in his children, the marriage was strained. Kingman says that by 1903 the couple were close to separation as they were "extremely incompatible". "Jack was still so kind and gentle with Bessie that when Cloudsley Johns was a house guest in February 1903 he didn't suspect a breakup of their marriage."

London reportedly complained to friends Joseph Noel and George Sterling:

> [Bessie] is devoted to purity. When I tell her morality is only evidence of low blood pressure, she hates me. She'd sell me and the children out for her damned purity. It's terrible. Every time I come back after being away from home for a night she won't let me be in the same room with her if she can help it.

Stasz writes that these were "code words for fear that was consorting with prostitutes and might bring home venereal disease."

On July 24, 1903, London told Bessie he was leaving and moved out. During 1904, London and Bess negotiated the terms of a divorce, and the decree was granted on November 11, 1904.

War correspondent (1904)

London accepted an assignment of the San Francisco Examiner to cover the Russo-Japanese War in early 1904, arriving in Yokohama on January 25, 1904. He was arrested by Japanese authorities in Shimonoseki, but released through the intervention of American ambassador Lloyd Griscom. After travelling to Korea, he was again arrested by Japanese authorities for straying too close to the border with Manchuria without official permission, and was sent back to Seoul. Released again, London was permitted to travel with the Imperial Japanese Army to the border, and to observe the Battle of the Yalu.

London asked William Randolph Hearst, the owner of the San Francisco Examiner, to be allowed to transfer to the Imperial Russian Army, where he felt that restrictions on his reporting and his movements would be less severe. However, before this could be arranged, he was arrested for a third time in four months, this time for assaulting his Japanese assistants, whom he accused of stealing the fodder for his horse. Released through the personal intervention of President Theodore Roosevelt, London departed the front in June 1904.

Bohemian Club

On August 18, 1904, London went with his close friend, the poet George Sterling, to "Summer High Jinks" at the Bohemian Grove. London was elected to honorary membership in the Bohemian Club and took part in many activities. Other noted members of the Bohemian Club during this time included Ambrose Bierce, Gelett Burgess, Allan Dunn, John Muir, Frank Norris, and Herman George Scheffauer.

Beginning in December 1914, London worked on The Acorn Planter, A California Forest Play, to be performed as one of the annual Grove Plays, but it was never selected. It was described as too difficult to set to music. London published The Acorn Planter in 1916.

Second marriage

After divorcing Maddern, London married Charmian Kittredge in 1905. London had been introduced to Kittredge in 1900 by her aunt Netta Eames, who was an editor at Overland Monthly magazine in San Francisco. The two met prior to his first marriage but became lovers years later after Jack and Bessie London visited Wake Robin, Netta Eames' Sonoma County resort, in 1903. London was injured when he fell from a buggy, and Netta arranged for Charmian to care for him. The two developed a friendship, as Charmian, Netta, her husband Roscoe, and London were politically aligned with socialist causes. At some point the relationship became romantic, and Jack divorced his wife to marry Charmian, who was five years his senior.

Biographer Russ Kingman called Charmian "Jack's soul-mate, always at his side, and a perfect match." Their time together included numerous trips, including a 1907 cruise on the yacht Snark to Hawaii and Australia. Many of London's stories are based on his visits to Hawaii, the last one for 10 months beginning in December 1915.

The couple also visited Goldfield, Nevada, in 1907, where they were guests of the Bond brothers, London's Dawson City landlords. The Bond brothers were working in Nevada as mining engineers.

London had contrasted the concepts of the "Mother Girl" and the "Mate Woman" in The Kempton-Wace Letters. His pet name for Bess had been "Mother-Girl;" his pet name for Charmian was "Mate-Woman."Charmian's aunt and foster mother, a disciple of Victoria Woodhull, had raised her without prudishness.Every biographer alludes to Charmian's uninhibited sexuality.

Joseph Noel calls the events from 1903 to 1905 "a domestic drama that would have intrigued the pen of an Ibsen.... London's had comedy relief in it and a sort of easy-going romance." In broad outline, London was restless in his first marriage, sought extramarital sexual affairs, and found, in Charmian Kittredge, not only a sexually active and adventurous partner, but his future life-companion. They attempted to have children; one child died at birth, and another pregnancy ended in a miscarriage.

In 1906, London published in Collier's magazine his eye-witness report of the San Francisco earthquake.

Beauty Ranch (1905–16)

In 1905, London purchased a 1,000 acres (4.0 km2) ranch in Glen Ellen, Sonoma County, California, on the eastern slope of Sonoma Mountain.He wrote: "Next to my wife, the ranch is the dearest thing in the world to me." He desperately wanted the ranch to become a successful business enterprise. Writing, always a commercial enterprise with London, now became even more a means to an end: "I write for no other purpose than to add to the beauty that now belongs to me. I write a book for no other reason than to add three or four hundred acres to my magnificent estate."

Stasz writes that London "had taken fully to heart the vision, expressed in his agrarian fiction, of the land as the closest earthly version of Eden ... he educated himself through the study of agricultural manuals and scientific tomes. He conceived of a system of ranching that today would be praised for its ecological wisdom." He was proud to own the first concrete silo in California, a circular piggery that he designed. He hoped to adapt the wisdom of Asian sustainable agriculture to the United States. He hired both Italian and Chinese stonemasons, whose distinctly different styles are obvious.

The ranch was an economic failure. Sympathetic observers such as Stasz treat his projects as potentially feasible, and ascribe their failure to bad luck or to being ahead of their time. Unsympathetic historians such as Kevin Starr suggest that he was a bad manager, distracted by other concerns and impaired by his alcoholism. Starr notes that London was absent from his ranch about six months a year between 1910 and 1916 and says, "He liked the show of managerial power, but not grinding attention to detail .... London's workers laughed at his efforts to play big-time rancher the operation a rich man's hobby."

London spent $80,000 ($2,280,000 in current value) to build a 15,000-square-foot (1,400 m2) stone mansion called Wolf House on the property. Just as the mansion was nearing completion, two weeks before the Londons planned to move in, it was destroyed by fire.

London's last visit to Hawaii, beginning in December 1915, lasted eight months. He met with Duke Kahanamoku, Prince Jonah Kūhiō Kalaniana'ole, Queen Lili'uokalani and many others, before returning to his ranch in July 1916. He was suffering from kidney failure, but he continued to work.

The ranch (abutting stone remnants of Wolf House) is now a National Historic Landmark and is protected in Jack London State Historic Park.

Animal activism

London witnessed animal cruelty in the training of circus animals, and his subsequent novels Jerry of the Islands and Michael, Brother of Jerry included a foreword entreating the public to become more informed about this practice. In 1918, the Massachusetts Society for the Prevention of Cruelty to Animals and the American Humane Education Society teamed up to create the Jack London Club, which sought to inform the public about cruelty to circus animals and encourage them to protest this establishment. Support from Club members led to a temporary cessation of trained animal acts at Ringling-Barnum and Bailey in 1925.

Death

London died November 22, 1916, in a sleeping porch in a cottage on his ranch. London had been a robust man but had suffered several serious illnesses, including scurvy in the Klondike. Additionally, during travels on the Snark, he and Charmian picked up unspecified tropical infections, and diseases, including yaws. At the time of his death, he suffered from dysentery, late-stage alcoholism, and uremia; he was in extreme pain and taking morphine.

London's ashes were buried on his property not far from the Wolf House. London's funeral took place on November 26, 1916, attended only by close friends, relatives, and workers of the property. In accordance with his wishes, he was cremated and buried next to some pioneer children, under a rock that belonged to the Wolf House. After Charmian's death in 1955, she was also cremated and then buried with her husband in the same spot that her husband chose. The grave is marked by a mossy boulder. The buildings and property were later preserved as Jack London State Historic Park, in Glen Ellen, California.

Suicide debate

Because he was using morphine, many older sources describe London's death as a suicide, and some still do. This conjecture appears to be a rumor, or speculation based on incidents in his fiction writings. His death certificate gives the cause as uremia, following acute renal colic.

The biographer Stasz writes, "Following London's death, for a number of reasons, a biographical myth developed in which he has been portrayed as an alcoholic womanizer who committed suicide. Recent scholarship based upon firsthand documents challenges this caricature." Most biographers, including Russ Kingman, now agree he died of uremia aggravated by an accidental morphine overdose.

London's fiction featured several suicides. In his autobiographical memoir John Barleycorn, he claims, as a youth, to have drunkenly stumbled overboard into the San Francisco Bay, "some maundering fancy of going out with the tide suddenly obsessed me". He said he drifted and nearly succeeded in drowning before sobering up and being rescued by fishermen. In the dénouement of The Little Lady of the Big House, the heroine, confronted by the pain of a mortal gunshot wound, undergoes a physician-assisted suicide by morphine. Also, in Martin Eden, the principal protagonist, who shares certain characteristics with London, drowns himself.

Plagiarism accusations

London was vulnerable to accusations of plagiarism, both because he was such a conspicuous, prolific, and successful writer and because of his methods of working. He wrote in a letter to Elwyn Hoffman, "expression, you see—with me—is far easier than invention." He purchased plots and novels from the young Sinclair Lewis and used incidents from newspaper clippings as writing material.

In July 1901, two pieces of fiction appeared within the same month: London's "Moon-Face", in the San Francisco Argonaut, and Frank Norris' "The Passing of Cock-eye Blacklock", in Century Magazine. Newspapers showed the similarities between the stories, which London said were "quite different in manner of treatment, patently the same in foundation and motive." London explained both writers based their stories on the same newspaper account. A year later, it was discovered that Charles Forrest McLean had published a fictional story also based on the same incident.

Egerton Ryerson Young claimed The Call of the Wild (1903) was taken from Young's book My Dogs in the Northland (1902). London acknowledged using it as a source and claimed to have written a letter to Young thanking him.

In 1906, the New York World published "deadly parallel" columns showing eighteen passages from London's short story "Love of Life" side by side with similar passages from a nonfiction article by Augustus Biddle and J. K. Macdonald, titled "Lost in the Land of the Midnight Sun". London noted the World did not accuse him of "plagiarism", but only of "identity of time and situation", to which he defiantly "pled guilty".

The most serious charge of plagiarism was based on London's "The Bishop's Vision", Chapter 7 of his novel The Iron Heel (1908). The chapter is nearly identical to an ironic essay that Frank Harris published in 1901, titled "The Bishop of London and Public Morality". Harris was incensed and suggested he should receive 1/60th of the royalties from The Iron Heel, the disputed material constituting about that fraction of the whole novel. London insisted he had clipped a reprint of the article, which had appeared in an American newspaper, and believed it to be a genuine speech delivered by the Bishop of London.

Views

Atheism

London was an atheist. He is quoted as saying, "I believe that when I am dead, I am dead. I believe that with my death I am just as much obliterated as the last mosquito you and I squashed."

Socialism

London wrote from a socialist viewpoint, which is evident in his novel The Iron Heel. Neither a theorist nor an intellectual socialist, London's socialism grew out of his life experience. As London explained in his essay, "How I Became a Socialist", his views were influenced by his experience with people at the bottom of the social pit. His optimism and individualism faded, and he vowed never to do more hard physical work than necessary. He wrote that his individualism was hammered out of him, and he was politically reborn. He often closed his letters "Yours for the Revolution."

London joined the Socialist Labor Party in April 1896. In the same year, the San Francisco Chronicle published a story about the twenty-year-old London's giving nightly speeches in Oakland's City Hall Park, an activity he was arrested for a year later. In 1901, he left the Socialist Labor Party and joined the new Socialist Party of America. He ran unsuccessfully as the high-profile Socialist candidate for mayor of Oakland in 1901 (receiving 245 votes) and 1905 (improving to 981 votes), toured the country lecturing on socialism in 1906, and published two collections of essays about socialism: The War of the Classes (1905) and Revolution, and other Essays (1906).

Stasz notes that "London regarded the Wobblies as a welcome addition to the Socialist cause, although he never joined them in going so far as to recommend sabotage." Stasz mentions a personal meeting between London and Big Bill Haywood in 1912.

In his late (1913) book The Cruise of the Snark, London writes about appeals to him for membership of the Snark's crew from office workers and other "toilers" who longed for escape from the cities, and of being cheated by workmen.

In his Glen Ellen ranch years, London felt some ambivalence toward socialism and complained about the "inefficient Italian labourers" in his employ. In 1916, he resigned from the Glen Ellen chapter of the Socialist Party, but stated emphatically he did so "because of its lack of fire and fight, and its loss of emphasis on the class struggle." In an unflattering portrait of London's ranch days, California cultural historian Kevin Starr refers to this period as "post-socialist" and says "... by 1911 ... London was more bored by the class struggle than he cared to admit."

Race

London shared common concerns among many European Americans in California about Asian immigration, described as "the yellow peril"; he used the latter term as the title of a 1904 essay. This theme was also the subject of a story he wrote in 1910 called "The Unparalleled Invasion". Presented as an historical essay set in the future, the story narrates events between 1976 and 1987, in which China, with an ever-increasing population, is taking over and colonizing its neighbors with the intention of taking over the entire Earth. The western nations respond with biological warfare and bombard China with dozens of the most infectious diseases. On his fears about China, he admits, "it must be taken into consideration that the above postulate is itself a product of Western race-egotism, urged by our belief in our own righteousness and fostered by a faith in ourselves which may be as erroneous as are most fond race fancies."

By contrast, many of London's short stories are notable for their empathetic portrayal of Mexican ("The Mexican"), Asian ("The Chinago"), and Hawaiian ("Koolau the Leper") characters. London's war correspondence from the Russo-Japanese War, as well as his unfinished novel Cherry, show he admired much about Japanese customs and capabilities. London's writings have been popular among the Japanese, who believe he portrayed them positively.

In "Koolau the Leper", London describes Koolau, who is a Hawaiian leper—and thus a very different sort of "superman" than Martin Eden—and who fights off an entire cavalry troop to elude capture, as "indomitable spiritually—a ... magnificent rebel". This character is based on Hawaiian leper Kaluaikoolau, who in 1893 revolted and resisted capture from forces of the Provisional Government of Hawaii in the Kalalau Valley.

An amateur boxer and avid boxing fan, London reported on the 1910 Johnson–Jeffries fight, in which the black boxer Jack Johnson vanquished Jim Jeffries, known as the "Great White Hope". In 1908, London had reported on an earlier fight of Johnson's, contrasting the black boxer's coolness and intellectual style, with the apelike appearance and fighting style of his Canadian opponent, Tommy Burns:

> [What won] on Saturday was bigness, coolness, quickness, cleverness, and vast physical superiority ... Because a white man wishes a white man to win, this should not prevent him from giving absolute credit to the best man, even when that best man was black. All hail to Johnson. ... superb. He was impregnable ... as inaccessible as Mont Blanc.

Those who defend London against charges of racism cite the letter he wrote to the Japanese-American Commercial Weekly in 1913:

> In reply to yours of August 16, 1913. First of all, I should say by stopping the stupid newspaper from always fomenting race prejudice. This of course, being impossible, I would say, next, by educating the people of Japan so that they will be too intelligently tolerant to respond to any call to race prejudice. And, finally, by realizing, in industry and

451

government, of socialism—which last word is merely a word that stands for the actual application of in the affairs of men of the theory of the Brotherhood of Man.

In the meantime the nations and races are only unruly boys who have not yet grown to the stature of men. So we must expect them to do unruly and boisterous things at times. And, just as boys grow up, so the races of mankind will grow up and laugh when they look back upon their childish quarrels.

In 1996, after the City of Whitehorse, Yukon, renamed a street in honor of London, protests over London's alleged racism forced the city to change the name of "Jack London Boulevard"[failed verification] back to "Two-mile Hill".

Eugenics

London supported eugenics, including forced sterilization of criminals or those deemed feeble minded. His novel Before Adam(1906–07) has been described as having pro-eugenic themes.

London wrote to Frederick H. Robinson of the periodical Medical Review of Reviews, stating, "I believe the future belongs to eugenics, and will be determined by the practice of eugenics."

Works

Short stories

Western writer and historian Dale L. Walker writes:

London's true métier was the short story ... London's true genius lay in the short form, 7,500 words and under, where the flood of images in his teeming brain and the innate power of his narrative gift were at once constrained and freed. His stories that run longer than the magic 7,500 generally—but certainly not always—could have benefited from self-editing.

London's "strength of utterance" is at its height in his stories, and they are painstakingly well-constructed. "To Build a Fire" is the best known of all his stories. Set in the harsh Klondike, it recounts the haphazard trek of a new arrival who has ignored an old-timer's warning about the risks of traveling alone. Falling through the ice into a creek in seventy-five-below weather, the unnamed man is keenly aware that survival depends on his untested skills at quickly building a fire to dry his clothes and warm his extremities. After publishing a tame version of this story—with a sunny outcome—in The Youth's Companion in 1902, London offered a second, more severe take on the man's predicament in The Century Magazine in 1908. Reading both provides an illustration of London's growth and maturation as a writer. As Labor (1994) observes: "To compare the two versions is itself an instructive lesson in what distinguished a great work of literary art from a good children's story."

Other stories from the Klondike period include: "All Gold Canyon", about a battle between a gold prospector and a claim jumper; "The Law of Life", about an aging American Indian man abandoned by his tribe and left to die; "Love of Life", about a trek by a prospector across the Canadian tundra; "To the Man on Trail," which tells the story of a prospector fleeing the Mounted Police in a sled race, and raises the question of the contrast between written law and morality; and "An Odyssey of the North," which raises questions of conditional morality, and paints a sympathetic portrait of a man of mixed White and Aleut ancestry.

London was a boxing fan and an avid amateur boxer. "A Piece of Steak" is a tale about a match between older and younger boxers. It contrasts the differing experiences of youth and age but also raises the social question of the treatment of aging workers. "The Mexican" combines boxing with a social theme, as a young Mexican endures an unfair fight and ethnic prejudice to earn money with which to aid the revolution.

Several of London's stories would today be classified as science fiction. "The Unparalleled Invasion" describes germ warfare against China; "Goliath" is about an irresistible energy weapon; "The Shadow and the Flash" is a tale about two brothers who take different routes to achieving invisibility; "A

Relic of the Pliocene" is a tall tale about an encounter of a modern-day man with a mammoth. "The Red One" is a late story from a period when London was intrigued by the theories of the psychiatrist and writer Jung. It tells of an island tribe held in thrall by an extraterrestrial object.

Some nineteen original collections of short stories were published during London's brief life or shortly after his death. There have been several posthumous anthologies drawn from this pool of stories. Many of these stories were located in the Klondike and the Pacific. A collection of Jack London's San Francisco Stories was published in October 2010 by Sydney Samizdat Press.

Novels

London's most famous novels are The Call of the Wild, White Fang, The Sea-Wolf, The Iron Heel, and Martin Eden.

In a letter dated December 27, 1901, London's Macmillan publisher George Platt Brett, Sr., said "he believed Jack's fiction represented 'the very best kind of work' done in America."

Critic Maxwell Geismar called The Call of the Wild "a beautiful prose poem"; editor Franklin Walker said that it "belongs on a shelf with Walden and Huckleberry Finn"; and novelist E.L. Doctorow called it "a mordant parable ... his masterpiece."

The historian Dale L. Walker commented:

Jack London was an uncomfortable novelist, that form too long for his natural impatience and the quickness of his mind. His novels, even the best of them, are hugely flawed.

Some critics have said that his novels are episodic and resemble linked short stories. Dale L. Walker writes:

The Star Rover, that magnificent experiment, is actually a series of short stories connected by a unifying device ... Smoke Bellew is a series of stories bound together in a novel-like form by their reappearing

454

protagonist, Kit Bellew; and John Barleycorn ... is a synoptic series of short episodes.

Ambrose Bierce said of The Sea-Wolf that "the great thing—and it is among the greatest of things—is that tremendous creation, Wolf Larsen ... the hewing out and setting up of such a figure is enough for a man to do in one lifetime. "However, he noted, "The love element, with its absurd suppressions, and impossible proprieties, is awful."

The Iron Heel is an example of a dystopian novel that anticipates and influenced George Orwell's Nineteen Eighty-Four. London's socialist politics are explicitly on display here. The Iron Heel meets the contemporary definition of soft science fiction. The Star Rover (1915) is also science fiction.

Apocrypha

Jack London Credo

London's literary executor, Irving Shepard, quoted a Jack London Credo in an introduction to a 1956 collection of London stories:

> I would rather be ashes than dust!

> I would rather that my spark should burn out in a brilliant blaze than it should be stifled by dry-rot.

> I would rather be a superb meteor, every atom of me in magnificent glow, than a sleepy and permanent planet.

> The function of man is to live, not to exist.

> I shall not waste my days in trying to prolong them.

> I shall use my time.

The biographer Stasz notes that the passage "has many marks of London's style" but the only line that could be safely attributed to London was the first. The words Shepard quoted were from a story in the San Francisco Bulletin, December 2, 1916, by journalist Ernest J. Hopkins, who visited the ranch just weeks before London's death. Stasz notes, "Even more so than today journalists' quotes were unreliable or even sheer inventions," and says no direct source in London's writings has been found. However, at least one line, according to Stasz, is authentic, being referenced by London and written in his own hand in the autograph book of Australian suffragette Vida Goldstein:

> Dear Miss Goldstein:–
>
> Seven years ago I wrote you that I'd rather be ashes than dust. I still subscribe to that sentiment.
>
> Sincerely yours,
>
> Jack London
>
> Jan. 13, 1909

In his short story "By The Turtles of Tasman", a character, defending her "ne'er-do-well grasshopperish father" to her "antlike uncle", says: "... my father has been a king. He has lived .... Have you lived merely to live? Are you afraid to die? I'd rather sing one wild song and burst my heart with it, than live a thousand years watching my digestion and being afraid of the wet. When you are dust, my father will be ashes."

"The Scab"

A short diatribe on "The Scab" is often quoted within the U.S. labor movement and frequently attributed to London. It opens:

> After God had finished the rattlesnake, the toad, and the vampire, he had some awful substance left with which he made a scab. A scab is a two-legged animal with a corkscrew soul, a water brain, a combination backbone of jelly and glue. Where others have hearts, he carries a tumor of rotten principles. When a scab comes down the street, men turn their backs and Angels weep in Heaven, and the Devil shuts the gates of hell to keep him out....

In 1913 and 1914, a number of newspapers printed the first three sentences with varying terms used instead of "scab", such as "knocker","stool pigeon"or "scandal monger"

This passage as given above was the subject of a 1974 Supreme Court case, Letter Carriers v. Austin, in which Justice Thurgood Marshall referred to it as "a well-known piece of trade union literature, generally attributed to author Jack London". A union newsletter had published a "list of scabs," which was granted to be factual and therefore not libelous, but then went on to quote the passage as the "definition of a scab". The case turned on the question of whether the "definition" was defamatory. The court ruled that "Jack London's... 'definition of a scab' is merely rhetorical hyperbole, a lusty and imaginative expression of the contempt felt by union members towards those who refuse to join", and as such was not libelous and was protected under the First Amendment.

Despite being frequently attributed to London, the passage does not appear at all in the extensive collection of his writings at Sonoma State University's website. However, in his book The War of the Classes he published a 1903 speech entitled "The Scab", which gave a much more balanced view of the topic:

> The laborer who gives more time or strength or skill for the same wage than another, or equal time or strength or skill for a less wage, is a scab. The generousness on his part is hurtful to his fellow-laborers, for it compels them to an equal generousness which is not to their liking, and which gives them less of food and shelter. But a word may be said for the scab. Just as his act makes his rivals compulsorily generous, so do they, by fortune of birth and training, make compulsory his act of generousness.
>
> [...]
>
> Nobody desires to scab, to give most for least. The ambition of every individual is quite the opposite, to give least for most; and, as a result, living in a tooth-and-nail society, battle royal is waged by the ambitious individuals. But in its most salient aspect, that of the struggle over the division of the joint product, it is no longer a battle between individuals, but between groups of individuals. Capital and labor apply

themselves to raw material, make something useful out of it, add to its value, and then proceed to quarrel over the division of the added value. Neither cares to give most for least. Each is intent on giving less than the other and on receiving more.

Legacy and honors

Mount London, also known as Boundary Peak 100, on the Alaska-British Columbia boundary, in the Boundary Ranges of the Coast Mountains of British Columbia, is named for him.

Jack London Square on the waterfront of Oakland, California was named for him.

He was honored by the United States Postal Service with a 25¢ Great Americans series postage stamp released on January 11, 1986.

Jack London Lake (Russian), a mountain lake located in the upper reaches of the Kolyma River in Yagodninsky district of Magadan Oblast.

Fictional portrayals of London include Michael O'Shea in the 1943 film Jack London, Jeff East in the 1980 film Klondike Fever, Aaron Ashmore in the Murdoch Mysteries episode "Murdoch of the Klondike" from 2012, and Johnny Simmons in the 2014 miniseries Klondike. (Source: Wikipedia)

NOTABLE WORKS

NOVELS

The Cruise of the Dazzler (1902)

A Daughter of the Snows (1902)

The Call of the Wild (1903)

The Kempton-Wace Letters (1903) (published anonymously, co-authored with Anna Strunsky)

The Sea-Wolf (1904)

The Game (1905)

White Fang (1906)

Before Adam (1907)

The Iron Heel (1908)

Martin Eden (1909)

Burning Daylight (1910)

Adventure (1911)

The Scarlet Plague (1912)

A Son of the Sun (1912)

The Abysmal Brute (1913)

The Valley of the Moon (1913)

The Mutiny of the Elsinore (1914)

The Star Rover (1915) (published in England as The Jacket)

The Little Lady of the Big House (1916)

Jerry of the Islands (1917)

Michael, Brother of Jerry (1917)

Hearts of Three (1920) (novelization of a script by Charles Goddard)

The Assassination Bureau, Ltd (1963) (left half-finished, completed by Robert L. Fish)

SHORT STORIES

"An Old Soldier's Story" (1894)

"Who Believes in Ghosts!" (1895)

"And 'FRISCO Kid Came Back" (1895)

"Night's Swim In Yeddo Bay" (1895)

"One More Unfortunate" (1895)

"Sakaicho, Hona Asi And Hakadaki" (1895)

"A Klondike Christmas" (1897)

"Mahatma's Little Joke" (1897)

"O Haru" (1897)

"Plague Ship" (1897)

"The Strange Experience Of A Misogynist" (1897)

"Two Gold Bricks" (1897)

"The Devil's Dice Box" (1898)

"A Dream Image" (1898)

"The Test: A Clondyke Wooing" (1898)

"To the Man on Trail" (1898)

"In a Far Country" (1899)

"The King of Mazy May" (1899)

"The End Of The Chapter" (1899)

"The Grilling Of Loren Ellery" (1899)

"The Handsome Cabin Boy" (1899)

"In The Time Of Prince Charley" (1899)

"Old Baldy" (1899)

"The Men of Forty Mile" (1899)

"Pluck and Pertinacity" (1899)

"The Rejuvenation of Major Rathbone" (1899)

"The White Silence" (1899)

"A Thousand Deaths" (1899)

"Wisdom of the Trail" (1899)

"An Odyssey of the North" (1900)

"The Son of the Wolf" (1900)

"Even unto Death" (1900)

"The Man with the Gash" (1900)

"A Lesson in Heraldry" (1900)

"A Northland Miracle" (1900)

"Proper "GIRLIE"" (1900)

"Thanksgiving on Slav Creek" (1900)

"Their Alcove" (1900)

"Housekeeping in the Klondike" (1900)

"Dutch Courage" (1900)

"Where the Trail Forks" (1900)

"Hyperborean Brew" (1901)

"A Relic of the Pliocene" (1901)

"The Lost Poacher" (1901)

"The God of His Fathers" (1901)

""FRISCO Kid's" Story" (1901)

"The Law of Life" (1901)

"The Minions of Midas" (1901)

"In the Forests of the North" (1902)

"The "Fuzziness" of Hoockla-Heen" (1902)

"The Story of Keesh" (1902)

"Keesh, Son of Keesh" (1902)

"Nam-Bok, the Unveracious" (1902)

"Li Wan the Fair" (1902)

"Lost Face"

"Master of Mystery" (1902)

"The Sunlanders" (1902)

"The Death of Ligoun" (1902)

"Moon-Face" (1902)

"Diable—A Dog" (1902), renamed Bâtard in 1904

"To Build a Fire" (1902, revised 1908)

"The League of the Old Men" (1902)

"The Dominant Primordial Beast" (1903)

"The One Thousand Dozen" (1903)

"The Marriage of Lit-lit" (1903)

"The Shadow and the Flash" (1903)

"The Leopard Man's Story" (1903)

"Negore the Coward" (1904)

"All Gold Cañon" (1905)

"Love of Life" (1905)

"The Sun-Dog Trail" (1905)

"The Apostate" (1906)

"Up the Slide" (1906)

"Planchette" (1906)

"Brown Wolf" (1906)

"Make Westing" (1907)

"Chased by the Trail" (1907)

"Trust" (1908)

"A Curious Fragment" (1908)

"Aloha Oe" (1908)

"That Spot" (1908)

"The Enemy of All the World" (1908)

"The House of Mapuhi" (1909)

"Good-by, Jack" (1909)

"Samuel" (1909)

"South of the Slot" (1909)

"The Chinago" (1909)

"The Dream of Debs" (1909)

"The Madness of John Harned" (1909)

"The Seed of McCoy" (1909)

"A Piece of Steak" (1909)

"Mauki" (1909)

"The Whale Tooth" (1909)

"Goliath" (1910)

"The Unparalleled Invasion" (1910)

"Told in the Drooling Ward" (1910)

"When the World was Young" (1910)

"The Terrible Solomons" (1910)

"The Inevitable White Man" (1910)

"The Heathen" (1910)

"Yah! Yah! Yah!" (1910)

"By the Turtles of Tasman" (1911)

"The Mexican" (1911)

"War" (1911)

"The Unmasking of the Cad" (1911)

"The Scarlet Plague" (1912)

"The Captain of the Susan Drew" (1912)

"The Sea-Farmer" (1912)

"The Feathers of the Sun" (1912)

"The Prodigal Father" (1912)

"Samuel" (1913)

"The Sea-Gangsters" (1913)

"The Strength of the Strong" (1914)

"Told in the Drooling Ward" (1914)

"The Hussy" (1916)

"Like Argus of the Ancient Times" (1917)

"Jerry of the Islands" (1917)

"The Red One" (1918)

"Shin-Bones" (1918)

"The Bones of Kahekili" (1919)

SHORT STORY COLLECTIONS

Son of the Wolf (1900)

Chris Farrington, Able Seaman (1901)

The God of His Fathers & Other Stories (1901)

Children of the Frost (1902)

The Faith of Men and Other Stories (1904)

Tales of the Fish Patrol (1906)

Moon-Face and Other Stories (1906)

Love of Life and Other Stories (1907)

Lost Face (1910)

South Sea Tales (1911)

When God Laughs and Other Stories (1911)

The House of Pride & Other Tales of Hawaii (1912)

Smoke Bellew (1912)

A Son of the Sun (1912)

The Night Born (1913)

The Strength of the Strong (1914)

The Turtles of Tasman (1916)

The Human Drift (1917)

The Red One (1918)

On the Makaloa Mat (1919)

Dutch Courage and Other Stories (1922)

AUTOBIOGRAPHICAL MEMOIRS

The Road (1907)

The Cruise of the Snark (1911)

John Barleycorn (1913)

NON-FICTION AND ESSAYS

Through the Rapids on the Way to the Klondike (1899)

From Dawson to the Sea (1899)

What Communities Lose by the Competitive System (1900)

The Impossibility of War (1900)

Phenomena of Literary Evolution (1900)

A Letter to Houghton Mifflin Co. (1900)

Husky, Wolf Dog of the North (1900)

Editorial Crimes — A Protest (1901)

Again the Literary Aspirant (1902)

The People of the Abyss (1903)

How I Became a Socialist (1903)

The War of the Classes (1905)

The Story of an Eyewitness (1906)

A Letter to Woman's Home Companion (1906)

Revolution, and other Essays (1910)

Mexico's Army and Ours (1914)

Lawgivers (1914)

Our Adventures in Tampico (1914)

Stalking the Pestilence (1914)

The Red Game of War (1914)

The Trouble Makers of Mexico (1914)

With Funston's Men (1914)

POETRY

A Heart (1899)

Abalone Song (1913)

And Some Night (1914)

Ballade of the False Lover (1914)

Cupid's Deal (1913)

Daybreak (1901)

Effusion (1901)

George Sterling (1913)

Gold (1915)

He Chortled with Glee (1899)

He Never Tried Again (1912)

His Trip to Hades (1913)

Homeland (1914)

Hors de Saison (1913)

If I Were God (1899)

In a Year (1901)

In and Out (1911)

Je Vis en Espoir (1897)

Memory (1913)

Moods (1913)

My Confession (1912)

My Little Palmist (1914)

Of Man of the Future (1915)

Oh You Everybody's Girl (19)

On the Face of the Earth You are the One (1915)

Rainbows End (1914)

Republican Rallying Song (1916)

Sonnet (1901)

The Gift of God (1905)

The Klondyker's Dream (1914)

The Lover's Liturgy (1913)

The Mammon Worshippers (1911)

The Republican Battle-Hymn (1905)

The Return of Ulysses (1915)

The Sea Sprite and the Shooting Star (1916)

The Socialist's Dream (1912)

The Song of the Flames (1903)

The Way of War (1906)

The Worker and the Tramp (1911)

Tick! Tick! Tick! (1915)

Too Late (1912)

Weasel Thieves (1913)

When All the World Shouted my Name (1905)

Where the Rainbow Fell (1902)

Your Kiss (1914)

PLAYS

Theft (1910)

Daughters of the Rich: A One Act Play (1915)

The Acorn Planter: A California Forest Play (1916)

CPSIA information can be obtained
at www.ICGtesting.com
Printed in the USA
LVHW040140031120
670493LV00015B/281